KINGDOM RULES

VOLUME ONE

DEREK L. BUILTEMAN

CONTENTS

Acknowledgments	vi
Prologue—The Advocate	1
1. The Stench In Crence	7
2. Dreams And Madness	21
3. The King's Son	31
4. The Seduction	39
5. Zoella	52
6. Glasha	60
7. Badek Rising	73
8. A Sword But Not A Kingdom	87
9. Lies	99
10. The Battle Within	114
11. Princess Mess	127
12. Invitation Only	150
13. Dungeon Of Blood	165
14. Enslaved	179
15. The Pirate Life	186
16. Crime And Punishment	200
17. Dangerous Women	211
18. Trading Places	219
19. Different Kind Of Truth	230
20. Forever Goodbyes	251
21. Bottom Of The Well	263
22. Road To Nowhere	272
23. The Coming One	285
24. Battle For The Ice Throne—Part One	298
25. Butchered	314
Epilogue	327
Glossary	333
Cast Of Characters	335
About the Author	339

The Kingdom Rules, Volume I
COPYRIGHT © 2024 by Derek L. Builteman
All rights reserved. No part of this book may be used or reproduced in any manner whatsoever without written permission of the author, except in the case of brief quotations embodied in critical articles and reviews.
Cover and interior design by Betty Martinez
Publishing History
First edition, 2024
Print ISBN 979-8-9909720-0-1
Digital ISBN 979-8-9909720-1-8
Copyright Registration Number TXU 2-436-994

ACKNOWLEDGMENTS

Thank you Shannon, for finding a story in my mess of a first draft. You challenged me to become the author I am today. Without your editing skills, there would be no Kingdom Rules.

Your eyes on my manuscript were very helpful, Aimee. Best of all, you got me past the "Author Imposter" syndrome!

You turned the Kingdom Rules into a stunning visual, Betty. Your suggestions and guidance were most appreciated.

Rachel, the talent you displayed when you wrote your novel in high school inspired me to do it myself when the time was right for me. I highly valued your input on the details when I drew a blank. I'm also challenging you to write whatever story is next for you.

Your support of my undertaking meant a great deal to me, JD. Conversations we've had over the years helped develop some of the dialogue in this book. Thank you for the father/son relationship we share. I hope there are many more years to enjoy!

Steve—Thank you for being a great friend across the years. Your encouragement meant more than you'll ever know.

Lance—Your humor and ability to make me laugh, especially at myself, relieved the stress of getting this done. Your friendship was invaluable. Here's to McGregor's!

Mark—Thank you for your friendship and rooting for my success.

Tony—Thank you for being one of the first people to read my book. The subsequent support and encouragement were key to continuing the process.

A special thanks to the Tuesday cycling group for keeping my head straight.

To everyone who gave their valuable time to read the book in its various forms—thank you! You helped shape Kingdom Rules.

Leslie—thank you for your unwavering support while I wrote Kingdom Rules. There were days I thought I was the worst writer ever and others when I thought I was great, but you kept me right in the middle, not too high and not too low. When I vented, you were there to listen and when I wanted to quit; you weren't having it. There will be people who read this novel and are shocked that I wrote it, but you will be the one who isn't. Even in the years leading up to the start of the manuscript, you praised my writing in the different avenues I was using it in. You knew I had it in me and never doubted it while I constantly worried. Thank you so much for being my wife and walking with me on the journey to the Kingdom Rules.

PROLOGUE—THE ADVOCATE

"What is your name?"
The man's voice was icy and detached, the question lacking any genuine interest.

"Brigida, Your Holiness," said the girl. The warmth from a slow-burning fire in the hearth did nothing to keep her from shivering.

"Brigida," said the voice. "Such an innocent name."

The teenager said nothing, too terrified to put thoughts into words. The room had a dim glow from the fireplace and candles. Brigida's brown eyes darted about. In the room that was once a greeting room, there was only a high-back chair and a bed that seemed out of place.

"Where are you from, Brigida?"

"The district of Euphorium, in the town of Prego, Your Holiness."

Tears streamed down her red cheeks and dripped onto her chest, causing her to shiver and making her even more miserable. She was tall for her age, with long legs, strawberry-blonde hair, and cheekbones that sat high on her pretty face.

"You have traveled a long distance."

Through her tears, she blurted out a plea.

"I ... I just want to go home, Your Holiness."

The Advocate, tall and thin, rose and glanced at the fire before he approached the trembling Brigida. He dressed in black from head to toe, including the veil that covered his face and shrouded his identity. No virgin ever saw his face ... ever.

"Did I ask you," said the Advocate, "about returning home?"

"No," she said, "you did not, Your Holiness."

"Do not speak to me unless I ask you a question."

A long, narrow gold chain dangled from the Advocate's neck down to the middle of his chest. Suspended from the necklace was a symbol resembling the statues and carvings Brigida had seen in and around Prego.

Brigida was doing her level best to cover her chest and pubic area with her arms and hands, while turning her body to the side.

"Do you know who I am, Brigida?"

"I do, Your Holiness."

"You don't have to worry, child; I won't hurt you."

"Thank you, Your Holiness."

"Well, who am I?"

"You are the Advocate, the most Holy One, Diviner of Wisdom, Interpreter of the Prophetic Word, and the rightful Ruler over Dapuin."

Memorized and spoken as taught by two women of the Sisterhood Order over the long trip from Prego. Comprised of women who renounced marriage and childbearing, the Order existed to serve the High Holy One. The two women who had accompanied Brigida guided her in the Oracle's way by reading the sacred text to her morning, noon, and night.

The black-clad knights stationed outside the room were members of the Sons of the Tower, the Advocate's personal bodyguards, whose primary duty was to safeguard the Advocate at all costs, even their own lives.

"Do you know why you are here?"

Brigida couldn't bring herself to say it out loud, but she knew the reason for her removal from her home and the escort to the Advocate's chamber. She wasn't the first summoned to the Advocate's bed.

"Speak up, Brigida," said the Advocate. "When I ask a question, you are to answer it."

"I am here," she said, fighting back more tears, "to bear you a son, so the prophecy may be true."

"Has the day of your first bleeding arrived? I'm sure you've heard the stories of those who've told lies to me."

Brigida didn't need to hear the stories; she only needed to remember the dead and broken bodies in Prego, the chosen city of the virgin, according to the Prophetic Word. They often labeled men who lied about the status of their daughters as treasonous and received the worst kinds of deaths, including impalement by large, rusty iron hooks forced beneath their ribs and then hung from a crossbar. Town folk heard screams of dying men losing their minds, and they now reverberated in her ears as she stood before the Advocate.

"Yes, Your Holiness, I have bled as a woman."

"Very good. Now go lie on the bed."

She shuffled over to the bed, still hugging herself, and lay down. Known as Brigi to friends and family, she closed her eyes and waited for the inevitable. The wait was not a long one.

"Touch yourself until you are moist."

The coldness of the command frightened Brigida. She used her fingers but stopped.

"I can't, Your Holiness."

"Here. Use this."

Again, the tone of the Advocate's voice did nothing to ease her panic. The Advocate, with his head turned away, handed her a jar of perfumed grease. Despite her naivete, Brigida knew how to use the scented oil. The young girl whispered, just audible enough for the Advocate to hear, "I smeared it on."

"Get on your hands and knees. You are not to look at me. When I am finished, I will leave the room. You'll receive new clothing and escorted to a room inside the Tower."

"When can I go home?"

"Do not ask me that again."

The tone this time was chilling. Everyone knew the power and position of this man and the authority he possessed. Brigida didn't understand what it all meant, but she knew enough to keep her mouth shut for the rest of her time with the Advocate.

Brigida positioned herself on her hands and knees and remembered the times her brother made her play the "doggie game" and how much she hated it. Shivers racked her body relentlessly, while a paralyzing fear consumed her. The room was silent, save for the crackling of the dying fire. The tall, thin man pulled up his cloak and pulled out his cock and stroked it until he was ready.

She felt hard, cold hands on her hips, signaling it was time for the misery to begin. As fast as he went in, he came back out after three or four strokes.

"They sent you to me untouched," said the Advocate, in a calm, yet detached voice.

"But I am, Your Holiness," said Brigida, beginning to sense something was wrong. Very wrong.

"Who has put their male member into your vagina?"

"No one."

"I will have your house burned to the ground with your family in it, if you do not tell me."

Brigida wept again, her body shaking uncontrollably. Despite her age, she understood that her family would serve as a public example for those who lie and keep secrets.

"Shall I ask the men by the door to help you speak the truth?" the Advocate said.

If she didn't tell the truth, who knew the terrible things they might do to her? She did not want to find out.

"My brother Joss," she sobbed.

With the truth established, the tall, thin man with the icy hands pulled his cloak down and walked to the door. As he exited the room, the two men outside entered and laid hands on Brigida, grabbing her biceps with rough leather gloves, then placing the black hood over her head again. The Sons jerked her out of the bed and carried her from the room without a word spoken between them.

The Advocate walked down a long, narrow hall lit with torches and into another chamber. In the small room was a male servant, along with a tub of warm water and the biggest collection of expensive and exotic soaps in all Acaria. The tall, thin man whispered into the young man's ear, and he began disrobing the man. The rite of purification had begun.

Two days later, the verdict came down from Atthal; Joss was to be put to death on the breaking wheel. On the day of the execution, the city guards forced the people of Prego to come to the town square. The rest of Brigida's family sat and watched their eldest son stripped of all clothing and lashed to an old, splintered wagon wheel with several radial spokes, which was anchored to the stage's floor.

With utmost brutality, the executioner tormented Joss, ensuring his survival despite the intense agony. The snaps of bones breaking, and Joss's screams echoed across the square, and seared the sounds into the minds of all who heard. The executioner put Joss on another wheel and raised him on a pole, leaving him to perish. Late afternoon was coming, and the crows would be on their way in search of a meal.

No one in Prego ever heard what happened to Brigida, nor the rest of her family.

After the sun chased the horizon for two fortnights, a man sat in a room within a massive palace. A fire in the hearth

warmed the room, but the strawberry-blonde teenager shivered despite it all.
"What is your name?"

CHAPTER 1
THE STENCH IN CRENCE

The two men began their walk from Chirlingstone Castle down Whore's Hallway, before turning left onto the narrow street that housed the King's Key, a small tavern catering to those who coveted privacy and had the coinage to pay for it.

"I swear," said Sir Terrin Omond, "the smell gets worse every time we come this way."

"This morning at the Council Meeting," Sir Renoldus Gwatkin said, "King Leander issued an order to establish a sanitation sherd. Apparently, you're not the only one tired of the smell."

"I assume authorities will levy fines against shop owners who refuse to keep their small patch of street clean."

"Its taxes, or more pigs."

People filled the cramped and busy streets of Crence. The smell of human waste emptied from chamber pots, animal dung, and trash was prevalent. Mixed in with the smells were the loud and dissonant sounds of daily life. Shouts of the town crier, church bells ringing the hour, and shop merchants bellowing out the virtue of their wares.

Tiny cookshops peddled steaming hot sheep's feet and

beef ribs. The scent of baking bread and roasting meat battled with the muck and smoke from wood-fires, the competing smells crashing together as swords do on shields.

"I'm convinced one day," said Terrin, "I'll receive a chamber pot to the head."

"Better you than me," Renoldus said, with a slight smile.

"What, the great Sir Renoldus can't take a chamber-pot to that thick skull?"

"No, but I've had enough shit slung my way today."

At this, Terrin fell silent as the two continued walking, dodging people and animals as they continued on their way.

Sir Renoldus Gwatkin was a hero to the people of Brüeland. Terrin, a hero in his own right, had never quite achieved the same level of fame—though that had never darkened their friendship.

Renoldus was a tall man, six-foot-two, strong across the back and shoulders, with superior speed and agility for a man of his broad build. The short, boxed beard he wore grew out of a strong, square face with blazing clear blue eyes. Renoldus's beard and hair were both rust-colored, with spots of gray around the temple and chin.

Renoldus slowed his steps just before reaching the King's Key, as did Terrin, when he realized his friend was not matching his stride.

"What's wrong?" said Terrin, checking the sky for an errant chamber pot.

"In the War Council meeting last week," said Renoldus, "there was talk of increased ship building in Flace."

"I remember. Lord Cagnat didn't seem concerned."

"What if the shipbuilders in Flace are building ships for the Acarian navy? They are the best the continent offers."

"I suppose it's possible. But why risk our peaceful relations?"

"Acaria will need more ships if they hope to challenge our

prowess on the seas. The treasure they can throw at them is immeasurable."

Terrin broke his gaze and looked up the street at the King's Key sign. Renoldus sensed his friend was unmoved by the idea of Flace building ships for the enemy. Terrin solely focused on his battle plan for land engagements and had little time for matters of the sea.

Renoldus was ready to let the matter drop, but not before making his opinion known first. "Never underestimate an enemy, especially one with the riches of the Advocate."

This is the information Watkin needs to pursue instead of the castle intrigue he is so fond of. Crence will burn while he insists on navel gazing.

As they arrived at the Key, Renoldus pounded his fist on the thick wood door and waited. "Open the damn door," he muttered. "I'm thirsty."

"Mind your manners," Terrin said. "The gods are always watching."

"Since when did you believe in gods?" said Renoldus.

"I prefer to hedge my bets," said Terrin. "A little religion would do you good, my friend."

You may have a point.

The two wore burgundy silk tunics embroidered with a golden stallion, dark black boots, beige pants, and coats with one large burgundy lapel folded down to match the tunic. The belts, made of black leather, held the sheaths for their respective swords—Renoldus carried his famous black sword, *Blackout, Conqueror of Evil.*

Oswald swung open the door, and Renoldus and Terrin entered the King's Key, passing under its well-worn wooden sign with a large key painted in red and outlined in black, with a modest gold crown perched on top. Leaves and branches hanging over the door indicated the Key sold wine, as well as beer and ale.

"Oswald, when are you going to replace your sign?" asked

Terrin, half-joking. "The wood's warped, and the paint has faded."

"Are you going to pay for it?" shot back the owner.

"I already have. How much ale must we drink?"

Oswald grumbled as the two men made their way toward the back of the room, where Oswald's two sons were quick at work clearing a table.

The Key was as comfortable as a worn glove. Large, rounded wood chandeliers hung from chains attached to timber beams, filling the middle of the tavern with a warm glow. The further back, the darker it became, though Renoldus took comfort in the shadows.

The scents of fresh straw, reeds, and rushes scattered on the floor muted the smell of the streets outside. Smoke from inside the central hearth lingered in the air like the morning mist.

Signs of wear and tear were clear. The stone floor was uneven, worn by generations of patrons' muddy boots—a vile sludge that had sunk into the cracks. If the straw, reeds, and rushes didn't get changed often, the smell would creep out and mingle with the wood-fire, an evil haze smelling of soot and a castle's moat.

Renoldus's eyes searched the interior for Johna, his onetime lover turned informant. He'd missed the sights and sounds of the Key, centered in one of the most important port cities on the continent. At the reading table beneath the window, five men of wealth were playing Raffle. Laughs and curses echoed off the walls as the dice clattered and coinage changed hands.

The beautiful and reserved Af'lam whore named Bex negotiated quietly for more coinage with a short, overweight nobleman at another table. Bex was a crossbreed, a half-orc father and a human mother. Her skin was olive, and her features were mostly human, except for large, pointed ears that poked out of her black hair.

At a table next to the back door, four merchants poured ale down their throats and laughed at their own crude jokes. The majority were at the expense of the whores upstairs. Renoldus's narrowed eyes lingered on their table, his brow furrowed.

The creaky wooden door at the rear of the tavern swung open, raising Renoldus's hopes. He realized it was not Johna, but the young daughter of the cookshop owner four shops down, who was there to deliver pies, roast chicken, and warm bread.

One of the innkeeper's sons brought three tankards of ale to the table—two for Renoldus and one for Terrin.

"I have a question for you, son," said Renoldus. The boy stuck his hands in his pockets and looked down at the straw on the floor. "Did you notice any unfamiliar faces recently?"

"I'm not sure what you mean, Sir Renoldus."

"Some men, maybe even a woman, who may have dressed and spoken differently? Who asked a lot of questions?"

"No, my lord." The boy turned, then paused. "Yesterday, a man arrived as it grew dark."

"Go on."

"He seemed angry. I don't know, he…he frightened me."

"What did he look like?"

"I didn't get a good look, but something was wrong with his eye, my lord."

Interesting.

"Here." Renoldus handed a shiny coin to the boy. "If you remember anything or see him again, you let me know. Okay?"

"Yes, Sir Renoldus. Thank you, I will."

"Don't tell your father what he gave you," Terrin added as the boy returned to work with a bright smile. Lowering his voice, he said to Renoldus: "A spy would be more subtle, don't you think?"

"True," agreed Renoldus. "You would want someone who blends in."

"Do you think he's one of Watkin's men?"

"Who knows? Perhaps he's grown lazy and overconfident about who he enlists."

"You know Evelyn. How involved is she with Watkin?"

Watkin was married to Lady Evelyn of House Rainstrong, a Lady once betrothed to Renoldus. The arranged marriage to Renoldus was called off because of unspecified complaints regarding House Rainstrong. The resulting complications created an acrimonious relationship between Renoldus and Watkin.

"It seems impossible for her not to be. How deep? I don't know."

"He's a vile creature. I always feel the need to bathe after I've seen him."

Renoldus chuckled and his bright blue eyes lit up for a moment. "No soap in the kingdom can wash his bloodied hands. But I'm sure we don't wish to speak ill of the king's closest advisor."

Renoldus caught the attention of Oswald and put two fingers in the air, which the owner acknowledged with a shake of his head.

"Two more ales so soon?" said Terrin.

"I'm thirsty, gods dammit."

Terrin held up his hands. "I'm your friend, remember? Are you eating much? You look thin."

"Are you my friend or are you looking to bed me?" Renoldus forced a laugh, but it fell as flat as day-old ale.

Terrin leaned in closer from across the table. "It is not the ale. It is the hole in your heart that worries me."

"Is there no end to the misery?"

Terrin eased back into his chair. This was how it always began: the ale flowed, Renoldus mourned the loss of Cecile, drunken arguments ensued. The same troubadour's song, the same chorus repeated ad nauseum.

Terrin shot a glance toward Oswald. The bald man gave instructions to his sons and weaved his way toward them, stopping at a few tables to greet patrons.

"Terrin," said Renoldus, "I know you mean well. You have stood by me when it was difficult to do so."

"I will always stand by you," said Terrin. "I only want all to be well within your soul."

The two men raised their tankards upward and clashed them together, sending a few drops of ale flying onto the straw-covered floor beneath their boots. Oswald shuffled over with more speed than one would expect from an overweight tavern owner and delivered two tankards of ale to Renoldus.

"Here you are, my lord," said Oswald, putting the two tankards on the table. "What news from the castle?"

"No news," said Renoldus, "which I count as good. What news on the streets of Crence?"

"Men are worried about the Acarian Empire. They fear the Blue Horde will cross the Blaen River, and your army cannot stop them."

The Advocate's army was frightening. Their penchant for burning down villages and crops reminded many of the infamous swarms of the blue vespera, a locust-type insect known to cut large swaths in fields.

"With Sir Terrin the Trusted and myself at the gate?" said Renoldus. "Rubbish. It'll never happen, my friend."

But it will. Thousands of men may die so that one may claim the largest throne on the continent.

"Oswald," said Terrin, "tell Sir Renoldus what the noblemen are saying."

"Sir Renoldus," said Oswald, "they don't want to lose their castles, nor the land granted to them by the king. These men are running scared and if they take their families, servants, and livestock and leave the kingdom, it's not good for business."

Fear was spreading from person to person, village to village, city to city. The anxiety crept across Dapuin, swelled through stories of brutality and cruelty practiced by the Blue Horde, and those of the One Faith.

"People fear what they don't know," said Renoldus. "A strange religion? A reclusive warlord? Once rumors begin, they grow larger and larger each time the story is told. Soon they'll call the Advocate a god himself, in a tower rising to heaven."

People have used terror to silence unrest since time began. But, soon after the prophetic voice of the Advocate spoke of the Faith and the One True God, dread became refined as iron ore was to steel.

"They are not the only kingdom to use fear, Oswald," said Renoldus, leaning in. "Wars are fought in the mind first. Planting dread in the hearts of soldiers weakens their will to fight. They know the power of my black sword and the fierceness of my army."

"There are rumors," said Oswald, "that Princess Ingrid's father has plans to send her to marry the Wolf Prince, son of King Rycharde of House Andairn."

Is Watkin the source? He's the only one with direct access to the king.

"Folk should mind their tongues," said Renoldus. "Slandering a prospective husband for Princess Ingrid is treasonous."

"But is it true?"

"I don't know King Leander's mind, but speculation on any alliance drives rumor and gossip."

"I'm sorry—I meant no offense—"

Renoldus's eyes narrowed, and his voice rose. The rumors wearied him, and his tone reflected his distaste for such gossip.

"No man is worthy of Princess Ingrid," he said, rising

from his seat. "It doesn't matter if King Rycharde's son was conceived in the belly of a Yelloweye or not."

"Easy gentlemen," said Terrin, "people are staring, and we don't need the attention."

"Sir Renoldus," said Oswald, "please forgive me. I'm only the messenger."

Renoldus sat again and questioned who Oswald's son had seen.

"Tell us about who your son saw," said Renoldus.

"Kids see things and exaggerate," said Oswald.

"I can assure you by the look on his face, he saw something that frightened him."

Oswald debated being truthful, contemplating the consequences if caught lying. He sighed and began.

"There was a man who came into the Key," said Oswald. "His face had scars."

"Did he say anything?" asked Renoldus.

"Not outside of asking for wine. He watched the back door, then left."

"But what scared your son?" asked Terrin.

"His appearance, I suppose. It looked like something had burned the man's face, leaving it scarred. His eye drooped and was milky white and didn't move as a normal eye would."

"Anything else you remember?" asked Renoldus.

"Yes. He was wearing a brooch in the shape of a snake. It was made of gold and shone bright off the lights of the candles."

Renoldus shifted in his chair, and he narrowed his eyes to a squint.

Have these men grown brazen enough to emerge from the shadows?

Renoldus pulled another coin from his leather pouch and slid it over across the table to Oswald, who shoved it into a pocket with the stealth of those practicing magic.

"Thank you, Sir Renoldus. Do the two of you require more ale?"

"Not for me," said Terrin. "I need to return to the castle before it gets too dark."

"Yes," said Renoldus, "more ale for me. I do not need to go home before it gets too dark."

There was an uneasy chuckle amongst the three men. Oswald left to fill Renoldus's tankard, leaving the two to talk alone.

"Renoldus, my friend," said Terrin, "I did not mean to offend by what I said earlier. I know how hard it has been for you."

"No need to apologize," said Renoldus. "We speak our mind. Subtlety was never my strong suit—nor humor, apparently." At Terrin's look, he rose unsteadily and patted Terrin's shoulder. "Good night, my friend. Tell Lady Gelen I send her my greetings."

Terrin hesitated as Renoldus dropped back into his seat.

"Your eyes trouble me, my friend," Terrin said. "They have lost their light. You spoke well to Oswald, but you risk your reputation. These words may sting, but the stripes of a friend bring healing."

Renoldus studied his tankard.

Terrin touched him on the shoulder, holding his hand there briefly.

"G'Night, my friend," he said.

Terrin turned and headed for the door and Renoldus watched, envious of the man now headed home to a wife, his children.

If only Cecile had a child, I'd still have a piece of her.

As soon as Terrin left, Oswald returned with two tankards of ale for Renoldus and set them on the table in front of him.

"I thought I might bring you two," said Oswald, "and save a trip."

Renoldus scowled. "What do you mean by that?"

"Nothing, my lord. I'm simply showing you a kindness."

Renoldus picked up one tankard and sipped the ale at first,

before gulping the rest down his throat and into his belly. He slammed the tankard down on the table and pushed it over to Oswald.

"Looks as if you will need to make another trip," said Renoldus.

"Yes, my lord," said Oswald, all the while muttering under his breath as he went back to pouring ales.

Where is Johna? I wonder about a connection between Sir Burned Face and her absence. I warned her when she saw men wearing the Broach of the Snake, it would be time to hie. Though no one wants to believe it exists, Brutrark Vercis is cunning and lethal.

The Brutrark Vercis: a gathering of disgruntled knights and noblemen dispensing their own brand of justice. But they sought more than mere justice—they wanted to rule the kingdom as if it were their own.

Another ale disappeared into the gut of Renoldus before Arlette, a whore from upstairs, approached his table. She pulled back her long auburn hair into braids and pinned them up with a large, gaudy bronze flower. Her dress was blue-green wool, cut low in the front to show off her ample cleavage. Long sleeves did not quite hide the ink on her arms, put there by the raiders who had bought her at a slave market in the free-trade city of Torn Cloak.

The big city of Crence had been unkind to Johna, a woman with big dreams who'd come to the city hoping to fulfill them. Arlette had befriended her, and the two had been close all the time Renoldus had known Johna.

"Sir Renoldus, Black of Brüeland," Arlette said, "may I sit for a moment?"

"Yes, you may," said Renoldus.

"Johna left this letter for you." Arlette held a parchment in her hand, rolled with a ribbon wrapped around it. It was a thin strip of the same purple material Johna often wore in her hair. "She wrote it in her own hand."

He pulled another coin out of his pocket and slid it over to Arlette, and she placed the letter into Renoldus's hand.

"Please forgive me if I am prying," said Arlette, "but are you feeling unwell? You appear to be ailing."

The remark caught Renoldus off guard, and so he answered truthfully.

"I am," he said. "I grieve for Cecile."

"Thank you for your honesty, Sir Renoldus. I believe without you, none of us would be alive and well in this city."

"I fear if I cannot heal the pain of loss, I will not be that man anymore."

Renoldus looked away, his soul tormented by the loss of Cecile.

What if I can't be that man again?

"I will leave you to your letter, Sir Renoldus," said Arlette, standing to head back upstairs.

"I fear it is not good news, but thank you," said Renoldus, also standing.

"Respectful, even to a whore. Johna was right in calling you a gentleman."

Renoldus could only smile. He was uncomfortable with such talk and eager to read Johna's letter.

Arlette smiled and gave Renoldus the once-over. "Should you ever require the solace of a woman …"

Arlette let the remark hang in the air before she turned and made her way seductively up the stairs and on to her room, leaving Renoldus laughing inside at the woman's frankness and boldness.

He untied the ribbon with great care and placed it in his pocket. Unwinding the parchment, he began to read:

My dearest Renoldus,

I'm sorry I couldn't give you a proper goodbye. I wanted to come to you tonight. But I understand the consequences. You have been called to greater things.

You were right about many things. I found out Brutrark Vercis is real. The men who compose this secret society aim to bring their own justice to Brüeland. I suspect these wicked men are to blame for the death of Cecile, even though I lack the evidence. Your fears were true. It runs deep within the walls of Chirlingstone Castle. Watch your step. Assume no one is your friend.

I know you are hurting more than words can express. Please don't fall into the rabbit hole of drink, or you may never escape.

I am headed for the city you named. When I arrive there, I will find work and wait for your next directive. I still have all the coins you gave me.

Please remember me always, my love.

Johna

Renoldus pulled out the ribbon and, with the same care, rolled up the parchment and stood to leave. The thought that he would not see Johna again released a flood of anger into his heart. The thought of slaying everyone in the Key crossed his mind to appease his hurt and anger at those who had forced Johna out of town.

Anger burns within me at the reprehensible men seeking to harm Johna. Yet I'm to blame for convincing her to embark on this perilous journey. Worse, I never loved her. I pretended she was Cecile at the cost of a broken heart for her if she ever were to return.

Renoldus consumed two more ales before he stood up to leave. He looked upstairs and wondered if he should climb the stairs and make good on Arlette's offer. Renoldus took one step toward the old wooden stairs but stopped to look around. Everyone was watching intently as the Black of Brüeland decided what to do.

I cannot do this. If I head up the stairs, it will mean I don't care about myself, and I must care. To do this would mean I have dishonored the Call.

Renoldus turned back and walked out the door without stopping to say goodnight to Oswald, as was his custom. He made it back to the castle, once again avoiding the contents of a chamber pot raining down from above. But there was a shitstorm coming and it would change the course of many a man and woman.

CHAPTER 2
DREAMS AND MADNESS

"Welcome, my brother-law," said Skuti. "It is good to see you again."

Jomar, Aeehrl of Iziadrock, smiled as he dismounted his horse with the aplomb of a skilled horseman of royal upbringing. He was a large man, over six feet tall, with a muscular frame and long, straight brown hair that fell below his shoulders. He could be a temperamental man, but today, at least, he showed only a jovial smile under mischievous hazel eyes.

"Is it me," said Skuti, "or are there more gray hairs in your beard since the last time we were together?"

"If it were anyone but you making such an observation," said Jomar with a laugh, "I would cuff them about the ears and have them put on the wheel! Dare you insult the greatest Aeehrl in all of Flace?"

"And when was this title bestowed upon you? Had I known, I would have objected."

The brother-laws laughed, embraced, and then shook hands with a grip that would have crushed the bones of lesser men. Jomar stood taller than Skuti by a few inches, yet the gods sculpted the shorter man from stone. He was as strong as an ox, with the stamina of a wolf on a hunt.

Skuti's lightheartedness vanished as he asserted, "We must have a serious discussion about unification."

"I've traveled four days to get here," snapped Jomar, "and you want to talk business before I've had my first ale?"

This was his brother-law's other face: the dark and brooding Aeehrl, loving and trusting none save himself.

I should've known better than to discuss this matter with Jomar before he's had an ale ... or five.

"You are right," offered Skuti. "Please enjoy the hospitality of Seaborne Keep until you are ready for such discussions."

Skuti waved to a nearby servant girl and two ales appeared moments later. The malt kilned over a fire produced a brown, smoky color, and flavor. Besides hops, juniper and bog myrtle also added to the taste of the ale.

"We will have much time to chat about this matter," said Jomar, "although I cannot imagine the Council of Aeehrls agreeing to such a thing. It's a fool's errand."

"Yes, but what if you and I stood together? The remaining Aeehrls do not have the numbers to defeat us. You'll be king and I will command our armies and we will unite Flace."

"Skuti, listen to yourself. Let's say we declare war on the other Aeehrldoms. They will retreat to their castles, and we have four sieges on our hands. That is not a viable strategy."

"War is coming, Jomar. If we do not unify Flace, we will become meat that is picked off the bone by Acarian vultures."

"War is coming, true enough, and I'm convinced Acaria will prevail. I would rather negotiate with them while there is peace than pick up arms against our brethren."

"Why, in the name of Aenta, would the Acarian Empire want to negotiate with six different Aeehrldoms? If we don't unite, they will invade Flace and drag back to Acaria our men who are strong, along with those skilled in a trade. They will take our land and use it is as a gong."

The two looked away. Only a fool would deny the Acarian Empire was preparing to expand its borders. The only question was how to respond to the empire's calculated erasure of land boundaries.

"I will speak on behalf of the six," said Jomar, "as if we were one."

"You want to negotiate with them?"

"Acaria needs ships, and our people build the best," said Jomar.

Skuti shot Jomar a sideways glance. "How can you trust them to honor any agreement?"

"The same way you trusted the Yelloweyes."

I had to because you weren't coming.

Although Jomar's words stung, Skuti made no retort. There were more pressing matters before them and no need to revisit the past and open old wounds.

"You have heard the stories about the Blue Horde," said Skuti, "as have I."

"They are just that," said Jomar, "stories."

"They can't all be false."

"Then weak men make up those kingdoms."

"They have forced every kingdom they have conquered to bend the knee to the Advocate. We will be slaves in our own land."

"That happens to conquered kingdoms. We negotiate from strength; everyone on the continent knows of our ships."

"I will not bend the knee to the Advocate, nor will I stop worshipping the true gods and goddesses as our forefathers have done since time began."

Jomar raised his hand, showing he was through with the whole thing. "You are just being obstinate," he laughed, "because you know I am right. Now, I will speak of this no more. Tonight, we eat, drink, and sing songs to the gods."

"I will do all three things," replied Skuti, "but more of the first two and louder on the last than you, Aeehrl Jomar."

Their eyes met and laughter followed. Wrapping their

massive arms around the other's shoulder, they headed off toward Zoella Heil in the inner ward of the castle.

Tonight was a night of honor and celebration of the goddess Zoella and her kindness and goodness toward the people of Ashul and Iziadrock. The two men strolled towards the Heil, continuing their conversation. Both felt their stomachs churn as the smell of cooking meat wafted from the kitchen. The growls from their bellies were loud enough to frighten a young child.

Rather than listen to their husband's conversation, Thora and Thorve made their way to the sweet-smelling trees in the near distance, close to the Heil. The twins were identical, down to the very essence of their bodies. They had blonde hair in long curls interspersed with tight braids that fell just below their chest line. They held it in place in the middle of their forehead with a golden headband.

The eyes of the sisters were aqua, the color of the seas, set atop a small straight nose and round lips, producing a sly grin in private, and a broad, warm, and genuine smile when in public. Their dresses were made of colorful imported material from the southernmost part of the continent. Cut to leave the upper chest bare, the dresses showcased gold and silver hanging jewelry, along with intricately designed collar necklaces.

"Thorve, my twin," said Thora, "it's so good to see you."

"Sister, it's been too long," said Thorve. "Far too long."

There was a calm silence in the air as the twins strolled along a footpath. The path weaved its way through a pleasure garden planted with fruit and shade trees, rosebushes, and wattle fences covered with honeysuckle. Arm in arm, the twins finished their walk under an arbor with long vines, which led to a circular arrangement of turf seats encircling a small fountain. The kitchen garden was not far away.

"The gardinarius did a fine job replanting the garden," said Thora. "I can smell the scent of flowers in the air."

"Yes, he did," said Thorve. "Skuti does not care much about appearance and comfort, but he knows the pleasure I receive from this well-planted herber."

Thora wore an ornate silver collar necklace, with a separate silver chain necklace soldered to the main piece. Dangling off the chain was a silver pendant of two axes crossed, the signet of House Throst. Thora, with great care, unlatched the silver collar and eased it from around her neck, which she craned toward her sister.

The story is told through my stripes.

"In the name of the goddesses," said Thorve, "those bruises are awful. Was it Jomar?"

"I swear he is going to kill me in one of his rages," said Thora. "If not for the Aeehrl's Guard, I wouldn't be here."

"Have his dreams grown worse, then?"

Thora nodded, briefly looking away. "Jomar spoke of casting his eyes upon a turbulent sea with waves as tall as a keep. Out of the tumultuous black water, the Leviathan of old rises and wraps its long tentacles around every ship it finds. The beast crushes each one as if it were a dry twig and drags the broken ship to the bottom of the sea."

"I remember Father telling us stories of this beast," said Thorve. "But Thora, that is all they are—stories. Dreams—"

"There is more," Thora said. "The ships are so many, he says they fill the sea and rise above the water. At last, the monster turns to Jomar and rides the waves toward him. He claims a goddess sits atop the beast's back with a spear."

Thora paused for a moment, allowing Thorve time to soak in the story of Jomar's dream and its implications.

There is one more piece of information my sister needs atop this telling.

"Jomar was a good man," said Thora, "when Father arranged the marriage …"

She looked away and shook her head slowly.

"Yes," said Thorve, "I remember being envious. You were married off to an Aeehrl and I, a shipbuilder."

"Now, I envy you."

"Sister, do not say such things. Your pain saddens me."

"Yes, but it's the truth."

It became quiet as the sisters struggled to find the right words. After a brief silence, Thora decided it was time to press forward.

"I have something else," said Thora, "that I've held back, afraid it would upset you further."

"Please," said Thorve, "talk to me."

"It's hard to speak of Jomar's accusations."

Thora glanced away and gathered her thoughts.

"Jomar believes, as sure as Vesceron rises in the sky each day," said Thora, "that I send him these dreams to torment him. And he believes I will take his crown, and you will claim Skuti's. That we plot to rule the Aeehrldoms ourselves."

"Absolute lie," said Thorve. "I'd do nothing to harm Skuti."

"But he has convinced himself. I can only hope he does not poison Skuti's mind."

"This cannot be. I will warn Skuti of Jomar's madness."

"You mustn't do that. It will only play into Jomar's hands. He will twist it and use it against you."

"Then what should we do, my twin?"

You have spoken as expected, and now I have an accomplice to eliminate Jomar. I must convince you the magic of Badek is the only means we have to kill Jomar without having his blood on our hands.

"I traveled to Evanora of the Forest," said Thora.

"Thora," said Thorve, "don't speak that name aloud. You know we cannot speak of what she does."

"It's the only way."

"Is there no better cure for Jomar's madness?"

"Cure? His mind has gone too far to return. We must have Jomar sleep with the dead."

I have planted the seed. Now is the time to water and watch it grow.

"Thora," said Thorve, leaning in closer to her sister, "how can you suggest such a foul deed as this? You'd have your own husband killed in cold blood?"

"I have no choice," said Thora.

She leaned her head to the side and touched the bruises around her neck. "He is going to kill me if I sit by idly and do nothing. Who knows if this will be our last time together before we meet again in the Beautiful Place? If Evanora takes his life, our hands will be clean."

"There is too much danger. You know how the magic of Badek works. She'll take years off your life in exchange for what she gives you. No one knows how long they have."

"I'll take that risk. An unknown fate is better than the death I see before me."

"Enough of this talk for now. We can speak of it tomorrow, but Thora, please think of the consequences."

If you only knew ...

Thora decided she'd done enough to draw Thorve into her web of deceit and engaged in small talk with her sister.

"What rumors do you hear of the coming war?" asked Thorve.

"I only hear what Jomar tells me," said Thora, "and he says the rumors of war are as a fire to dry timber."

"Skuti thinks war is coming and wants to unify Flace. It's the only way to protect the Aeehrldoms from an army with greater numbers than grains of sand on a beach."

Thora shifted on the turf seat and looked wistfully at the fountain. Her voice trailed off as she spoke.

"I don't trust Jomar, but I do trust Skuti ..."

It's more than trust I want from him. If only he were —

"Thora?"

"What?"

"You're distracted."

"I am sister."

"You've become obsessed with what our laws forbid. I've never seen you act this way."

Thora gave a nod and a smile. Her smile appeared as it always did, easy and sincere, but Thorve knew her sister and it was anything but.

Thora, get your mind right or Thorve is going to catch on. Don't say something stupid and ruin your trap before it can be sprung.

The sisters stood and locked arms, pretending all was normal for the moment. They headed toward the Heil and the night's celebration, listening to each other's stories of their children's deeds and gossiping about what nobleman was bedding which servant girl.

JOMAR AND SKUTI were strolling toward the Heil in merriment, laughing at the same stale jokes, when Jomar abruptly ceased laughing and clutched Skuti's arm, his gaze swinging back and forth as if searching for eavesdroppers.

Jomar, what in the —

"There is one more thing I need to tell you," said Jomar, "but you mustn't speak of it to Thorve."

What have you done this time?

"What is so important," said Skuti, "that I shouldn't tell my wife?"

Jomar's voice dropped to a hoarse whisper. "Thora is trying to drive me mad."

"What? How could she do such a thing?"

"She's always blamed me for the death of their father. She wants vengeance … and while it grieves me to tell you this, I believe Thorve is helping her."

Skuti delivered a sideways glance at Jomar.

"Have you gone mad?" said Skuti. "Thorve would never join Thora on such a thing, if it's happening at all."

"I am deathly serious, Skuti," said Jomar. "She sends me nightmares."

"What's Thora's motivation for doing this, even if she's capable?"

"She wants to overthrow me and sit on the High Chair."

"This strains all credulity, Jomar."

"You don't understand! I saw the beast of old come out of the sea and destroy all the ships ever built until they filled the waters and reached the sky. Worst of all, a beautiful woman dressed in magnificent colors sat on the back of the horrific monster as it stormed across the waves, seeking to devour me. Though the woman is bewitching, she spat vile curses at me. She carried in her hand a magical three-pronged spear, by which she swears I will die."

Skuti waited for a moment with his eyebrows furrowed. After a quiet moment, with only birds singing, Skuti tilted his head back and laughed loudly.

Jomar reached out with his long, powerful arms, grabbed Skuti by his colorful mantle, and pulled him in close. The strength of Jomar caught the amused Skuti by surprise and snapped his head forward. "Shit, Jomar—"

"Do not make light of this, Skuti Ingimund, or I swear you and I will become enemies."

"Calm yourself," said Skuti. "You do not want others to see us like this."

Jomar eased his grip on Skuti and took a step back. His hazel eyes were ablaze, and his long hair fell into his face. He resembled a man on the verge of rage. A scowl replaced the slight grin that normally graced his face and his body tightened as if ready to fight.

"I'm sorry, Jomar," said Skuti, "I see now there's truth in your words."

Maybe the dreams are driving him mad. This is a Jomar I don't know.

"I must ..." said Jomar, unable to finish his thought. The blank stare of Jomar reminded Skuti of the men he'd seen at the asylum.

Where is Jomar at?

"What is your mind on the matter?" said Skuti.

As a trap snatches a rat, Jomar's senses returned. "I must do away with Thora."

"What are you saying?"

"Do not play coy with me. You know what I mean."

"You cannot speak of murder—"

"I am."

The unexpected turn and tone of the conversation shocked Skuti, and so he paused briefly.

"Jomar," said Skuti, "forget about that thought. You know how much Thora means to the people of Iziadrock. They would rip the crown from your head and hang you in chains if they discovered you were the culprit."

"I would rather be a vagrant than an Aeehrl plagued with a curse," said Jomar. "I will end the life of Thora."

"How can you even think about it? Send her to a monastery. Find some trumped-up charge to bring against her. You are the Aeehrl. All must do as you say, including your wife."

The men had wandered closer to their wives, and Skuti saw movement within the garden.

"Look, the women are preparing to leave the garden. Let's end this discussion and go to the Heil."

"We're done for today, but we will talk tomorrow on the subject."

I am sure we will. How can I talk unification with you now? Your focus is on how to kill Thora and end her plan of driving you mad. I will have none of it. Storm clouds gather, and if we don't unify Flace, they will leave us to starve in the cold aftermath of wars fought without our involvement. Then, will it really matter?

CHAPTER 3
THE KING'S SON

*P*rince Rycardus, the heir to the Andairn throne, scooted away from his parents' sight, riding his hobby horse named Knight. He waved his wooden sword, imagining it to be his father's black sword as he galloped Knight out of the courtyard into a dark, quiet garden area. The four-year-old boy slashed his weapon at invisible enemies at his feet, shouted "Take that!" as he rode by.

A small, round leather ball rolled from the bushes and stopped at his feet. Rycardus glanced at the ball and then at the figure emerging from trees.

"Hello, Prince Rycardus," she said. "I believe this belongs to you." The brief greeting caused her small yet sharp-as-nails canines to flash.

"You're not supposed to be here," said Rycardus. He took an unsteady step back and dropped his hobby horse to the ground, almost causing him to fall on the hard dirt.

"Don't be afraid, young prince," she said. "I won't hurt you."

She was a smallish female, her yellow eyes wide and bright, set in a face with little hair, and it resembled a man's whiskers after a week of growth. Her lips stretched around her mouth, making them grotesquely thin. Reddish-brown hair hung down to her shoulders, and triangular ears sprouted from the top of her head. She wore a black tunic and short gray belted pants.

"My father says the Yelloweyes kill people," said Rycardus. He was unusually big for his age, with a shock of black hair on a pale face.

"Your *father*—" she started harshly, then caught herself and cleared her throat. Your father is wrong. We're quite nice, actually."

Delinda cast her eyes around the area and crept closer to Rycardus. An ever-growing sense of fear froze the young prince in his tracks.

"Do you want to be king someday?" she said.

"Don't come any closer."

"You didn't answer. Do you want to be king?"

"Yes, but first I want to be a noble knight." Rycardus flashed his wooden sword and moved it about.

She scooted another foot forward while he played with his sword.

"I bet you'll be a skilled knight someday."

In an adjacent garden, Lady Sela of House Trulbosh had her arm tucked into the arm of her husband, King Rycharde, as they strolled along on a peaceful evening with the glow of torches lighting their pathway. The two were silent, savoring a pleasant evening without meetings or entertainment. Suddenly, Sela stopped and put a finger to her lips.

"Did you get closer?" said Rycardus.

"You can trust me," she said. "I didn't move any closer."

"Father said that he doesn't trust you."

Delinda stared at the dirt under her large feet, let her jaw quiver for a moment, and managed not to bare her fangs. Taking a moment to collect herself, she continued. But it was time. It was past time.

She smiled. "Have I lied to you?"

"No," he said, "but your eyes are mad at me."

The sound of boots against the adjacent walking path and bushes was loud enough to grab the female's attention. Startled, she dropped herself into a squat and then lunged at the young boy.

"Rycardus," yelled Rycharde, "get back."

Rycharde broke through the waist-high hedge with his sword positioned above his head, and he brought the black blade down full force at the same time she sprang forward. The blow's power sent the head, with rage-filled yellow eyes, rolling a few feet away. Blood pulsed from her neck, forming a puddle at Rycardus' feet.

Rycharde kneeled and pulled his son in and held him tight as ever. Lady Sela slipped in behind Rycardus, surrounded the heir with her arms, and placed the side of her face on Rycardus's back. Rycharde felt a warm, sticky substance on his neck where Rycardus had wrapped his injured arm.

"Shit!" he yelled.

"Father," said Rycardus, "it hurts."

"I know, son, hold on. Sela, give me your scarf."

Sela ripped off a gold broach, tearing her imported gown, and handed the silk scarf to Rycharde. "How deep is it?"

Without a word, he turned their son's forearm bottom side up.

"Oh my," she said, placing her hand over her mouth.

Rycharde frowned, ripped off a piece of the scarf, and tied it tight on the bicep above the wound on his son's forearm.

Tears cascaded down Rycardus's red cheeks. "Ow, that hurts!"

Rycharde picked up his son, threw him over his muscular shoulder, and ran toward the Healer's laboratory beneath the castle. Sela walked hurried toward the chapel to offer prayers for her son as tears ran down her own flushed cheeks.

"Rycardus," said Reyna, "you're going to get me in trouble with Karles."

"The slaughterer?" said Rycardus. "He's lucky to have you."

Rycardus smiled at Reyna as young men do when they're in love. He grabbed her hand and pulled her along as they ran toward the orchards. Reyna laughed as they went, in the way young women do when they're in love.

This wasn't their first visit to the king's private orchard. Hidden from view, they went to the orchard's edge and sat beneath an apple tree on the cool grass.

"Do you remember when we first met?" said Reyna.

"How could I forget," said Rycardus, "catching the contents of a chamber pot on my head and then falling into the disgusting mud and you frantically trying to clean me up?"

"Well, you were the prince," said Reyna. "Even as a boy."

Reyna covered her mouth and laughed. Rycardus feigned offense and then joined Reyna in snickering at his misfortune.

"When I got older, I'd ride into the city," said Rycardus, "and you'd sneak out of your grandparent's cookshop and meet me."

"My grandparents knew what I was doing," she said. "They just didn't say anything."

"You never told me how you ended up in the Knife's Edge."

"I had nowhere else to go."

"But the Knife's Edge?"

"Rycardus, I don't want to talk about that awful place. It upsets me still."

Tears welled up in Reyna's eyes and instead of turning away, she made sure Rycardus saw them. It was a sensitive subject, but Rycardus was growing troubled by the lack of answers. Initially, he grasped the freshness of the emotional wound and the healing time required. Now he thought she was stonewalling him.

You're hiding something from me, and I'll figure it out.
In the meantime, Rycardus did what he always did.
"I'm sorry," said Rycardus, "I didn't mean to upset you."
"I know," said Reyna.
Reyna sensed Rycardus was angry underneath his apology, and so she eased the conversation toward the physical.
"Remember our first visit here?" said Reyna.
"Of course I do," said Rycardus, "I'll always remember it."
"We were so innocent when we were first naked together, exploring our bodies out in the open."
"Right over there, under that tree. I was so nervous."
"My passion was like a fever, burning through my body. And when you slid into me …"
"No feeling in the world is better."
Rycardus glanced at the tree where their love began, then back at Reyna. The desire started at the soles of his feet and made its way up his body as heat rises from a fire.
"You're staring," she said, "at my breasts."
"I know," said Rycardus. "I can't help myself."
Another smile, this one sly and playful, caused Reyna to laugh. Rycardus worshipped at the altar of Reyna's body. She differed from the young women of Wolfden, and certainly different from Princess Ingrid, Rycardus imagined.
Her body was long and lanky, but the muscles in her arms and legs were a sign Reyna was cut from a different cloth. Her strength was almost that of Rycardus's, a fact she reminded him of often. He felt it when their passion became physical, almost animalistic. Multicolored bruises on his torso, deep scratches on his back to the point of scarring, and curious bite marks which resembled a dog's bite pattern more so than a human's.
"Bed me as though it's our first time," said Reyna.
"There, under that same tree?" said Rycardus.
"No, right here."

Seconds later, clothes littered the ground. Rycardus caressed Reyna's body, trying to repeat what happened that afternoon in the early Dead Months before the brutal cold made its assault on Wolfden.

Their hands and mouths traveled over the contours of each other's body in ways that were rough yet pleasing. Rycardus quickly stiffened, excited by the thought of the first time they were in the orchard. Reyna's soft moans only made him desire her all the more. His touch made Reyna ache, and she guided him inside, which produced a moan from Rycardus.

"Being inside you …" whispered Rycardus, unable to finish his sentence.

"Don't stop," said Reyna, "I want all of you in me."

"You want my seed inside you, don't you?"

"Yes … give it to me."

Reyna's passionate cries became louder, as did Rycardus's groans. He pushed harder and faster until one last stroke gave Reyna what she wanted.

"Oh, the gods," said Reyna, "you felt so good."

"So did you."

They quickly dressed and lay on their backs looking up into the trees and sky; without words, they held hands and allowed the moment to seep into their memory. Rycardus had blown past the point of no return in his love for Reyna and moved further and further away from his obligation and duty to marry Princess Ingrid.

Rycardus turned his head toward Reyna.

"There's a council meeting in the morning," said Rycardus.

Reyna turned her head toward him, staring at him with soft green eyes.

"Don't let him bait you into another ugly confrontation," said Reyna. "Let him call me a *duhbrarei*. That's what I am. I can live in either world."

"The word signifies more than that. It means you're a dirty whore and a liar too."

"It doesn't matter. I know you love me."

Rycardus turned his head and fixed his gaze on the tree once again. He furrowed his brow as the last confrontation flashed in his mind.

"He always brings up Princess Ingrid," said Rycardus, "and the importance of the alliance."

"Will you let me be your mistress?" said Reyna with a wide and open smile.

"Hilarious."

The afternoon light was fading, and a slight chill snuck into the shaded grove. They moved closer and cuddled for warmth.

"It's getting stronger inside me," said Rycardus. "Every day, it seems."

"What of Delinda's attack?" said Reyna. "Do you remember any more of it?"

"Who?"

"Umm, yeah, Delinda. I heard it was the name of the assassin sent to kill you."

"What are you talking about?"

Reyna glanced away. "It's just hearsay from people. It's not important. Forget I said it."

"Forget it?"

"Don't be angry with me. I care about you, and I want to know what happened that awful night."

"All I see are yellow eyes. They turn angry, and she leaps at me with fangs bared."

No one will reveal the truth about that night to me. I know she left some of her venom inside me. Its power has been growing silently for years. It's changing me, I can feel it. I try to control it, but one day the beast will conquer. What will happen to me then?

"I believe you have a destiny to fulfill," said Reyna.

"You've said that," said Rycardus. "But destined for what?"

"Maybe you'll be a bridge for peace between the forest and the castle."

A bridge for peace with the Yelloweyes? A bridge for an alliance with Brüeland to wage war and defeat an enemy? I feel the weight of the Wolfburn Valley on my shoulders.

Rycardus unfolded his tall frame from the ground and stood. The beast inside was evolving, and its force was placing untold pressure on his bones and joints, causing the prince to stretch out unnaturally.

"Oh my god that hurts," said Rycardus.

"What hurts?" said Reyna.

"Nothing, never mind. We should go before it gets dark. Let me help you up."

Reyna grabbed his hand and used the momentum from being pulled up to wrap her arms around Rycardus's neck.

"I love you," she whispered in his ear.

"I love you," said Rycardus. He kept his eyes, increasing in yellow hues, hidden from Reyna to avoid her seeing the tension written across them.

The couple held their embrace for a moment longer before leaving the orchard and returning to face a reality Rycardus had been avoiding. Clenching her hand, he feared that letting go would shatter their illusion of a deceptive reality. Life with Reyna was not the enticing fantasy it seemed. When stripped down to its core, it was only a muddled delusion full of lies and deceptions.

Rycardus remained silent on the way back to the castle.

CHAPTER 4
THE SEDUCTION

*T*he apartment Renoldus called home in Tarquin Tower was as good as it got for anyone not named King Leander or Queen Vanora. His living quarters faced south toward the Great Ocean of Kura, with its deep black waters, volatile undercurrents, and enormous waves that punished and crashed against the granite cliffs below the castle.

It was a large apartment with a sizable bedchamber and roomy solar; double doors opened to a veranda that allowed Renoldus a clear view of the seas and the ships on its waters. Cecile's bath and dressing room remained untouched since the day she died. Two maids lived in a small adjoining chamber; Renoldus kept Cecile's maid, unwilling to let her go for the sake of Cecile's memory.

Three rapid knocks on the door jarred Renoldus out of his mindless reading of letters. He glanced toward the door with dulled blue eyes, sitting at his trestle desk of oak stained with wine, candle wax, ink, and black marks from scorching. If only desks could speak, it would tell the tales of one Sir Renoldus Gwatkin, the Black of Brüeland and Lord Commander of the king's army. But tables do not talk, and the secrets inside this spacious apartment at the top of Tarquin Tower would be safe. For now.

Renoldus, instead of approaching the door, turned his attention back to his desk overwhelmed with a multitude of papers and letters hiding its past.

"I am the commander of the fucking army," he said, "not the scribe."

Renoldus reached for the bottle of wine on his desk and peeked inside, then poured the last of its contents into a hand-crafted wine goblet. The pure gold vessel was embossed with free-running stallions, the heraldry of House Blackwood. The goblet was a gift from the late King Tarquin Blackwood, marking Renoldus's ascension to knighthood.

With the goblet raised to his lips, three more raps sounded on the large, heavy door. Once more, he glanced at the door, but stood up this time, accidentally toppling the chair onto the stone floor.

"Damn it to judgement," he said, effortlessly lifting and replacing the bench.

At this late hour, who could it possibly be?

With a chuckle, Renoldus stumbled towards the door, already on his second bottle of wine. With his tall frame, he leaned against the door and pressed his ear to it. The same three quick raps turned into a balled fist pounding on heavy wood.

"Who's out there?" said Renoldus through the door.

The voice was familiar, but faint, and the words were unclear.

"Speak again, louder."

"Renoldus, open the door," said Princess Ingrid.

Ingrid?

"Ingrid, what are you doing out there?" said Renoldus, continuing to lean his powerfully constructed body against the door.

"Someone is following me."

"If you were not outside your chamber, no one would follow you."

"Please, just let me in and I will explain."

Reluctant to do so, but not wanting to create a scene or draw unwanted attention, Renoldus cracked the door open with no intention of allowing Ingrid entry. As the door opened, Ingrid swiftly darted like a cat, maneuvering past Renoldus to reach the chair farthest from the door. Surprised, the best Renoldus could offer was a sardonic smile and growing irritation.

"Lady Evelyn allows you to leave your chambers dressed in this fashion?" said Renoldus.

Princess Ingrid wore a peasant blouse with large open sleeves and a low-cut neckline showing off her cleavage and freckled chest. Her waist was bound in leather, matching her pants and knee-high boots.

"She is asleep," replied Ingrid, "and what does it matter to you what I wear?"

"You're right, it is not my concern what you wear. You say someone is following you, young princess?"

"Drop the young. I am a lady, not a maiden child."

"By the way, what are you planning to do with that dagger strapped to your boot?"

"Watkin's spies are within the castle too, and they wait and watch, chatting up men and women, all in the name of finding a piece of dirt to hold over one's head."

Renoldus was in no mood to discuss Ingrid's knowledge of Watkin's web and he wasn't about to reveal he had his own spy. "Were you going to stab one of them?"

"Why do you make levity at my expense?"

Bemused, Renoldus smiled at Ingrid. "While Watkin has spies, they are not within these walls."

Pushing her auburn-red hair curls off her shoulders, Ingrid paused and raised an eye at Renoldus. "Do I know more about the castle than the Black of Brüeland? Your drinking has blinded you to the political intrigue that plagues this castle."

What does Ingrid want? It's not about being followed or Watkin's spies. I will not respond to Ingrid's nonsense any further, especially when I am tired and feeling drunk.

"Princess, please, not tonight," said Renoldus. "Why is it you came here?"

"I told you I am being followed," replied Ingrid.

Renoldus stuck his head out, checked the hallway, and saw no one. When he turned back, Ingrid had moved from the chair over to his desk, where she picked up the golden goblet and turned it in a circle, examining the detail. Renoldus closed the door, realizing he could not shoo the princess out of his apartment as quickly as he intended.

"So," said Ingrid, "this is it?"

"This is what?" said Renoldus.

"The wine goblet my grandfather gave to you."

"Yes, and what of it?"

"One more reason for my father to hate you."

The princess brought the goblet to her lips, swallowed the last of the wine, and wiped off her mouth with the sleeve of her blouse. She moved away from the desk and toward Renoldus's bedchamber, ignoring his voice from behind.

"Don't go in there."

Renoldus grabbed a candle and peered into his bedroom and through the shadows saw Ingrid sitting in a chair next to a small table he used for reading or drinking wine, or sometimes both. She motioned with her hand for him to light the candle sitting in the middle of the table.

"Princess," said Renoldus, "you did not come here to tell me someone was following you. Now, state your purpose to me."

"Are you that blind," said Ingrid, "that you cannot see your own flaming desire for me?"

"That's quite enough, princess. Come on, let's go. I'm

tired, and Lady Evelyn will search for you soon." Renoldus turned his back and started toward the front door, but stopped once more at the voice of Ingrid.

"Why are my advances to you ignored or met with condescending remarks? I can tell by the way you look at me, you find me desirable. I know you want to bed me. Tell me so or I'll say liar."

"For the love of the gods and goddesses, Princess Ingrid. If your father the king finds out you were here—"

"He will not, I promise."

"Promise?"

This conversation has gone on too long. Why am I enabling her to continue in this fantasy? Bedding Ingrid makes me no better than the pigs in the city.

"Renoldus," said Ingrid, "I will not be without an answer from you any further. Will you take me as your lover or not?"

"Ingrid," replied Renoldus, "do I need to explain to you the consequence of such an act?"

"Consequences don't matter to me."

Regrettably, I care little myself anymore. If I did, you wouldn't be here.

"You are a bold young woman," said Renoldus. "Do not tempt me with this. It will ruin the both of us and the kingdom I swore to protect."

What knight dishonors his kingdom by bedding its princess? How can a supposedly honorable and brave man stoop to depending on a seductress to halt her allure, not for moral reasons but for political convenience? I have lost my ability to say "no" and my will to say, "This is wrong."

"I am bold," Ingrid said. "And I will do whatever it takes to share your bed."

"You seduce me with your vine-like allure and its illicit wine. As you stand there, you expect me to become intoxicated by it."

"You're already intoxicated by my wine. Come, teach me to be a whore in your bedchamber and show me how to please a man. Make me feel like a woman, give me your passion, and I'll embrace it all."

"What are you doing?"

"I'll show you what all the men in Brüeland desire. Then I am going to open my legs and allow you into a place no man has ever been."

Ingrid removed her boots and peeled off her clothing, one layer at a time, starting with her leather waist piece and finishing with her blouse. As she removed the last of her garments, Renoldus approached Ingrid, taking in the contours of her body from head to toe.

"Do you approve?" she whispered through a dry mouth. Ingrid's heart-shaped lips opened slightly, and the amorous and seductive expression grabbed Renoldus by the loins and drove his lust to the point of no return.

Ingrid shivered despite not feeling a chill, and her freckled chest flushed as Renoldus stepped out of his pants and revealed his approval. The two embraced, and the warm feel of Ingrid's ample, still-blossoming breasts caused a fleeting remembrance of a young Cecile. Renoldus briefly paused, pulling Ingrid closer, desperately grasping onto the transient moment.

Ingrid nervously groped for his cock and, with an iron grip, yanked it up and down a few times until Renoldus intervened and placed his hand over hers, guiding her into the proper feel and motion. Her soft hand relaxed, and with the proper grip, moved his shaft up and down, producing the pleasurable groans and words she wanted to hear.

"I am intoxicated by your wine," said Renoldus. "I will drink of it until I have had my fill."

"Renoldus," she breathed, "please drink from my cup."

Ingrid fell back onto the bed, and Renoldus followed, running his hands over her curved waist and hips. She was not skinny, nor was she plump, but her stomach was soft and testified to a life of luxury. Ingrid's longing for Renoldus to be inside her intensified as they kissed, intertwining their tongues and exploring each other's bodies with their hands and mouths.

Tonight, every inch of this woman will be mine. Damn it all to darkness.

"You will feel like a woman tonight," whispered Renoldus.

"Do to me as you want," said Ingrid. "I am eager for you."

Ingrid opened her legs as promised and moaned ever so softly as Renoldus eased himself into her. She bit her lip and winced as Renoldus moved in and out of her, slowly at first, then more rapidly as Ingrid moved past the pain into pleasure. Soon Ingrid matched the rhythm of the movements and lifted her ankles into the air.

"Oh, to the gods," said Ingrid.

"Ingrid," shouted Renoldus, shooting his seed into her belly.

∽

RENOLDUS WALKED down the long winding staircase and entered the belly of Chirlingstone Castle but had not one idea why. It was cold, dank, depressing, dark, terrifying, moldy, and odiferous among many other unpleasantness's. He stood at the entrance to the Crypt of Kings, a long, narrow hallway full of cobwebs, an occasional shiver-inducing breeze, and eerie sounds and echoes.

"Who has called me here?" said Renoldus. "King Tarquin?"

He was familiar with the ins and outs of the Crypt from his childhood. Renoldus's father, along with other high-ranking officials in the king's court, lived in apartments within the Tower. The sons of the officials played in the bowels of the castle despite the warnings not to. Despite the admonition, they, of course, played beneath the castle, trying to scare the shit out of one another.

But they saved their best attempts at fright for the scrawny young Prince Leander. All the boys knew the king, his father, would be unsympathetic to his son's sobbing and whining; nor were his older brothers any help, often joining in the misery inflicted on poor Leander. As the boys left to squire for knights, Leander stayed behind, brooding and plotting his revenge.

"Why am I down here?" said Renoldus.

"Renoldus," Cecile's faint voice called.

The feeling of deep dread enveloped him until it settled in his bones, yet there was this unyielding need to press forward. It was the voice. It was always the voice calling him from somewhere in the distance, its echo reminding him of all things beautiful and pleasant about her. Alongside the good, there was apprehension and foreboding about another failed rescue attempt for his wife.

"No, please," said Renoldus, "I beg you, Cecile, not down here."

The odd caretaker, Droart, held a torch by the crypt, wordless and fixated. Renoldus seized the torch, while Droart, being a short and weak man, held on tightly.

"Droart, give me the torch," said Renoldus as he tugged again, still unable to pry it loose. "Damn you to darkness, Droart, give me the torch."

Droart's sudden head turn caught Renoldus off guard. His face, gray as clouds in the Freezing Months, had eyes black as night and ooze running down his chin. Night crawlers as big as a finger crept from his nose.

"I've already been," said the voice, devoid of humanity.

Startled, Renoldus jerked the torch and pulled it loose, along with Droart's arm, up to the shoulder. The dark ooze squirted from his shoulder and sprayed the side of Renoldus's face. The liquid smelled of death and rotting corpses.

"Shit," said Renoldus. "Gad, the stench."

The voice came calling once again, and the perfumed spirit and essence of Cecile erased, at least for the moment, the smell of all things opposed to her greater qualities. The sound of her song floated in the air like a puffy white cloud on a bright day in the Growing Months.

"Renoldus ..." called the voice somewhere near and far.

Despite his strength, Renoldus could not pry the dead hand of Droart from the torch. Left with no choice, he trudged ahead down the hallway with the arm of the strange little man hanging from the long wooden handle topped with rags soaked in a fluid mixed with sulfur and lime.

The recumbent effigies reflected each king in the prime of his life, carved in stone and placed atop tomb-chests. Each statue held a torch via an outstretched arm, and it angled the illumination from the flame such that each king stared down at Renoldus. It felt as if they examined his soul for worthiness and found it lacking.

The deeper he ventured into the hallway, the more the stone effigies increased in height and size, with each one towering over Renoldus by four body lengths. He dared not look at them for fear of worse condemnation, and so he ran toward the end of the hall but made little progress even as his legs churned faster and faster. The statues chanted as one: "We have found you guilty of violating the Code of the Black."

"Stop accusing me!" said Renoldus.

With urgency in her words, Cecile silenced the kings. "Renoldus, hurry."

Exhausted, he ran on weary legs toward the voice, which seemed closer than before. Each time he put his foot down, there was the sound of splashing water and another foul smell emerged from the stone beneath him. Renoldus peeked down at his feet as he slogged on, and he felt his pace continue to slow, as if his feet were cast in iron.

"What happened to my boots?" said Renoldus. "And why am I running barefoot?"

The stone floor was cutting the bottom of his feet each time they hit the ground. Then realization set in.

"For the sake of the gods," said Renoldus, "I am running in the ruin of the moat water."

"Renoldus," Cecile's voice called urgently, "come quickly and save me, as you failed to do before."

The weight of guilt and shame landed on Renoldus's shoulders, creating a steel yoke, and it abated his gait even further. This additional burden forced him to use his full strength to take one step after another as the load became heavier with each plodding stride.

"Renoldus," said the spirit of Cecile, "faster, do not fail me again."

Remorse, regret, disgrace drove Renoldus further and pushed his wearied body forward in a flowing muck, gaining speed and depth. The discharge of vile and filthy water was up to his chest, yet the flowery scent of Cecile had replaced the stench.

"Where are you, Cecile?" shouted Renoldus. The slime had long since swallowed the torch. He only hoped to follow her voice. There was no reply, and now Renoldus encountered an outcome resembling the first.

"Cecile," he said, panicked by the possibility of a second failure.

"Renoldus," said Cecile, "here I am, but quickly. It's almost too late."

Renoldus turned in the mire but saw nothing but the black horrific water around him stretching forever in front of him. He hoped to be in the castle recesses, but doubt now troubled him.

"Where am I?" said Renoldus. "Am I in the place of punishment? Is this my lot for eternity, to swim in the shit of others while Cecile begs me to help?"

Two arms shot up out of the water and wrapped themselves around his neck from behind, and the figure entwined its legs around his midsection like a child riding their father's back. The additional weight was not quite enough to pull Renoldus backward into the dung-filled water, but it was close. A woman's familiar voice whispered in his ear.

"She is already dead," said the voice. "Come with me and let me love you."

"Johna?" said Renoldus.

The name of his former-lover-turned-spy had just left his tongue when another set of arms held to his neck and the rest of this other body encased Renoldus from the front. The face of the woman in front of him had never looked as gorgeous, even though most of her body was dangling in the foulest of waters.

"Ymenia?" said Renoldus.

"Forget about her," said Ymenia, one of the servants in the castle. "I am the only one who can care for you now that your wife is dead."

"What are you saying? How do you know she is dead?"

"Because she is, love," said Johna, "and who is this whore?"

While fighting to rise above the two heads competing for his attention, leg irons clamped around his ankles.

"Cecile," said Renoldus.

"No, please do not kill me!" screamed Cecile. "Have mercy on me, I beg you!"

"Let me go free," said Renoldus, "she is not dead. You lied to me."

Renoldus struggled to get free of the women, but it only weakened his already tired and wearied body, and they held on even tighter.

"She is already dead," echoed Jonah and Ymenia. "The voice is coming from the grave."

"Lies," said Renoldus. "Neither of you speaks the truth."

She rose behind Renoldus, with her red hair visible first, followed by her face and then her freckled chest, until only her lower body remained beneath the putrid water. Wary of making a sound, she slipped a leather collar around Renoldus's neck and snapped the lock into place. Upon seeing her, the other two fell from him and into the water.

"No," screamed the voice of Cecile one last time, before going silent.

"Cecile, wait," yelled Renoldus.

The woman with red hair turned, holding a long chain, and walked through the water as if it didn't exist. As the chain became taut, she jerked it downward and pulled Renoldus under.

"You belong to me now," said Ingrid.

Renoldus shot up from his pillow, gasping for air, and gulped in as much as his lungs could hold. He reached for the goblet of wine on the table next to his bed and gulped down the rest. Renoldus was wearied and worn down by the onslaught of almost nightly dreams and their growing sense of doom and failure.

I am losing my mind. Since I began bedding Ingrid, these nightmares have plagued me. Can Cecile be speaking to me from the grave, causing guilt in my mind and soul?

The affair was in its fourth week and growing in its insanity. Over the last week, the two were extreme in their recklessness with discretion. The allure of an illicit affair only intensified their propensity to live on the edge of sanity. Lady Evelyn skillfully used her husband's connection to the darker side of Crence to prevent the exposure of the princess's ongoing desire for near daily fulfillment.

Unable to sleep, Renoldus opened another bottle of wine and sat alone with his thoughts. He sat in near darkness and examined his life for what it had become; an attempt to use wine and now the princess to fill the void left by the death of

Cecile, only to be racked by guilt. Yet there was something about Princess Ingrid he loved.

Why can't I release Cecile? Will she haunt my dreams from here to eternity? I cannot open my heart and mind to a woman for fear of Cecile's jealousy and her memory. And this from the grave? Love lost has pierced my heart, not by steel or iron, but by something much stronger.

Ingrid has become a sweet cress to my wounded soul. The rhapsody in it relieves the pain, but payment for its pleasure is found in its enslavement. Is this what I have become? Slave to my body's desire and fulfilled in Ingrid? Yet, do I not find pleasure also in bedding King Leander's daughter as revenge for the murders I know he arranged?

CHAPTER 5
ZOELLA

The two Aeehrls and their respective ladies met at the courtyard side of the screens passage at one end of Zoella Heil before entering the large rectangular room. The length was two and a half times the width, with a taller vaulted ceiling. They crossed the hall and approached the dais on a raised platform. The castle staff arranged the Aeehrl's High Chairs behind the long, hand-carved oak table, which had legs shaped like the eahrshe, the great black-and-white whale found off the coast of Flace.

"The mullioned windows are beautiful," said Thora.

"As you know, glass is expensive and scarce," said Thorve, "but they provide substantial light to keep the Heil from becoming the Great Cave."

"The placement of the large bay window is very well done, and the design is quite original. You opted to remove the central hearth and replace it with fireplaces and chimneys. Well played, sister."

"Skuti's dedication to his work with the architects matches his attention to detail in ship design and construction. The central fireplace is spacious enough for a person to stand and move around."

"Perhaps we could entice Jomar to walk into it."

"Thora, watch what you say. You never know when the ears of the wrong person might be open."

The two sisters smiled together as they did when they were young girls planning to do some deed outside of proper behavior, as children do. They would spend hours in conversation, carefully planning to avoid any blame. Not once were the twins ever caught in their childish games.

Ah, Thorve, you look at me as you did when we were just young girls. How much fun we had tricking adults with our cunning. Nothing has changed, my sister, only the stakes have increased. They did not find us out, even after we—that was dreadful, and I am sorry we ever did such a thing. She was such a nice old woman.

"The Heil at Saeehrspire is dark and dank," said Thora. "One might assume Jomar in his vanity would command a new Heil constructed, but he is too busy planning for—" Thora caught herself at the last moment, stopping before revealing a fact best kept for later. It was far too early in the game for such a play as this.

"Planning for what, Thora?"

"I will speak on the matter later. It's time to take chairs next to our husbands."

Thora, you need to pay greater attention to what you are saying. Don't ruin everything with a careless word. Hmmm ... maybe, on second thought, sharing it with Thorve might help convince her of our need to act now against Jomar.

Thora and Thorve walked the three steps up to the platform and took seats next to their respective husbands. The chairs were befitting of their standing as ladies, but not as large or ornate as the High Chairs of the Aeehrls. Further down the dais on either side of the Aeehrls were the members of Skuti's court and their wives.

"People of Ashul," said Skuti as he rose from his chair, silencing the den of noise from the sounds that filled the air of a hall preparing for a feast. "Today we celebrate the abundance of the harvest and give thanks to Zoella, for we have found favor in her eyes. She found the aroma of our sacrifices on the altars pleasing."

Skuti raised his leather tankard to the roof and shouted, "All praise to Zoella, goddess of the Abundant Harvest!" Those in attendance rose as one, lifted their goblets and tankards upward, and shouted: "Praise Zoella!"

After giving thanks, the people toasted one another and sang the traditional songs passed down through the annals of time. Two minstrels walked and played lutes, leading guests in old and new songs.

"Well-spoken, Skuti," said Jomar, as Skuti sat back down in his High Chair. "The gods and goddesses have shown us great favor."

"Yes, my brother-law," said Skuti, "they have indeed."

Servants used petals from sweet-smelling flowers and rushes to throw on the slate floor, disguising unwanted odors and to soak up spills. On the wall opposite the windows were decorations of intricately woven tapestries, weapons, and murals. The artists painted the coat of arms in black-and-white and emblazoned with an eahrshe, the sigil of House Ingimund.

Guests sat on benches at long trestle tables. The aroma from roasting meats came from the kitchen and wafted through the hall. In addition, vegetables from the kitchen's garden were prepared, including peas, beans, carrots, cabbage, and spinach. Dessert included wafers, pastries, and fruit from the trees on the castle grounds, among other delicacies.

After the feast, it was customary to resolve minor petitions or disputes of the commoners. Jomar's reputation for revelry preceded his coming, and with him present, those in attendance could expect him to share plenty of counsel. However, there was usually little wisdom to go with it.

"Aeehrl Jomar, are you ready?" said Skuti, smiling at his brother-law.

"I am!" said Jomar, toasting his leather jack full of beer to the sky and taking a large gulp. "Bring out the first victim!"

"If you don't get serious, I am going to throw you out of the Heil."

"Then throw me out, if you dare."

The two men, now drunk, almost fell onto the floor in hearty laughter. It would be up to Thora and Thorve to restore a semblance of order to the proceedings. Skuti earned a reputation as a just and fair ruler of disputes, but a drunken Jomar ensured that the business portion of the evening would descend into folly.

"Jomar, stop behaving like a common drunkard," hissed Thora. "You are embarrassing me with your behavior."

"Skuti!" said Thorve. "Don't turn Aeehrl Jomar into a court jester; you're upsetting Thora. Take care of this business and then drink the rest of the night if you must."

"I am leaving the Heil," said Thora, leaning toward Thorve. "I cannot stand Jomar's duplicity. At one moment, evil darkens his world, and the next he loves the world and everything in it. Except for me, I'm sure."

"You act as if this has never happened before," replied Thorve. "Sit there and let the boys have their fun."

"At the end of this madness, he won't care where I'm at, or even if I'm in bed with another man."

"Thora, that's not how ladies should speak," Thorve said, giggling. But Thora found it less than amusing.

"But is it acceptable for an Aeehrl to allow his whores and bastards to roam the city freely?"

"No, it is not, Thora. I'm sorry I made light of such a thing."

"It's not you, Sister. The weight of Jomar's sins has crushed the spirit within me. I'm leaving."

As she departed, Thora turned her face toward Skuti as he prepared for their so-called court session and, in near disgust, glanced at Jomar, inebriated, and having quite the celebration and then some.

I would allow Skuti to bed me anytime he wanted to, unlike Thorve. But Father gave me this piece of shit instead.

Skuti cleared his throat and made a motion for his assistant to call the cases to be presented this evening. He peeked over at his wife and caught Thorve's shaking head, then glanced at Thora's seat, empty. Skuti ignored the oddness of Thora having left the Heil and plodded forward.

"Aeehrl Skuti," said Sigfast Grimkel, castellan of Seaborne Keep, "the first order of business regards if in fact Serk Gaut stole a sheep from Oddleif Larund's farm."

Both men approached the elevated table to plead their cases. Serk, a short, bald man, had a scarred face and a reputation for poor character. Still, Thorve pitied the disliked man. Oddleif, a respectable man, had a farm and a family in a nearby village.

"State your case against Serk Gaut," said Sigfast.

"Serk stole one of my sheep out of its pen," said Oddleif, "and sold it down at the harbor to a sea merchant. I have a witness."

"Serk, what is your defense against this serious charge?" said Sigfast.

"I am guilty and throw myself at the mercy of the court," said Serk. "I stole the sheep and sold it, so I would have coinage for a roof over my head and food in my belly."

"Then why were you caught at the brothel with your head between a whore's legs?" asked Oddleif.

"See. I got a roof over my head and something to eat."

The audience erupted in laughter, almost bringing down the roof of the Great Heil. Skuti and Jomar shared a look and joined the uproarious noise with their own loud guffaws.

Thorve smiled, suppressing a laugh. Oddleif could only watch with a look of disgust on his beet-red face.

After the howling had died down, Skuti, with his best serious face, turned and conferred with Jomar. The two whispered as if they were seriously considering the matter, when they were, in fact, talking about the shape and size of two well-endowed maidens seated nearby. Thorve looked on, her unease obvious in the way she shook her head and stared at her husband.

At last, the quiet talk stopped and Skuti pronounced his judgment: "The court says you are to perform the walk of shame, as is the custom for cases of thievery. In addition, you are to repay Oddleif for his sheep and if you cannot do so, I will throw you into debtor's jail until at such a time you can repay the amount. Aeehrl Jomar, do you have anything to add?"

"Indeed," Jomar said, eyeing Serk. "If you sought a bedmate, why not keep the sheep?"

At that, the entire hall erupted in laughter again. Laughing, Skuti almost toppled from his chair and onto the platform. Jomar was bent over in laughter, causing himself a coughing fit that only added to the hysterics.

After the riotous crowd settled down once more from its uncontrolled hooting and howling, they presented several other cases to Skuti. It was a fortunate turn that the following cases required little thinking. Skuti and Jomar were incapable of serious thought on any matter. By the time the court session was over, Skuti and Jomar had worn themselves out from ale and laughter. Jomar, drunk and tired, stepped a few feet from the platform, laid himself down, and passed out on the cold slate floor.

Again, Jomar? For as big as you are, your ability to stifle drunkenness is quite low. Now to get you on a rug.

"Bardi!" shouted Skuti to a warrior across the Heil chatting with a female servant.

"Yes, my Aeehrl," replied Bardi, ignoring the servant girl for a moment.

"Fetch the bearskin blankets near the fireplace and bring them here. I need help with Aeehrl Jomar."

Bardi excused himself from the attractive brown-haired girl and promised to return as soon as he finished the Aeehrl's business. Bardi grabbed another man, and the two carried the heavy fur blankets over to where Skuti was standing while Jomar snored as if he were a bear.

"Help me roll Jomar atop the one," said Skuti, "and we can cover him with the other."

After some strenuous effort, the three men were able to move the large frame of Jomar onto the thick rug without waking him.

"Well done, Bardi," said Skuti. "Find the servant girl. Tell her of your good deed and the Aeehrl's great appreciation of such help. Perhaps that will help convince her what a good man you are. If not, she is not worth having."

Bardi almost ran as he moved away to find the servant girl he'd left minutes ago. The other man turned and walked away. Skuti realized his error and called the man back.

"What is your name, young man?" asked Skuti.

"Egil, if it pleases you, my Aeehrl," replied the young man.

"Egil, I did not grant you anything for your service with Bardi."

"I require nothing, my Aeehrl. My service is enough."

"Well said. Nonetheless, I would be remiss if I granted Bardi a kindness and not you. A red-haired girl from an excellent family stands against the far wall. They are seeking a husband for her. It is clear you come from such a family, and I am guessing your father has enough coinage for her dowry. Go introduce yourself and tell her how impressed I am with your diligence."

"May your name, my Aeehrl and lord, be exalted above all others in Flace."

Skuti nodded at the young man as he set a beeline for the red-haired virgin. "Perhaps Father would have approved of that," said Skuti to no one in particular.

CHAPTER 6
GLASHA

The fourteen-year-old princess ran through the village streets and straight for the Tree of Whispers, one of the large, majestic trees making up the Groves of Sorrow. The trees were massive, with trunks so wide one could march an army through them. In the Tree of Whispers lived a blind old woman, named Shadbak, in a rickety makeshift treehouse.

If her father, *Chouufsuoum* Sarg, found out his daughter was again visiting with the seer, his anger would burn hot against her. He was a violent warrior king, with angry black eyes and a lust for power outside of the Af'lam village he had ruled for twenty years with an iron fist.

His desire to be accepted by kings as an equal turned into an obsession that one day would consume him and unhinge him from sanity. His hopes for legitimacy lived in the growing beauty of his daughter and her ability to attract a prince or king to wed. The arranged marriage and subsequent alliance would enable Sarg to escape the hidden groves and build a kingdom of his own.

"Shadbak," said Glasha up to the treehouse, "send down the rope."

"What are you doing out here?" said Shadbak. "Your father will be angry with you if he finds out."

"He is always angry with me. And everyone else."

"Then why do you make it worse, child?"

"I like the stories you tell."

"They are not stories. They are history waiting to be written."

"Please?"

Shadbak lowered the rope, and Glasha scrambled up to the treehouse. She was not the usual princess, wearing dresses, sewing clothes and the like. Glasha, a warrior at heart, fought like every other Af'lam woman.

Each day, she spent her morning's training under the tutelage of the best fighter in the village, a warrior named Ditru. Her accuracy in throwing a small axe was impressive, especially given her age and gender. Males her age rarely hit the target while Glasha was throwing bulls-eyes straight down the middle. As her adult muscles grew, her ability to throw a double-bladed axe and wield a large sword would increase tenfold.

"Thank you, *Cimcier* Shadbak," said Glasha with wide emerald eyes, expecting more stories from the books. *Don't say stories*, she thought, correcting herself.

Shadbak sat at a wobbly table on a chair not appreciably much better. The table was littered with herbs, berries, roots, leaves, and random pieces of lizards and snakes.

"You're welcome, my child," Shadbak said. "But this is the last time. Your father has already made threats against me for telling you lies."

"What are you making today?" said Glasha.

"A remedy for quick healing of wounds."

Shadbak held up a container of a mysterious liquid held in an old cracked waterskin which somehow was not dripping any of its contents onto the floor.

"What's that one with the X on it?"

"You need not know what it's used for."

"Please? I'm not coming up here again."

"Suit yourself. They use it in the ceremony to honor Gydia, goddess of fertility."

The girl approaching her teenage years looked away and giggled at the mention of Gydia.

Glasha had determined to ask of her own future before she scooted up the rope. She feared disliking what was to come, but her father's plans were not her own. Rising from the floor, she gazed at the endless trees, it seemed, with no end. "Will I ever leave this grove of trees? I want to see what else is out there."

"Oh, my child," said Shadbak, "you will flee from this grove of trees, forced to roam the continent, pursued by enemies, including your very own people."

"I wanted a happy life, not one of running from my people."

"You will witness the unimaginable."

"What caused all this?"

"Not what, but whom?"

Shadbak turned her attention back to her table filled with herbs, flowers, and roots, continuing her work on potions and concoctions. One jar on the table drew Glasha's attention momentarily while she waited for Shadbak to continue. When the old seer didn't respond, Glasha started anew.

"I don't want to marry a human prince or king," she said. "They won't treat me well. I'll just be a curiosity for people to see."

Shadbak kept working and didn't bother to look up. "You'll wed neither prince nor king."

"I don't want to wed anyone in our tribe, either. Ditru wants to mate with me. It's the only reason he teaches me how to be a warrior."

"You'll not marry an Af'lam warrior."

"Then who?"

"A man you've seen, yet don't know."

"That's not much help."

"Both of you will do something unforgivable in the eyes of the king you serve and, as a result, forced to leave the kingdoms you were born into."

"How can I do something that's unforgivable, *Cimcier*? This is getting worse."

The room went quiet as Shadbak continued her work and Glasha contemplated what Shadbak said. Unable to stand the silence, Glasha pressed forward despite her growing dread.

"What else is there about the man?"

"It'll be up to you to restore him to whom he once was."

"That's something I can do."

"There's one last thing."

"What's that?"

"You must receive the blessing of a woman no longer amongst the living."

Glasha rolled her eyes and squealed. "That's impossible."

Shadbak didn't want to crush the young woman's spirit, and so she smiled and added one last tidbit. "Not impossible, but you'll need to prove your worthiness."

Shoulders slumped, Glasha sat on the floor.

I shouldn't have asked these questions.

"Do you know," said Shadbak, "why the others hate you?"

"I have light-colored skin," said Glasha.

Shadbak moved closer to Glasha to get a good look into her eyes; despite her blindness, she still possessed the ability to look into one's soul. There was no getting used to the seer's smell, but Glasha ignored it best she could to hear what she had to say.

"Do Sarg and Ushat have light skin?"

"No, but Father says my light skin is a gift from the gods."

"Does anyone else in the tribe have light skin?"

"Just me."

"When the time comes for you to leave the village, a slave

will attend to your wounds. When your eye considers her, you will see a wide smile and from her eye, a tear will roll down her cheek."

"What are you saying, *Cimcier*?"

"You can figure that out for yourself."

Glasha furrowed her brow and cradled her chin in the heel of her palm. Hurt and feeling embarrassed, she tried to bury herself into an old rug filled with stains and holes covering the old wood floor underneath.

"I should not have come here today."

"You asked, and I have told you, Glasha. Return to the village, as I am weary and must rest."

After speaking these words, Shadbak crawled into her ramshackle bed and fell asleep. Glasha eyed the potion bottle labeled X and the container of liquid used in healing. Glasha calculated in her mind the best way to slide down the rope with two delicate items in her hands.

As Glasha was considering her crime, Shadbak shivered and produced a prolonged cough as if she were deathly ill. The loud sound caused Glasha to flinch, and the floor responded with a creak. Still, Shadbak continued sleeping and moments later rolled herself over such that her back was facing Glasha.

With great care, Glasha snatched the two items, slid down the rope, and ran for the village, disturbed by everything she had heard.

Shadbak rolled over again, and a smile creased her face.

∼

Sarg Thall, Glasha's father, had a face with more scars and age lines than unblemished skin, evidence of a life filled with violence. Two long, deep, parallel scars marked the left side of his face, from hairline to eyebrow. The deep gouges came courtesy of a masked assassin with an axe, attempting to turn Sarg's head into a canoe.

The failed attempt rattled Sarg and led to an even greater mistrust of those close to him, exacerbating his already unpleasant personality. As it was, Sarg could be merciless, vindictive, arrogant, violent, unbending, murderous, deceitful, prone to bouts of severe depression, and abusive. All within the same day.

Chouufsuoum Sarg had the appearance of a hardened military commander, with deep-set angry black eyes and a perpetual snarl. Underneath the thin eyebrows and eyes was a small triangular nose with flared-out nostrils and a short, scraggly beard graying with age, as was his thinning straight hair pulled back around his pointed ears, although they were close to those of a human. Small tusks came from his lower jaw and over his upper lip, creating indents in the skin beneath them. His once-medium-toned olive skin was turning tan from age and the unrelenting rays of Vesceron.

"Where is Glasha?" said Sarg. "I swear to the unlistening gods I will chain her to a tree for her disobedience."

"Why do you speak like that?" said Ushat, his wife. "You never disciplined your daughter a day in her life. And now you expect her to come when she is called?"

"Shut your mouth, you insolent whore."

"She's just a little bitch who thinks everyone should worship her."

"Shut your mouth."

"Why? Is it because I dare to speak the truth when nobody else does?"

Sarg stared at his wife for a moment with his black eyes and furrowed brow, a look he often used to bend men to his will. Ushat glanced up, shaking her head like a mother would to an annoying child, before returning to a letter from the court of eldresses.

Glasha's boots lightly clacked against the rough-edged

stone floor, signaling her entrance into the throne room and her reluctant approach towards her father's throne.

Sarg's deep booming voice thundered in the small throne room with few adornments and nothing to absorb sound. Sarg built his castle with both stone and wood on a raised dirt mound, surrounding it with a walled courtyard, a protective ditch, and palisade. The repairs needed on the *Chouufsuoum's* timeworn residence would take coin and skilled labor, which was in short supply within the tribe.

"Where have you been?" he said.

Glasha sauntered across the stone and stopped before the stairs leading up to her father seated on a throne made of stone. It was primitive compared to the thrones made from marble and gold of kings and queens, but it was a High Chair and represented the unquestioned power of the man seated on it.

What does he want now? If this is another of his desperate attempts to wed me to an old man calling himself a king, I will not do it. I've wearied of squeezing myself into a dress that doesn't fit and being paraded around like some sort of animal.

"Are you going to answer my question?" said Sarg. "I sent word to you over an hour ago."

Glasha stood before her father with arms folded across her chest. "Can't you see the sweat on my body? I was breaking in the new bow Ditru gave me."

"Watch your mouth. I'm the *Chouufsuoum* and your father. I'm in no mood for your churlish behavior."

Get on with it. I know what you are going to say.

Sarg's eyes narrowed, and he began his dance with destiny and daughter once more. It was an awkward frolic where the movements never quite matched the music.

"I've found a king who wants to ally with our tribe," said Sarg. "He's under attack and needs our fighters."

"Another old man?" said Glasha, "Father, please don't put me through this again."

"He's a young king. His father recently died."

"No one, old or young, desires me as a mate. My skin is a different color. I'm taller, more muscular, and in my heart, I'm a warrior. I've no interest in going to dinners and galas."

"When I arrange introductions such as this, you undermine me from the beginning."

"I don't undermine you. They don't want to marry me."

"Of course they don't when you behave as you do. Guzzling wine out of fine vessels, then spilling drink and food all over yourself as if you're a barbarian. You will embarrass me no further."

Embarrass you? You've been embarrassing me since I first bled. You know females are mature at fourteen, and now I'm sixteen. I'm a grown female, not some little princess. I've had enough of your silly attempts at marriage for me.

"You've embarrassed me my whole life. Each time you drag me in front of those lascivious men who want to bed me so they can brag about taming a savage with their cock is humiliating. *Cimcier* Shadbak told me I won't marry any of them. She also told me I have seen the man that I shall marry, and he has bright blue eyes."

"Dare you speak to me with such audacity and tell me lies from the master of false prophecy?"

"She doesn't lie. You both know Ushat is not my mother. My light skin is not from the gods, but of a human slave."

Sarg ripped the rust-marked steel crown from his head and slammed it to the floor, sending it bouncing off the stone. The old steel crown, made a century ago, passed by Glasha and landed several feet away.

"*Kumm omie si kurrmuss!*" said Sarg. "You make my ears bleed with your lies and profane words about your mother."

"Everyone in the tribe hates me," said Glasha, "because I'm not a true Af'lam princess. They know Ushat isn't my mother. They just don't say it out loud."

Oh, no. What have I just said?

Glasha's beautiful bright emerald eyes became even wider, and she felt as if her legs had turned to the pudding she found so tasteful. The confidence she brought into the throne room was gone in a matter of seconds. Her bravado withered like a flower in the heat of the Burning Months.

The silence following the echoing of Glasha's last words seemed to last an eternity. She knew she was in trouble but couldn't have imagined what was to come. The curtain Glasha had just ripped in two revealed secrets no one could know, let alone say them in front of Sarg and Ushat in the throne room.

Glasha wanted to seek forgiveness, but the look on her father's face frightened her into silence. She didn't move but an inch, so panicked and afraid of Sarg's reaction and what he might do to her. But it was Ushat who responded first. She rose from her smaller stone throne, took a few measured steps toward Glasha, and slapped her across the face.

Whack! The sound of flesh on flesh rebounded off the walls and enhanced the power of the blow and what it symbolized. Glasha was no longer a princess; the lie had been breached and there was no repairing it.

The blow knocked Glasha off-balance, but she remained standing. She felt shaken, not from pain, but from Ushat's boldness.

"I'm not your mother, thank the gods," said Ushat, remaining calm. "You're nothing more than a spoiled little bitch."

The warrior in the princess rose from her core, and anger overtook her. She righted herself and pulled her arm back, balled up her hand and—*Blam!* She flew across the room and landed with a thud on the stone floor. Sarg used the momentum of jumping from his chair and blindsided his daughter with a lowered shoulder. The unevenness and sharpness of the stones cut Glasha's arms and legs and opened gashes above her eyebrow and on her head.

"How dare you raise your hand to the *chouufsuoumuss,*"

bellowed Sarg. "I should have you executed for such impudence."

"Beat her and send her away," said Ushat. "The sight of her disgusts me."

Ushat walked over to Glasha and spit on the side of her face, then rubbed it in with the bottom of her dusty boot.

"I always hated you. Good riddance."

Ushat exited the throne room and ascended the stairs to her solar, leaving Glasha alone with her father.

"No, Father," said Glasha, "please don't."

"Shut your mouth," said Sarg, "you are no longer part of this family. You're a mangy street dog, beaten and spit on. I have no use for you."

"I will leave today. Only let me go."

Glasha realized she was moving and not of her own accord. Sarg was dragging her across the floor by her hair until he dumped her unceremoniously to the ground. She got to her feet, dazed, and with legs that threatened to fail her. Sarg sent her back down to the hard stone with a powerful backhanded slap to the other side of her face. The rings Sarg wore on his hand cut her cheek and jaw, and blood trickled out of the cuts. It was the last thing Glasha would remember.

Several hours later, Glasha stirred. Every inch of her body hurt from the vicious blows of Sarg. As she came to, she could sense someone was kneeling beside her.

"Please," said Glasha, "don't hit me."

"I won't, sweetheart," said a quiet human voice.

Wait. The voice is familiar to me. I can hear it sing to me from the past; it's faint, but I know it.

With one eye swollen shut, Glasha opened her other eye and looked up at the woman beside her. She wore a smile wider than the woman ever thought possible again, and as she did, a tear rolled down her cheek.

Cimcier Shadbak?

"Mother?" Glasha whispered, "is that you?

"Yes, my dear," she said, "how'd you know?"

Glasha only smiled, cracking open the cuts on her bruised and swollen lips.

"You've been badly beaten," her mother said. "Let me clean your wounds. I have some water and herbs."

Glasha's lips hurt, and it was difficult to speak through them. "How'd I get out here?"

"Two guards dumped you here. They laughed and said you belonged with us."

"Here?"

"You're in the slave's pen. Who beat you?"

"My father."

"He is a brutal man."

Glasha paused for a moment. *Do I want to ask? But I must know.*

"Did my father rape you?"

The exhausted slave, once the most beautiful girl in her village, nodded her head and shed painful tears. The memories of being summoned to the keep and sexually assaulted by the *Chouufsuoum* until she became pregnant stayed with her. She never spoke to him again after that and tried her best to avoid him when working in the castle. They prevented her from seeing the child once she finished nursing. If Glasha's name formed on Ela's lips, a beating, or worse, would await her.

"I'm a bastard princess."

Uttering the words brought the stigma to life. Glasha, a bastard child of the *Chouufsuoum*, never imagined herself in this manner.

No wonder they all hated me.

"Don't say that," said the slave. "You are still the princess."

I'm not the princess, but you're my mother.

"I don't even know your name," said Glasha.

"My name is Ela," she said and smiled at her daughter.

"That's beautiful. Do I have a human name?"

"Yes. It's Miriella."

"It's a wonderful name, Mother. Someday when I find the man who's mine, I'm going to have him call me by that name."

"I hope you find love one day."

"I will, and I know the man. Shadbak told me."

Despite the slight exaggeration, Glasha had decided since she last saw Shadbak that Sir Renoldus was the man she was to marry. Even lying in the dirt, hurting from head to toe, she recalled, as if it were the previous day, locking eyes with his bright blue orbs. The moment seemed to last an eternity and as she held his gaze; it convinced the young Glasha, there was a deep attraction between the two. Her emerald eyes had slain the famous knight, or so she thought, as easily as a rabbit by one of her arrows.

It must be him. Who else could it be?

Ela smiled again at her daughter, and despite her bruised and swollen face, she still found beauty in her Miriella. "I hope you find him soon."

Glasha ended her daydreaming, realizing she needed to leave the tribe as soon as she was able.

No later than just before Vesceron rises. I must go before the darkness departs.

"I'm leaving the tribe," said Glasha. "I will need to move quickly."

"You must," agreed Ela. "If you stay in the village, death awaits you."

"I will not die at the hands of my father, or anyone else."

Glasha's mindset changed. She was determined to escape her punishment and flee into the night and on toward Brüeland. She didn't know what she would say or where to look for Renoldus once she arrived there. But there would be plenty of time to figure it out on her horse ride west.

"Ditru, I think that's his name, came by while you were still sleeping. He brought your horse and your weapons and some clothes, I believe. He must've paid off the guards, although he carries a very large sword."

"Did he say anything?"

"He said he would come find you someday. That's about it."

He'll never see me again.

"Here, let me help you up," said Ela. "I see some women of the tribe walking this way. You can rest in my tent, and I'll finish cleaning you up. I will give you my dinner later, meager as it is. Sleep for a few hours and you can be on your way when the time is right."

Glasha struggled to her feet, wrapped an arm around Ela, and limped toward her tent. Glasha felt uplifted when she found her mother, despite her condition. Later that night, she escaped as planned and galloped her brown and white spotted palfrey as fast as he could go. Glasha needed separation from the warriors that her father would send after her once he was told she'd escaped.

Ela sobbed uncontrollably as her daughter left, draining every last drop of her tears. When she finished, she found a long, thick rope and a sturdy tree limb.

CHAPTER 7
BADEK RISING

Celebrating Zoella's goodness had turned into a Boccromol, as the ancients named it. As Skuti observed the revelers, he could only hope and pray no enemy marched against Ashul in the next week. Skuti was feeling the effects of ale himself, furthered by the emotional mayhem of Jomar. All the theater had distracted Skuti from any realistic hope of forging a plan with Jomar to unify Flace.

It's time to walk the strand and clear my head. Mead should help.

Skuti chuckled at his reasoning but motioned the new servant girl over to where he was standing. The young woman was petite, with few curves, and lacked the height of the strong, big-bodied women populating Ashul. She stood out from amongst the gathered crowd yet did not garner many second looks.

"What is your name?" said Skuti.

"Astrid, my Aeehrl," she said.

"Your accent is not of this land. Where do you call home?"

"Taazrand, from across the waters. My father sold me for coinage, and I eventually ended up here."

"Very well, Astrid, bring me one of our fine mead vessels.

Tell the alewife I want the vessel marked with X-X on its side."

"Yes, my Aeehrl."

Astrid headed off for the buttery, and Skuti watched her take every step. Her light reddish-brown hair fell just below her small breasts and to the middle of her back, and her hips swiveled in just the right way.

What am I doing? Father told me affairs begin within the mind long before they become real in the flesh.

Skuti turned his head away and spotted Thorve alone on the platform with a silver goblet, sipping wine and watching her people enjoy themselves on another pleasant evening in Ashul. He decided to join her and get his mind off Astrid.

"Where is Lady Thora?" asked Skuti.

"She is not quite herself," replied Thorve. "She's run off and I don't know where she went."

"That is not like her to leave, nor you to not seek her. Does she have a lover in the city?"

Thorve shifted her gaze from Skuti to the crowd in the Heil, tears welling in her eyes.

"I was only jesting," said Skuti. "Please forgive me. Her disappearance must have more to it than I imagined."

"I cannot speak of it now," sniffled Thorve, "but I'm not angry with you."

Skuti glanced back over his shoulder and noticed Astrid in front of the wood curtain leading to the buttery. She held the jar of mead in her hands and smiled at Skuti.

"I am going out to the strand," he said, "and for you, my lady?"

"I am sorry, my Aeehrl. Soon, I will retire to the keep."

"As you desire, Lady Thorve of Ashul."

"I watched the new servant girl disappear a moment ago, and now she is over by the curtain holding a jar of mead, I believe. Don't pass out drunk before coming back to the keep. It is unbecoming for the Aeehrl of Ashul to be so drunk."

"I prefer the days when no one cared who I was or what I was doing."

"But the gods have chosen you for a higher calling."

"While true, I am still a warrior at heart."

"That's why Ashul loves you. Never lose sight of that."

"I may fail, but you will always be there. In the eyes of the people, you're faultless."

Tears started anew and rolled down Thorve's cheeks. She dabbed at them with a small, square kerchief, cleared her throat, and attempted to regain her composure. After giving herself a moment, Thorve adjusted herself on the chair and smiled.

"Speak truthfully, Thorve," said Skuti. "I swear by the gods in the heavens you have heard disturbing news from Thora."

"I have," said Thorve, "but I don't want to talk about it. I will not cry as if I'm watching the funeral pyre of a loved one. Not here, in front of our people who rely on me for strength."

Skuti nodded and paused, thirsty for his mead and more conversation with Astrid.

"I can only assume Jomar has told you his version of the truth," said Thorve.

"He has," said Skuti.

I swear we are being lied to again, and unification is at the center. There is evil behind their exaggerated claims of madness and murder. I swear in the dark, secret places of my soul, Thora is the one behind Jomar's failure to aid my rebellion against Vott, a vile man who killed the sisters' father, Eldgrim, to claim the High Chair for himself. I know Jomar, and in his heart, he's still a warrior. His lust for war is like a man's desire for a beautiful woman. As a young man, Jomar would fight just to fight, always searching out bigger opponents to test his skills.

Despite the sadness written on her face, Thorve held back her tears. Skuti placed his hand on Thorve's shoulder, and with her own she grasped it tight for several moments until easing her grip and bringing it to her lips. Thorve kissed Skuti's hand with tenderness before releasing it.

"Go, Skuti," said Thorve, "perhaps the smell of the sea will help clear your head, although the mead will fog it back up."

Skuti chuckled before he added, "Would you have me find the healer and fetch you the dream savory to ease your tensions and help you sleep?"

Despite desiring the herbal remedy, she still needed to stay in control. "No, but thank you for the offer."

With a quick nod, Skuti headed for Astrid and the jar of mead. The servant girl was waiting with her smile as the Aeehrl of Ashul approached.

"Here it is, my Aeehrl," said Astrid, "just as you asked."

"Well done, Astrid," said Skuti.

"Is there something else I might do to please my Aeehrl?"

I need to walk straight for the door and outside to the ...

"I trust your father was poor," said Skuti.

Astrid was quiet for a moment before remembering what they had spoken about earlier.

"Yes," she said, "he knew I would fetch the most coinage among the children."

"Age?"

"I can glimpse the spiritual realm and foresee the future. I think you refer to my kind as a Þuriðr."

Her green eyes are different, intense. Perhaps there is a power in them. Or, perhaps, I have had too much ale and am full of lust.

"Prove yourself to the Aeehrl of Ashul."

"If it pleases my Aeehrl, I will do as I am told. May I ask my Aeehrl to step outside for a moment?"

"Why is that, servant girl?"

"If I may, my Aeehrl, the Lady of Ashul is staring over here. I'll slip out through the buttery if you'd rather, and you can exit through the door."

Astrid curtsied to Skuti, then exited through the curtain

and back across the buttery. Skuti did not look back at Thorve and, despite his reservations, left the Heil. Skuti walked to a quiet spot inside the garden, far away from prying eyes. He leaned against a half-wall when Astrid came near and stood close to him.

"Your looks are exotic compared to the women in Flace," said Skuti.

"The rest of Ashul's men have a different opinion," Astrid said.

"Then they are not men, but boys."

"May I touch your hand, my Aeehrl?"

Skuti extended his hand and Astrid took it and used it to move in closer, and as she did, Skuti noticed her eyes were darker, harder, with more of an edge. The angled brows and dark lines drawn around her eyes on her light brown skin ignited a fiery desire in him.

Astrid peered into Skuti's eyes as if she was going to gaze into his soul. In that instant, he perceived nothing, not even the revelers' noise. He saw only the deep green eyes.

"Do I frighten you, my Aeehrl?" said Astrid.

"Nothing frightens me," said Skuti.

"Your eyes are saying something different."

"Maybe you should look closer."

Skuti pulled Astrid in, sharing a deep and passionate kiss.

"I can feel you want me," whispered Astrid into Skuti's ear, "and I you. But not tonight."

Skuti pulled back and caught a twinkle in Astrid's eyes and a seductive smile on her face.

"You have led me to water like a horse," said Skuti, "yet you will not let me drink."

"Trust me," Astrid said. "Eventually, my well will satisfy your thirst."

Skuti folded his muscular arms across his chest and cast a suspicious eye at the young seer.

"Well?" he said.

"Let me hold both of your hands this time," said Astrid.

This woman has duped me for certain.

A wry smile formed on Skuti's face, somewhat up, somewhat down, but it was a wrinkled smile.

"See anything?" he asked.

Astrid ignored the question and continued to peer into Skuti's green eyes, which were much like his smile: somewhat open, somewhat closed. She stared intently, searching with her eyes.

Astrid hoicked her hands away from Skuti's and backed away. She placed a hand over her mouth and gasped. Skuti, surprised at her panicked state, cast a sideways glance at the foreign seer.

"What did you see?" said Skuti.

Astrid shook her head back and forth before taking several deep breaths.

"You need to stay away from Thora, my Aeehrl," said Astrid, speaking as if she had run a good distance. "She has brought an ancient, yet powerful magic to Ashul. There is a witch hiding in Iziadrock, and she has made a deal with this devil."

"How do you know it was Thora?" said Skuti, skeptical at the insinuation. "Thorve is her twin."

Astrid couldn't shake what she saw after the veil of evil disappeared, and she remained visibly upset.

"When I brought ale as you dined, I felt a sinister power fall over me. When I glanced over at Lady Thora, darkness enveloped her."

"This means?"

"Avoid going to the strand tonight."

"Why?"

As Astrid regained her composure, she still felt chilled by the glimpse of Evanora, the witch hiding in Iziadrock, conspiring with Thora. The threat from the witch was real, and Astrid understood her powers wouldn't be enough against the ageless and experienced Evanora. All she could do was warn Skuti and hope it sufficed.

"Doing so will cause a haunting deception that lingers forever."

This is too vague.

"You speak vaguely. What is this deception?"

"I cannot say for sure. The witch I spoke of caught me staring into your future and threatened to kill me. I had to escape before the witch revealed the deception."

"You must've seen something."

"The Reaper of Souls is on his way to collect the soul of one innocent man. If you don't go, he will be sent away empty-handed."

"Still more vagaries. How can I trust what you are telling me?"

"You've chosen not to believe me, so I will leave something for you to remember my words."

Astrid grabbed Skuti's forearm with one hand and ran one of her long nails from the other down his forearm. The painful, burning sensation made him attempt to pull her hand off, but it would not budge.

"Let go, damn you," said Skuti.

Astrid released her grip; a long red streak ran down his forearm, from the crook of the elbow to his wrist. Skuti looked at the mark and then back to Astrid several times before speaking.

"What is wrong with you?" said Skuti. "I should have you arrested."

"This shall vanish," said Astrid. "Yet upon its return, you'll remember my words. When you're in need, call for me, and I shall come."

"I'd rather not remember any of this. I'm heading for the strand where I will drink the mead and forget what you've told me."

"Remember what I said. Thora is not to be trusted."

Skuti shook his head and noticed more people entering the garden area, and some were staring at their Aeehrl and the mysterious servant girl. He looked at his arm again and the wound was gone.

"I've spent too much time with you," said Skuti. "Pack your bags and go back to wherever it was you said."

"I will do as you say, Aeehrl Skuti," said Astrid. "Our paths will cross again someday."

"Goodbye, and good riddance."

He stumbled away, unsteady from drink, hearing Astrid's voice one last time, its echo lingering in his mind for a long time.

"One soul shall perish tonight," she said.

Despite trying to ignore the words, Skuti turned around before leaving the castle, as he always did, and stared at the walls. They were marred from the short but intense battle waged by Skuti the night he and his men took control of Ashul. The mason wanted to repair the damage, but he would have none of it.

"Those battle scars," Skuti said with a sense of humility, "remind me of where I came from and why I am here."

Nodding to the men of the night watch as he walked out of the gate, Skuti intended to follow the stone road leading toward the harbor, then turn down a wide footpath leading to the nearby strand. However, just before he could act, a voice emerged from the wall.

"Aeehrl Skuti," shouted the captain of the watch from atop the castle wall, "where is your guardsman, Sir Alfarin?"

"Why, Sir Eirik," said Skuti, "are you saying I cannot defend myself? As for Sir Alfarin, one might assume he is at home with his wife, guarding her belly with his naked backside."

"I am concerned for your safety, my Aeehrl," said Eirik.

Skuti pulled his sword and pointed it upward at Sir Eirik.

"Come down here and do battle with me, and I will prove your concern to be false."

"Aeehrl," shouted the captain, over the top of loud laughter from his men, "no offense meant. But the hour is late, and darkness has fallen."

"Do you still believe in monsters from children's tales? I have my sword and am ready to meet the Leviathan should she feel hungry."

Skuti walked away, but the bellowing voice of Sir Eirik drowned out the rollicking laughter of his men and brought Skuti to a halt.

"What now, Sir Eirik of the Windy Words?"

"Aeehrl," said Eirik, "at least take one of my men with you to stand guard. I will not have the Aeehrl of Ashul dead on my watch."

"If it were to silence you, I would take the whole of your men with me. Tell him to keep his distance."

"Thank you, my Aeehrl," said Eirik. "You know not when enemies will present themselves."

Eirik is overzealous, but he means well. He has risen through the ranks as an arrow flies through an open field. I have seen what he can do. Eirik's sword and axe skills rival the best in Ashul.

Skuti walked toward the quiet harbor that would bustle with men, women, children, and animals by the time the morning light cracked the sky. Merchants with goods from all over Flace came to sell their wares to buyers from the castle. Traders from nearby towns and villages brought their goods to sell or barter with the people of Ashul, as well.

Skuti continued his walk, never once keeping a straight line. With sword in one hand and mead in the other, he reached the strand. He listened as enormous waves pounded the shoreline repeatedly as if catapulted from the sea, a siege engine beneath them, intent on destroying the rocks and sand. The crashing waves formed a rhythmic sound, and with it, a measure of solace washed over Skuti as he stopped to observe the waves as they crept up to his bare feet.

What am I to do about Jomar? Is he losing his mind? If we do not unify and come together to make a stronger cord, we will be as single strands snapped with little effort.

Stars filled the northern sky, and a half-moon provided enough light for Skuti to walk along the sand, although he could have traced his route by feel. He climbed a grassy knoll and sat down to admire the harbor view, filled with anchored ships of various sizes in the bay and port.

"Skuti," called Thorve at a distance, "where are you?"

"Up here," replied Skuti.

Skuti grabbed his mead jar and took a swig, savoring the flavor and the warmth of the liquid as it passed down into his belly.

Ah, this mead is the best batch the alewife has tipped in some time. She tipples better than her deceased husband.

"There you are," said Thorve, out of breath and eager to sit down.

"Changed your mind, did you, my lady?" said Skuti.

"Yes, yes, I did. Were you going to offer me a taste of your mead?"

"When did you start drinking mead? You hate the concoction."

"I am only thirsty. Should I drink of the salty water from the sea, my love?"

"You sound like your sister when you say that."

"Say what?"

"My love."

Skuti passed the jar to Thorve, who threw back her head and gulped down the mead as if she were an experienced drinker of the strong honey-based mix. Satisfied with the taste, she passed the jar back to Skuti, who shot her an odd glance. Thorve stifled a belch and giggled like a little girl would.

"Did you find your twin?" asked Skuti.

"Uh, no, I did not," replied Thorve.

"You were quite upset about her when I left you."

"I was—and still am. Did I say anything about her? I'm sorry, my husband, but I am worried, and my mind is floundering."

Thorve must be upset. It's been some time since I've seen her like this. Something doesn't seem right.

"You didn't tell me anything," said Skuti, "other than it was neither the time nor the place to talk."

"For now, leave it at that," Thorve said. "Once they leave for Iziadrock, I'll explain my sister's unrest."

Skuti brought the jar of the fermented mixture of honey, water, and yeast, brewed with spices and fruit, to his lips and breathed in the sweet scent of the mix. Tilting his head back, he poured a good measure into his mouth, allowing it to flow down his throat with the smoothness of a woman's back.

The warmth of the mead countered Astrid's prophecy, if it could be called that. He had rolled the meaning around in his head while walking and since sitting down.

"Allow me one more swig," said Thorve.

Skuti gave the jar to Thorve, who held it with one hand and retrieved something from her dress pocket with the other. She sipped and extended the bottle. "Here, finish it."

Skuti had looked away toward the sea. He took in a deep, relaxing breath and held it before blowing it back out again. The sea completed what the mead began. He finished the rest of the mead and threw the empty jar down into the sand below.

"Thorve, you don't seem right."

"Why do you say that?"

"I suppose it's the worry over your sister."

"It is. Jomar is a problem; he hates ... *her*."

"They both are a problem. Do you think they have attempted to play us as a lute again?"

Thorve was silent for a moment. She floundered for an answer, surprised by Skuti's rebuke of Jomar and Thora.

"Is it necessary to discuss this now? That's not the reason you invited me here."

"True, but it bears further discussion."

Thorve ignored Skuti's remark and pressed forward with a different agenda.

"What did you want with me, my love?"

"Thorve, you know why I asked you out here."

"Then do what you will with me. The festival has turned my desire toward you."

Skuti stared at Thorve's chest as she stood and pulled her gown beneath her ample, rounded breasts and wiggled out of the multicolored dress she was wearing. The strange behavior of Thorve no longer mattered to Skuti as his own craving, unquenched by Astrid, started again at the sight of his naked wife. He felt his cock stiffen as his hands squeezed hard on her tits. Thorve pinned him beneath her firm body and rubbed it against his.

"Thorve," said Skuti, "your body still creates desire within me."

"I know, my love," said Thorve. "I saw the way you looked at me earlier."

Thorve pulled Skuti's trousers down and eased him into her.

"My god," whispered Thorve, "you are rather large."

"What?" said Skuti.

"Shhh. Just take me."

Ignoring everything around them, they passionately made love on the beach, consumed only by each other. Thorve stayed on top of Skuti and enjoyed every minute of pleasure until they were both satisfied.

Thorve kissed Skuti and stood and put her dress back on. Before leaving, she kneeled by Skuti.

"You were even better than I imagined," said Thorve.

"What did you say?" said Skuti, fighting off sleep.

"Nothing, my love. Sleep well."

"I thought you didn't want me to sleep out here?"

"I changed my mind. Sweet dreams, my love."

It was almost light by the time Sir Eirik and several of his men reached Skuti. Still asleep on the sand, the morning fog blanketed his body and muted the sounds of Eirik and his men shouting his name. Good fortune smiled on Eirik's men when one tripped over Skuti's leg and planted himself face down on the sand.

"Aeehrl Skuti," said Eirik as he tried to wake his Aeehrl and fearing he was dead at the same time. "This cannot be. How could the gods ordain this?"

Why do I hear his voice and why am I asleep on the sand? Damn that mead to darkness. What in judgment did the gods ordain?

"Eirik," said Skuti, "you are making my ears bleed."

"Thank the gods," said Eirik, "you are not dead too."

Skuti slowly opened his eyes and saw Eirik's men peering down at him. At the last minute, he realized his trousers and undergarments were down at his ankles, so he decided against attempting to stand up.

Why are my pants down? Is this some sort of jest?

"What do you mean 'dead too'?" said Skuti. "Explain yourself, and the rest of you back away and turn around."

Skuti yanked his trousers and undergarment up and cinched them with his belt. With a look of disgust, he grabbed his sword out of the sand and slammed it into its scabbard without wiping off the granular substance.

Skuti circled around, ensuring eye contact with each man, and said, "If anything you've seen gets back to me, you'll end up in a dark, dank cell under the castle. Am I clear on this?"

Each man at least nodded and most added, "Yes, my Aeehrl."

"Very good," said Skuti. "Sir Eirik, explain to me what has happened."

For the love of the gods, don't become the man of windy words.

"My Aeehrl," said Eirik, "when the man I sent to look after you did not return, I sent two more to check on him, expecting a report he was sleeping—"

"Do not draw this out; tell me how the guard died."

"My Aeehrl, someone stabbed him twice in the heart with a dagger."

How does someone get close enough to stab an armed guard in the chest?

"Did the guard have his sword drawn?"

"No, he did not."

"Then surely he must've known his assailant."

"My Aeehrl, I cannot say, but he was partially undressed."

What circumstance be this? Did a seductress come and murder him?

"Did the man have a wife?"

"Yes."

"Did he speak of a mistress?"

"Not to me."

"I need one of your horses, preferably the fastest one."

"Grim," said Eirik, "give your horse to Aeehrl Skuti."

"Yes, Sir Eirik," said Grim, a young soldier, "anything for my Aeehrl."

"Sir Eirik, return the body to the castle," said Skuti, "and inquire about any mention of a mistress or any grudges held against him. Tell his wife he is dead and pay attention to how she responds. Who knows, she could be the guilty one."

"Yes, my Aeehrl."

Skuti swung his leg up over Grim's black-and-white palfrey and had the horse galloping away all in one motion. There would be no more celebration of Zoella's abundance for Skuti Ingimund. He had a brother-law to keep from losing his mind and prevent him from murdering his wife, all the while getting him to agree to unify Flace. A foreign seer, possibly correct about the Reaper of Souls in Ashul, added to the growing trouble.

CHAPTER 8
A SWORD BUT NOT A KINGDOM

"You don't look well," said Sir Renoldus, as Lord Watkin, the King's Advisor waddled into the room. "Have you seen the healer?"

"Are you my wife?" said Lord Watkin. "Mind your own affairs."

Walking in, sitting down, and retorting to his nemesis made his face turn red and purple, triggering a coughing spell.

"Lord Watkin," said Valter Cagnat, the Master of Merchants and Trade, "I believe Sir Renoldus was paying you a kindness by asking about your health."

Valter had built one of the best merchant fleets on the Western Seas and profited greatly from it. The apartment he shared with a woman half his age spoke to his wealth and health, as did his collection of artifacts from around the continent.

"Fuck off," said Watkin, wheezing out his words. "Worry about who buys and sells. Sir Renoldus is biding his time until I die so he can have my wife. There is no kindness in his asking. He is nothing more than a vulture circling in the air."

"If I wanted Lady Evelyn," said Renoldus, "I would

simply take her from you. However, she's a virtuous woman, and I couldn't do that to her."

"What is wrong with you Lord Watkin?" said Lord Searl Brewburn, Prime of Law, a man of average height, but quite thin. "It's no wonder people despise you. You're full of bitterness and hatred. You're as likable as a porcupine."

Seven men from King Leander's council sat in a room near the Great Hall. They surrounded a long rectangular table which sat eight men around it with a raised seat at the head for King Leander. Lord Watkin, the King's Advisor, sat to the right of Leander.

The ornate chairs looked important with their high backs but gave little comfort to the person sitting in one. A drapery of fine material, featuring gold fringe that extended to the floor, adorned the sides of the table.

On one side of the table hung a large tapestry from the wall. It matched the table's length and had half its height. Bold and striking colors made King Leander look quite grand as he accepted the crown to replace his fallen father as the king of Brüeland.

Across the room, a tapestry immortalizes the Battle at the Western Wall. Celebrated on the handsomely woven fabric were King Tarquin, Sir Jeames Gwatkin, Sir Wylymot Ormond, and Sir Renoldus Gwatkin in the last battle all four would survive.

Large windows were at the opposite ends. One had a sea view of the sea, the other a view of the castle grounds, easy distractions for those with shorter attention spans.

"If you're done insulting one another," said Leander, "let's talk the business of the kingdom and be done with it."

The king wore a golden crown featuring twelve heraldic stallions equidistance apart atop a band that rested on his head and over his shoulder-length brown hair. Under each stallion was a circular ruby. The sparkling red gems matched the rubies interspersed with gold clam shells on a golden necklace reaching down to his chest.

With piercing brown eyes, Leander searched the room briefly before starting. His face, covered by a beard with gray around his chin, showed little emotion. "Eunuch, my wealth?"

Arnet Chatard received training at the Citadel, the largest and most prestigious bank on the Western Continent. As part of their oath, graduates were cut before leaving for service in a noble's or king's court.

"Gold production continues in the Rox Mountain's mines," Arnet said.

Watkin played the good soldier, allowing the king to stay above the fray. "How much a day?"

"Two to three rouls."

"Why the decrease?"

"One of the mines is flooded."

"You said that last time we met."

Leander crossed his arms with an artful smile on his face. The room stared at Arnet, who squirmed in his chair.

"Our king is preparing Brüeland for war against the empire," said Watkin. "How much of the war can we fund with loans from the Citadel?"

"Perhaps a small amount as a favor to me."

"What do you mean 'favor?' What in damnation does that mean?"

Arnet perspired, causing droplets of sweat to form on his forehead.

"The arrogance of the Citadel is beyond measure," said the king. "In the bank's dull mindedness, they believe the silly man in the tower has the power to force my kingdom to bend the knee."

Arnet cleared his throat. "Yes, my king. Unfortunately, that is their opinion."

"Sir Renoldus, your opinion on the matter?"

"My army will defeat the Acarians because of King Jamettus's conceit. The fight within a man matters the most. I know our soldiers and there is no fear in them. Acaria will sue for peace and King Leander will make the Empire pay homage, and in doing so, take the money the Citadel loaned them."

"I suggest you talk to your friends at the Citadel," said the king.

"I will sail to the Ivory Isles by week's end," said Arnet.

"What about the mine?" said Watkin.

"What about it?"

"Look, you cut bastard. Stop playing word games and give me a straight answer. When will the flooded mine become operational again?"

"I'm not sure."

"That's not an answer."

Eyes were back on Arnet again. The nonconfrontational man hid behind the importance of his work and his supposed neutrality as an emissary of the Citadel under the employ of the king.

"The chyef of one of the mines," said Lord Valter, "is a relation of mine. I'll see what the situation is."

"Thank you, Lord Valter," said Leander. "What news on the seas?"

"As strange as it sounds, there's a pirate wreaking havoc on the Western Seas. I've heard several variations of the same story. The fog rolls in, you hear strange sounds, and his ship is upon you. Travels with some kind of siren of old."

"Come now," said Seral. "You don't believe this, do you?"

"Where there is much smoke, a fire must be."

Renoldus looked square at Watkin. "What do you hear about this pirate?"

"Whispers of the sea don't speak to me."

"I suppose you know nothing of Flace building ships for the Empire's navy."

"Were you not—"

"I've heard rumors about this Sir Renoldus," said Valter. "Nothing substantial, but it would make sense."

The room became quiet in anticipation of Leander's next question, that didn't materialize. "Business is done for today. Take leave of this room. Renoldus, you stay."

Watkin, wearing a wide smile, was the last to leave the room. He nodded at Renoldus. "When you're finished with the king, I'll be out in the Hall waiting for you."

The king brought one of his mangled hands, covered by a black glove, to his chin. His gaze swept the room, lingering on his tapestry before turning to Renoldus. "You're having an affair with my daughter."

"Is that what Watkin said?"

"It's the worst kept secret in the castle."

"Worse than how you killed your brothers?"

Leander locked eyes with Renoldus for a moment, but couldn't hold his gaze.

"You're just like a dog returning to its vomit," said Leander.

"If you consider vomit to be the truth, then yes," said Renoldus.

Without realizing it, Leander had leaned forward enough to have his forearms on the table. He eased himself back into his chair with his back straight and a slight grin eased on to his face. The conversation lulled, and Leander allowed the silence to hang in the air before starting up again.

"It's become clear that your self-righteousness is nothing more than a sham. You're everything you once hated."

You're right, but I will not admit it to you.

Renoldus tightened his eyebrow and met the eyes of Leander. The king smiled in return.

"It will not work. Your stare has lost its power."

"That's not what your eyes say."

Leander coughed into his hand, then briefly lowered his

head. The smile on his face suggested he had swallowed the proverbial canary.

"I've made in alliance with king Rycharde of Aflana. His son Rycardus will marry my daughter and you'll lead her retinue to the Wolfburn Valley."

Is this a joke?

"I find your jesting out of place."

"Do you see a cap 'n' bells and not a crown atop my head?"

"During war preparations?"

"I'm also sending you into exile if Ingrid makes it safely to Wolf's Keep."

"This is sheer madness. Have you lost your mind?"

"I have not, but I am losing the man who took the virginity of the Princess. You better hope Prince Rycardus has no experience in his chamber. If so, I'll leave it to you to explain exactly why Ingrid is no longer chaste."

Renoldus left the table and went to the window, gazing at the castle grounds.

This is what I've earned. I should be a knight-errant.

"You'll lose the crown you so cherish without me."

"Sir Terrin will lead my army to victory."

Renoldus turned and walked to the door, disregarding Leander as he departed. As he reached for the handle, Leander stopped him.

"I'm not finished. If Ingrid doesn't make it to Wolf's Keep, my men will hunt you down and execute you. You will also be executed if the Prince rejects her for her lack of chastity. Am I clear?"

"I hope the Advocate puts your head on a pike."

Renoldus rushed out of the council room as the door slammed shut. As he headed down the Hall, Renoldus's boots made a click-clack sound against an old stone floor. King Brüiant, grandfather of Leander, had built the castle with a flair for the austere, and the Great Hall bearing his name was no exception.

Renoldus stopped at two wooden chairs with cushioned backs of burgundy, one of which was occupied by Watkin. In front of them was a large square tapestry featuring the late King Tarquin with the great black sword in his hand atop a black stallion and with bloodied enemies at his feet.

"Lord Watkin," he said, "you wanted to speak with me?"

"Yes, is there a problem with that?" said Watkin, not bothering to stand.

"None, only surprise."

"Quite. I surprised myself by asking."

Watkin appeared to be in no hurry to start. Disinterested in small talk, Renoldus sat and pondered what King Tarquin would think of his son's reign. The voice inside his head rebuked him swiftly and mercilessly.

What would he think about you bedding his granddaughter? Why don't you explain what you've done to Ingrid? Even whores won't do such things.

"Sir Renoldus," said Watkin, "that's quite a frown on your face."

Renoldus shuffled around in his mind like a drunkard trying to remember where they were and how they got there. It took a moment, but he recovered his mental balance.

"The confrontation with King Leander has me on edge."

"That's what you get when you bed our king's virgin daughter."

"Did you want me to put you out of your misery?"

Watkin raised his eyes and nodded his head toward the tapestry behind Renoldus. The smug smile melded onto his face said it all. "King Tarquin wouldn't approve of stabbing a helpless old man."

Renoldus snapped his head away and stared at Tarquin's tapestry and then lowered his head. *If he were to rise from his tomb-chest, he would have me executed.*

Watkin sighed and began. "I called you over to settle accounts. You're leaving, not to return …" Watkin's voice trailed off, perhaps not wanting to dwell on the grim image of a fallen hero executed in the country he had faithfully served. At least until the end.

You're right, I'm not coming back. A man with a sword but without a kingdom.

Watkin's hacking cough echoed throughout the Hall, making it sound worse than it was, but it was a painful cough and a tough reminder of his grim condition.

Renoldus took a flask of wine from under his tunic and handed it to Watkin.

Watkin nodded his head in appreciation and took a long sip. "And of course I'm dying."

Renoldus produced a smirk and shrugged his shoulders. "A funeral awaits us all."

Watkin smiled and shifted in his chair. "I owe you a debt of gratitude. You sullied your reputation and got yourself exiled. By making use of every resource and coin, I potentially could have achieved some level of soiling. But exile? Not a chance."

"I stand in judgement of King Tarquin regardless of what I do to you. Why not suffocate you? It will look like a natural death."

"Angry with me, or the truth?"

"Both."

"Actually, you owe me a debt of gratitude. The king wanted you killed, but I advised him that exiling you was a better choice."

"Are you certain it wasn't the opposite?"

"I didn't want to see you hurt or betrayed. You've been Brüeland's heraldry come to life, a heroic stallion to the masses. The choice you made to bed the princess was a terrible mistake, but one unworthy of death."

Renoldus leaned his head back against the wall and pondered the moment he succumbed to the crushing weight of his physical desire. The sight of Ingrid's naked body and her willingness to experience it all in his bedchamber shattered what remained of his fragile will.

That wasn't it. You decided to bed Ingrid months before that night. When you allowed yourself to think about it, to let your eyes linger on her curves, to daydream about what it might feel like, to indulge yourself in dark fantasies of revenge against King Leander. Those were the times you said yes to Ingrid.

After a pause, Watkin spoke while shifting his eyes to the tapestry in front of him. "There's a woman who works at the King's Key as an alewife. I believe you know her."

Renoldus folded his arms across his chest and answered as if uninterested. "Only by name."

"I've been told she's asking questions an alewife shouldn't ask."

"Is that so?"

"It is."

"Recently, a man entered the Key and scared one of the owner's sons. Had a droopy eye; face was badly burned. The owner told me he was asking questions that had little to do with eating or drinking."

"This alewife, did she tell anyone where she went?"

"Not that I know of."

"So if you find out anything … I hear she might be in danger."

"I will pass it on. If the droopy-eyed man comes back to Crence, an angry man awaits him, eager to speak to him."

The large hall remained silent for several minutes until Watkin cleared his throat and took another sip of wine. He handed the flask back to Renoldus with a slight grin.

"Who killed Cecile?" said Renoldus.

"Ah, the question of all questions," said Watkin.

"Don't stall."

"I don't know. That's the simple truth."

"That's convenient, considering you're the King's advisor."

"King Leander had nothing to do with killing your wife. He had nothing to gain from it."

"He did if you consider a punishment delivered to be a gain."

Eyes closed, Renoldus breathed deeply, transported back to the Hall, trading insults with Leander.

"You smug bastard," Renoldus said. "Not even a tear for your father, the king?"

"I'm the king now," said Leander, "and I hold your life on a string, and I will cut that string when it is no longer useful to me."

"I pray Blackout doesn't come to you. You are unworthy to even look at it, let alone carry it."

"Perhaps I will allow you to grab the handle and watch your hands burn beyond recognition. Who needs a knight with no hands?"

The crowd surrounded them, chanting for Blackout to be presented to Leander before the formal ceremony.

"Bring it," Leander said. "I want Sir Renoldus to watch this up close."

They sheathed Blackout in an iron case to prevent a stray hand from touching it. It had been placed on a rolling table of gold with cut-outs to rest the famous Black sword upon it. As the table glided closer, an exaggerated smile broke out on Leander's face. Renoldus folded his arms across his chest, bemused by Leander's arrogance.

The king's own guards maneuvered the cart through the crowd and stopped it in front of Leander with the handle pointing toward him. A momentary look of uncertainty appeared on his face. Without a smile, he drew the sword out of its iron case and raised it to the sky.

"Long live the king," shouted Leander.

His face revealed that all was not well for the new king as he turned toward Renoldus. "No, gods, no!"

No one knew for sure what was happening except for Renoldus, who laughed at Leander much as he had all those years ago in the bowels of the castle. Leander panicked and brought his free hand up to pry off the hand holding the suddenly blazing handle. Leander screamed at the knight, hands stuck to the inferno.

"Renoldus, do something, damn you!" he said. "I command you!"

"My king," said Renoldus, "I cannot, and you know that. The sword will let go when it's ready."

Leander struck the sword against the iron case, hoping to free his hands, but only saw sparks. There were cries from the crowd to bring water, but before any of the liquid arrived, the sword mercifully released Leander's hands and fell to the ground with the handle pointed toward Renoldus.

The smell of burned flesh filled the front part of the Hall, causing many in the crowd to recoil. Leander fell to his knees, rolling onto his back, staring at his burned and bloodied hands, as the shout went out for the royal healer.

Renoldus stared at Blackout for a moment and pondered if it was he whom the sword had chosen to wield it. With the crowd focused on the wounded and suffering king, Renoldus picked up the sword and held it in his hand, checking its weight and balance. The healer urged the crowd to move away from Leander. Meanwhile, Renoldus emerged from the Great Hall, wielding his sword and history before him.

"Even today," said Renoldus, "I still vividly recall *Blackout's* choice in this Hall, as though it was yesterday. That day's events reveal everything about King Leander. Arrogant, full of himself, and far too hasty in his decisions. That is the king you serve."

"Yes, I've heard about that day. I'm convinced your arrogance shows every time you recount the story, if today was any sign."

"Only those on the wrong side of *Blackout's* choice. The lot of you look at it as if I stole it from Leander somehow."

"I fear I must draw this conversation to a shrewd focus."

"Yes, we're done here."

"Best wishes in exile."

"The same to you in the darkness that will become your new home."

Renoldus stood and thought one last time about killing Watkin. Instead of ending the sick man's life, he left the Hall and stepped into the afternoon sunlight, his hand tightly gripping Blackout as if strangling a viper.

CHAPTER 9
LIES

Skuti flew up the uneven stone stairs with powerful legs. The spiral stone staircase was built clockwise, leaving predominantly righthanded swordsmen moving up the stairs with no room to wield their swords.

It was not the only defensive stratagem Eldgrim Hastein had built into Seaborne Keep and the two towers containing the living quarters of Ashul's most important men and women and those who served them.

Skuti burst through the door and past the two guards while shouted over his shoulder, "Find Sir Alfarin!"

The Reaper of Souls took what was his, leaving Skuti questioning his hasty dismissal of Astrid's words. He hoped for a coincidence, but his heart tugged against it.

"Thorve," said Skuti.

She was standing on the veranda of the great chamber overlooking the harbor as Vesceron fought with the clouds to shine its light. She did not notice the activity below. Instead, last night's events consumed her, but it was the inability to find Thora that upset her the most. Skuti's voice cut through the mental inertia and brought Thorve from inside of her head, churning like a storm-driven sea, back to reality.

Exiting the veranda, she entered a square room with a table and chairs, enough for four individuals. To her left was the royal bedroom. It was twice the size of the waiting room, adorned with curtains for privacy, a canopy bed, and two harbor-facing windows. She also had her own chamber, as did Skuti.

"Thorve—"

"I can't find Thora," said Thorve. Her eyes, red and swollen, held the same kerchief from last night.

"What?"

"I don't know where Thora is."

How could you not know? You know where she's at, even when she's not here.

"Isn't your bond so close that you always know where your sister is?"

"This is not the time for your hurtful words."

Without realizing it, Skuti clinched his jaw and ground his teeth, a common occurrence when Thora became a topic of conversation between husband and wife.

"When did you last see Thora?"

"As she left the Heil last night."

"You don't know where she is?"

"I don't know, Skuti Ingimund. Do you?"

No telling where she's at.

Skuti shook his head and rubbed his temples with both index and middle fingers to soothe a headache from the previous night's consumption of alcohol and stop whatever madness had befallen him.

Every time Jomar comes, I end up with the curse that comes from drunkenness.

"Where's Jomar?" said Skuti. "Maybe Thora is with him."

"He's down at the livery," said Thorve.

"Who told you that?"

"He did."

Skuti paused for a moment to regroup. He was growing

more and more frustrated with Thorve's inability to put together a cohesive telling of events.

"Why did Jomar say that to you?" said Skuti.

"Jomar awoke in the middle of the night," said Thorve, "and started jabbering about the woman of his torment. She had landed in the harbor and was going to kill him."

"Did he strike you?"

"No. He muttered about building ships for someone so they could kill her. Jomar paced the floor and occasionally poked his head outside the Heil until Vesceron rose."

"Was the someone Acaria?"

"I don't know, Skuti. I could barely hear him. He was whispering as if the woman could hear him."

Wait. What were you doing in the Heil last night after I left?

"You told me last night you were retiring to the keep."

"Thora asked me to watch Jomar sleep so I could see what happens when he has the nightmares."

Thorve lied to me. Damn Thora to the depths.

"You didn't return to the keep to sleep. You stayed in the Heil and watched Jomar sleep."

"Call me a liar."

The word "liar" almost slipped out of Skuti's mouth, but he reconsidered. Thorve's protective instincts took over whenever he mentioned Thora. Engaging in name-calling would not help, and so he let Thorve's challenge pass by.

"You chose a fool's errand," said Skuti, "over telling me the truth."

"She's in distress," replied Thorve, "over Jomar's destructive behavior and needed my help."

"Did you consider the two have concocted the stories they're telling us?"

"Skuti, I won't engage in an argument about Thora and her supposed actions."

"Thora and Jomar are the focus here. They have pulled us into a world of deceit and murder. Thora has manipulated

Jomar before. The last time, I had to make a deal with the beasts of the forest to help liberate this castle."

"What would motivate Thora to do that? Why, in the name of the gods, would she stop Jomar from marching his army to help you take back the castle from that awful man?"

Thorve paused briefly, not because she had nothing to say, but because she recognized that the conversation was heading down a familiar rabbit hole where anger and bitterness lurked. But it was only for a moment as she decided, perhaps in ways she didn't understand, to jump into the hole and drag Skuti with her.

"You are a bastard," said Thorve. "I told you I would have no part in it."

"You're allowing Thora to manipulate you," said Skuti.

Thorve raised her arms, let out a series of curses, and returned outside. Skuti followed, determined to make his point known and felt.

"You think you know your twin," said Skuti, "but you do not. On the outside, you are the same. But inside—I think not."

"This always happens when you drink too much mead," said Thorve. "You turn spiteful."

"Why do you raise your voice to me? I'm attempting to find out what is going on within my Aeehrldom. Sir Eirik sent a guard to watch over me on the strand last night. I awoke to hear someone had stabbed the guard in the heart."

"I warned you not to fall asleep out there."

Skuti sucked in a breath, exhaled, and turned his attention to the harbor as it sprang to life. Morning clouds parted, revealing Vesceron's light on the bustling scene below. Fishermen were taking their ships into the waters near the harbor, while others headed upstream with smaller boats sailing the river nearby the harbor.

Shop owners were opening doors and readying themselves for the day. One level above a shop, a woman looked both ways before dumping the contents of a chamber pot onto the street below, narrowly missing her husband, a blacksmith.

Jomar and Thora come to Ashul, and shit rains down on me.

"Last night, a guard met his demise," said Skuti. "The servant girl who fetched the mead is a seer from Taazrand. She saw—"

"Wait," Thorve said, "did the little whore inform you of what occurred last night beforehand? Was this before or after she sucked your cock?"

"Are you accusing me of breaking our vows?"

"I saw the way she was smiling at you. When she saw me watching, she quickly disappeared, and you as well."

"You have lost your mind."

"You have not denied it."

"I did nothing with the girl, but you've made up your mind."

Thorve pushed past Skuti and headed straight for the bedroom and closed the curtain. She wept gently, recalling the night the castle fell to Vott's men. A mortified crowd watched as Vott's men took her father outside the keep and beheaded him. By then, Skuti had taken her to safety and spared her the indignity of watching her father's undeserved and horrid demise.

"I miss my father," she whispered. "None of this would've happened if he were alive."

Skuti exited the apartment without consoling Thorve, proceeded down the stairs, and headed to the guest livery by the Gate of Triumph. When he sprang through the door leading outside, Vesceron shone brightly in the sky, but Skuti noticed clouds on the horizon.

Storms are heading for Ashul. Can the gods make what is about to happen any clearer to me?

"Aeehrl Skuti," said Thora.

And here's my storm cloud.

"Lady Thora," said Skuti, "where have you been?"

"Watching your little seer kill that guard last night."

Did Astrid bedevil my guard and stab him to death?

"Did you see it happen?"

"Yes, and more. The little whore boldly seduced you, in full view of everyone, including myself."

Did Astrid follow me, kill the guard, and then allow me to quench my thirst? I can't remember anything after leaving the castle last night. Astrid was right; I can't trust Thora. There is no telling what the truth is.

"This talk is nonsense," said Skuti. "Nothing you're saying is true."

"Is it?" said Thora. "I saw you get cozy with her."

"Is that what you were doing last night? Following me?"

"Only out of concern did I follow you. I did not want you to fall upon an injury."

Skuti paused and looked up toward the apartment he shared with Thorve. Thora's accusations had quickly caused a large knot in his stomach.

Lie or not, Thorve will take her sister's word over mine.

"You know this is a lie. For all I know it was you, Thora. You also know Thorve will take your word over mine."

"That's true, she will."

I knew while I was engaging my lust with Astrid outside the Heil, it was a mistake. This jackal now holds something over me.

"What is it you want? A trial so Astrid will be found guilty and put to death?"

Thora produced a smile of deception. "You can have a trial, but testifying about what I witnessed would be necessary, and I assume you prefer otherwise."

"Do not play games. State it plainly."

"Have the girl sleep with the dead."

You want an axe over my head? Not this time.

"Had you been listening close enough," said Skuti, "you would know I sent her packing last night."

"I heard," said Thora, "but not good enough. You must bring her back and take care of your little problem."

"I'm certainly not going to bring her back."

"You will, unless you want me to share what that foreign whore did to the guard and then to you. Trust me, the story I tell will be much worse."

Skuti stood motionless. Within minutes, Thora had blackmailed him into finding and dragging Astrid back to Ashul. With a frown, he shook his head and glanced at the clouds gathered above his head, then turned to Thora.

"You would force me to kill innocent blood," said Skuti.

"Innocent?" said Thora. "I heard what she said about me. But she is the one practicing dark magic and not to be trusted. And I want evidence she is dead."

Thorve made her way down the stairs, still angry and upset with her husband, but having pulled herself together enough to look for her sister again. She made it three steps from the door before noticing Thora and Skuti.

"Thora," she said, "where have you been?"

"I was just telling Aeehrl Skuti where I was," said Thora.

Thora swung her eyes back toward Skuti, filled with a twinkle and a smile on her face. Skuti shot Thora a deadly look, but she only smiled wider in response.

"Is somebody going to tell me?" she said.

"Thora says she saw Astrid," said Skuti, "kill the guard with a dagger to the heart."

I should tell you the truth and be done with Thora holding me hostage. Better to deal with the consequences now instead of later.

"You saw it?" said Thorve.

"I did, sister," said Thora. "Come, I will tell you all about it."

Thora sensed Skuti's intentions and interrupted before he replied. She grabbed Thorve's hand and pulled, but could not get her sister to move.

"Skuti," said Thorve, "have you had her arrested?"

I should have your sister arrested.

"No," he said, "she left Ashul this morning."

"Skuti will find her," said Thora, "and the whore will pay for her crimes."

I will not send men in search for her. Who knows where she traveled to?

"As soon as she arrives," he said, "she will be hanged on the pier."

"Skuti," said Thorve, "you can't do that. It's against our laws."

"Sister," said Thora, "it's the best for all of us."

Thorve eyed them and said, "What in the name of the gods is going on with both of you?"

"Let's walk down to where Jomar is and I'll explain," said Thora with a confident smile.

"Skuti?" said Thorve.

"Your sister knows better than I," he said, a side of his mouth raised. "She was there."

"Are you coming with us?" asked Thorve.

"No," he said. "I will meet you down there."

I have gone from zero to two colossal problems. Why am I not surprised both involve Jomar and Thora? No way Astrid killed the guard. Her face was aghast at whatever she saw. No one is that good of an actor, except Thora. She is the one I should have sleep with the dead.

Skuti, out of breath from running, met Jomar outside the side gate where he and his well-stocked retinue were preparing to return to Iziadrock. Jomar's men were near finished securing the last of the gear.

"What is this, brother-law?" said Skuti.

"What does it look like?" said Jomar, standing alongside his horse.

Gad Jomar. Angry already?

"I see what you're doing, but why?"

"Ask Thorve."

Jomar's short, clipped words caused Skuti to bristle. Why

Thorve was watching Jomar sleep was already part of a larger argument, and Skuti did not need to be reminded of it through Jomar's flippancy.

"I know what happened," said Skuti, "but I want your version."

"Did I not tell you," said Jomar, "Thorve was conspiring against me with Thora?"

"Jomar, listen to yourself. There is no conspiracy between the two. This is outrageous talk."

"Only to you. Thorve came to harass my sleep, while Thora was out beseeching the gods to bring terror to your harbor, furthering her cause—with Thorve—in tearing the crown from my head."

"Jomar, for the love of the gods, stop this talk."

I'm getting nowhere. Is this an act to manipulate unification? But why? None of this makes any sense.

"See for yourself," Jomar said. "Three ships anchored in the harbor. The enticing woman with the spear is aboard one of those ships."

Sharing my knowledge about those ships will only worsen my problem.

"The three are large merchant vessels," said Skuti, gazing out toward the harbor. "They bear no colors except the flag of neutrality. Who can blame them for flying that flag? There are rumors of a great pirate lord attacking and looting ships on the open waters."

Jomar glanced around as if some unknown enemy was lurking in the shadows. He was growing agitated; every sound caused him to turn his eyes toward it.

What is wrong with you now?

Jomar whispered, "The beast is in these waters."

"What beast lurks in the harbor?" said Skuti, himself drawn into a whisper. "And how do you know it's there?"

"My dream. I smell the stench of its breath as we speak. That's why we're leaving."

I swear you are mad.

"Jomar, please calm down. Do not let your men see you like this."

"You underestimate this threat. The sisters are determined to usurp my authority. It's another reason I'm leaving. Your brother-law is telling you evil is about, and you care not and blame it on my supposed madness."

Skuti realized there was no sense in continuing to engage Jomar in his raging against unknown enemies and a monster lurking in the sea.

"Do you intend to kill Thora?" said Skuti.

"She will die," said Jomar, "whether by my hand or another's, I don't know. Perhaps a fatal disease will fall upon her as a punishment for what she is intending to do."

As Skuti endured Jomar's rants, Thora made her move to draw Thorve into her own madness of ancient magic and the plot to murder Jomar.

Thora and Thorve walked at a snail's pace, arm in arm, stopping before they reached their husbands as a throng of people gathered. Thorve's head was spinning from Thora's story about what Astrid said and how she killed the guard. She had left out Astrid's seduction of Skuti—for now—but it remained as a dagger tucked inside her belt.

"I am sorry you had to see such evil," said Thorve, "but it may have saved Ashul future trouble. I knew that whore had her sights set on my husband."

Enough about Astrid. I need you to agree to my plan.

"We must act on the Badek," said Thora.

"Thora don't say that," said Thorve. "Somebody will hear you."

The Gate of Triumph loomed, with its silver bars reflecting the late morning sun. Skuti ordered the gate built as a tribute to the fallen men who help reclaim the castle from

Vott. It was where the sisters said their goodbyes and blessed the gathered crowds.

"You saw for yourself," said Thora, "how troubled Jomar is."

Jomar was not the only troubled soul. Thorve felt her spirit darkening, and unease settled over her. She tried to put the whirlwind of the past day out of her mind but was unable. Jomar's frightful dreams, the fight with Skuti, Thora's accusations regarding Astrid. This was after Thora expressed her desire to use the ancient magic of Badek to kill Jomar. They all convened in her stomach and stirred it as a stew made of angst, worries, and fears.

"Upon my return to the castle," said Thora, "I will arrange a meeting with Evanora."

"We did not finish talking about this," said Thorve. "You could lose your life."

Here goes, sister.

"Would you ... no, I cannot ask such a thing from you."

"What? We have kept nothing to ourselves."

"You're right, we have not."

I need you to say yes. This is the right time. Skuti and Jomar are about to become enemies and it will end in war. Jomar wants Ashul for himself and has banded together with the other Aeehrldoms to do so. Skuti's hatred for Jomar will rise out of his soul when he figures out the other Aeehrldoms are building ships for the Empire. I cannot have Skuti killed in battle.

"Please share in the cost of years it will take from my life to have Jomar killed."

The stew had received the last ingredient. Thorve's jaw dropped indiscernibly, and her eyebrows raised and arched as she stared at her sister.

"I feel like I am going to vomit," she said.

"What's wrong, sister?"

"I don't—"

Thorve fell to her knees and gave up the contents of her

stomach, some of it landing on Syr Grima Ernmun, the Shy, her guard and childhood friend from Iziadrock. The tall, big-boned woman, with the strength of any man, kneeled with one leg; her sizable back and black cape blocked most from seeing Thorve on the one side. One of Thora's guards, Sir Saxi Alrik, covered the other side in the same manner, forcing Thora to squat on her knees at her sister's head.

"Sister, what happened?" said Thora. "Did I upset you?"

Thorve coughed and nodded her head up and down. Using the back of her hand, she wiped away the spit and vomit from her lips. Tears flowed from reddened eyes, adding to the misery of regurgitating in public. The words came out in a hoarse whisper.

"How can you ask that of me?" said Thorve.

Syr Grima yelled at the crowd, "Back away and give our lady room to breathe!"

The scene deteriorated into chaos. Word was out the Aeehrl and Lady of Iziadrock were leaving the day after the feast, and people were pouring into the area to see the two ladies. The twins' haphazard walk to the gate was created by Jomar's insistence on leaving early, with little warning. With Thorve down, the closest people stopped, causing a large group to push and shove while others behind them pushed to get closer.

"Step back," shouted Sir Beiner Gudmund, the other of Thora's two guards, "or this will be your last day above ground."

The knight drew his sword and used it flat to push people backward, threatening each time he pushed forward. The foot soldiers with them used their shields to press forward and opened enough space around Thorve to keep her from getting trampled.

"You better get her up and out of here," said Beiner. "The crowd is going to squeeze the shit out of our arses if we don't."

"What do you want to do?" said Sir Thormar Balki, Thorve's second bodyguard.

"I'll throw Thorve over my shoulder," said Syr Grima. "These soldiers can lead the way."

"We'll take Lady Thorve," said Thormar, "and get her to safety. Take Lady Thora out of this mess."

Despite Thora's size, Beiner wrapped an arm around her waist and pushed his way forward, using the butt end of his sword. Thora was nearly off her feet, walking on air as she contorted her body to look back at Thorve.

"Sister," she said, "please don't be angry with me."

DISTRACTED by the commotion for a moment, Skuti regained his focus, but not his patience. Jomar appeared to have recovered from his fit of fear driven by the supposed presence of the monster of old and its rider.

"I can no longer abide in this nonsense," said Skuti. "What of our talk in unifying Flace?"

"There will be none," said Jomar. "I knew your self-righteousness would prevent you from aligning with the Advocate."

Skuti eyeballed Jomar with suspicion as he readied his horse.

"The Council of Aeehrls has agreed," said Jomar, "to unify Flace, and I will act as king until a vote can be taken to name who will sit on the Ice Throne."

"Why wasn't I involved?" said Skuti. "I'm an Aeehrl, same as everyone else."

"There was a majority. Why would we want to have your false morality present?"

False? You coward.

"You are a madman and a bastard."

"When I return home, I am sending a signed letter to King Jamettus accepting their proposal to build the ships. They have promised to defend Flace against any enemy that marches against our borders. It's our only way to protect our people from slaughter."

This day is nothing more than the shit flying down the garderobe.

"You knew this before you even set foot in Ashul," said Skuti. "Knowing your penchant for lying, I'd say you're already building ships."

"It is time for us to leave. You have a fortnight to decide on joining the new Flace."

"I don't need that much time. Ashul will not be part of any agreement with Jamettus, nor their Advocate."

Jomar turned and mounted his horse without a glance or word to his brother-law. After giving the command, he and his guards moved out first, leaving Seaborne Keep and headed for Iziadrock. Skuti turned and walked away, a cauldron of anger and resentment churning within his soul.

Jomar and Thora have lied to me and shit on Ashul as if our mouths were a collective moat. I played the dutiful brother-law, accepting them as truth even when I knew they were not. I've avoided confronting the two to maintain peace with Thorve. I'm going to war with Jomar's miserable alliance, and I do not care who I have to ally with to win.

Beiner and Gaut delivered Thora to her entourage after sneaking her through a passageway to the livery. She was dirty and angry, yet continued to scheme as she mounted her horse. Her dapple-gray palfrey with its smooth, ambling gait caught up to Jomar at the front of the retinue. Thora's blue eyes stared at Jomar.

"Stop with the dreams," said Jomar. "I've done as you asked."

"I've sent you no dreams," said Thora. "Why do you insist upon it? You tried to strangle me over it."

"If not, then who?"

"Your own paranoia."

You've wearied me your stupidity.

"Because of your embarrassing, frightful behavior," said Thora, "I couldn't finish properly with Thorve."

"They were in the harbor," said Jomar.

The Leviathan is nothing but a myth. Why are you fixated on the monster and its rider? I'm watching a man losing his mind.

"For the love of the gods, Jomar. Set this nonsense aside."

Jomar sat up straight in the saddle and adjusted the half-helm, half-crown, complete with nose guard, resting atop his head. It was forged in gold with little adornment, but noticeable battle scars were on it.

"Did you tell Skuti?" said Thora.

"I did," said Jomar, "and he reacted as I expected."

"Don't underestimate him. He'll find an ally and challenge you if you're not careful."

I've looked into the future with Evanora, and I've seen things.

"The Yelloweyes will get slaughtered as would anybody who sides with him."

It's not the Yelloweyes this time.

Thora eased her horse back and away from Jomar. She grew tired of her husband's words and instead counted the days until the magic of Badek was to be released.

"I have a dagger," said Thora under her breath, "just for you."

CHAPTER 10
THE BATTLE WITHIN

King Rycharde and his inner circle sat at a solid oak rectangular table, off to the right of the throne room. Rycharde sat at the table's end, with his wife Sela to his right. She was a tall woman, thin, with modest curves, and a pale angular face, framed by raven-black hair. But it was her deep blue eyes that set her apart. Sela was an exquisite woman of taste, intelligence, and served the kingdom with grace. But most importantly, she cared for her eldest son with all her heart.

The king and lady sat atop a raised platform in high-backed chairs made of oak with purple-dyed fabric sewn into the cushions. Prince Rycardus sat at his mother's right, and next to him was Sir Evrardin the Wolf. Despite his fierceness, he was a well-read man with a particular interest in the history of the Wolfburn Valley. A few spread rumors of the Curse's blood running in his veins, insisting they saw his eyes turn yellow in town, despite being two generations removed.

Lord Jasce, Keeper of the Wealth, sat to the king's left. Jasce was an average-sized man, perhaps overweight, with sad brown eyes and thick reddish-brown hair worn beneath the ears. Bookish, with little personality to speak of and in fear of his own shadow, he lived with a plump, nagging wife and four daughters, two of whom he had recently arranged marriages for.

Seated next to Jasce was Lord Wymon, a curious man, short and thin, with a pencil mustache and long, straight black hair. He consistently donned the trendiest attire and refused to settle for anything less. Although not a handsome man, women flocked to him because of his style and coinage. No one knew the number of wives he left behind in various port cities and towns, nor did Wymon.

Next was Sir Raiimond of Winter, a large and towering man, unmatched in strength and height among all in the kingdom. The single man with aqua-colored eyes and long, flowing blond hair past his shoulders, often pulled back into a ponytail, was a magnet to the women of Wolfden. The problem for Raiimond was a total lack of self-awareness. It led to his mouth speaking stupidly and arrogantly, causing women with any sense to turn and run. He sat next to Jasce, often eyeing the Keeper of Wealth with suspicion.

Seated beside Evrardin was Lord Brice, the most reserved and private among them. He was the castle steward and ruled it with an iron fist. Rycardus had been finding out just how iron the fist was with his attempts to sneak Reyna up to his room.

His hardened upbringing, mixed with the mockery he had endured in becoming a nobleman, left him with a permanent frown. Brice was disciplined in every aspect of his life and feared no man save the king, and only then because of his great respect for Rycharde.

"How bad is the next year going to be?" said Rycharde, addressing Jasce. "Crops, animals, people ..."

His words trailed off, and he paused. Even kings struggle to grasp their people's losses.

"Not as terrible as I might have expected," replied Jasce. "The policies you instituted a decade ago, requiring ten percent of each harvest to be held in reserve, have no doubt saved our people from serious hardship in the months and years to come."

"We must rebuild and increase the reserves," said Rycharde. "We need wheat, rye, barley, and oats to yield a plentiful harvest in the Dead Months."

The king spent much of his time within his own head, observing and brooding. Rycharde, a quiet man, preferred to keep his thoughts private until he felt all the facts had been presented to make his decision. His reputation was one of aloofness and arrogance, but neither was true. Still, it was a reputation he couldn't shake, not that he minded.

"It will be done as you say," said Jasce. "I will begin work on the details as soon as we are finished."

I wonder how much you pilfer of the coinage paid in taxes. If you are, my father will find out and you'll spend the rest of your life in the debtor's prison.

The rest of the council eased back in their seats, figuring Lord Wymon would be next to speak, and he was certain to have a story or five.

"Lord Wymon," said Rycharde, "what are you hearing amongst the merchant sailors and traders?"

Without a doubt, Wymon was the best listener in the kingdom. Blessed with an innate ability to draw people into telling him even their most intimate details, he turned his skill into a seat within Rycharde's small council. At one time, he was a hugely successful merchant prince; he was now Rycharde's Master of Trade and Information. When questioned about his knack for gathering information, he simply answered, "I ask the right questions, in the right way, at the right time."

"I hear stories told with fear in the eyes of the teller," said Wymon. "They say the Advocate is demanding merchants sell nothing but Acarian goods abroad. They force ships to pay exorbitant port taxes if they hail from a kingdom not under his thumb."

"It would appear that the Man in the Tower," said Rycharde, "is seeking to control trade and lay siege to his enemies' ability to buy and sell. That's why our alliance with Brüeland matters. Three strategic kingdoms remain to be conquered. Flace, because of their shipbuilding. Brüeland for their vast supply of resources, and ourselves for the gold and silver. The remaining kingdoms will either bend the knee or suffer the consequences."

Silence filled the room as the council members considered Rycharde's assessment and its significance for the kingdom. The silver and gold mines to the north and east had always been the backbone of trade for Andairn kings. If the precious metals market vanished, dire consequences would affect not just Wolfden but the entire Wolfburn Valley.

Raiimond jumped awkwardly into the middle of the silence with a question he, and everyone else in the room, knew the answer to. "When do you expect Princess Ingrid to arrive?"

The prince stared back, contemplating how to respond to Raiimond's antagonistic rhetorical question with one of his own. Evrardin sensed Rycardus was on the verge of engaging Raiimond in an emotional confrontation surrounding his impending marriage to Ingrid.

Instead, Rycardus turned to his father. "My king," he said, "need we discuss this matter again? The princess will be here before the Burning Months."

"This is an important matter, my king," said Raiimond. "The alliance between Brüeland and Wolfden is critical to our survival, and theirs as well."

Evrardin tapped the thigh of the muscular prince, but to no avail.

"Sir Raiimond," said Rycardus, "you know the answer. Worry about yourself and stay out of my—"

"Enough," said Rycharde. "Rycardus, watch your tongue with Sir Raiimond."

"You know what he's doing," said Rycardus, shifting left toward his father, "yet you allow him to shame me in front of these men."

"My king," said Evrardin, "if it pleases you, this conversation is best had outside of the council."

Rycharde eyed his son and said, "Prince Rycardus, we will discuss your behavior later in my chambers."

You are oblivious to Sir Raiimond, Father. If you only knew some of the murderous deeds he commits in your name.

"Lord Wymon," said Rycharde, "is there further information we should consider?"

"Strange rumors continue amongst the sailors," said Wymon. "Persistent enough that these stories have my attention."

"Continue," said Rycharde. Wymon's information, at its worst, was entertaining. Rycharde needed something to ease the tension created by his son and Raiimond.

"There is a pirate on the seas," began Wymon, "calling himself Lord Commander, and he has a growing fleet of ships under his command."

"A pirate?" said Raiimond. "And you expect us to believe such nonsense?"

"Mind your sword," said Wymon. "Let it do the speaking for you."

The smile on Rycardus's face was quite wide, and he made sure Raiimond saw it, exaggerating the smirk when he glanced over. It was met with an icy stare.

"It's not the typical pirate story," Wymon said. "There is often a fog which accompanies his attacks, granting him an obvious advantage over his target. Further, his crew comprises ruthless island warriors who have a reputation for brutality."

"Have you lost your mind?" said Jasce. "This is pure fiction."

"Mind the coinage," said Wymon, "and let me finish."

Even Rycharde, known for his stoicism, smiled. Sela, who

always distrusted the man's intentions towards her husband, had to muffle a giggle.

"Last," said Wymon, "is the woman traveling with him. Some say she is a goddess, some claim she's a witch, and others say she is a siren of old. Regardless of her nature, she carries with her a special three-pronged spear that she uses to work her magic."

"Surely you don't believe that?" chuckled Rycharde while the others laughed, except for Raiimond, still seething over the insult of Lord Wymon. The table's occupants couldn't stomach a story about a woman with magical powers, rolling their eyes in unison, even if only in spirit.

"Laugh," said Wymon, "but he has made it known he opposes the Advocate."

"Does he have a name?" said Jasce.

"Lord Commander Taylor Denton. Perhaps we might arrange a meeting, my king, between our representatives and his."

"I'll take it under consideration, Lord Wymon."

If I were king, this is a meeting I would gladly take. If Wymon speaks the truth, this man may become our continent's strongest ally. Even I've grown weary of the stories about Acaria's supposed great navy.

Rycharde was done with Wymon and his story yet hoped it had served its purpose.

"We've had our revelry for the moment," said Rycharde. "Let's get back to the business at hand. I think it's obvious now, war is coming to this part of the continent. As stated, it's imperative that we increase the reserves. A religious lunatic in a tower won't starve my people."

Jase smiled and nodded toward Rychard. "Agreed, my king," he said. "I will ensure we increase the reserves."

Sela brought an eyebrow down and stared at Jasce. He cleared his throat and removed the silly grin from his face, the one he wore like a boy telling his father what he wishes to hear. Jasce turned awkwardly away from Sela's disapproving glare and looked down at the table, where his books and papers stared back at him.

"What of the Forest, Sir Evrardin?" said Rycharde.

"The Gray Claws lost too many lives, given their ability to adapt," said Evrardin, "but they were unprepared and didn't react well during the storms. Instead of behaving like a pack, a good number of males took the lone wolf approach, leaving mates and children behind."

"Good," said Raiimond. "Only the gods know how many wives and children suffered because those bastards killed their husbands and fathers."

"I'm sure you've avenged those deaths," said Rycardus, "and countless others."

"Rycardus," said Rycharde, "I've already warned you."

Raiimond's eyes and voice showed anger as he asked, "Are you a sympathizer?"

"Sympathizer?" said Rycardus. "If standing against your slaughtering of their women and young who pose no threat to you makes me a sympathizer, so be it."

"Damn you, boy," said Rycharde, glaring at his son, "not one more word out of your mouth."

Rycardus pushed his chair out and faced Raiimond. "You enjoy killing. I know the things you've done."

Raiimond stood and pointed his finger menacingly at Rycardus. "Your dark-haired bed swerver tells you lies. You're bedding a *duhbrarei* and she's nothing but a whore who opens her legs and mouth—"

"Shut your vile mouth. You're the animal. You kill for pleasure, and you do it in the king's name."

Rycharde stood, his handsome face contorted and red. "For the love of the gods, mind your tongues in front of the queen. I swear I'll have both of you sent to the cells for this madness."

Sela sprang to her son's defense. "Rycharde," she said,

"you'll not throw our son into a cell. Sir Raiimond's foulness provoked him."

In a matter of seconds, the anger and bitterness of Rycardus and Raiimond, simmering in their hearts for what seemed like forever to Rycardus, boiled to the surface like water over a fire. Rycharde's consistent pattern of siding with Raiimond was too much for Rycardus to abide by any longer.

"You have no idea who she is and what she's doing," said Raiimond, wound as tight as a top and unable to stop. "Sneaking her up to your room; everyone knows what you're doing. Am I right, Lord Brice?"

"I will not provide an answer for you to bully the prince any further," said Brice. "He's the prince and next in line to succeed our king, whether or not you like it. I swear if you don't stop this lunacy, I will remind everyone of the women you've brought into the castle."

Lord Brice was not one to be trifled with. He wasn't the size of the bigger man, but there was no fear nor quit in him. If he had to, he would gnaw on the leg of Raiimond like a dog until he cried for mercy.

"Put an end to this shameless affair," said Raiimond, turning back to Rycardus, "and marry the princess before you doom yourself."

"Sir Raiimond," said Sela, "sit down and silence your tongue."

"Lady Sela," said Rycharde, "please—"

"I will not stand for Sir Raiimond's behavior as a member of your council."

Rycardus tried to get past Evrardin over to Raiimond, but the Wolf grabbed him in a bear hug and held on tight.

"Don't do this," said Evrardin into his ear, "you'll regret it."

Rycharde had seen enough and pulled open the doors and shouted for the guards.

"Get in here at once," he said. "Take Sir Raiimond out and prevent the prince from going after him."

Two burly guards proceeded to Raiimond, who complied without resistance but maintained a smug expression while exiting through the heavy oak doors. Two more guards, just as powerful, approached Rycardus, who halted his aggression and raised his hands in a gesture of surrender. Evrardin released him with caution, and the guards blocked his path toward the door.

"The council is done," Rycharde said, frustrated by his inability to rein in the chaotic meeting. "I'll convene the next meeting before the week is out."

Evrardin pulled Rycardus's head toward his shoulder. "Consider your actions today," he said under his breath. "You're doing yourself no favors with the king."

Nodding his head, Rycardus kept his eyes fixed on the stone floor.

Even those I consider friend take up sides with my father.

Evrardin exited the room and Rycardus followed, only to have his father stop him at the door.

"Not you," he said. "Sit down."

Sela shot a stern glance at Rycharde, then turned her head, and smiled at her son. She sat between the two, an apt position for the woman who was quite familiar with acting as mediator between her husband and son. Now more than ever in the past year.

"Son, what is wrong with you?" said Rycharde. "Why must you quarrel with Sir Raiimond every chance you get?"

"Wrong with me?" said Rycardus. "Ask him why he feels it's necessary to antagonize me."

"Antagonize?"

"Yes. He hates Reyna and takes it out on me."

"As do I. She stands in the way of our survival as a kingdom and as a family."

Sela regarded her son with the eyes of a loving mother,

conflicted by who he was and who he might become. She knew from the night of the attack on her precious young boy he was going to change one day, although she fought with her heart to deny it.

The years of denial within her soul buried the facts of what happened that night, and now she was unwilling to dig deep into her heart to unearth them. Even now, as she looked at Rycardus, the truth called out from the depths of her inner being.

Sela blamed herself for what happened, but the self-loathing did not change the damage by Delinda, the assassin sent to kill the young prince. The healer did his best, but it wasn't enough, and she knew it, though she pretended not to. Even her unending prayers went unanswered.

Rycardus put his head down and shook it before raising it with a sarcastic smile.

"Both of you deny in your minds," said Rycardus, "what you know to be true in your hearts."

"Enlighten me, son," said Rycharde. "Please tell me what's in my head and heart."

Tears welled up in Sela's eyes. "Rycharde," she sniffed, "you know exactly what he's talking about."

Rycharde placed a tender hand on her shoulder. Sela's sadness over Rycardus was another reason for Rycharde to take his guilt out on his son, perverse as it may be. Rycardus was innocent in everything that occurred on that fateful evening. Yet he bore the burden and the pain of a clever were-wolf intent on killing the son of their dreaded enemy.

"I heard another tale this week," said Rycharde, "of your changing."

Rycardus did what he often did when the stories of his aggressive nature were told by his father. He hung his head, understanding the story to be told would contain either words of disappointment or anger, and more often, both.

"Sir Raiimond had to pull you off your opponent," said

Rycharde. "The boy told him your eyes turned yellow, and you pummeled him with your fists after you knocked the sword from his hand."

Rycardus's head remained bowed, and anger burned at the mention of the name.

"I know you hate Sir Raiimond," said Rycharde, "but can you try to understand his perspective?"

Rycardus raised his head, and three sentences came out of his mouth summing up succinctly the truth of his relationship with Raiimond.

"Father, he's hated me my whole life," said Rycardus. "He knows what you won't admit to. I'm going to turn."

"Rycardus," said Sela, shifting her eyes between Rycardus and a tapestry on the far wall, "you can still fight it."

He switched his attention to his mother, exhausted by her constant refrain of overcoming what was inside him. *If only she could look and feel inside my body, then she wouldn't say such stupid things.*

"Mother, for the sake of the gods, don't say that anymore. There is no fighting it. I've read all the books in the castle and …" Rycardus stopped. If he said the name, the accusations would begin. It didn't matter.

"Talked to Reyna," said Sela, finishing the sentence.

Rycardus shifted in his chair and thought about making a run for the door. "Mother," he said with a grimace on his face, "please don't start."

"We need to," said Rycharde. "She is a part of this, an enormous part."

I should leave right now.

"Father," said Rycardus, shrugging his shoulders, "what's the point?"

"Son," said Sela, "let me explain Reyna's actions from a woman's perspective."

"I swear to the gods, Mother," he said, shaking his head, "you don't understand."

"Rycardus," said Rycharde, "watch your swearing, lest the gods bind you to it."

Rycardus eyed his father for a moment. What he wanted to say and what he said were entirely two different things.

I swear, I swear, I swear, I swear upon each time I bedded Reyna in your orchard.

"Please forgive me."

"I understand the ways of a woman," said Sela. "Reyna whispers sweet words into your ear, words she wants you to believe. She uses her body, exchanging it for your love."

"Oh, for the sake of the gods and goddesses, Mother," said Rycardus, "you're making her out to be some sort of villain."

"Consider your mother's words," said Rycharde. "Once she spread her legs, you became intoxicated, under the influence of her plans for you."

You're making me sick to my stomach. I want to vomit after hearing from you what it means when a woman spreads her legs for a man.

Rycardus became red in the face, and he broke eye contact, shifting his gaze to where Raiimond was sitting earlier. "My god, you two, what is wrong with you? Please stop with this kind of talk."

"We're merely trying to explain to you the nature of how things are," said Sela.

"Well, try something else," said Rycardus.

Rycharde and Sela exchanged dutiful glances and pressed forward. They both spoke at the same time, but Rycharde deferred to his wife, believing her kinder words would have a greater impact.

"Rycardus, my son," she said, "you must put your affair with Reyna behind you and focus on Princess Ingrid. I hear she is quite beautiful."

"Mother, I don't—"

Rycharde, in an instant, decided shouted words were more effective and nearly flew out of his chair in a rage to prove it.

"You're going to marry the princess," he said. "End of story."

"I told you no," said Rycardus, "and I meant it."

"I don't care if I have to stick Heartstriker up your arse. You will marry Princess Ingrid and solidify the alliance between the two kingdoms."

Rycardus's eyes turned yellow, and he bolted for the door. As the door slammed shut with a loud thud, his body cramped, and he battled the foreign invader from taking over his body with all the strength he could muster.

I can't hold him off very much longer. It's going to consume me ... and soon.

CHAPTER 11
PRINCESS MESS

Clarenbald Atwood waved toward Renoldus as he dismounted his riding horse, a black palfrey named Blackwind, and made his way over to where Clarenbald was standing alongside a perch.

"Lord Clarenbald," said Renoldus.

"Sir Renoldus," said Clarenbald.

"Is she for our king?"

"No, this regal raptor will be a gift to King Andairn when his son marries Princess Ingrid."

"Will we be taking this gift to him when we escort Princess Ingrid?"

"No, she won't be ready in time. I will accompany King Leander on his trip to Wolfden for the wedding."

No matter where I go within the castle walls, I receive a reminder of who it is I'm bedding and how ruinous it is.

Clarenbald's brown eyes were always wide open and appeared as if they never blinked nor closed. People encountering them often felt uncomfortable when talking with him. Some averted their gaze when speaking, and others stared into his eyes, longing for the rarest of things—a blink from the Master of Mews.

His brownish-blond hair was unkempt, as was his beard, which formed a point just below his neck. Gray was in his hair and beard, but only on one side of his face and head. Clarenbald was intelligent, quiet, and unassuming despite the importance of his art and the coinage he was paid for it. He held forth at the king's table often, and when reminded of this, he shrugged his shoulders and smiled.

"This raptor will be a memorable gift," said Renoldus. "Gyrfalcon?"

"Very good, Sir Renoldus," said Clarenbald. "I'll turn you into a falconer yet."

Both men enjoyed an honest laugh. Renoldus held tremendous respect for Clarenbald's skill, and he respected Renoldus's military might.

You're a nice man, Lord Clarenbald. May the world never corrupt you.

"Sir Renoldus!" shouted Teebald, Clarenbald's oldest son. "I brought Myst for you."

Renoldus eyed Clarenbald and smiled.

"Thank you, lad," said Renoldus, "let me put my glove on properly."

Myst was a beautiful saker falcon with a pale head, and when in-flight, her wings were broad with dark underwing coverts. When Teebald got close enough, Myst glided over to Renoldus's left arm, covered with a large leather glove, and perched there.

"She should be ready to hunt," said Teebald. "She's hungry and eager to find food."

"Well done, lad," said Renoldus.

"I have to get back to the mews, Sir Renoldus. Good luck."

Renoldus shook his head and smiled.

"You are doing a fine job raising your son," said Renoldus.

"Thank you, Sir Renoldus," said Clarenbald, "he is a nice boy and should do well with the family business someday."

With firm grips, they shook hands before Renoldus headed back to his horse with his falcon.

"Be cautious," Clarenbald warned as Renoldus walked away.

"Any reason in particular?" said Renoldus.

"Sightings of the Beast again."

"I swear these sightings have become more predictable than the sun rising."

"I am only a messenger."

"Don't worry, I won't kill the messenger."

Both men shared another laugh and Renoldus, with Myst perched high on his raised glove, strode to his waiting horse.

"Are the two of you going to work together today?" said Renoldus, moving his head back and forth between the two. "I'll take your silence as yes."

Renoldus mounted his black horse and gave his saker falcon a command. "Myst, find me this mythical beast and we'll kill it, and you can gorge on its flesh."

Renoldus sat tall in the saddle and ambled away from the mews toward the King's Forest. He preferred Blackwind on his hunting trips, especially when riding into the forest with one of his raptors. His smooth, ambling gait gave Renoldus additional comfort in the saddle. Myst flew off to search for prey while Renoldus and Blackwind followed behind.

It was warm for this time of year in the southernmost part of Brüeland, with a balmy breeze blowing inland off the Nask Ocean. Renoldus worried Myst might lack the energy to hunt in the warmth. If she didn't, it wasn't a lost day, as he was more interested in clearing his head than sitting in a clearing.

As his horse walked along, a tall figure sat atop a brown and white spotted palfrey and followed at a distance behind him.

I will ruin an alliance between the two kingdoms, if I haven't already, if I don't stop bedding Princess Ingrid. I took Ingrid's virginity without nary a second thought and gave her nothing in return. What can she offer her future husband now?

I must not care. While I think little of King Rycharde's army, I still need his men to hold off the Acarians. If Rycharde were to call off the alliance, I would have made my life even more miserable. Acaria has already added men by enslaving soldiers of the kingdoms they have defeated. If I don't get extra men, I've doomed my army and my king.

I don't believe in anything anymore except for an excellent wine and Ingrid in my bed. There are no noble causes left. Leander is evil. The advocate is worse. Yet evil is still evil.

Renoldus shook his head in despair, contemplating the choices and consequences that awaited him, affecting those he cared for, and the kingdom he risked his life for. He continued to sit high in the saddle and allowed Blackwind to walk forward.

So, I fight on the side which will do less slaughtering, commit fewer brutalities, and keep more promises? Once, fighting for a kingdom held value. During King Tarquin's reign, we fought to unite the kingdom for the people's betterment. We believed there was a better way to live, a better way to treat one another, a better way to govern ourselves. It was mere dust blown by the wind to some unknown place, never to be found again after the assassin's arrows took down King Tarquin.

My father was next, my wife thereafter, and I never figured out how to live after the mourning was done and all the tears were cried. Continue to mourn some more? Drink the pain away? Find a woman each night to spread her legs and feel comforted? None of this taught me the art of living and loving again, nor will it ever. How do I break the chains of enslavement to my pain?

As was becoming his norm, Renoldus shook his head and despaired over his losses for a moment before questioning his future motivation.

Without purpose, I'll perish on foreign soil, slain by an unworthy squire. Since I don't know how to live, I won't know how to die either. If there are gods or goddesses in the heavens, please give me a purpose again.

Renoldus dismounted his horse in a clearing and walked

over to Myst and her quarry, a plump grouse who fell victim to the saker's sharp talons. Distracted by his thoughts and focused on following his falcon, he had lost track of where he was, leaving him in a part of the forest he was unfamiliar with.

"Where in the name of the gods am I?"

Renoldus turned toward a high-pitched squeal and the cracking sound of twigs and sticks breaking on the forest floor. A gray-haired boar was almost on him, giving him no time to pull *Blackout* from its sheath. The boar pointed its long, dirty, and sharp curved tusks at Renoldus and clipped him below the knee, sending him sprawling to the ground.

Positioned several yards away, the bulky and massively built boar was ready to charge at Renoldus as soon as it detected any movement. With deceptively tiny legs, the beady-eyed beast stared him down and dared him to stir. Its large snout blew out air in contempt at its human target.

Damnable beast is real.

Renoldus tried to get to his feet, but the beast saw the movement and readied itself for another run. Huffing turned to screeches as the boar gained speed and prepared to strike as it had before, tusks straight and raised.

Loud sounds from the boar rushing forward drowned out the whizzing of two arrows racing through the air. Small broad-heads at the tip of each arrow pierced the boar's tough hide at the midline. The first strike was the shoulder's back crease, followed by a lower, rightward strike. The timing of the loosed arrows was perfect, entering the beast while its leg was forward, leaving the heart exposed.

After a few more steps, the hog, weighing two-hundred pounds, collapsed. Renoldus was stumbling forward but lost his balance and fell face first to the ground. The hard landing rattled his body, yet he had the sense to scramble to his knees even though the pain burned like fire. Catching his breath, he realized the fletchings were unique, and nothing he recognized.

These arrows are not of our hunters.

"Who's out there?" said Renoldus. "Show yourself."

Renoldus heard rustling noises again and caught movement out of the corner of his eye. As the sound grew close, he readied himself for a strike at another fast-moving hog.

This is no boar.

The tall figure walked on two legs and wore a short black cape with its hood pulled down low enough to disguise the face. In one hand was a bow; the other was empty. Renoldus tightened his grip on *Blackout* and prepared for the worst.

"Sir Renoldus Gwatkin," said the voice as the figure approached, "the Black of Brüeland."

"You have me at a disadvantage, friend," said Renoldus. "You know me, but I cannot see your face."

The figure stopped, pushed back the hood of her cape over the ponytail on top of her head, and allowed the rest of her raven-black hair to cascade down to the middle of her back. With a coy smile, she untied her cape and let it fall to the ground.

"Who are you?" said Renoldus. He paused for a moment, but there was no mistaking the eyes. He sheathed his sword and a slight smile formed on his face.

Surely it's her. There's no mistaking those eyes. I don't care how long it's been.

"Glasha?" he said. "Princess Glasha, Brovas's daughter?"

"Yes," she said. "You remembered."

"One cannot forget your eyes."

"Nor yours."

There was much to forget the day Renoldus arrived at Brovas's castle within the Groves of Sorrow. Terrin, along with a dozen handpicked knights and thirty of the best horse archers in Renoldus's army, accompanied him to a large, overcrowded village frozen in time. Perhaps it was too many men, but with the Af'lam, a show of force lowered the probability of steel clashing.

Upon Renoldus's arrival, the Bravos family and the highest-ranking elders of the tribe gathered in front of the old motte-and-bailey castle desperately in need of repair. The *Chouufsuoum* had lived in the castle for twenty years and by the shape of his body and the look in his eye; he had no intention of leaving anytime soon.

The western kingdoms knew the Af'lam for their resentment, shifting eyes and perfunctory greetings, which created an unfriendly tone. As much as Bravos wanted acceptance, he often repelled those who had the power to help him with his arrogant and condescending views of humankind.

Once the drink flowed, a stream of sexual vulgarities mixed with a pinch of belligerence created a failed recipe for success with potential allies. Brovas's acts of defiance created opportunities for possible alliances to turn adversarial instead.

Renoldus performed a brief search of the area for anyone who looked out of place or behaved in such a manner to arouse suspicion. Among the gathering of royalty and aldermen stood a tall girl with wide, expressive green eyes. Renoldus completed his first pass and saw nothing unusual. He brought his attention back to the girl with the emerald orbs.

The pair locked eyes and after a few moments, each smiled as strangers do. But Renoldus felt drawn to the girl in a way he couldn't explain. Terrin came near and asked his commander a question that swayed his attention. When Renoldus turned around, the girl had vanished amidst the crowd.

"Renoldus," said Glasha.

Renoldus, shaken out of his recollection of their first meeting, turned the other way, expecting another angry boar.

"No, turn back to me. It's your leg. Lie back and let me look at it."

Renoldus ignored Glasha's request. "Your aim is true and

better than my most skilled archers. None of them would've dropped a boar with placements such as yours."

"I worked twice as hard as anyone else. Archery doesn't come easy for me, and I needed to prove I belonged. It's not easy to be the princess everybody hates."

"Hates? You?"

Renoldus sensed Glasha was in no mood to share the reasons for which they hated her, and he let the subject drop.

"Renoldus, lie back," she said. "I need to look at your leg."

Renoldus lay back this time, acknowledging that the boar's puncture wounds hurt. "Are you a healer, too?"

"You better hope so."

Renoldus smiled, but it quickly left his face when he noticed Glasha reaching for a knife attached to her belt. The adrenaline masking the pain was fading, forcing him to realize this was no mere flesh wound.

"We can do this two ways," said Glasha. "Either I cut your trousers with my knife, or you can take them off."

"For the sake of the gods," said Renoldus, "are you serious?"

"Very."

Whatever fondness he felt for Glasha was dissipating like the morning mist. "Help me with my boot and I'll pull my leg out of the pants."

Sliding his leg out of his pants proved no simple task, but when finished, "Clearly, the gods are angry with me," said Renoldus.

"That I know nothing about," said Glasha, "but I know the wound on your leg is very angry."

Glasha moved closer to Renoldus and picked up his leg and examined his shin and calf where the beast's sharp cutters had lacerated the skin, creating two deep gores. The blood from the wounds ran down his leg, veering at the curvature and into the grass beneath him. She inspected the rest of his leg for swelling, redness, minor cuts, and the like. Finding nothing of a serious nature, outside of the gores, she eased his leg down and whistled for her horse.

"That's a nasty wound filled with whatever filth was on the boar's tusks," she said. "I'll need to clean it out."

Glasha's horse, Klando, trotted out of the trees and into the clearing as an actor enters the stage. The Af'lam crossbred the breed as a multipurpose horse, capable of being trained for war but primarily used for hunting and travel. They were light, fast, and strong, the perfect steed for the warrior princess.

"That's a very handsome horse," said Renoldus. "The markings are unique."

"He was a gift when I turned of age," said Glasha. "He has a good heart and will fight when needed."

Glasha stepped to her horse and Renoldus watched her every step, amazed by her muscular build through her thighs, arse, and upper back.

The gods sculpted you. How else to explain your strength ... and beauty?

She returned with several odd-looking items and set them down next to Renoldus. He eyed them with suspicion and gave her a sideways glance.

Glasha ignored his questioning look. "I'm going to heal your wound as the Af'lam do."

"How's that?" said Renoldus.

"Over time, my people used various herbal mixtures to heal wounds and ease pain. After we were separated and sent into the wild, our ancestors discovered the perfect combinations of herbal mixtures. Our fierceness is unmatched, yet we are few. We needed the injured fighters back in battle quickly."

"But I'm fully human. What if it doesn't work?"

"Did you want the alternative?"

Renoldus laughed and thought, *Beggars cannot be choosers, especially deep in the King's Forest.* "If it's death, then no."

Glasha gave Renoldus a smile, then busied herself with

crushing herbs and berries, and added the strange-smelling liquid she had stolen, blending it into a paste. Out of her belt pouch, she retrieved two almond-shaped objects, holding one back and giving the other to Renoldus.

Renoldus rolled the almond-shaped pill in his palm. "What is this?" he said.

"It's something to help you stay calm," said Glasha. "It's made from the simples."

Glasha paused briefly, lifting her head as though seeking guidance from an unseen presence.

"Is there a problem?" said Renoldus.

Glasha flashed an uneasy grin. "No, not at all. Do you have ale or mead with you?"

"I have wine."

"Wine is rare to us, but I suppose it will do."

"It's in the flask hanging from my pommel."

Renoldus held the pill between his fingers and brought it to his nose. The pill's faint aroma was both familiar and elusive. *What is in this thing?*

She returned from Blackwind with a reassuring smile. "Here it is. Put what I gave you in your mouth and drink it down with the wine."

Don't do it. It's time for you to refuse, Renoldus. This pill might contain death. She might have been sent to avenge the warriors who were killed in the skirmish. She did track me down ...

The wine was sweet, and the pill slid down his throat. He took one more gulp of his wine for the taste and effect and kept the flask within arm's reach.

I am an utter fool for taking a pill I know nothing about and mixing it with wine.

Glasha went to work but stopped. "May I try some of your wine? I'm thirsty."

Surprised, Renoldus smiled and handed her the flask. "Here you go."

With one hand over her mouth, Glasha brought the flask

to her nose and made a sour expression but still drank from it. "Too sweet."

Glasha set down the flask, diligently working on the paste until it formed a thick, square shape.

"Now what?" he said.

"I'm going to pour this liquid on your wound and suck out whatever poison the hog had on its tusks. Humans ignore what's inside the wound before it's closed, and we're called ignorant. The paste goes on last."

"I suppose this might hurt."

"I'm going to give you a powder to inhale. Just a small amount should do."

"What is it?"

"An ancient powder discovered by the first of our people. The powder puts a warrior into a state where pain is unfelt, allowing the healer to clean the wound."

She poured the gray powder into her palm and extended her hand out. He stared at the contents in her palm and the powder stared right back at Renoldus.

"I swear an oath to the gods, if they do exist," said Renoldus. "If you've given me the powder of death, I will come back and haunt you for the rest of your days."

Glasha avoided eye contact by staring at the powder in her hand. "I will not kill you; quite the contrary. I believe there is a destiny that awaits us."

Renoldus effortlessly consumed the powder, surprising himself and causing a chuckle. "If I die, I can meet my destiny."

Glasha was not laughing with him. "Mock if you must, but you will soon see it is true."

After a moment, the powder worked its magic, instantly calming his body and relieving the pain.

"Your eyes are alive," said Glasha. "How are you feeling?"

"It's impossible to describe," said Renoldus.

"Your mask of pain is gone."

"I feel free from all that troubles me."

"Our people say it's living as the gods do."

Renoldus soaked in the mystery of Glasha's powder, and as he did so, she began tending to his wound, cascading the mysterious liquid over it. She removed the poison with her small tusks and applied the paste she had crafted together over the wound.

"How do you feel now?" said Glasha.

"Strange," said Renoldus, "but there's no pain in my leg."

"Soreness may occur like a bruise later, but it heals quickly."

Renoldus's rugged smile served as his thank you. Despite the effects of Glasha's herbal remedies, he was lucid enough to ask the question of why she had traveled to find him. "What made you decide to fulfill your destiny now?"

Glasha paused, staring at the ground briefly. "I didn't know when I would search for you, but I had to flee when my father became violent. He sent warriors to track me down and drag me back to the Groves. Although I traveled for several days, I needed a place to hide for a few more, and I slipped into the forest to escape them."

"You're at least a half-fortnight ride from the Groves. How long have you been here?"

Glasha glanced over at the dead boar and admired her near perfect placement of arrows, avoiding the gaze of Renoldus. "Only a few days."

"You face harsh judgment for being here without the king's permission."

Glasha shifted her gaze back to Renoldus with a quizzical look. "The king's permission? I thought forests were for all people to enjoy and hunt in."

"This land is the King's Forest."

Something about the time you've spent in the forest doesn't ring true. I swear I've felt eyes in the forest on more than one occasion.

Glasha pivoted the conversation away from the King's

Forest, preferring a topic she'd be able to control. "The glance we shared that day was powerful. We share a common, greater destiny. How else can you explain why I was here to save your life?"

Figurative rolled eyes were in his voice as Renoldus became irritated by Glasha's stretching reality to fit her narrative. "I was thinking the same thing. How did our random encounter a few years ago lead us to this day?"

Wait. My desire burns like a fire within me.

"I just told you. Destiny has brought us together."

Renoldus felt arousal within his trousers. "You've put me under the power of an enchantment, haven't you?"

Glasha paused for a moment and gave Renoldus a curious look. "I've done nothing of the sort. Why would you ask such a question?"

"I have this burning desire for you, yet a hog has gored me. This is not how one recovers from a wound."

"You've wanted me since that day. I saw it in your eyes."

"How can you be serious? You were only a girl then."

"Only? I was nearly a woman then. You know Af'lam females mature faster than human women."

"What does this have to do with today?"

"Answer me this and tell me the truth, Sir Renoldus. Have you desired me since that day?"

He raised his eyebrows and shook his head. He had enough of love-at-first-sight talk, a silly idea from romantic authors. "What was the first pill for?"

Glasha eyed the ground for a moment and played with her long, wavy black hair, swishing the ponytail atop her head back and forth. "I already told you it was to calm you."

It was more than calming. But I'll play along.

"Do you think your life is driven by random events?" said Glasha.

You're posing a question that the halls of history have passed down without finding a satisfactory answer. And you're asking me under these circumstances? "I suppose. Had thought little about it."

"There is a purpose to life. It would be foolish to think otherwise."

Renoldus frowned and looked away. He disliked being labeled foolish, and the implication was clear. The discussion of purpose seemed pointless amongst the bloodied and battered bodies, and the listless warriors, victims of *Blackout*. In his dreams, they approached him, haunting him, with corpses piled high behind them, stretching far into an open battlefield.

You want to talk to me about purpose? What is the point of young men dying at the end of a steel blade because a king wanted to show another his cock was bigger?

"Your face reveals disagreement with my words."

Time had passed faster than either realized, and dusk had arrived. The sky was stunning, with its bright colors changing from blue to orange and purple. It was into those wondrous hues Renoldus shifted his gaze and searched for an answer in nature's beauty why wars and death marred such loveliness.

I've killed men in war so often it's lost all meaning to me. Yet, the murders of my father and Cecile have set my life on a course with no compass; and worse, I continue to ruminate on the authorities, doing nothing about it. Is this a penance of sorts? I pay for creating enough widows and fatherless children to last ten lifetimes over? Perhaps Glasha has the answer, but I don't want to ask the questions for fear of the change I would need to make.

"Where are you?" said Glasha.

Renoldus said nothing but looked again to the sky and its wonder. It caused him to think more deeply about divine providence and, if so, did it have any relevance to life as he experienced it?

Why isn't it obvious whether gods and goddesses exist? If so, we could move forward in life. But it's not and we can't. If there is a purpose behind the death and destruction I've witnessed, I refuse to be associated with those responsible.

A frustrated frown hung on Glasha's face, a sign of her growing impatience. "Renoldus, did you hear me? Where are you?"

Renoldus nodded his head toward Glasha and in his mind he opened the door to a room filled with dusty old memories, forgotten feelings, and stories never told. The room was a mess. Grief out of place, anger hidden underneath sorrow, love thrown in a corner, and an enormous pile of guilt in the middle of it all.

Renoldus had fallen again into his cycle of cynicism and self-pity. "I've fought and killed men forced to serve their yearly time in the king's army. Those men, even some boys, had no place on a farmer's field far from home, clashing steel with men like me. Talked into a sense of bravery by commanders who knew they were sending sheep to the slaughter. There was no purpose to the cycle of war befalling men before I was born, and it shall certainly continue after I die."

Glasha remained silent. There was no question to be answered, no comment to be made. But she did her best, given the circumstances. "Without evil, how would we recognize good? Searching for what is good sparks hope and without it you fall into bitterness and resentment, which I feel is where your heart lives."

I'm bitter, hopeless, and sitting here wallowing in it won't help either of us. I came here to clear my head and all I've done is add more shit to the moat.

Renoldus struck a conciliatory tone and offered some hope, at least for him. "Then again, perhaps I am wrong. You've searched for me, the man with blue eyes whom you once saw."

Glasha's circular eyes came alive, likely excited by the chance to share her afternoons spent with Shadbak, *the Cimcier* of the whispered Tree.

"There is an old blind woman living amongst us we called

Cimcier," said Glasha. "Although you might call her a seer or prophetess."

"Seer is our word. Now go on."

"Her name is Shadbak. No one knows how old she is or where she came from."

There is something endearing in your enthusiasm, I'll give you that. Even if it is a lie, you have my attention.

"She lives in a treehouse nestled in what our ancestors called the Tree of Whispers. I liked to listen to her stories, which she called history, waiting to be written."

Renoldus sat up as if Glasha's recounting her time with Shadbak was pulling him forward into the mysterious world of the seer in the Tree of Whispers. None of the seers, prophets, witches, interpreters of dreams, and fortune tellers who called on King Leander had ever piqued Renoldus's interest, but Glasha's tale of Shadbak spurred his imagination.

"My father forbade me to visit Shadbak," said Glasha, "accusing her of telling lies. I kept going until he started making threats against her. The day she foretold my future was our final meeting."

"Your father tends to get angry and lash out." Renoldus's stab at humor was like a stone thrown into the sea. Glasha raised an eyebrow, ignored the remark, and continued to share her story.

"My father disliked Shadbak's predictions about his future, so he deemed everything she said was false."

"What'd she say during your last visit?"

Sensing the right time, Glasha moved closer to Renoldus and rested her hand on his arm. The sensation of her powerful hand was pleasurable and heightened his challenge of suppressing longing and passion.

"Shadbak told me I would marry neither king nor prince, nor anyone from my tribe. She said I'd already seen the man I was to marry."

"That's it?" said Renoldus.

"No, there's more. She said you would commit something unforgivable in the eyes of your king and he'd force you to leave. They said you were bedding—"

"Wait," said Renoldus. "Who's they?"

Renoldus narrowed his eyes, questioning how Glasha got that information without visiting Crence. *Her kind are not well-liked, and if they're in the capital, they are whores like Bex. But forced to leave? Was it the old blind woman who told her?*

"Uh ..."

"Go on. You've shown no signs of shyness to this point."

Glasha swallowed hard and plunged forward as a woman jumps into an ice-cold lake. "I've overheard conversations with men out hunting in the forest. These men must've had a great deal of treasure by the way they dressed and by their servants who did the actual hunting."

Renoldus gazed into the woods and imagined Glasha's perspective on such a thing and failed to stifle a laugh.

The frown on her face preceded what Renoldus knew would be the next question. "Are you laughing at me?"

"Absolutely not. Your innocent eyes truly captured the truth of the hunting parties of the nobility. But go on, let's hear what they said about me."

The interruption caused a pause in Glasha, and her demeanor changed. "I'm not sure I want to tell you what they said. Their words were mean and unkind."

"You won't be telling me something I haven't heard before."

"The accusations were mostly about your drunkenness. They say you cannot get over the death of your wife. I believe her name is ... C ... es ..."

"Cecile."

"Yes, that's it. They also said you were bedding the red-haired princess, Ingrid. She's being sent somewhere to marry a prince to form an alliance, but she is no longer a virgin. You used to be a hero, but now you're more like a drunken fool spending all your time at the King's ... Keyhole, I think is what they called it."

Glasha's words cut Renoldus to the quick and embarrassed him. What they said was true, but for Glasha to hear it from others was more painful than he expected.

I'm worse than a fool because I knew better and did so anyway. I've sullied my reputation beyond what I can repair in a lifetime. Clearly, I'm not the man for this woman, no matter how much I'm attracted to her.

"Those things are all true and I'm sorry you had to hear it from them. I think your Shadbak meant someone else."

"Now I'm sure you're the one."

Your eyes say, "Believe me, it's true." My mind, heart, and soul argue over what to believe now. I have not seen eyes as clean as yours since Cecile. I yearn for your touch, yet I swear you gave me more than a calming pill and lit the fire within my inner parts.

"What makes you so sure I'm the one?" said Renoldus.

"Renoldus," said Glasha, "there are other things about your life which correspond with what Shadbak said about the one."

"Is it still possible I'm not the one?"

"No. Everything the *Cimcier* said about the one tells me it is you, without a doubt."

The conversation lulled, and the two became quiet. Despite the strangeness of the day, Renoldus found himself drawn to Cecile as usual. All women faced comparisons, fair or unfair. Of course, no one could pass the test, given the absolute perfection of the slain woman.

"The day's randomness reveals your gods' power to position you perfectly," said Renoldus.

The smile across Glasha's face grew, and she came to life. "Now you believe."

"I'm not totally convinced, but you're persuasive."

And so is whatever you gave me ...

"I'm only saying what history will reveal as true."

What she swallowed down with the wine produced the

same results in her innermost places as it did for Renoldus. Under a cluster of small trees was luscious ground covering, and she fantasized about lying back onto it as Renoldus made the love of the gods to her. "Is your leg strong enough to limp over to those trees?"

Renoldus smiled and feigned greater pain than he was in. "Will you carry me?"

"I doubt you desire rumors of being carried by a woman from a distant land. It might ruin your reputation."

"I'm doing a fine job of tarnishing my reputation. What's one more story to add to it?"

Glasha shot him an odd look, but Renoldus laughed and, as he did, walked with a slight limp over to a spot underneath one of the trees. Glasha smiled with bow-shaped lips slightly parted, and Renoldus allowed his thoughts and imagination to roam free.

Drawing closer to Renoldus, Glasha shifted her shoulders forward while he leaned against the tree for support. "Tell me, Sir Renoldus. Do you like what you see?"

"You're alluring and intriguing, and it makes me want to know every inch of your body from head to toe."

Glasha's cheeks reddened, and she glanced away for a moment, then brought her attention back to Renoldus. "Your eyes tell me you want to see what's under my armor."

Renoldus was eager, but tried to conceal his escalating desire, pushed forward by the little pill. "My eyes do not deceive you."

Glasha took her time in unhooking the steel clasps, keeping the piece of hardened leather tight against her forearms. When both were off, she playfully tossed them at his feet with a sly smile.

The chest armor was one piece of hardened leather, formed to fit her upper body. It was held together at the top via a piece of thin but sturdy chain hooked to steel loops sewn into the leather on each side. On the bottom part, two bigger steel loops fit through open tabs in the leather. As with the top portion, a chain, this one with bigger links, hooked to the loops. Shoulder guards were attached to the top of the chest armor with leather straps.

Renoldus eyed Glasha as if he were dying of thirst and she held in her hand fresh cool water just drawn from a well. "Allow me to do the rest."

Glasha smiled demurely and lifted her arms to the sky as if she were surrendering. Renoldus opened the clasps and held the armor open, allowing her to slither out. Amazed by what he saw, he kneeled and removed her shin guards and left the princess in her battle skirt and nothing else.

Glasha locked eyes with Renoldus and ran her tongue over the top of her lip. "Do you approve of what you see?"

"Approve? That wasn't the word I was thinking of," said Renoldus.

He pulled his dirtied burgundy tunic over his head and cast it aside. Glasha moved forward into the powerful arms of Renoldus and kissed him softly on the lips.

"The warmth of your skin feels good against mine," said Glasha.

"You're driving me insane with want of your body," said Renoldus, "its curves, its strength, its color."

"The words you speak seduce me," whispered Glasha, "and I want my need satisfied."

Glasha wore a defensive battle skirt made with leather strips protecting her hips, thighs, and sensitive areas. Without shame, she shimmied out of the skirt and stood in front of Renoldus.

Renoldus was down to his pair of black trousers, with one leg out and a boot. *Blackout* was still on his hip, and so he undid his belt and dropped it to the ground. Glasha removed the other boot and pulled down the pant leg. Somehow, it looked more like a dance and less like a man removing his pants.

Glasha laughed at Renoldus attempting to disrobe. "This is not the time for dancing. You might hurt yourself worse than before."

"You could've helped me more," laughed Renoldus, "and instead you allowed me to look like a jester out here."

Glasha grabbed Renoldus by the hand and led him to a large patch of ground covering made primarily of thage grass, blue tulsi, and purple moss. Together, they produced a heady scent and, as both breathed it in, they became further intoxicated with desire. Glasha laid her back against the mixture of grass and flower and pulled Renoldus down on top of her.

Renoldus smiled and kissed Glasha's neck and whispered words of love in her ear. She pulled him up to her lips by his rust-colored hair and became the aggressor, kissing him with unexpected intensity. The force of Glasha's kisses, spurred on by her once-hidden and pent-up craving for his touch, caused her petite tusks to cut into his lips and mouth.

The pain feverishly fanned the flames of the furnace of his sexual wanting of the exotic Af'lam woman. Even thoughts of Cecile were forced to seek refuge at the strength of the knight's desire.

Two people, two different cultures, two skin colors became one in the middle of the King's Forest for one glorious night. They exhausted themselves, giving all in body and soul, as Vesceron chased away the night. Both got dressed and prepared to leave but stood to watch the rise of the brilliant star, squeezing every ounce out of their encounter as fruit is for its juice.

The princess flashed a flirtatious smile at Renoldus. "How does your leg feel, Sir Renoldus? It gave you little trouble during the night."

Renoldus returned an affirmed smile mixed with a touch of desire. "It feels good. But not as good as when I first felt the warmth inside you."

As quick as a thunderstorm blows in from a cloudless sky,

Glasha changed the intimate playfulness. "I need to tell you something."

"Uh-oh," laughed Renoldus.

"I am a bastard of Sarg and a human slave."

Renoldus was quiet for a moment. "Your revelation doesn't change my feelings for you."

"I will tell you the story later, but I want you to use my human name, Miriella."

"That's a beautiful—"

Snap!

Both froze at the sound of a stick breaking.

Glasha turned her head toward the sound and peered into the forest. "Sounds like we might have a visitor."

Renoldus did the same and scanned the tree line for movement. "If someone sees us, I can be hanged."

"For having a swive in the forest?"

"It's the King's Forest, and it's who I'm with."

Glasha swung her head back to Renoldus. "Me?"

He maintained his focus and did not look at Glasha. "Not everyone appreciates you as I do."

Add to my sins the taking of a woman unacceptable to society.

There were no further sounds to show anything other than a random stick breaking in the forest. The two relaxed for a moment and Renoldus explained what it meant for a knight of his standing to be caught with a woman in the King's Forest. Worse yet, to be caught in the act with a *kirattu* was a sin beyond forgiveness.

"In our society," said Renoldus, "you're considered a—"

The distant sound of horses' hooves caused a frenzy of motion. Renoldus mounted Blackwind and called for Myst. The saker falcon glided down from a tree as Renoldus rushed to put his glove on. "When can I see you again?"

Glasha looked back before sprinting away. "Come out here again. I'll find you."

Renoldus regained his bearings and raced away on a

different route than he had meandered on at the start. Amid his return to the castle, he realized the true nature of his involvement with two royalties, each extremely dangerous in their own ways.

If there are gods, my condemnation will be swift and the punishment severe. The lust of my flesh has ruined me. I search for a woman to replace Cecile, knowing full well that it's a futile exercise. Yet I eagerly chase the dream, foolishly risking my life and ruining my standing as a heroic knight.

Glasha could've been an assassin and ended my life. Perhaps that type of death would've been an apt finish to this inexcusable behavior. But in the morn' my thoughts will return to Glasha and our next meeting. Even the gods cannot save me from myself.

CHAPTER 12
INVITATION ONLY

Two days ago...
Skuti headed for the stairs leading to the battlement facing the sea, seeking a better view of the three mysterious ships anchored in his harbor. In his crowded mind, thoughts moved in and out. Worst-case scenarios played to their not-so-logical conclusions, and Thora's less-than-subtle blackmail hung over his head like an executioner's axe.

"Aeehrl Skuti," called Sir Harald, "no one has seen the girl."

"What girl?" said Skuti.

"Thora didn't tell you?"

"Tell me what, damn you?"

"She told us to find the servant girl, the skinny one who works with the alewife."

Harald was a large man, a head taller than any man in Flace, and his muscular frame put the fear of the gods into the heart of many a man standing in front of him. His graying hair made him look older than he was, and the lines on his face did him no favors. Harald's guardsman's clothes were at least a size too small, and he was no longer as formidable as he once appeared. The fire had left his eyes, and he walked with a hunch as he moved around.

Skuti's sudden burst of laughter startled Harald and put a curious look on his face. "No, she didn't, but nothing surprises me with her."

Skuti plowed up the steep staircase and to the top with ease. Sir Harald huffed and puffed his way up, stopping twice to catch his breath.

"Whose ships are these?" said Skuti.

"They belong to the Pirate Lord," said Nasi Geirleif, Commander of Ships, "and the witch he travels with."

Nasi was a tall, thin man with hands perpetually held behind his back. His weathered face did not differ from other men of the sea, and like most sailors, he wore a beard. He kept his beard trimmed, unlike other Flacian men of rank, keeping it close to his face. Nasi was a smart man, although he preferred instinct and experience over traditional ways of fighting. His uncanny ability to predict weather and ocean currents left him with few peers.

"I thought this Pirate Lord," said Skuti, "was a figment of everyone's imagination."

"No, my Aeehrl," said Nasi. "He is very real, and he and his barbaric crew sailing into our port is an ominous sign."

"How did they pass three ships through the Key Hole?"

"Fog," said Harald, joining the discussion. "They say the woman with him conjures up a thick mist and shrouds the ships in mystery."

"So, the stories are true."

"It would seem so, my Aeehrl."

Weaving and ducking in between men, a young boy raced up the stairs and onto the battlement walkway. Loud voices from two guards in pursuit gained the attention of Skuti and Nasi just as the boy reached his destination.

"I've been given this message for Aeehrl Skuti," said the

boy, standing as tall as he could despite catching his breath at the same time.

Skuti squatted down, matching the height of the boy. "Who gave you this message?" he said.

"I don't know, my Aeehrl," said the boy. "A woman emerged from the sea and handed it to me."

All who gathered around laughed and poked fun at the boy and his fantastical story, except for Nasi.

"A woman out of the sea? Are you sure?"

"Yes. The colors of her eyes were different. They made me stare into them."

"The boy saw the witch," said Nasi. "The stories of those who have seen her always mention the eyes. Did she have a spear?"

"I don't know, Lord Nasi," said the boy. "I didn't see one."

"Enough questions," said Skuti. "Give me the message."

"Here, my Aeehrl."

"The man who wrote this spares no expense," said Skuti. "This is written on vellum, the best quality of parchment, and it certainly has not been in the water." Skuti looked down at the boy before he pulled the black ribbon from around the rolled-up parchment and read.

Dear Aeehrl Skuti, the esteemed warrior king of the mighty city of Ashul,

I trust this letter finds you in good health, with a sound mind and stable hands.

As you know by now, three of my ships sit in your harbor. We are not here to do battle with your ships nor to engage your army on shore. As you can see from the wall, I have lowered my colors and have hoisted the yellow flag of neutrality in its place. I have nothing to gain by attacking your city and I promise not to do so while I am anchored in your waters, unless, of course, we are provoked.

Please dine aboard my ship, the Vendetta tal-Mejtin, tomorrow evening. Arrive no later than three hours past the apex of the noon sun. If you do not accept my invitation, I will sail peacefully away from Ashul.

I write this in my own hand.
My highest regards to the Aeehrl of Ashul and to his Lady.
Master of the Seas,
Lord Taylor Denton

"What is your name?" said Skuti.

"Kolbein, my Aeehrl," said the boy, "but everyone calls me Kolbe."

"Kolbe," said Skuti, "here is a gold coin for you. Stuff it in your pocket and run directly home. Understood?"

"Yes, my Aeehrl," he said. "I will run as fast as I can. Thank you."

Kolbe bolted into motion, running on the walkway toward the stairs like a young man with his pants on fire, and kept running all the way to his home near the docks. As he did so, Skuti rolled up the message with care and slipped the ribbon into place.

"Watch the ships with sharp eyes," said Skuti, "but do nothing aggressive toward them."

"As you command, my Aeehrl," said Nasi.

Skuti ventured one last look at Taylor's ship, but also noticed storm clouds bearing down on Ashul. Harald, a man without fear, seemed unnerved by the dark clouds gathering in the sky.

"I fear this may be a Salis, my Aeehrl," said Harald.

"Yes, it is, Harald," said Skuti. "Yes, it is."

"Should I have my men prepare the castle, my Aeehrl?"

"No, Harald. I sense this storm will blow over the sea, away from us."

"Are you certain, my Aeehrl?"

You? Afraid of a storm?

"Quite, actually. The man and the so-called witch won't permit it."

"I believe Aeehrl Skuti is correct," said Nasi. "It will sweep out to sea away from here."

"Sir Harald," said Skuti.

"Yes, my Aeehrl."

"Go see the healer and have him check your humors."

"Yes, yes, indeed I will, my Aeehrl."

"Pay heed to his words," said Nasi. "You look dreadful, and I have no desire to see your body on a funeral pyre." By the time Harald absorbed Nasi's words, Skuti was halfway down the walkway and headed for the stairs just as quickly as Kolbe, the young messenger.

I can only hope if we ever have to engage an enemy in battle, Harald can rally himself one more time. He deserves to die as a warrior and not in a bed pissing down his leg.

Skuti continued running and didn't stop until he reached the livery and his long overdue confrontation with Jomar.

~

TAYLOR DENTON HAD A SHROUD of mystery surrounding him. No one knew anything about the man until he appeared on the seas captaining the *Vendetta tal-Mejtin*. It was as if he had manifested himself out of thin air. It was not long after he arrived on the seas that both captains and sailors alike were speaking his name and that of his ship in hushed tones, convinced if they spoke any louder, he might soon find them.

"Stay here," said Skuti as he motioned to tie the boat off close by.

The man nodded and barked commands to his crew. Skuti climbed up a rope ladder unfurled over the side of Taylor's ship. He made it halfway up the ladder when he stopped for a moment before finishing his climb.

I've never seen a ship like this. No one west of the Great Expanse possesses the ability to create this design. But I can have one built larger, though, and quicker.

The *Vendetta* was a three-masted warship, full-rigged, with sleek lines and bowlines, and a sternpost rudder. She was faster, sailed in straight lines longer, and made precise turns, all vast improvements over the best of ships sailing the four seas.

Skuti completed his ascent up the ladder, and Taylor greeted him at the top.

"Aeehrl Skuti," said Taylor, "it is a distinct honor to meet you. People who depend on ships for their way of life widely recognize your name."

"Lord Taylor," said Skuti, "I have heard much about your prowess on the sea, and now I know why men fear you."

I would run from this ship too.

"Much of my reputation comes from the tongues of enemies."

"I am not here to cast judgment; only the gods may judge a man. I am here as a guest at your behest."

"You are indeed a wise man; the stories are true."

The smell of the sea mixed with that of roasted meat rose through the open doors to the cargo hold. It was warm on the deck of Taylor's ship, but soon the afternoon breeze would pick up and temperatures would dip. The setting sun, with little cloud cover, would be a spectacular sight.

"Follow me," said Taylor. "Dinner will be served shortly in my cabin. While we dine, I will explain the nature of my invitation."

You're not what I expected.

"Lead the way," said Skuti. "I'm hungry—the appetites of Flacian men are quite large."

The men climbed two sets of short staircases and made their way to the captain's quarters. Two guards met them at the door, and the servants inside sprang to life once the men passed through it. The lead servant, an older man with a sincere smile, seated Taylor at the head, with Skuti opposite him. The rectangular mahogany table could accommodate six additional guests, three on each side.

As Skuti scanned the room, wine in an engraved golden goblet magically appeared on the table.

"I hope you approve," said Taylor. "This is one of my favorites from a vineyard off the coast of Nocleace. Have you been there by chance?"

"Although we build great ships," said Skuti, "our people rarely sail that far. I fear the days of raiding and exploration are long gone."

"It's a shame, Aeehrl Skuti. There's so much to see and be amazed by. This is why I am in love with the sea."

Taylor dressed in a waistcoat and breeches made of velvet in a rich, deep navy color. His face was angular, accented with a full mustache and goatee; the trimmed facial hair was close to the face and had a touch of auburn when the light was right. He pulled back his long, shoulder-length brown hair into a ponytail, securing it with a light blue scarf made of the finest silk.

"I propose a toast," said Taylor. "May the seas be ever calm, the wind always at our back, and the enemy beneath our feet."

"Hear, hear."

Both men raised their glasses and sipped the wine.

"This is quite good," said Skuti, "although I am not an expert."

"Ah, but you are an expert at the design and building of ships," said Taylor. "You have continued what your father was renowned for."

So, we begin.

"I was, but as Aeehrl there is no time," said Skuti. "Dedicated and loyal men have taken over."

With a sip from his goblet, Taylor confidently smiled, aware of the high price his offer would fetch. "I won't waste your time with truth or fiction tales. You've heard the stories, seen the ship, and now you've met the man behind it all. Wisdom will be your guide."

"You did not invite here to discuss your past, nor is it my business."

"I need ships, and I want them constructed in Ashul."

Asking means no turning back. But what am I to do? My people are alone. How soon until Jomar and his council attempt to take Ashul by force? My warriors are strong and fearless, but the numbers are against us. Still, some circles will hate me because I allied with a pirate.

"You are deep in thought, Aeehrl Skuti," said Taylor. "Please, speak your mind."

Under a furrowed brow, Skuti continued to mull over his options, but always landed on the same answer. Taylor prodded no further and settled back into his chair. A quick nod to the servant standing close by, and more wine found its way into his golden goblet with inscriptions in a language owing itself to the people of *Gżira tal-Kranju*. Taylor moved the goblet toward his lips and the movement broke Skuti's attention away from his dilemma.

"What language are those inscriptions written in?" said Skuti.

"You pay attention to the details," said Taylor. "Important, yet too often ignored."

Skuti lifted his eyebrows and leaned forward in his chair.

"*Utathi* is the language," Taylor explained, "and those of *Gżira tal-Kranju* are the people."

"Is this where your warriors are from?" said Skuti.

"It is. But we digress. What is on your mind?"

The captain's quarters were quiet again. The ship rocked in the harbor, with creaking wood and occasional commands breaking the silence.

"I want to forge an alliance with you," said Skuti.

"Interesting," said Taylor. "What do I gain that I can't achieve on my own?"

"All of Flace's shipbuilding capabilities. Six Aeehrldoms constructing ships for you instead of only one."

"Hmmm. Go on."

"Not only that, but it will also force Acaria to look elsewhere for shipbuilders. Doing so will require both time and money."

"How will you go about this?"

"With your warriors and my men, I will take the rest of Flace by force, and the Ice Throne will be mine."

"So it is the Ice Throne you seek."

"It's not for vanity's sake, but for the survival of the Flacian people."

Skuti drank from his goblet, forgetting for a moment he was drinking fine wine and not mead. Taylor watched, bemused by Skuti's rougher edges but impressed by his tactful and thorough thinking. It made Taylor think of something his father once said: "The things unseen within a man are often his best weapons."

A brown-haired woman in strange attire slipped into Taylor's quarters via a false wall, constructed using one of the large bookshelves framing his bed. It turned just enough to allow a person to slip into an open space with stairs leading to the next level above and below. The mysterious woman strolled over and stood behind Taylor, placing her hand on his shoulder.

Is this the witch? Where in damnation did she come from?

Skuti stared at the woman and tried to make sense of what she was wearing. He'd seen nothing like it before, nor would he on anyone else. Whatever it was fit tight against her body, almost as if it were her skin. Aware he was staring, he abruptly stood.

"I am sorry," said Skuti. "I did not stand for you as our customs dictate."

"Aeehrl Skuti Ingimund, it is unnecessary," said the woman with a smile. "My name is Calena."

"Lady Calena?"

"Call me Calena for now."

With a slight grin, Taylor stood and proposed another toast. Wine showed up again, this time in front of Calena.

"Let's raise a toast to the seas and their hidden mysteries since the Number of Days began."

All three lifted their goblets to the sky and sipped the wine, and the men took seats while Calena opted to stand to the right shoulder of Taylor.

"Calena," said Taylor without looking at her, "Aeehrl Skuti has proposed an alliance."

"Aeehrl Skuti Ingimund needs to align with someone," said Calena, focusing her eyes on him. "His brother-law, Aeehrl Jomar Throst, has betrayed him and left him isolated and on his own."

"How long?" said Skuti.

"How long for what?" interjected Taylor.

"How long has he been building ships for Acaria?"

"The first ships they constructed," said Calena, "left port nearly a year halved."

"Cargo or war?"

"Both," said Taylor.

Skuti shook his head in disbelief, pushed away from the table, and walked away toward the forecastle windows. The sun's radiance cascaded off the blue water of the harbor, creating silver ripples for as far as the eye could see. In the near distance was Ashul's busy port with people bustling about the shops and docks.

"They have taken me for a fool," said Skuti, as he returned to the table and took his seat. "In order to keep the sisters from quarreling, I played the dutiful husband and brother-law, deferring to Jomar's decisions."

"Tragic mistake," said Taylor.

"In the worst ways," said Skuti.

There was a change in Skuti's countenance, something no one would notice except for those closest to him. Gone was the sly, confident half smile, replaced by narrowed eyes with no attempt at even a grin.

"The wars promised long ago are coming," said Skuti. "Where do you stand?"

"Taylor and I stand against Acaria and its malevolent man of religion," said Calena.

"Are you on the same side as the rest of the continent?"

"Neither," said Taylor with no emotion. "The rest of the continent is no better with its corrupt kings and rulers."

"We will take the continent for ourselves," said Calena, "and provide the people what they deserve, Aeehrl Skuti Ingimund."

"Deserve?" said Skuti.

"Yes," said Taylor. "You'd do anything for Ashul's people. We will do likewise for the continent."

"How would you know?" said Skuti. He shifted his eyes back and forth between the two. The two clearly knew more but refused to disclose it. Skuti's eyes stayed with Calena as she was prepared to speak in a voice that was deep and authoritative.

The young boy was right. Her eyes demand your attention. As does her voice.

"All spoken words reach the seas in the end, Aeehrl Skuti Ingimund," said Calena. "Sailors speak amongst themselves on the waters and their words come to me as the wind does."

"The Great Hall's fiery destruction is legendary," said Taylor. "So is the mystery behind your enemies' retreat from the forest and their attempted surrender in the Heil. Your people refused to believe rumors about men fleeing inevitable death from those with yellow eyes."

If the fist crashing down on the table startled Taylor and Calena, they did not show it. Skuti was standing and pointing a finger toward the two.

"Why is it you know everything about me," said Skuti, "and I know nothing about you?"

"Listen, Aeehrl Skuti Ingimund," said Calena, "and you will learn everything you need to know."

"We hoped to have you build ships for us from the beginning," said Taylor. "You will not hoard the increasing wealth but will use it for the benefit of your people. You have no fear of other's judgments regarding who you ally with."

Skuti listened but didn't like what he heard. "What are you implying?"

"You are a man who is ruthless with his enemies," said Calena, "and will do whatever it takes to deliver his people from evil and make them prosperous and glad."

Taylor stood with a large smile on his face. "Let's go up top," he said, "and discuss matters further while watching the sun take its dive into the horizon."

The servant by the door opened it and nodded to Skuti, who left and waited outside. He felt refreshed immediately by the cool afternoon sea breeze. Skuti grew uncomfortable and anxious sitting for extended periods of time.

Why am I surprised and irritated that others know about Vott's destruction? Still, I know little of their story. Despite the rumors, they didn't mysteriously appear out of nowhere.

The three stood on a private balcony overlooking the harbor and Seaborne Keep. Calena was tall, two fingers taller than Taylor, a man half a head taller than Skuti. Her suit resembled tight-fitting mail, only made of smooth interlocking clam shells, brightly colored in the blues and greens of the sea. The mail was not heavy nor burdensome, and she moved about freely and easily as if it were her skin.

"Ashul is perfectly located," said Taylor. "The narrow passageway into the harbor provides a defense against an enemy trying to invade by sea. Land forces face difficult terrain if an army wishes to attack inland."

Even with natural advantages, a force such as Acaria could conquer his land by simply overwhelming with man power. If Jomar and the Five Armies were to attack, they would have an advantage. It would be difficult to defend against their knowledge of the area and larger numbers.

When I strip it down to the core, my options are limited. I can't call on the Yelloweyes again. Pirates are bad enough, let alone the other choice. But I will not give up my Aeehrldom until my stiff body is ready for the grave.

"Let's talk alliance," said Skuti, "as it will soon be dark."

"These are my terms," said Taylor. "I will give you enough of my warriors for you to crush Jomar and his group of Aeehrls. My ships and men will protect Flace from attack by sea or land. You will fight alongside us when it is time to expand borders."

"What is enough?"

"One of my warriors is worth ten of Jomar's men."

"Have you not heard of Flacian fighters' courage and toughness?"

"Jomar doesn't understand how loath his men will be to fight against you. There are blood relatives on both sides. My men will put the fear of death into those opposing you. They will fight with fear and either get slaughtered or drop their weapons and flee."

"Your men, Aeehrl Skuti Ingimund," said Calena, "will always fight with fire in their bellies for you. With the Serpents, the blood will flow as if it were a river when you have defeated those who shunned you. This I have seen."

Afternoon was on its way out as evening chased after it. Skuti gazed out at the water and then toward his Aeehrldom one last time before confirming what he knew when he accepted Taylor's invitation—Ashul would form an alliance with the Pirate Lord.

If my people hate me for it, they can subject me to the executioner's blade. Flace will be whole. Beware those who believe Jomar can become king.

"I accept those terms," said Skuti, "but those who construct should be paid for their work."

"Of course I will pay them," said Taylor, "and your people

will experience riches beyond their dreams. The boat you arrived on will have a large chest aboard it. Payment made in good faith for future work."

"I will agree—"

"There's one last thing. I want to have a piece of land next to the sea where I will construct my castle. My colors will be visible from the height of its keep, and it will fly above the Flacian flag."

I expected you to ask for something. It's always this way when negotiations reach their end. This is a steep price to pay, a price I will not pay. It will take years for your castle to be built—longer when I hinder its construction. No flag will ever fly above the united flag of Flace.

"You're asking Flacian people to sacrifice their pride," said Skuti. "It is a difficult thing you ask for."

"Aeehrl Skuti Ingimund," said Calena, "without an alliance your people will be dead. There is no pride beyond the grave."

Taylor and Calena shared a confident glance and waited for Skuti's response. The Aeehrl of Flace remained silent, giving the impression he was still mulling the offer over. There was no place to turn for Skuti, and his two counterparts knew it long before the *Vendetta tal-Mejtin* set sail for Ashul.

"Your terms are acceptable," said Skuti. "It's the custom of our people to make a blood oath together as a guarantee."

Skuti pulled his dagger from behind his back as Taylor slipped his from a sheath attached to his belt. They sliced their palms, locked hands, and stared into each other's eyes. Calena's large, calloused, and bloody hand snuck in and gripped the top of the handshake, surprising Skuti, and he watched her as she raised her head to the heavens.

"We may not undo what we have promised here," said Calena. "A blood oath has sealed the agreement and anyone seeking to break the oath will face certain death."

Wind rushed out of nowhere and blew hard against the

ship and continued raising a fast white-capped wave, and it raced across the harbor and crashed against the rocks, sending water and foam high into the air.

What have I done?

CHAPTER 13
DUNGEON OF BLOOD

The king's solar was down a short hallway and to the left of Rycardus's chamber. On the short walk over Rycardus told himself to stand firm and leave before getting so angry as to provoke the changing's powerful impact and the pain it brought with it. After a warm greeting from his father, the two sat. It was apparent Rycharde was attempting a new tack with his son.

Don't stray from what you've decided. Be unyielding to father's strong will.

"When your turn is complete," said Rycharde, "you can still live amongst humans. You know that is true with Sir Evrardin."

At one time I considered him a friend and ally, but after the fight with Sir Raümond, I don't know.

"That's different," said Rycardus. "There were two generations before him."

Silence enveloped the room, leaving Rycardus anxious and uncomfortable. Even in good times, the fear of a misstep always loomed, the hammer always above his head.

"Either way," said Rycharde, "it can be done."

Rycardus leaned back in his chair and folded his arms across his chest. "How many times must we discuss this?"

"Until you realize the consequences of your actions and the nature of your betrayal—not only to me, but to the kingdom and the alliance with Brüeland."

"Did you tell King Leander about my condition? Isn't that a betrayal of your own word?"

"I promised him my son, and that is what I'm going to give him."

"Isn't there a measure of deceit in what you told him? What will he say when Ingrid tells him?"

The king's solar grew quiet again. In his heart, Rycardus knew he was winning the battle, but the war had already been decided unless he surrendered to the king and married Princess Ingrid and everything else be damned.

Somberness fell over Rycardus as he realized intrinsically that he needed to choose one of two paths. The revelation of a third path where all benefited was only a deception he played on himself. He rolled around the idea of keeping Reyna as a mistress after marrying Ingrid, but his conversion was the issue, not the arrangement.

"Why did you allow me to make my own choices?" said Rycardus.

"Making good and sound decisions marks a great king's reign," said Rycharde. "I wanted to see what choices you'd make given difficult circumstances."

"But that's not fair. I did not ask for the attack nor want it."

"Faire is where you sell your pigs."

Anger was building within Rycardus, and as it did, the beast stirred. "Maybe you just lacked the courage to kill me when you knew I was doomed."

"Watch yourself, Rycardus. I am not only your father, but also your king."

"You always say that when I strike a soft spot in your armor of righteousness."

"Are you saying the king has a soft spot?"

"Not the king, but the father."

I've made my decision, so why am I sitting here trading insults with the king?

The king, who spent much of his time within his own head, rubbed his chin, showing to Rycardus he was mulling over the argument and barbs in his head. He hated his father for it, when an emotional and raw conversation might better serve the two men. Instead, he appeared calculated in whatever he offered, using it to elicit a response for which he was prepared.

I don't know what it is, but it gets more emotional when Mother is here.

"Where is the queen?" said Rycardus.

"That's an odd way to ask for your mother," said Rycharde.

"Damn it to utter darkness. I don't act right, say what is right, and everything that goes wrong is my fault."

Oh, no. The cramping is starting.

"Perhaps it is true, then."

"Only to you."

"Ask the council members and see if they concur."

"Undoubtedly, they will see it your way. They are your servants."

Rycharde stood up and held his son's gaze. "Twenty-four hours."

Muscles in his legs and arms began to twitch and spasm, and unable to keep it under control, he bolted for the door, but not before blurting out, "I don't need twenty-four hours. You know what my choice is."

You can make it to your room.

As Rycardus struggled to make his way down the hall toward his room, his body spasmed and jerked hard enough to knock himself to the cold stone floor. Burning pain pulsed through the muscles and joints, as if fire were rushing through his veins.

This hurts like hell unleashed. My bones, muscles ... teeth. I feel like I can't move.

As quickly as it started, it stopped. Reyna's scratches and bites had heightened Delinda's venom working inside of Rycardus, but even together they lacked the power to sustain a full change in a large and still growing Rycardus.

It's starting, but I feel as if I'm stuck between two worlds.

Rycardus braced himself against the corridor wall and stood. The first two steps felt awkward, and Rycardus was about to land hard on the stone floor if it weren't for a barrel next to an arched wooden beam that he grabbed onto. The corridor was empty, allowing the prince to escape the gossip that would surely follow such a fall. No doubt its spreading would be like a wildfire in a forest, burning everything in its path.

He began the walk back to his chambers again and used the corridor wall to steady himself as if he were drunk. The rest of his steps carried him to his room where he fell on his bed, exhausted by the process of changing and the stress induced by the anger he felt toward his father and his place in life.

Lying on his bed for a few hours of intermittent sleep filled with dreams of yelloweyed beasts and kings, he awoke to the reality of needing a plan to leave the castle without a word getting back to Rycharde.

If I know my father, he is going to track me at least because he will need to show he tried to intercept me. He'll tell Sir Raiimond and the White Guardians, and say I ran off without his knowing and that I'm a danger to myself and others.

There were dark circles underneath Reyna's eyes when she met Rycardus at the start of an old corridor added to the castle, dating back to the time of Richard-Richer, Rycardus's great-grandfather. "Are you positive this leads to an exit? You know how I am about tight spaces."

Rycardus, irritated by the lack of sleep and Reyna's incessant chatter, sent her the eye of evil. It was about an hour before Vesceron would rise and take over the night, and he wanted to leave as soon as it did.

"Yes, stop asking me."

"You don't have to snap at me."

"Then quit asking me the same question."

The thought struck him hard, like a blow landing on its target. It was a simple question but demanded a more complex and nuanced answer.

What am I doing? Really, Rycardus, what are you doing?

"Rycardus," said Reyna, "what's wrong? Your face has gone pale and you're staring out in the distance."

"Maybe because I am trusting my future to you, and I don't know if I can even trust you with today."

"How can you say that to me? I love you with all my heart."

"Have you been dishonest and hidden certain things from me?"

Reyna glanced at the stone floor, searching for answers, or buying time. Either way, Rycardus was in no mood for any more subverting the truth or circling around a question. "I know I've not always been truthful, but when it's just you and I together alone, I will stand by you and be truthful even if it's painful."

"I wish I could believe you."

It's too late now. I've sold my soul to the devil and can only hope she does what she just said.

"But I believe you have a greater destiny to fulfill."

"Let's go, Reyna. I don't know how much time we have."

Rycardus lit his torch with Reyna's candle and hurried down the corridor until they found a doorway at the end of the long hallway. The linen paper in his hand held the answers he believed, and for the moment, there was nothing to deny it.

Upon opening the door, it instructed the reader to turn right down another corridor until it reached its end, and a left turn became necessary. Rycardus said nothing to Reyna, folded the paper as one might fold a map, and stuck it into his tunic.

After coming to the end and turning left, the two weaved their way through various passages and cramped walkways. Reyna, appearing tired and frustrated, complained. "Are we almost there? I've told you I don't enjoy being in confined spaces."

"Shhh," said Rycardus, "do you hear voices?"

"What? No, should I?"

"I don't know. That's why I'm asking you. You've got the ears."

"No. I hear nothing."

I swear I heard voices. Am I getting paranoid?

Rycardus was regretting his choice for an escape route as the two squeezed through the tight space. "I didn't realize this was a pathway for dwarves."

Several paces later they made it to the last door, and Rycardus put a skeleton key inside the lock and pushed the door open. Chilly air rushed by the two, as did an unpleasant smell. Rycardus said nothing and entered, but Reyna stayed outside and peered in with her candle.

"Are you sure we're safe down here?" said Reyna.

"No one remembers this old dungeon. Up those stairs and we'll be at the backside of the stables."

"How can you be sure?"

"Are you questioning me? I know this castle better than anyone."

Reyna entered the dungeon without a smile, shifting her eyes around the room before she caught his gaze. "You seem uncertain."

"As do you."

"This is difficult for me. I fear I'm ripping you from your family and you'll regret it someday. You'll hate me for the rest of my life."

Rycardus pulled Reyna's strong body close to his and kissed her softly on the lips. Although it was cold and dank in the old, creaky, smelly dungeon, Rycardus felt oddly warm and revitalized after the lack of sleep, and despite his irritation and frustration with Reyna, he felt passion rising within his loins.

Why am I feeling this desire for Reyna?

"I made a choice for love over my standing as heir apparent," said Rycardus, "but it's not too late for me to turn around if you don't share the same love."

"You know the answer," said Reyna. "I am dead to my grandparents and assassins will be sent to kill me. If sacrifice means love, then I have sacrificed it all for you."

"I need to hear the words."

"I love you, and may you be damned for even questioning my love for you."

Rycardus pulled her in again and passionately kissed Reyna as if this one kiss were an accurate measure of his deep love for her. They clung to each other tightly, yearning for the moment to last forever.

"Do you love me," said Reyna, "as I love you?"

"I have given away my inheritance for you," said Rycardus, "rejected my family, and have refused to marry the woman my father has chosen."

"You made me say the words. It's your turn."

"I love you."

The animal lust in Reyna and Rycardus took over despite the need to flee. Each tore the clothes from their body and flung them across the cold, hard, and filthy stone floor. Neither was ashamed by their nakedness and so the two stood and stared at each other while allowing their lust to burn as a smoldering fire within their loins.

"Your exotic beauty tantalizes me," said Rycardus.

Reyna's beauty was exotic, setting her apart from other women in the Wolfburn Valley. Everyone knew it but said nothing. She did her best to blend in with loose-fitting dresses and garments, but her muscular limbs, pronounced curves, and round breasts would not stay hidden.

"I am like no other woman," said Reyna, "and if you let me be your chosen one, I will willingly be your whore for eternity. Plant your seed in me so I can bear you the son you deserve. He will enjoy the best of our worlds."

While the words were still in the air, a sudden and blinding pain jolted her body, and she doubled over in pain. Reyna looked up at Rycardus with confused yellow eyes.

"What happened?" said Rycardus.

"Oh my god, Rycardus," said Reyna, "I have never felt the change come on as it has now. Please … Rycardus. My desire for you is so strong it has released the beast inside me."

The two youthful bodies came together with a ferocious hug that both held for a moment before their mouths collided in a vicious kiss, more painful than pleasurable. Reyna's claws crept from her nail beds, and she ran them down Rycardus's back. His arousal for pain grew as he spent more time with Reyna. She eased her head away from the taller Rycardus, standing on the tip of her toes to whisper in his ear with a raspy and deeper voice.

Reyna pulled away, grabbed his hand, and led him over to an old barrel where she positioned herself for Rycardus to take her from behind. She held on to the edge of the barrel, which was thick with dust and cobwebs.

Reyna's face faced downward, and her yellow eyes peered out across the stone floor, as if she had lost something of value. A tingling sensation began flowing through her body as never before.

In the shadows of a cold, dark, damp, musty and silent dungeon, only the sound of moans and Rycardus's pelvis banging against Reyna's firm backside echoed throughout the room. The tingling sensation filled her shaking body, causing a violent reaction to start within her.

Reyna's muscles were starting to spasm, slight and inconsistent from holding the barrel in an awkward stance. Reyna kept her face looking downward, her yellow eyes shut tight, her face contorted into a mask mixed with pleasure, driven by sadistic pain. The tingling feeling became more intense than what Reyna's body could tolerate, causing her head to jerk up; her eyes opened, full of life and animal lust.

Each thrust of Rycardus into Reyna's body was like an ember setting her ablaze as a dry forest does when a fire burns through it. The sensation reached her deepest regions, sending words out of her mouth that were unintelligible, a cross between growls and passionate cries of an orgasm to follow.

As Rycardus continued to bang his muscled abdomen against her, her body became engulfed in flames of overwhelming passion and satisfaction. But there was something else flowing through Reyna's veins, much more sinister and darker.

Reyna's glowing yellow eyes turned from lust to menacing. Small red pupils stared out into the black. With a deformed hand and menacing claws, her left arm warned others to stay away from the barrel. Her right arm still held the barrel, but it grew more muscular, sprouting hair down the forearm, and claws formed at the end of her hand.

Reyna's lips were nothing more than a thin line of black and her open mouth revealed small sharp fangs. Triangle-shaped ears rose out of her hair just enough to see the tips. Her eyes roamed the room, seeking someone. With heightened senses, Reyna could feel another was in the large, dark, and foreboding dungeon.

Rycardus was oblivious to it all. Eyes shut, mind distant, it would require a day's ride to return him to the present. The sexual gratification within his loins was growing more intense and the feel of his seed begging to be released overwhelmed any and everything else, although Reyna was ready to pull away. Someone was in the dungeon, the wrong man at the wrong time.

Reyna turned her werewolf's head to the side, to listen for the unmistakable sound of boots against stone stairs. Rycardus was unaware of the faint sound of leather on stones, but he was the man she least desired to encounter, especially not engaging in such actions with his son.

Rycardus pushed one last time, hard as humanly possible, and shot his seed into her belly. The force of the last crash of his body against hers knocked Reyna off-balance, and she lost control of the barrel and her body. Both came crashing down to the unforgiving stone floor, smashing the old wooden cask. Reyna cried out like a dog getting smacked on the nose.

"Rycardus," shouted Rycharde, "what goes on down there?"

"Father," said Rycardus, "do not come any further. You risk your life down here."

"You would turn on your father?"

"I don't want to hurt you, but I can't speak for Reyna."

Reyna's deep growled echoed in the small chamber, warning King Rycharde to step no further. In return, Rycharde placed his hand on the hilt of his black sword, *Heartstriker, Scourge of the Wolf*, but left it in its sheath. Reyna's yellow eyes pierced the darkness, finding Rycharde midway down the stairs. The staircase winding down to the dungeon was narrow, and it would be impossible for Reyna to escape without knocking King Rycharde out of the way or to avoid the legendary blade from piercing her transformed body.

"You know what she is, Rycardus," said King Rycharde. "She is a *duhbrarei*, and her loyalties lie with the Yelloweyes. She's using you for her own purposes."

"Reyna, no," said Rycardus.

Reyna bolted for the stairs on two legs, unable to contain her anger and contempt for King Rycharde any further. As she prepared to leap at Rycharde, the door at the top of the dungeon opened and light invaded the stairs. At the top was Sir Raiimond, torch and sword in hand.

The sudden light revealed Reyna and Rycharde drew his sword, but in the process banged his hand and forearm against the uneven stones in the sidewall. The blow caused him to loosen his grip on *Heartstriker*. Reyna lost her focus in the light, and instead of hitting Rycharde dead on she caught more of the wall and less of the man, but enough to knock him over and send his body down the uneven and jagged steps, his sword trailing behind him.

"Rycharde!" shouted Raiimond, too late to matter.

Reyna's body was stunned by the impact, and she fell into a heap on the same hard steps. With Reyna down, Raiimond saw his opportunity to provide justice for his king and allowed the hate and contempt he held in his heart and soul to come rushing out.

"I should've killed you when I had the chance," said Raiimond. "You have ruined the king's son, and now I will send you to the place of suffering." He kneeled next to her, wanting to savor the moment as one savors a fine wine.

"When I am done with you," said Raiimond, "I'm going into town to burn your traitorous grandparents' shop to the ground with them in it."

"Raiimond!" said Rycharde from the bottom of the stairs. "She's moving!"

But it was too late. Reyna had put her lightning-quick reflexes in motion. While still on her back, she brought an arm around and, with razor-sharp claws, tore at Raiimond's face, bowling him over at the same time. The cuts were deep to the bone, and blood poured out of the wounds.

"Shit," he spat out, "you little cunt of a girl."

Reyna's guttural voice cursed, "You bastard! You prefer the company of mothers and men. Wherever you go, I hope my kind are there to greet you."

Before finishing the wounded man, Reyna looked down at Rycharde, who watched helplessly at his longtime friend on the precipice of life. For a moment, Reyna and Rycharde locked gazes. Her eyes did not differ from the others he encountered. Hate, vengeance, murder, evil. Yet she smiled with thin lips at Rycharde, showing him she understood the emotional pain she was about to dump on his head as if the hurt were in a barrel being poured out.

Reyna nearly ripped Raiimond's head off with the power of her jaw and fangs, pulling skin and bone from the body. She clamped down ferociously on his neck and windpipe, crushing his larynx. Rycharde looked on in horror, unable to speak while she kept her viselike grip around Raiimond's neck.

When Raiimond's soul was on its way to its ultimate destination, she released her jaws and chewed on what she took from the skilled warrior's neck and face. Without swallowing, she spit the disgusting mix from her mouth toward Rycharde.

"That's for your intention of murdering both of us," barked Reyna.

Spinning, she rushed to the door and escaped to freedom, growling and cursing at Rycharde before leaving.

Rycharde picked himself up and climbed back up the stairs to reach Raiimond, but as he expected, it was far too late. The Advisor to the King of Andairn was dead. Rycharde lowered his head and wept bitter tears at the loss of his friend and confidant.

"This is your fault," said Rycharde. "My Advisor lies dead, killed by the Yellow-eyed dog you bed."

"It's always my fault," said Rycardus. "I suppose I'm responsible for allowing the Grayclaw to attack me when I was but a little boy."

It's coming on. I can feel my anger changing me.

"Don't be obstinate with me, son. You're not to blame, and I've never said otherwise."

"I knew there was something different about me when you did not send me to another house for training. You lied about that too."

"True—what would you have me do?"

"Tell the truth. Everyone knew what I was but said nothing for fear of your wrath."

"There's more to it than that."

"Is there more to the truth? You owed me that."

Oh, god, this hurts. If gods and goddesses exist, please ease the pain.

Extreme leg pain, burning muscles, and a splitting headache dropped him to the floor. "Why didn't you just kill me when you saw there was no saving me? You can't fathom the pain of morphing."

"Fight it," said Rycharde, "you can fight it!"p

"Not this time. My anger is against you. Leave or you're going to get hurt."

Silence came over the dungeon, and darkness consumed the light after Raiimond's torch burned out. Rycharde groped for *Heartstriker* before finding it at the bottom of the staircase. He pointed it out toward where he last heard his son speak.

"I have *Heartstriker* with me. Do not force me to use it."

"Don't come any closer. I can see you."

"Let's talk this through, son. If you leave the castle and take the whore with you, we will become enemies."

"We are not talking. I can't trust a word you say."

"If not for me, then at least do it for your mother. She loves you deeply and defended you even when it was difficult to do so."

I didn't turn all the way. Dammit. My hands and arms are half human, half wolf. The strength to transform is not there. Shit ... I have to make my move now before I go back to human form.

Yellow eyes were the last thing Rycharde saw before his son's big body slammed against his and drove him into the wall. Rycharde crumpled to the ground, knocked out by a blow to the head from the collision of bodies and crashing into the wall.

Rycardus lost his balance and fell to the ground but found his bearings and stumbled up the stairs and out the door. Outside, Reyna walked away from a row of tall hedges wearing the tight-fitting clothes of a servant girl. Rycardus jumped behind the same hedges and eased back into human form with less pain.

"Holy shit," he said, "what happened?"

The clawed body of the servant girl lay amongst the hedges.

"Wrong place, wrong time," said Reyna.

"You killed her for her clothes?"

"I needed clothes, and she walked by."

"Look at her. We can't go around killing innocent people."

"You did not change all the way, did you?"

"No, I did not."

"When you do someday, you'll think differently."

Is this what I have sold my soul for? Random killings for clothes, food, and whatever else is needed? What kind of life awaits me?

"C'mon," said Rycardus. "We need to go. Once the bells ring, we need to be outside of the castle walls and as far away as possible."

CHAPTER 14
ENSLAVED

*I*t was only three days since his death, but they laid Watkin Dernesch to rest in the burial grounds outside the Cathedral of Eternity, close to the Stallion's Keep within Chirlingstone Castle. A man of Watkin's status normally lay in state for seven days, but Evelyn wanted Watkin in the ground in the shortest time possible, raising questions about the decision. But the choice had the king's backing, and that was that to the life of Watkin Dernesch, who lived and died in mystery.

It had been a week since Renoldus's revealing discussion with Watkin, and he was knee deep in preparation for Ingrid's trip to Wolfden and her subsequent marriage to Prince Rycardus. Ingrid's constant interruption of the development of his plan to escort her did not help in the least. Nor did the time spent attending Watkin's burial ceremony and all that accompanied it.

Renoldus had just picked up his jacket and sword when the dubious knock came at the door. He didn't even have to ask who it was.

"What, Ingrid?"

"I need to talk to you," said Ingrid.

"I'm busy."

"Too busy for me?"

"If I don't get your little trip planned, it will not be good for either of us."

"Especially you. Now let me in."

The gods decidedly hate me. It's my punishment for dishonoring the Code while bedding the once-fine virgin, the princess of Brüeland.

Renoldus looked hard at *Blackout*, for a moment wondering if murdering Ingrid, riding out to the forest, and leaving this all behind with Glasha might be the best answer. Instead, he pulled open the door and Ingrid ducked in.

"Why do you hold *Blackout*?" she said.

"Merely checking its balance. What can I do for you?"

"What's with the coat?"

"I can't wait for volunteers to show up. I need to inform the men I want to accompany me."

If I could only get one decision back ... I've told so many lies and mistruths to you, I can't keep track of them.

Ingrid grabbed the coat of Renoldus and threw it on his desk as if it were her apartment. Her clothing continued to be a hodge-podge of styles, and today's garb included a leather tunic not buttoned to the top with an undergarment of blue cotton with tight sleeves to her hands. The pants and boots remained, but around her waist was a brown leather belt which held a sheath.

"Put the sword away," said Ingrid. "I want to talk to you about Evelyn."

"Why are you carrying the sword you borrowed from my collection?" said Renoldus.

"I didn't borrow it. You said it was a gift," said Ingrid.

"I never said that. The castle blacksmith forged a sword which I gave to you, Ingrid. You wielded it when we trained, and it was to be your sword to carry. I want you to leave the sword on your hip with me before you go tonight."

"Since it was a gift, I can do whatever I want with it. Let me tell you about Evelyn."

What was I thinking? I've made more poor choices with Ingrid than in my whole life to this point. Renoldus gave little thought to the poisoner of Watkin. Frankly, he didn't care who it was, only that a villain was dead, and the world was better for it. It was a long march to death, and he died as the last ember in what was once a raging fire in the hearth. The only time Renoldus allowed himself to speculate on the culprit, he toyed with the idea that Evelyn poisoned her husband. It was plausible; he thought.

"You're going to tell me Evelyn poisoned her husband, and that's why they put Watkin in the ground as fast as they could."

Ingrid met his gaze as if he were a drunkard coming out of his apartment after a weeklong binge. "Everyone says that. I'm surprised the town crier hasn't shouted it out for all to hear. You must quit sitting here, constantly drinking wine. This will end once we're married."

Anger at Ingrid's accusation he was a wine-guzzling drunkard not knowing what was going on around him, snapped him back to his only way out from underneath her bondage. "You're going to marry Prince Rycardus."

"You're going to add to your plans our escape route. The thought of being mounted by the Wolf Prince disgusts me."

"Fugitives fleeing from the king's command lead very short lives. Maybe we can seek asylum with the Advocate."

"Renoldus, you're not helping me in the least."

"My job is not to help you but to get you to Wolf's Keep."

"No, it's not. It's doing as the princess desires."

"Now you're telling me you take precedence over the king's command?"

"What does it matter to you? He's already exiled you. He lacks jurisdiction over wherever you travel."

Renoldus rolled his eyes to the sky, exhausted by Ingrid's

constant arguing and her self-serving assumptions. "It's about honoring the Code of the Black. I owe obedience to the oath I swore to uphold."

Ingrid didn't miss a beat, seeming to expect Renoldus's thoughts. "I suppose fucking me in every way possible was part of the Code?"

"Damn you. Are you going to torment me until death?"

"If I have to. I gave myself to you and you promised to love me until the end of time. Just give in to it, my love. Make me your bride and I will bear you sons and daughters. You need an heir, and I will give you a son of royal lineage."

And so I did, foolishly, driven by the surrender of your body to mine. It's deliver you to Wolfden or I'll be praying for the end of time.

"For the love of coinage, Ingrid. Your father, the king, has given you to Prince Rycardus for marriage. This will form an alliance with the Andairns and save the continent from the Advocate and his growing army."

"It's a lost cause without you leading the army. So I will marry who I want, and it's you."

"If you don't do your duty for the sake of Brüeland, we'll be speaking the native tongue of the Acarian Empire."

"What do you care? You're a man without a kingdom to serve. We can go anywhere we want outside of the Advocate's long arms."

Why am I arguing with you? You get what you want, ignoring the impact of your choices on others. I hate and desire you at the same time.

With a growing headache and wearied from Ingrid's nonstop assault on his emotions and mind, her "give in to it" sounded like a perfect pardon from his sentence of loneliness in exile. He dismissed the notion as more condemnation than escape and a way to further dishonor the Code in one last act of disobedience.

After telling his mind no to the easy way out, his thoughts drifted to Glasha.

Glasha is a woman worthy of desire and respect. A woman to fall in love with. *Perhaps her prophetic claim can break the chains of desire Ingrid has wrapped me in.*

"Where were you at?" said Ingrid.

"Nowhere good," said Renoldus. "What of Evelyn?"

"I'm sure you don't know this either, but she is sleeping with my father."

Renoldus narrowed one eye and tilted his head. "What did you say?"

"It's true. She's sleeping with the king, and he has promised her the position of Advisor to the King."

Renoldus found the irony amusing and used the chance to make light of the situation. "It's probably not the only position he wants to put her in."

"Renoldus, that's disgusting. No one wants to think about their father in the marital bed."

Renoldus stroked his boxed beard and considered Evelyn for a moment as the reason for his father, Sir Jeames, to ultimately turn down the offer of Lord Peares of House Rainstrong. The Rainstrong name had a strong reputation and the marriage of Renoldus and Evelyn had seemed a logical fit. Lady Evelyn was eager to marry the dashing and handsome man who'd someday become the hero of Brüeland.

What did you see, Father, that made you change your mind? Was it something Lord Peares said? Did Evelyn's dark side come into the light and get exposed? You knew people who were experts in what you called research. Did they find something? King Tarquin also knew there were those who secretly opposed him. Was one House Rainstrong?

The princess ran her fingers through her curls and gave Renoldus a quick smile, an idiosyncrasy she had when preparing to talk about difficulties involving herself. "I'm going to Evelyn's apartment tomorrow to have a nice little chat. There is some information she needs to hear because she is spreading lies. Evelyn has done some terrible things that I plan on confronting her with."

"Slow down. What lies are being spread? What information do you have?"

"I can't tell you the details now, but I will later, I promise."

"And the terrible things?"

"Same."

"Answer me true. Are you going to do something you'll regret later?"

"Of course not, but Evelyn will regret the things she's done."

"Are you going to kill her now that she's leading *Brutrark Vercis*, a group you fear?"

The twinkle in Ingrid's eye proved he was on to something. "You've been paying attention all along. But don't be so sure she's leading that group of criminals."

"I only pretended to be a drunken, broken-down knight to get you to talk."

Ingrid smiled, with only one thing on her mind. The princess's attention span was that of a child bouncing back and forth between different subjects. She often flipped from serious discussion to physical desire, confounding and unnerving Renoldus. The behavior kept the once powerful and righteous knight off-balance and at odds with his morality and honor toward the Code he dutifully swore to uphold.

Just as he had made up his mind to be done with Ingrid, she turned up the heat, as if she sensed his commitment to ending the affair needed to be broken. Perhaps it was happenstance, or maybe it was intentional. In the end, it didn't matter. Either scenario left Renoldus in his bedchamber and questioning himself all over again.

The alluring princess moved temptingly close to Renoldus and kissed him on the lips. He tried to deny himself, but the burning desire beneath his belt said otherwise and he fell to the temptress once again. Ingrid swept the papers and the coat off his desk and rapidly unbuttoned her tunic …

Therefore, you have me enslaved. There can be no other woman like you, turning your body into a religious ritual where I worship at the altar of what lies between your legs. I must have you again and again. May you be damned for turning me into nothing more than a man who craves you more than food and drink. I would rather starve to death than miss a meal that is you. I am ruled by what lies between my own legs and its deep aching to be inside of you.

CHAPTER 15
THE PIRATE LIFE

Skuti rapped on the solid wood double doors with three quick knocks and cleared his throat.

"Commander," said Skuti. He was in lighter armor than usual but still too heavy for close-in hand-to-hand combat aboard a ship subject to the sea's mood.

"One moment," said Taylor.

There were two voices coming from inside the captain's quarters. The female was less than amused.

"I told you this would happen," the voice hissed. "Someday you're going to have this thing up your ass."

Turning away from the door, Skuti tried to suppress a laugh. It didn't work.

Don't laugh. You'd do the same with the devilish mystery woman.

The doors to Taylor's quarters opened, but not wide enough to allow Skuti into the room. Behind Taylor, a curved shadow crossed the floor and was out of sight in seconds, and as it disappeared, Taylor swung the doors open wide and allowed Skuti in before he pulled the doors shut.

The two men greeted the other with a firm grip on their forearms.

"Aeehrl Skuti," said Taylor, "come in."

"Good morn," said Skuti, stepping across the threshold, hoping to get a glimpse of Calena.

Taylor wore chocolate-brown felt breeches that were tucked into brown leather boots, cuffed just below the knee. Underneath a double-breasted green vest was a white linen shirt with cuffed sleeves. A dark green silk sash wrapped around his waist covered by a brown leather belt with a large gold buckle, with daggers tucked into the sash just before the hips.

Taylor led Skuti over to his desk under the glass windows and extended an arm with an open palm toward the chair with facing him. "Please have a seat, my esteemed Aeehrl."

"Those clothes," said Skuti with a smile, "appear as if a great deal of coinage was used to purchase them."

"Only the lives of the men who were wearing them."

"Sounds harsh."

"Do you not take dead men's valuables on the battlefield?"

The room briefly fell silent as Skuti shook his head and chuckled.

"Very true, Commander."

Taylor snatched a dark bottle by its long neck and two glasses from a cabinet across his quarters and sat across from Skuti. He poured a small amount of the liquid into each glass.

"May the seas be calm," said Taylor, "and our aim be true."

"Alas," said Skuti, "here, here."

The men clanked their glasses together and threw back the sweet-tasting fermented liquid.

"Some call this the drink of—"

Three rapid and concise knocks on the door interrupted Skuti.

"Who is it?" said Taylor.

"It's Barre, Commander," said Delvin "Grisly" Barre, quartermaster of the *Vendetta tal-Mejtin*.

"Enter," said Taylor. "What news?"

Barre entered and nodded to the two men. Aged and leathered, the face told the tale of a man who only knew the seas.

"The Artist has her measure," he said. "He says we be ready."

Taylor's sly grin returned as it always did when they needed the Artist, Barlow Thorne, a man of inexplicable talent. There was no one better on the Four Great Seas when it came to reading nautical charts and navigational instruments.

"Did he actually say that?" responded Taylor.

"You know he rarely speaks," said Barre. "I knew what he meant by how he nodded his head."

"Very well. Set the course and get the men ready, quartermaster. I'll be up on the bridge momentarily."

"Aye, Commander. Should we expect fog, sir?"

"No, there shall be no fog today. We'll take her straight up."

Barre's leather boots clacked against the planked wood floor with brisk steps fading as he made his way down the hallway. The long ends of the knot tying the teal paisley scarf to his head trailed behind as he exited.

Skuti nodded his head and leaned forward in his chair. "My Commander of Ships heard tale of the evil mist."

Taylor shook his head in silence before speaking. "Lies dominate discussions on the matter."

"Men fear what they don't know."

"Men of the sea fear one thing. What lurks below the surface."

Taylor rose and walked the few steps to a long wood bookshelf lining the wall and reaching the ceiling with a seemingly endless supply of books and neatly rolled scrolls of maps. In the middle of the shelving was a deep green curtain made of velvet.

The commander opened the curtain and disappeared for

a moment before stepping back out with a coat, hat, and scarf, and a sword with gold hilt and polished bone pommel resting in a black sheath.

There it is. Darkheart, Oath of the Leviathan.

"Your deeds must be great," said Skuti, "to merit a black sword."

Taylor pulled the curtain closed and paused for a moment before stepping back to the table.

"Those shall remain private for now," said Taylor.

The six words from Taylor took Skuti aback for a moment.

What man doesn't boast of his deeds.

"Can you describe her appearance?"

"Who?"

"Grala."

"Grala who?"

Skuti glanced askew at Taylor. "Grala. Goddess of Weapons. Didn't she appear with your sword?"

"Enough of this goddess talk. We've got a big day ahead of us."

This conversation doesn't feel right to me. The vagueness of you and Calena creates more questions than answers.

Taylor smiled; this time a more authentic grin cracked his face. He stuck one arm through his dark gray wool coat, then the other, and shrugged so it hung correctly off his shoulders. The coat featured small black diamonds in an even pattern festooned with gold buttons shaped like skulls, bordered by black stitching.

"Today we battle," said Taylor, "and tonight we'll celebrate as if the morrow may never come."

Both went down a spiral staircase and entered a small room occupied by the sailing master and navigator of the *Vendetta*. Barlow sat on a rickety chair with his arms folded, with his navigational maps laid on an old wooden desk taken off some ship years ago. He had laid his inventory of maps, rolled up into scrolls, in pigeonholes carved into the wall behind him.

"Master Barlow," said Taylor, "I hear you plotted the ship's course."

Barlow nodded, never taking his eyes off the charts. He was a different animal for sure, strange to the rest of the crew, but he was the best navigator on the seas, maybe ever. Barlow walked a fine line between genius and insanity, but Taylor felt Barlow still had more genius than insanity.

"I take it we have the wind at our backs," said Taylor, "and the weather in our favor?"

Barlow raised his eyes and nodded, incredulous at the question.

"Well done, Master Barlow. May we expect you on deck to watch the festivities?"

One more nod.

"Very well, Master Barlow. Carry on."

This ship is full of untold stories.

The quartermaster assembled the men as commanded, and they were eager and ready to hear their commander's last words before engaging the enemy. Taylor and Skuti made their way up the stairs to the deck, where Barre was waiting for them. Skuti scanned the fighters' faces, pausing on as many as possible.

Skuti leaned over to Taylor. "I've never seen eyes so eager to fight as those of your Serpents right now."

"Blood's in the water," said Taylor, "and these men are as sharks starved."

Skuti remembered from his youth the familiar sights and sounds of wind whipping the sails, and seawater spraying into the air from the continual up and down pitch of the vessel. Taylor mounted the last step and made his way to the helm; Skuti followed and stood to the side of Taylor and surveyed the crew once more, searching for fear in any of the men. He saw none.

Anyone who thinks the stories of these men are exaggerated tales from the sea best beware. I see death in their brown eyes.

"Men, your killing day has arrived," said Taylor over the sound of the wind.

The sea churned and swelled, as if it knew death was sailing in its waves. Taylor motioned for quiet. Taylor's voice carried as if a strongman had grabbed it and thrown it over the men on deck.

"We have the wind and Vesceron's light in their eyes. Drummers, strike your drums and sing your songs."

The crew erupted in uproarious applause with loud shouts of invective directed at the Advocate. An effigy of the religious zealot, complete with black robe and outsized headpiece, swung from a noose hanging from the crow's nest.

I doubted all the stories surrounding you. In fact, I believed none of it, including your existence even, until you sailed into my harbor one night. Drums, strange singing voices, fog, Calena, and even dark-skinned warriors eating dead men's hearts ...

"What of stories of your men," said Skuti, "eating the hearts of the dead?"

"Aeehrl Skuti," said Taylor, "don't ask questions when you are in fear of the answer."

Add another one.

Taylor clasped his hands behind his back and nodded his head. The wind did its best to blow off the black broad-brimmed felt hat, which fit snug against the sea-green scarf covering his head. Exotic feathers adorning the hat threatened to do the same, but undeterred, it stayed on his head as if held there by magic.

Taylor pulled out the spyglass from his coat, extended the lens, and glimpsed the *Espléndido* at a distance of about three nautical miles. Their crew was scurrying around like ants to change course in a last-ditch effort to evade the *Vendetta*.

The *Espléndido* was a medium-sized cargo ship, powerful on its sides, built with strong timbers, much like all Acarian ships. But she was very weak on her stern, and that was what the *Vendetta* was after.

She was sailing the seas without challenge even if it was a poorly kept secret that she carried large amounts of gold, silver, coinage, and jewels. But the ship flew the colors of the Acarian Navy, and no one dared steal homage or anything else shipped to the Advocate. Such an act would be a declaration of war against the empire, and no one save the Brüeland Navy stood a chance against their ships.

The crew of the *Espléndido* was well-trained, but lost their edge over time, placing too much confidence in the flag it flew and not enough in their own readiness. Drills weren't as sharp. The drink flowed from dusk till dawn, and even its captain imbibed too often, bored by the same routes carrying cargo back and forth, desensitized to the large amounts of wealth in its hold.

Taylor's *Vendetta* tracked the *Espléndido* for several moons after being tipped off as to her port of departure and on which day she was setting sail. Not that it was any great mystery. The ship was smaller, lighter, and faster than Taylor's *Vendetta*, but the wind and weather conspired to take the advantage of speed away from the *Espléndido*.

Taylor offered Skuti the spyglass, and he zeroed in on the chaos amongst the crew members of the *Espléndido* attempting to ready a defense against the fast-closing *Vendetta*.

That ship reminds me of the type we made when Father yet lived. The vessel's workmanship is poor, though, unlike anything we built in Flace.

The wind and sea warred against her crew and prevented enough archers from manning the fore-and-aft castles to stave off their attackers. Those who did so picked up bows and arrows that hadn't been touched in months.

"The crew onboard are nothing more than condemned men," said Skuti, "waiting for their sentence to be carried out."

Kingdom Rules

"Indeed," said Taylor, taking back the spyglass.

Taylor sensed the time was right. The fact he knew when the time had come to press the attack would be another mystery for Skuti to solve later.

"Bosun," yelled Taylor, "show them the black."

Dyson "Coxswain" Crowley walked the short distance to where two men were aft and relayed the order to hoist the flag of Taylor's growing fleet. The flag's background was black with a sword and a three-pronged spear crossed in the middle. Above the point of sword and spear crossing was a white skull. The eyes and nose were black, but its demented smile had long, hanging white teeth. No sailor wanted to see that flag.

"Haul on the main brace," said Taylor. "Make ready the dragons and run out the sweeps."

As quick as the order came, the crew came to life in strict discipline, unlike the men aboard the enemy vessel. The Serpents pulled back on the ropes holding the main yard, tightening them so the sails would be ready and steady to catch the wind for the next maneuver.

Taylor motioned to Skuti, and the two descended a set of stairs to the main deck. Four large brass tubes, mounted on wheeled carts, sat back from four square holes cut into the hull of the bow.

"What is this?" said Skuti.

"This is what the Serpents call the Dragon's Lair," said Taylor.

Skuti, wide-eyed as a child, scanned the deck, but it was the four brass tubes which held his attention. Six-man teams worked each tube, preparing to "feed the dragon," a phrase Skuti heard from one of the Serpents working nearby.

One man from each team brought a large pewter cup containing a thick red liquid. There were several of the cups, all with equal amounts of liquid, stored in a room close to mid-deck. Another man stuffed rags and pieces of cloth into the tube and jammed them in with a long wooden tool.

"What is this red liquid?" said Skuti.

"This is Dragon's fire," Taylor said, "if you will."

Six-pound iron balls sat in brass racks next to each tube; one man in each group put a ball into the tube, and two more men moved the brass tubes forward into the square holes.

The blacksmith making the brass tube drilled a small hole through the wall of the tube near the closed end. Through the opening, the "fire starter," as he was called, used a slow match at the end of a long stick to wake the dragons from their maritime slumber.

"What are those iron balls for?" said Skuti.

"Destruction," said Taylor.

After the first shots of the iron balls, the oarsmen were ready to put out the oars for a speed boost to get past the *Espléndido* in preparation to make a slight turn to become perpendicular to her.

The *Vendetta* had closed to within a few hundred yards of the *Espléndido*, and she was perfectly in line for the brass tubes to let loose the six-pound iron balls loaded inside.

"Wait on my command," said Taylor.

Taylor eyed the sea and the pitch of the *Espléndido* and waited until the stern pitched downward and the *Vendetta's* bow pitched upward.

Skuti kept his eyes on the brass tubes with a sense of dread and wonder.

"Fire," yelled Taylor.

Fire and iron flew out of the mouth of the brass dragons with an awful sound, much like peals of thunder. Plumes of white smoke belched out of the tubes, turned orange by the fire preceding it. The sounds emanating from the Vendetta reached the ears of the crew on board the *Espléndido*, prompting them to turn and gaze at the approaching ship.

Three iron balls obliterated four of the five large windows at the backside of the stern, sending wood and glass flying into the sea. The fourth missed its mark, flew over the weather deck, and dropped into the waiting sea.

"What just happened in the name of the gods?" said Skuti.

Taylor offered no answer as he flew by Skuti and up the stairs to the top deck. He pulled out his spyglass and surveyed the damage. Skuti followed, shaking his head.

"Three hits and a miss," said Taylor under his breath. "Good enough—for now."

Skuti eyed the destruction of the iron balls on the *Espléndido*'s stern. He stood frozen, stunned by the sight of splintered wood and shattered glass floating on the sea.

What is this magic?

The crew on deck of the *Espléndido*, or worse, those in the path of one of the round projectiles, faced certain doom. The opposing captain, Grayson Ainsworth, descended from the helm and stared back at the enemy ship.

"What in the name ..."

By instinct alone, he pulled his spyglass from his coat pocket. The fast closing Vendetta was heading straight for the side of the *Espléndido*, and he realized he was too late to make a maneuver to save his ship. The Vendetta had the drop over the Espléndido, leaving no option but to prepare for impact.

Its designers integrated into the hull of the Vendetta iron plates, enabling it to ram and disable ships in the water. Taylor's ship was bearing down fast on the *Espléndido*.

"Brace yourselves!" shouted Taylor.

The *Vendetta* rammed her opponent near the stern on the port side and the crew of the wounded ship were unprepared for the blow delivered by Taylor's ship. The force of the blow knocked men standing and staring at hell unleashed down onto the deck. Those stationed on the platforms fell to the deck with a thud or into the sea with a quiet splash.

Serpents hidden under the rail of the *Vendetta* came up, looping ropes with hooks over to the stern of the *Espléndido* and pulled the damaged ship toward their own. When the two ships were broadside and secured, the crew slid boarding planks across to the *Espléndido*. The Serpents crossed over to the enemy ship like the unholy dead crawling out of the underworld.

Shouting words in their own dialect, the Serpents attacked their opponents with a ferocity unseen and unheard of in naval circles. Laughed off by pompous admirals in Acaria, the stories became a desperate and agonizing reality for the men aboard the *Espléndido*. Swords clashed, axes struck shields, and shouts of confused and desperate men punctuated the fighting. Soon, the groans and curses of the dying men replaced the sound of swords clashing in a one-sided fight.

The battle ended abruptly, leaving no time for anyone to catch their breath. Stepping over debris, limbs, and dead bodies, the Serpents completed their work, going from body to body to finish those who were still alive. The only person surviving the onslaught on the top deck was Captain Grayson, left alive by Taylor's orders. Two Serpents grabbed the older man, dumped him into an old chair, and bound him with rope.

The Serpents on board cleared the hold and the lower decks until they secured the ship, and everyone gathered on the top deck. Taylor, followed by Skuti, walked over to the *Espléndido* using the planks left by Taylor's men.

"We deal in the currency of fear," said Taylor over his shoulder. "It produces scared men who lack the will to fight."

"They would've been better off surrendering," said Skuti.

Grayson from his chair eyed the carnage—the blood, body parts, and dead men sliced up as if they were cattle being prepared for a meal. As he surveyed the slaughter, he met eyes with Calena standing on the railing of the *Vendetta*. She held the three-pronged spear firm in her hand, its handle resting on the rail and its three tips pointed to the clear blue sky.

Skuti kept his eyes trained on Calena and the spear in her hand.

Jomar's dreams ...

"It's her," said Grayson. "I've heard the stories of her control of the seas and the weather. She is pure evil."

Taylor walked over to Grayson, drew *Darkheart*, and placed it under Grayson's chin, nicking the soft flesh underneath. The blood rolled down his neck and over his Adam's apple and disappeared under his grimy shirt. The man and his captain's coat were both bloody and dirty.

"Is this how you do it?" said Grayson.

Taylor removed his black blade from under Grayson's chin and sheathed his sword.

Grayson, unable to finish, said, "You are nothing but—"

"You are charged with captaining a ship of the enemy," Taylor said.

Grayson shrugged his shoulders as best he could, given the ropes tied tight around his body and the chair.

"Is the vessel under your command?" said Taylor. "Flying the colors of Acaria."

Grayson looked up with a blank stare. All he could see was the wanton devouring of human life by the man in front of him. Tears poured out of his eyes as the beleaguered captain broke down and sobbed. Taylor turned to walk away, but stopped.

"Mercy does not sail onboard the *Vendetta*," he said.

Skuti stared for a moment at Taylor and turned his head, choosing to gaze out at the sea instead of watching the Grayson's humiliation.

What have I agreed to?

"In truth," said Taylor, "I am disappointed the Advocate's men are weak in heart and soul."

Calena leaped from the railing of the *Vendetta* onto the deck of the *Espléndido* with ease. The sound of her landing caused Skuti to turn his head around as if it were on a swivel.

Who is this woman?

Calena smiled and walked over to Grayson and stood before the weeping man. She wore the same suit made of smooth interlocking clam shells, brightly colored in the blues and greens of the sea. Leaning her spear forward, she placed one tip on his forehead.

"Captain Ainsworth Grayson," said Calena.

The heat from the tip of the spear seared his head, and he jerked it to the side to escape the pain.

"What is your response to the charges?" said Calena, turning an ear toward the beleaguered captain.

Grayson did not answer the question. Instead, something deep within him welled up and screamed from the depths of his soul. "All of you be damned!"

"You are guilty as charged and the deep shall take you," said Calena.

Calena banged the handle of her spear onto the deck one ... two ... three ... four times, pausing after each strike.

"Return to the ship, men," said Taylor. "Bring what was in the hold over to the *Vendetta*; leave the rest."

As fast as the Serpents landed aboard the *Espléndido*, their exit was just as rapid. Several Serpents carried the haul of treasure found in the hold over to the *Vendetta*, while others retrieved their weaponry out of lifeless bodies. The last of the Serpents kicked the planks into the sea and cut the ropes holding the two ships tethered together.

The *Espléndido*, driven by the sea's waves, gradually drifted away from the *Vendetta*. Grayson, the lone survivor, sat in the chair with his chin finding rest on his chest. Skuti wondered about the death of the man, destined to float on the sea, oft attacked by birds until dying from lack of water and exposure.

Why not run a sword through him?

Skuti, Taylor, and Calena gathered near the railing of the *Vendetta* as the *Espléndido* floated along. Something passed under the boat and caught Skuti's eye as it sped through the water.

"What is this dark spot passing through the sea?" said Skuti.

"Watch and learn," said Taylor, passing the spyglass to Skuti, who promptly pointed it toward the *Espléndido*.

"In the name of the gods," said Skuti, amazed and aghast. "It's real."

Into the air rose a giant tentacle one hundred times the size of any squid he'd ever seen. The brownish-red flesh with suction cups as large as any giant's face continued its way up into the sky as a ladder extends toward the heavens.

Skuti handed the spyglass back to Taylor and waited for the inevitable. The tentacle flew down from the sky as fast as a falcon chasing its prey and crashed onto the ship, splitting it in two. While it did so, a second tentacle snaked onto the deck, grabbed Grayson, and dragged him down into the deep, dark sea. More tentacles sprang out of the water and wrapped themselves around the battered ship and pulled it down to the depths.

Jomar's dream ...

Watching from the deck, Master Barlow applauded.

CHAPTER 16
CRIME AND PUNISHMENT

*O*ne Faith Hall was the largest Great Hall ever built on the continent and as ostentatious as anyone had ever dreamed, save the Advocate who designed it. The king's taxes, along with the homage due the Advocate from conquered kingdoms and the amount of treasure hauled back from each kingdom felled by the empire's military, meant coinage was never in question nor doubt.

Magnificent braziers encompassing each of the eight onyx columns lit up every part of One Faith Hall and mantled it in warm reds and yellows. Huge chandeliers hung from the embowed ceiling, dancing in the flickering light while stone sculptures of Wymir, the god of Life, and his wife, Vaona, the goddess of Birth, with their son Aerin, god of Beginnings, looked down on the obsidian floor of the radiant One Faith Hall.

A verdigris rug that was matched by thinner rugs on either side of the hall halved the cavernous room, while square dag banners with embellished symbols of the Faith, the Brotherhood, and the Sisterhood drooped from the walls. Between each banner sat a small altar full of candles, many of which had been lit, and they illuminated the statues of the legendary creatures that roamed the continent before the Number of Days began.

A lavish throne of gold sat in front of a large window that radiated the light of Vesceron onto the throne by day and the stars and moon by night. The throne was covered in hallowed sculptures of the six gods and goddesses worshipped by the members of the One Faith. Fixed on the wide backside were several rather large symbolic diamonds formed into a firebird (sometimes referred to as the phoenix), with the rays of Vesceron rising behind it.

As the hallowed sculptures did, so did the six stone steps leading up to the throne, representing the number of gods and goddesses within the One Faith. Positioned beside the throne were six knights, all of whom were members of the Sons of the Tower, the Advocate's personal guardians.

On days the Advocate sat on the throne and taught from the Oracles of the One, many people chosen to attend filled the gilded and extravagant oak benches, all facing the center of the Hall. Those of higher standing sat in the more luxurious balconies overlooking the Hall.

Sitting off to the right of the Hall was a large room, home to the Holy One's council. Two broad windows shared a view of the One Tower, the tallest keep on the continent by good measure. On this day, verdigris curtains, matching the banners in the Hall and embellished with golden symbols of the Faith and decorative tips, concealed the windows.

The Advocate sat at the head of the long rectangular oak table on a raised platform, in a high-back chair made of gold with silk verdigris cushions made in Ougrar, the renowned kingdom in the Eastern Desert famous for its ivory, marble, silks, and jewels.

King Jamettus sat at the far end of the table, facing the Advocate, and stroked his rust-colored beard. Council members sat beside and opposite each other on the long sides of the table. Sir Melcher Blackburn, the Lord General of the Army, sat at one end of the table to Jamettus's right.

Melcher was a survivor of the first wars when the Acarian army first began its conquest to make the Western Continent one under the Advocate's thumb. Through the deaths of some commanders, his own success on the field of battle, and assisted by his ability to play the political game, he soon found himself at the top of the army's food chain.

White, flowing hair pulled neatly into a ponytail showed his advancing years, as did a long, lived-in face. An enemy dagger left a scar stretching from just under his right eye to the bridge of the nose, leaving a visible reminder of his good fortune in not losing one of his distinct amber eyes.

Seated to his right was Lord Sanders Lynch, Master of Wealth, who, moments ago, presented the council with the financial standing of the empire. Sanders spoke with arrogance, taking credit for a wealth that he believed was solely his responsibility. Acaria's treasury surpassed the combined wealth of all remaining unconquered countries and kingdoms. Every man in the room knew Melcher's conquering army filled the vaults with treasure. The only entity with more assets within its walls was the Bank of the Citadel, and it was close.

Whispers were increasing in volume about Sanders's own wealth. The once-thin man's stomach was larger and rounder now, and his clothes were made of imported fabrics of the utmost quality. The trips to an upscale, secretive house of pleasures turned out to be less than secretive. Of all people, Sanders knew the Advocate had eyes and ears throughout the city and about everywhere else he wanted to. The wisdom of the Oracles proved true once again by saying a man's sins chase him until he falls exhausted into a den of vipers.

On the other side of the table sat Sir Alleyn Hewelet, Admiral of the Seas. His brows were furrowed even before entering the council room. Thinning, long black hair hung down to his shoulders, framing a leathered, hardened, and beardless face. Bright Azul eyes turned women's heads everywhere he traveled, and, like many seafaring men, he had no wife, but a woman in every port.

When it was his turn to speak, Alleyn wasted no time. He spoke the truth even when it was difficult to do so, as it was today. Alleyn said, "Your Holiness, we have lost the Espléndido."

Although he used the word as a question, he kept the same stern face, neither surprised nor angry at losing enough gold, silver, coinage, and jewels to fund a small kingdom for a year. "Lost?"

"Yes, Your Holiness," said Alleyn. "I know Captain Grayson, and he's not the type to sail away with a fortune in the hold. Too risky for a man nearing the end of his career."

"Mutiny?" said Melcher.

"Always possible," said Alleyn, "but I just don't see it. The men are paid a good wage, and they know stealing from His Holiness will end in an excruciating death."

"That leaves the weather or an attack," said Jamettus.

"Weather is mild this time of year," said Alleyn, "and that shipping lane is close to the shore."

"Then she was preyed upon," said Melcher.

"There has been talk of a pirate," said Alleyn, "and with him is a witch—maybe one of the mermaids or sirens of old—but they say she practices the dark arts."

"You of all people put stock in that notion?" said Melcher.

"It gets worse," said Alleyn. "The crew is made of dark-skinned barbarians who eat the hearts of their slain enemies. But it is the iron balls erupting from this pirate's ship and destroying everything in their path that scares those on the waters."

"In the name of the gods, Sir Alleyn," said Jamettus, "do you believe this stuff?"

I knew you'd be back someday to settle scores, Rand Driscoll. I didn't expect you to sell your soul to that whore of the seas. Your father would be so disappointed.

With the personality of a stone monument, the Advocate spoke in his stern voice as if he were a teacher and the council were his students. In fact, it was the way he thought, always above all, and the great teacher of the masses in the Acarian Empire and beyond its ever-expanding borders. "Sir Alleyn is correct. Never doubt, nor underestimate the dark powers, which are always at war against the light of the One Faith."

If the Advocate was without his religious finery, his narrow face, sunken cheeks, and perpetual five-o'clock shadow, he might well fit in with the Acarian poor. His gray hair was cut short, as were his arching eyebrows; his nose was thin, but the nostrils flared, giving his face an unusual appearance best matching the Af'lam people he so despised. One of his brown eyes had a smaller pupil than the other but was almost impossible to detect, not that anyone could get close enough to see for certain.

The room fell into a hush brought on by the Advocate's decisive acceptance of the pirate lore as authentic. The so-called experts of the seas and the ships floating on them dismissed the absurd tales until it was too late. With drums beating and unfamiliar singing, the black ship arrived shrouded in mist.

The Advocate stared at Sir Alleyn and delivered what would be life-altering words. "I don't care how long it takes, how many men die, or how many ships are lost. Locate this pirate's ship and send it to the bottom of the sea. Don't return here until it's done. If you cannot stop this man, he will rule the seas and render your navy useless. You are no longer needed here."

Every man in the room swallowed hard and watched Sir Alleyn rise, as if being sent to the gallows. He bowed his head and acknowledged no one as he left the room and began his trek to the harbor.

"Sir Melcher," said the impersonal voice, "what of the unification you're going to prevent?"

"There are only two roads leading into Wolfden, unless, of course, one will travel through Trynt's Forest. I have commanded Sir Balan to head up these units posted on each road, far enough from King Andairn's scouts so as not to be noticed."

"Put another on the road leading into the despicable wolf god's forest. It's difficult to say for certain what the Andairns have worked out with the yelloweyed monsters."

"It will be as you say, Your Holiness."

The Advocate's vast knowledge and his ability to memorize the smallest of details, combined with a nimble mind, made him a worthy adversary for anyone who wanted to test his ability to galvanize his people. His years of bending Acaria into his vision of religious piety by any means possible gave him the ability to use an iron fist to keep his followers in line. Over the course of his time as Advocate, the need for ironfisted rule decreased and instead, much like obedient sheep, they followed their master wherever he went.

Perhaps the virgin princess from Brüeland is the one to bear me a son as prophesied in the Oracles. Vaona has not approved of the virgins brought to me so far. I'm running out of patience and time.

"I want Princess Ingrid brought to me unharmed," he said. "If your men harm Princess Ingrid, you will bear the burden of their mistakes."

Stroking his beard again, Jamettus nodded his head and spoke for Melcher. "I will bring the princess to you untouched, Your Holiness."

The king's attire was stripped down; only his royal blue tunic over a darker blue undergarment with long sleeves, with a royal blue cape over top and a brown leather belt wrapped around his waist. The Hall and council room did not allow any weapons inside since the king of Acaria and his brother assassinated the Advocate of a century ago.

Jamettus was stocky and his strength was in the chest and shoulders. He didn't wield the fastest sword, but he was exceedingly effective with his war hammer, bludgeoning enemies with blows to the helmet, piercing armor with the pick opposite the hammer, and using a leaf-shaped spike at the top to thrust at the opponent. Close-in fighting was where his body type and strength were decidedly in his favor. Foes found it nearly impossible to move Jamettus around.

"Take your leave, King Jamettus and Sir Melcher," said the Advocate. "I need to talk with Lord Sanders."

Jamettus and Melcher stood and bowed to the Advocate before departing. "As you wish, Your Holiness."

Although I don't need a new king or general, I need a new Master of Wealth.

Six of the Advocate's bodyguards, out of twenty-four, waited for the two men. The Sons of the Tower earned their reputation as the best of the best in all the land. They wore black cloaks with the customary insignia of the red firebird outlined in white and the rising sun and its rays behind it. Complex suits of flat black scales protected their chests, and blacksmiths adorned their armor with fastenings and other hardware made of pure gold. The shields they carried were also black and emblazoned with the red firebird and golden rays rising.

"Walk with me, Lord Sanders," said the Advocate. "I want to tell you a story."

A pleasant smile crossed Sanders's face as he walked, chest puffed out. "Yes, of course, Most Holy One."

I will soon turn your pride to humility and suffering.

The two walked for several minutes before the Advocate spoke in his dull, monotone voice. The High Holy One permitted himself no emotions. Ever.

"There was a man who enjoyed wealth and power," said the Advocate.

Sanders stared at His Holiness with a wide smile as they

strolled out of the Hall through an unfamiliar door. Sanders was too busy strutting and gawking at the Advocate, as if he were an awestruck child to notice the different exit. The Advocate stared straight ahead, never once looking over to Sanders.

"In fact," said His Holiness, "he sat on the king's council in a position that required his utmost honesty."

Sanders continued to place his gaze on the Advocate, rapt in the attention from His Holiness and the story being told. "Everyone held him in high regard."

"Yes, this is true. The king and the other council members trusted him."

If it were possible, Sanders puffed his chest further out, and his smile was broad across his face. The Advocate kept his steady gait, hands behind his back, and did not break a sweat even with his layers of clothing and the warmth of Vesceron upon him.

Your pride increases, yet the time you have left decreases.

"This same man hosted a grand feast for all of his wealthy friends. He had large flocks and herds, high-yielding crops, and sun-drenched orchards. Yet days before the feast, he had his men raid the herds and flocks of his poorer neighbors, who had little compared to the rich man."

"He," said Sanders with a smile, "shouldn't have taken from his neighbors. His own bounty was plentiful."

"In fact," said the Advocate, "he decimated their livestock, crops, and orchards; when the Freezing Months set in, they didn't have enough food to survive, and these neighbors died of starvation."

Sanders' gradual change in countenance revealed itself in the dissipation of his smug smile and the widening of his eyes. One guard opened a door to a set of stone stairs leading to a hallway lit by candles and a few dying torches. Stopping, the Advocate locked eyes with Sanders and insisted on an answer. "What should happen to the rich man?"

Sanders paused for a moment before he answered in a faltering voice. "He and his family should be killed for such a horrible deed."

"You have named your sentence, for you are that man."

The words' weight needed a moment to sink. "I?" said Sanders. "How can it be, Your Holiness?"

The Advocate's words were perfunctory and factual. "You had everything you needed. I richly rewarded you for your stewardship of my wealth, yet you found it necessary to steal from my flock."

It was clear in Sanders's hazel eyes that his heart had sunk to the deepest depths of the sea, never to rise again. Trembling with guilt, he mustered the courage to ask, desperately hoping for a different accusation to defend against. "How did I steal from your flock?"

You're a lying coward, and soon to suffer for it.

"It's pointless for you to ask me a question that you already know the answer to. You tell me what you are guilty of."

Sanders's mouth had become as dry as the desert soil, and so he swallowed to generate saliva, licked his lips as best he could, and spoke just loud enough for the Advocate to hear. "I taxed the flock beyond the designated rate. The additional coinage I wasted by spending lavishly on myself. You're right in condemning me for stealing from your flock and Your Holiness."

"You say lavish, but there is one thing you used your ill-gotten gains for, which is forbidden in the *Chronicles of Ethics and Morality*."

"I paid for whores who were races unlike our own."

The Advocate raised an eyebrow in silence.

"Whores from the deserts with brown skin, of the islands with black skin, and even the dirty race of green whores with tusks and pointed ears."

There is a last deed with an animal which is beyond forgiveness and death.

"You left one out."

"No more, please, your High Holiness. I am ashamed of my actions and betrayal of the One Faith."

"If you're ashamed now, why did you do it?"

"I fell in a moment of weakness."

You disgust me. It will be my pleasure to condemn you to the Double Suffering written in Laws and Judgment.

"Several moments."

"Holy One, please spare the recounting of this ugly sin."

"Waste no more of my time with your begging; begin."

The tears rolled down Sanders's red cheeks as a child's does when caught red-handed. "I was bedding a *duhbrarei* whore, part-Yelloweye, part-human, who would change into a were …"

Sanders fell to his knees and wept and begged for mercy. He reached for the bottom of the Advocate's robe and kissed it to prove his outward contriteness. In response, two guards grabbed Sanders and flung him into the air, sending him sailing for several feet before he slammed into the stone floor and bounced to a stop near the door.

Sanders could not get his fat hands out in time and the stones opened a large gash on his chin, scraped the side of his face, and opened minor cuts on his forehead. Bruised and beaten by the stones, he whimpered, "Please no, no more, in the name of our Holy One."

The guards remained silent as always. They only spoke when directed by the Advocate, and even then, only rarely.

"Do not injure him any further," said the Advocate. "He has a baptism of suffering to endure."

Two guards picked him up, carried him to the entrance, and lowered him down to the guards waiting below. Once at the bottom and on his knees, a guard slapped an iron collar around his thick neck, giving Sanders little room to breathe.

"I can't breathe," said Sanders, trying to gulp down oxygen in the air-deprived hallway.

Another guard forcefully jerked Sanders upright by using the chain that was welded to the collar. That same guard pulled back on his hair, so Sanders's face was looking upward. The Advocate stood outside the door and pronounced judgment.

"The Captain of Punishment," said the Advocate, "has the order to carry out your sentence as it is written in the *Book of Correction and Punishment*. Yet, he has freedom to act as he deems just for your offenses against the One Faith."

Sanders took a last horrified look at the Advocate, stoic and stone-faced, before the guards pulled the chain and dropped Sanders to the floor. The sound of the door banging closed represented the start of the long end Sanders faced.

The guards cut off his tunic and undergarment and stuffed a gag into his mouth, dragging him naked and bleeding down the rest of the short hallway until Sanders was face to face with a small wooden door stained with the blood of those too fat to pass cleanly.

It forced all who passed through the door to crawl like a dog through it, subjugated into a place of brutality so horrible those forced to watch often had to close their eyes at the sight of human degradation. Yet there were those who cheered the humiliating torture and death of high-ranking officials who ran afoul of the Oracle's laws.

The guards used their boots and shoulders to push and shove Sanders through the door, causing his skin to tear off as he moved. As soon as Sanders flopped onto the dusty dirt floor of the small amphitheater, he heard the screams of his wife before a loud cheer erupted from the crowd. Soon after, the gathered viewers erupted in shouts, demanding no mercy for Sanders, and as if on cue, his screams pierced through the clamor of those in attendance.

CHAPTER 17
DANGEROUS WOMEN

*I*ngrid stormed into the Dernesch apartment as a fast-moving storm blows through a town unexpectedly. She burst through the unlocked door to the apartment and found Evelyn on her veranda sipping a goblet of wine. She was facing outward, watching the repetitive crashing of the waves against the shoreline, when she heard the click-clack of boots across the stone floor. Startled, she instinctively stood and spilled several drops of wine down the front of her fashionable green dress.

"Damn it," said Evelyn, "look at my—Ingrid?"

"The dress," said Ingrid, "is your last worry."

The short sword on Ingrid's hip caught Evelyn's eye, and she viewed it with suspicion. "You're carrying a sword now. Are you afraid of someone?"

"Are you afraid of me?" said Ingrid.

Ingrid tapped on the pommel of her sword, waiting for Evelyn's sarcastic laughter to end. The weapon had a bronze casting, with ten scallops around its perimeter and colored in burgundy enamel. A stallion stood in the middle, looking back at its holder. The sword itself was a work of art and made by the finest bladesmith in Crence from a drawing of Cecile's.

Remember what Renoldus told you. If you draw the sword, you intend to use it. Don't deploy it as a threat.

Evelyn blunted the over-the-top laughter, and a frown crept down her face. "That's Cecile's sword you're carrying. I recognize the lobes. Did Renoldus give you her sword?"

Looking past Evelyn and out at the beauty of the sea, Ingrid caught a whiff of the briny smell of the ocean air, reminding her of the nights spent with Renoldus in his apartment. The rhythms of their bodies mixed with the smell of the sea caused Ingrid to feel the same warm feelings that was the prelude—

"Are you going to say something," said Evelyn, "or are you going to stand there with that silly smile on your face?"

Ingrid didn't act like a haughty princess, but she could play the part when required to assert her authority. "Renoldus has found a love greater than his first wife."

The change in Ingrid's speaking pattern caused Evelyn to pull her eyebrows down and shoot an askew glance at her. "If he truly loved you, he'd have a sword made especially for you. You took this one from his collection and didn't give it back. I know how Sir Renoldus is about his swords."

Ingrid shook her auburn curls, threw her head back, and continued in her role, attempting to unnerve Evelyn much as she had with Renoldus. "He had one made for me, but I prefer this one. Besides, what do you know of Cecile? The two of you weren't friends. She always eyed you with suspicion and told Renoldus to stay away from you. She didn't fear an affair, but she feared you or your maniacal husband harming him in some significant way. Ultimately you did, by taking her life."

The accusation hit a nerve within Evelyn, as evidenced by the narrowing of her gray eyes. The few friends Evelyn had in the castle suspected her husband was involved in the slaying of Cecile and didn't believe the death was an accident despite the declaration of Lord Searl Brewburn it was so.

"I would report your unlawful entry to my apartment," said Evelyn, "but you're leaving in a few days, never to be seen again."

"The kingdom will see me again," said Ingrid. "In triumph when I return home and take the throne."

"You're delusional."

Evelyn bumped shoulders with Ingrid as she left the veranda and made her way to the sitting room, where she stood with hands on hips and waited for Ingrid to follow. The princess paused for a moment and corralled her emotions before leaving the veranda.

"We're done here, princess," said Evelyn. "Leave and don't trouble me again."

Whatever Evelyn saw in the eyes of Ingrid caused her to glance away, and her words were less than forceful. "I asked you to leave."

"Do you see me moving?" said Ingrid.

Evelyn lost control and screamed at the top of her lungs. "Get out, damn you!"

Vesceron broke free of the morning marine layer and glowed in the sky, and its rays soaked the sitting room through the opened double doors to the veranda. The sudden burst of light caused Evelyn to squint and bring her hand up as a shield against the light.

Seizing the initiative in an altercation, as Renoldus called it, Ingrid stepped forward and punched Evelyn in the face, striking her in the jaw. The blow snapped Evelyn's head back and sent her staggering backward, but the strike was not substantial enough to knock her to the ground.

With wild eyes opened as wide as possible and focused on Ingrid's hands, Evelyn dabbed at the blood trickling from the corner of her mouth with her fingers. Instinctively, she rubbed them together as if she needed to confirm it was blood.

"You're terrified right now," said Ingrid.

Furniture sat in the sitting room, with Evelyn's chamber

entrance on the opposite side, hidden by a linen curtain. Ingrid familiarized herself with the settings and headed toward the front door she'd left open.

"What in the name of the gods is wrong with you?" said Evelyn after her. "Women don't hit one another."

After popping her head outside, Ingrid closed the door and glared at Evelyn as she walked. Evelyn's wide, dilated pupils darted around the room, and her agitation was obvious to the princess. Ingrid acted as if nothing happened while addressing Evelyn. "There are things we need to discuss."

"You're a barbaric whore," said Evelyn.

Ingrid continued to speak in a calm and reasoned voice. "Name-calling will not help you."

"Just get out."

"Not until we're finished."

Evelyn's mouth was dry, and she slumped her body while backing up toward the table and chairs. Ingrid slid toward the veranda doors and closed them with a shove, and a loud clash followed, leaving the doors shaking in their stops.

"Did you poison Watkin?" said Ingrid.

"Of course I poisoned him," said Evelyn. "Even he knew it."

Ingrid raised her voice and stared at Evelyn. "You're a liar and you've always been one. I poisoned Watkin in revenge for House Dernesch's role in killing my grandfather and Renoldus's father."

Evelyn fidgeted with her necklaces and looked away. "That's preposterous. I was the only one close enough to him to carry it out. Honestly, the notion House Dernesch authored some plan to get Leander on the throne is pure fantasy."

Ingrid cocked an eye at Evelyn and crossed her arms under her breasts. "Ameave is a poison made from the rare deadnettle. There is a disgraced healer living in the city who makes ameave. The bane works best in wine, something Watkin has—or once had—a passion for."

"What does this have to do with anything?" said Evelyn.

"Did Watkin have red marks on his left arm?" said Ingrid.

"Yes, but what does that prove?"

"It proves ameave poisoned him, something you know nothing about."

"You killed my husband, the King's Advisor? That's nonsense."

"I can kill whoever I want, including you, if I feel inclined to do so."

"You're mad. I knew you were unstable, but your erratic behavior suggests some time in the Raven's Nest might do you well."

Red curls fell down into Ingrid's face, which she swept back behind her ears, and she smirked at Evelyn. Lady Dernesch trembled noticeably, and the flush of stress and chaos from the last several minutes rose to her cheeks.

"My father always had an odd obsession with you, something I couldn't figure out. I read everything related to the Blackwood family history, including the writings about his brothers, Ancelin and Henriot."

Evelyn rolled her eyes and walked a few feet away before turning around to face Ingrid. Her breathing was quick and heavy, but she spoke in a voice higher than normal. "If you're going to suggest I or Leander had something to do with their accidental deaths, then you're truly deranged."

The princess ignored Evelyn's remarks and moved a step forward, then stood straight, head held high. "You were friends with Henriot first," said the princess, "but you piqued my father's interest somehow. One day the two of you told Henriot you'd dropped something into the old well where the gardens used to be. When Henriot craned his neck to look, the two of you grabbed him and sent poor Henriot to his death at the bottom of the pit."

"You have crossed a line," said Evelyn, "in accusing me of helping the king to murder his brother. How dare you?"

Ingrid offered no response and instead continued on with Ancelin's story.

"Ancelin grew wary of the two of you, figuring he might be next. The two of you needed to add a friend, someone trustworthy, to put Ancelin at ease. Terrin was the obvious choice, and when Leander promised him a position of authority, someday you had your third partner. The three of you decided the Gilpar River was a perfect spot for another 'accident.'"

"If I had to guess, you stripped down and encouraged Ancelin to jump in. You kept Ancelin occupied while Leander and Terrin snuck in from behind and sent him down the river and into the rapids, and the rocks did the rest. People claimed they couldn't recognize Ancelin when they discovered his body. The episode adds new meaning to Sir Terrin's christened name, the Trusted."

Ingrid pulled her hair over to one side, adjusted her leather corset, and waited for Evelyn to respond. The only sound was the consistent rattle of the double doors against their stops when the breeze kicked up.

"You violent and lying cunt," she said. "I hope the Wolf Prince is a devil and shreds your body with his claws and teeth."

"I may be violent, and Prince Rycardus may be a devil, but a liar I'm not."

"Then maybe you're a writer of fantasy stories."

"Are you telling me my late Grandmother Alexia's diary is pure fantasy?"

"Alexia had gone mad by the end, and you know that to be true."

"They sent Grandmother to the Raven's Nest because she allowed her son's crimes to go unpunished and it haunted her. Leander feared she was going to tell someone, hoping to get it off her chest. Those cruel and despicable people in the Nest destroyed the rest of her mind."

Evelyn bowed her head and shook it back and forth while she laughed at Ingrid sardonically. "You've gone mad just like Alexia. Now get out."

"I'll leave, not because you told me to, but because I'm done with you."

Ingrid turned to go and as she approached the door, Evelyn's voice called for her to stop. When she turned, Evelyn was approaching with a wide smile, as if she just remembered a joke.

"I hear Sir Renoldus has a paramour," said Evelyn.

"What?" said Ingrid.

"They meet in the King's Forest."

Nice try. Do you think I'm this stupid?

"That's pathetic," said Ingrid. "I'm supposed to fall for this absurdity? I have him watched when he's not with me."

"Perhaps your watchers are drinking ale instead," said Evelyn.

Surely not. They receive handsome pay, and if I discover any negligence in their duties, I will have them killed.

"What are you getting at, damn you?" said Ingrid.

"It's obvious he's meeting someone," said Evelyn, "and I'm concerned it might be dangerous for Sir Renoldus, given his drinking habits."

The red hair atop Ingrid's head might as well have been a fire as she nearly erupted at Evelyn for the swipe at Renoldus. Her words sounded as if a snake spoke them, particularly the name of her love. "Watch what you say about Renoldus."

"It's not in dispute," said Evelyn. "He enjoys the company of a woman and wine to go with her."

He's no longer a drunken stalðun. I've tamed him.

"End this evil charade and tell me just who it is you think he's bedding."

"The dirty green *kirattu* princess. I'm sure you know about the history between our kingdom and the Af'lam tribe in the Groves."

Ingrid laughed but did so in such an exaggerated manner, one might think she was an actress in the king's court. Evelyn put her hands behind her back and waited for Ingrid to finish.

"If you're finished with this fairy tale," said Ingrid, "I'll be leaving. Renoldus will find this story quite amusing."

"He won't when he's given you the *birmems dekaaka*. You should see the healer."

The expression on Ingrid's face landed somewhere between disgust and fear. Evelyn smiled and turned, leaving the princess standing in the doorway with a twisted look on her face. Feeling stupid with nothing to say, she spun and began the walk to Renoldus's apartment. Every rub of her leather pants against her sensitive area as she stepped convinced her she had contracted *birmems dekaaka*.

Surely he ... there's not a chance he dipped his yard into a green-skinned whore. That's disgusting, and he's the Black of Brüeland, not a stalŏun. Evelyn fabricated that story solely to provoke me. Still, I'll be inspecting his cock when I get there.

CHAPTER 18
TRADING PLACES

No animal in an Aeehrldom matched the horse's importance, and Seaborne Keep's stables never compromised on the quality of its horses. Skuti was absolute and spared no expense in doing whatever was necessary to pursue excellence in the care of his own.

Alrik Orri was Marshall, the best in all of Flace, trained by his father, Isulf, a legend within the Six Aeehrldoms. Alrik was in charge of all matters relating to horses, including the specific care of the Aeehrl's and lady's horses.

"We need more horses," said Skuti. "It's going to be a war of attrition, especially if we have to lay siege to more than one castle."

"Yes, my Aeehrl," said Alrik, "there are horses on the way from the Af'lam tribe to the east."

"Was King Brovas at his insulting best?"

Alrik chuckled and rolled his eyes. "Of course. He'll do anything to prove his standing amongst us."

"I've heard tell he would sell his balls if he could marry his daughter off to even a small house."

"She is exotic with a very firm body, if you find their type enticing."

It was Skuti's turn to have a laugh. "I'll stick to blonde hair and blue eyes."

Unless Calena was about to ask me into her bed.

"Speaking of those traits," said Alrik, "Lady Thorve is walking over."

Skuti's body tensed as he turned to face his wife. Alrik sensed there was unpleasantness between the two and wondered what caused the tension. He hoped it was only a pothole in the road given the buildup in the looming civil war.

"Lord Alrik," said Thorve, "ready my traveling horse."

"Of course, my lady," said Alrik. "I will have one of the grooms bring it straight away."

The light mood of his chat with Alrik dissipated the moment Thorve walked up. Skuti had been waiting for this moment and feared his marriage was on the verge of breaking apart emotionally. There would never be a divorce, as was the custom amongst Aeehrls and Ladies, but with the popularity and mystique of the twin sisters, Skuti risked running afoul of his people if he publicly despised Thorve.

"I have to go," said Thorve, "my sister needs me."

"What did I say?" said Skuti.

"What you always do. Thora's a liar and a manipulator."

"I don't think Jomar is dead. It's only a smokescreen to lull me to into a false confidence."

Can't you see the deception?

"It's always about you."

Thorve wore her riding clothes: a sleeveless, blue-patterned skirt stopping at the thighs over a tight undergarment of a thin black material extending into her knee-high brown leather boots. She wore her long vest unbuttoned but kept it in place with a wide cloth belt. Colorful arm warmers completed her outfit.

"This is not the time to go to Thora," said Skuti. "I just returned after a fortnight at sea and war is looming. The people look to you for strength."

"I'm not the one who set off on a pirate adventure," said Thorve, "and left me here alone to answer the questions."

"I told you about our meeting. Taylor may be our salvation."

"The people will never accept the dark-skinned men on our soil."

"They will if they don't want to bend the knee to Jomar and his knaves."

"Others might prefer that—I would do it."

"Until you and the others are worshipping the Advocate."

Thorve's cheeks were flushed, and her blue eyes narrowed. She was livid once again, and her anger flowed without hindrance from a heart soaked by bitterness. The departure of Jomar and Thora brought an insidious darkness to their marriage. Skuti's trip aboard the *Vendetta* hardened his perspective on life with the realization the alliance with Taylor was more vindictive and violent than he expected. Calena's leviathan was the berry atop the pastry of dread.

"You've changed, Skuti Ingimund," said Thorve, "since the little foreign cunt seduced you after I told you not to go out there."

You haven't been the same since you fell into the trap of your sister's lies. The ancient magic Thora wields threatens the safety of everyone. Including you.

"Lies," said Skuti, "which you've believed over your husband's word."

"The word of a passed-out drunk?" said Thorve.

"Watch yourself. I am still your husband—and Aeehrl."

"You resort to threats to silence me?"

Skuti tried a different angle but expected the same result. "Jomar wants to cause me pain, and he does that by holding you for ransom or killing you. He wants to kill Thora; what makes you any different?"

"I'll take the risk," said Thorve.

"If it happens, don't expect to be ransomed until the war is over."

"All you're concerned about is the Ice Throne you want so much."

"We agreed war was our only option to remain free and unite Flace."

Thorve stomped away toward the groom who held her horse, and Skuti followed in pursuit. She took her horse from the groom and dismissed him, and he disappeared when he saw the look on Skuti's face.

She cursed at the gods for allowing events to occur, which put Flace on the verge of civil war. Worse, Skuti and Jomar were on opposing sides, meaning the losing sister was bound to become a widow, and maybe dead as well.

"You've changed ever since you met Taylor," said Thorve. "Angry, moody, and brooding."

"Jomar and Thora have made me what I am," said Skuti. "I will have my vengeance for their wrongs and uniting Flace against me."

"Even you admit to your temperament."

I'm done arguing with you. Go run off to help your lying sister and leave me here alone to stand against my enemies. Whatever happens in battle happens. If I kill Jomar and Thora, so be it; the gods and goddesses have ordained who shall live and die.

"Go," said Skuti, "don't come back."

"Skuti Ingimund," said Thorve. "You're a bastard."

Thorve swung her leg over her horse and rode out toward her guards and maiden waiting for her. In an instant, the four departed towards Iziadrock. Skuti stood alone with his thoughts, which he soon directed towards Thora.

I will kill you and I will not stop until I do. You are a poison, killing off everything you come in contact with. I admired Jomar at one time and look at what you've done to him. You've finally corrupted Thorve with your evil potion. May the gods bring you to me so I can end your evil existence.

"Lady Thora," said Sir Beiner, "your sister is at the gates."

"How many guards are with her?" said Thora.

"Only two and her maiden, Lady Thora."

"Very well. You know what to do."

"Yes, Lady Thora."

Beiner pivoted and hurried out through the door to the solar and down to meet Thorve and her guards. Thora examined the room once more, stopping at a table in the center to read the letter she had penned earlier. Finished, she put the letter back on the table meticulously and picked up the quill pen and the small inkpot with a smile bigger than a child's when receiving a gift.

Oh, my sister, the time is nigh.

Thora dropped the inkpot and pen to the floor, breaking the pot and spilling the iron gall mixture all over the floor. As she examined the mess, Thorve's and Beiner's voices were getting louder as they moved closer to the solar. Thora walked across the hallway and climbed the ladder to where one of the last rungs leaned against the timber beam stretching across the room and listened and waited.

"Lady Thorve," said Beiner, "I will leave you with your sister Lady Thora. By the way, how are you feeling?"

"I'm much better," said Thorve. "I don't know why I became ill. Perhaps my humors caused the sickness."

"Very well, Lady Thorve," Beiner said. "Always a pleasure to see you."

Thora listened for the sound of Thorve's boots on the stone floor down the hall. Abruptly, the noise stopped. Thora maneuvered herself on the ladder as she had practiced, pulled the noose over her head, and let it rest on her chest. She waited once more while Thorve read her letter across the way.

My dearest and beloved Thorve,

I murdered Jomar using the magic of Badek. After he was dead, I realized what a great sin I had committed. Never should I have agreed with Evanora to kill Jomar. What kind of woman trades years off her life to murder her husband?

You will find me in my chamber. I could not bear a public death, so I've decided to hang myself for the crime. Although I will miss you horribly, I must pay for what I did.

I will take your greetings to Mother and Father.

Your sorrowful sister,

Thora

When the sound of Thorve's boots began again, Thora tightened the noose and knocked the ladder to the ground with a loud crash. Thorve entered, screaming as never before.

"Thora," said Thorve, "please no, don't do this. Let me cut you down so we can talk."

"Don't touch me," screeched Thora. "I deserve to die."

"Please. I'm begging you not to."

Thorve picked up and replaced the ladder. She climbed up with heavy legs but stopped, exhausted, before reaching Thora. With an odd, almost painful look on her face, and with Thora staring down at her sister while struggling to breathe, time seemed to stop for a moment. A hard, icy wind blew through the room and knocked Thorve from the ladder to the ground with a thud.

But instead of lying on the ground, Thorve's neck was in the noose, and it was her body swinging from the beam as Thora lay on the ground coughing. She looked up at her sister with a wry smile even though her neck was burning from the rope's reeds and fibers.

Thorve grasped for the rope above the noose, attempting to pull herself up to the beam and salvation.

"What have you done?" said Thorve, struggling to speak. "Get me down!"

"I'm afraid I can't," coughed Thora. "I've already paid the devil."

"You're using the Badek to kill me instead of Jomar?"

"Skuti will kill Jomar in battle for me."

"How could you?"

"Father should've given you to Jomar; you were the first out of the womb."

The Reaper of Souls, dressed in a dirtied and tattered black cloak, had entered the room unseen by the two women. Within his skull, deep-set black orbs floated in their sockets and stared at Thorve. In one hand was an old, rusted sickle on a crooked piece of wood and in the other, an open book bearing names, weathered by time immortal. The hourglass around his waist was almost empty.

"This is about Skuti." said Thorve, forcing out the words one at a time.

"He will be the one to sit on the Ice Throne, and I his queen," said Thora, with a wide smile. "I've seen it."

"He will know the difference."

"I killed the guard, not Astrid. I went to Skuti that night on the knoll and seduced your husband. He knew no difference."

The last words Thorve heard crushed whatever was left of her heart and soul. *Skuti was right*, would be the final thought of her life. Thorve's face appeared purple, and her tongue protruded from her mouth. Her blue eyes bulged as her life ebbed away.

Everything turned black for Thorve, and the Reaper made a move towards the soul of the older twin, daughter of Aeehrl Eldgrim Hastein and Lady Dotta Sigfus. But as strong as she was in life, Thorve's inner strength did not release it. It was a troubled and angry soul, and she stared down at the Reaper, took the book from his hand, crossed out her name, and took a new one. She would be Anshee in the afterlife. *Saeothephol Fleshae*, as the people of Flace named it, would have to wait.

The Reaper fled and left Anshee's bitter soul to remain in the air, able to move about in arid places. She would make her presence known and felt throughout Flace from the other side of the grave.

The only sound left in the room was the rhythmic creaking of the beam as Thorve's empty vessel swung back and forth from the tussle with the Reaper. Thora watched her sister's body and hoped for a moment that Thorve was alive, and it all was a dream.

"What have I done?" said Thora, staring at her dead sister. "I murdered my twin, and it hurts all over."

Tears welled up in Thora's eyes and she wept, repeating those same words over and over. Thora cried her river of tears until reality hit. Adrenaline spread across her body, and her mind raced.

Calm down. Follow the plan. This is what you wanted.

Standing with confidence, she tiptoed over to Thorve, wrapped her arms around the dead woman's legs, and gave her sister one last deceitful hug. But as she pulled away from her sister, she paused and stared at the back of her hands as if she had contracted the Avian Death.

"No," said Thora, "please, no. Not now."

Evanora, you didn't explain this. You deceived me.

Panic set in. Thora set about the room, shocked, mind swirling, and searched for her small looking glass, a mirror encapsulated within two flat round disks made from ivory. The case, small enough to fit her hand, would suffice for now.

She proceeded to her cedar chest, delved into the jumble of ordinary items inside, and found the mirror case. Unsure if she wanted the truth, Thora cautiously brought the mirror to eye level.

Before taking a peek at the mirror, an odd feeling passed over her body, and sensing something was not right, she turned around and looked back at Thorve's hung body. The mirror case dropped out of Thora's hand and broke on the hard stone floor beneath her. Both hands covered her mouth, waiting for a scream that did not come.

Anshee had taken control of the shell that once held her heart and soul. The spirit cast her deep-set black eyes down on her sister.

"This is only the beginning," said Anshee.

The voice was unfamiliar, not like before. In its place were tones once unknown to Thorve. Condemnation, indignation, regret, guilt, hate, desperation, vengeance, violence ... all were rolled into a voice that shouted even when it was quiet.

"I will haunt you for the rest of your life and make you cower like the little cunt you are. You murdered me with dark magic and stole my husband. There is no fouler deed than what you have done to me. Skuti will come to know it's you and in despair you will throw yourself from the highest tower. Dogs will gorge on your flesh."

The raging, revenge-filled eyes of black snapped shut before Thora could say a word, not that her voice could have produced anything intelligible. Terrified, she could not move, frozen in front of her dead yet threatening twin sister.

This can't be real. Get ahold of yourself. Thorve's dead and the dead don't speak. It was only your guilty conscience.

Thora backed up while keeping her eyes on the motionless body hanging from a rope tied around a wooden beam. Upon reaching the door, she hurriedly fled the room for help.

This is it. Thora has passed away, yet a new Thorve has been born.

"Help!" said Thorve. "Thora has hung herself!"

Thorve continued to run down the stone floor, shouting for help. Moments later, Sir Beiner arrived out of breath from his sprint up the stairs.

"Lady Thora—Thorve," said Beiner, "what's wrong?"

"Thora has hung herself," said Thorve, "as planned."

"No, my lady. You've grown older."

"What?"

"Your face has aged since I saw you earlier."

"How bad?"

"Who am I to judge?"

"Damn you, Beiner, I'll look for myself!"

Thorve ran off toward Thora's bedchamber, where a larger mirror awaited her. Thorve threw any object she could lift at the mirror, shattering the glass and causing shards to fly and crash into the walls and floor. "Evanora, you deceived me. You told me years would be taken from my life and I would die ahead of my time. Yet, the years have abruptly deserted me."

Thorve flew out of the room and bumped into Beiner, who was responding to the loud destruction coming from Thora's bedchamber. Beiner saw bloodstains amongst the glass and turned to Thorve, who had blood dripping from her fingers.

"You have blood all over your hands," said Beiner. "Get the towel over by the basin."

"I don't have time for this," said Thorve. "Cut my sister down and take her clothes off."

Beiner exited the room and Thorve, ignoring the bloodstains, rapidly stripped off her clothes. She then ran across the hall without glancing at the remains of the mirror. Entering the room, she tossed her clothes next to her dead sister. "Get out of the way; I'll do it."

Steiner stood back and turned his head away as Thorve tore off the rest of her sister's clothes and put them on herself. *Damned clothes are tight. Now I've aged and gained weight.*

"Beiner, look at me. Do I look fat in this?"

"Why no, my lady."

Thora knew Beiner was lying, but it mattered little at this point. The plot and execution relied on lies, so adding one more about her weight was the least of their problems to maintain the murderous charade.

"Is my maiden in the boudoir?"

"Yes, bound and gagged."

"Pull her out. Tell her Thora's dead and you need these

clothes put on her. When she's done, throw her out the window. She committed suicide when she saw Thora dead."

Beiner left to carry out his duty, leaving Thorve to look around once more before exiting. Casting her eyes at her sister's naked and blue body, Thorve instantly recalled the frightening encounter with Anshee and turned to leave. The voice resumed before she reached the threshold. Thorve froze in the doorway, unable to move, as if she were stuck in a dream.

"When did you decide it was easier to use the Badek on me, murdering whore?" said Anshee. "You're not getting out of this castle, stupid bitch. Jomar is going to keep you for ransom. He's always wanted to sard me. You'll be spreading your legs for him again."

The laughter was as hideous as it was chilling to the bone. Thorve tried to scream but nothing came out, and her legs of lead refused to move. Tears dripped out of her eyes and rolled down her face as the laughter became more sinister and crueler.

"Thorve," said Beiner, returning from the boudoir with Thora's maiden over his shoulder. "What's that awful sound?"

Beiner's voice stopped Anshee's hideous laughter and released Thorve's body, paralyzed by fear. She crashed to the floor and banged her head against the stone floor, opening a cut between her eyebrow and hairline on the side of her face.

Oh, gods, what have I done? Please bring her back to life before I die of fright.

CHAPTER 19
DIFFERENT KIND OF TRUTH

Rycardus grabbed Reyna by the hand and jerked her behind him, nearly pulling her shoulder out of its socket with his ever-increasing strength as he led them to the stables. Rycardus knew they had little time before his father sent word to the bell tower to sound the alarm. But Rycharde was also lying near the tunnel entrance underneath the castle, nursing whatever injuries he had sustained from Rycardus and Reyna as they both fled.

How badly are you hurt and how long will you stay down?

Without Raiimond, Rycharde would need to gather the White Guardians himself and plan the details of the hunt for his son. It would take him time to look over the maps and escape routes Rycardus might take. His son was well-versed on the roads and paths leading in and out of the castle and it was possible, given the circumstances, they could head for Trynt's Forest. Valgerd, King of the Bloodmoon Wolves, could either kill the prince in revenge or initiate a ransom demand. Neither was a good outcome.

Rycardus raced to the stables with Reyna in tow until she pulled back on his arm, bringing him to an awkward stop.

"What are you doing?" said Rycardus.

"These shoes are too small and you're going too fast," she said.

"Reyna, let's go," said Rycardus, "just take them off."

Rycardus noticed the dark spots on Reyna's hand as she grabbed for him again.

"Is that blood on your hand?" he asked.

She looked despite not needing to. "Shit, yes."

"For the sake of the gods, wipe it off. There's some around your chin too."

Reyna spat on her hand and wiped the blood streak away, repeating the action on her chin. "Did I get it?"

"Good enough. C'mon, let's go."

The bells had yet to be rung as the two rushed into the royal stable where Rycharde, Rycardus, and Ricaud kept their war and riding horses. It was a simple building, with wide entrances and two walls separating the barn into three rooms, including haylofts. The stable boys often slept in the hay.

Mace and Peirce, the stable boys, hurried over to saddle Rycardus's riding horse.

"Prince Rycardus," said Mace, the senior of the two, "I didn't get word you wanted to ride. I'm sorry your horse is not saddled and ready."

"Change of plans, Mace," said Rycardus. "Lady Reyna will ride Indigo. Peirce, come with me."

Mace eyeballed Reyna with suspicion for a moment before running to fetch Indigo's saddle. Her ill-fitting clothes stood out to the smart young man, along with what looked like small blotches of blood on the dress she was wearing.

Peirce followed Rycardus into the next room and walked over to the stall of his brother's riding horse, a handsome palfrey named Bolt.

"I'll help you saddle Bolt," said Rycardus. "We're in a hurry to get started."

"Um, yes, my prince," said Peirce.

"Is there a problem?"

"No, my prince. I thought you would ride Damien since Rey—uh, Lady Reyna, was riding Indigo."

"You thought wrong. Now hurry over to the equipment room and bring back my damned saddle."

"Right away, Prince Rycardus."

Hooves pounded the dirt path and headed away from the castle and toward Trynt's Forest. Rycardus had his mind set to turn east before reaching the forest and heading for a trade route leading up and through the Northern Steppes.

He'd heard about the road during one of Lord Wymon's meandering stories one afternoon over ales at the Snakes and Stones Tavern across from the castle. It was an "easy place to hide if one ever needed to do such a thing," he said with a wink. Everyone at the table laughed, knowing Wymon had done the very thing himself.

The riding path narrowed as it entered a wooded area, ending the ability of two horses to gallop side-by-side. Reyna's inexperience on horseback and the uncertainty caused by the speed at which they were traveling left her holding the reins so tightly her hands became raw.

Rycardus looked back and glimpsed Reyna's face and knew it was time to ease up. They'd gained enough space since leaving the castle to slow for a bit and give themselves and the horses time to rest. He remembered a stream running next to the path at some point where they could water the horses and take a breather. As Rycardus was doubting his memory, the sound of running water filled his ears.

It was past noon when they reached the stream, Reyna was quiet when the pace slowed, shutting down any conversation Rycardus attempted to start up. Reyna's silence irritated him and the time to find the water source only added to it. After taking care of the horses, he met her next to the stream.

"What's wrong?" he said.

"Nothing," she said, staring at something upstream. "I'm just tired."

Kingdom Rules

This is where I always give up. No more.

"It's more than tired," he said. "There's something wrong."

She looked at him uneasily, like a guilty child. "I need to tell you something, and it will not be easy."

As if on cue, a large knot developed in Rycardus's stomach, and all the butterflies in the kingdom landed in his belly at the same time.

Now what?

"What have you hidden from me?" said Rycardus.

It was too difficult for Rycardus to see in the shade of the trees, but the tint in Reyna's eyes lightened and also widened. Whatever doubts he had circled his head like vultures waiting for his hopes to be dashed.

"Please remember, no matter what I say," she said, "I love you with all my heart."

For the sake of the gods, whatever she has concealed is worse than those before it.

Rycardus swallowed hard and prepared for the worst. "Go ahead."

Reyna stared at the ground and only looked up after she said it. "There's something I've wanted to tell you for a long time. I am Delinda's bastard daughter."

The relaxing sound of the stream flowing rhythmically clashed, even raged against the static, foul-smelling water of shit that was Reyna's deception. Rycardus stood motionless, stunned beyond a whack on the head from a war hammer. The knot in his stomach became so large it threatened to erupt like a volcano out of his arse.

The silence threatened to unnerve Reyna and so she spoke, not to comfort Rycardus, but because she needed to feel in control. "I know this is difficult."

"Difficult? You know this is difficult? You just told me you're the child of the yelloweyed whore who tried to kill me. Yes, this is fucking difficult!"

Reyna gazed into the distance and muttered. "There's more."

"What did you say?"

Reyna cleared her throat. "There's more."

"You mean more duplicity?"

Reyna nodded her head and cleared her throat once more. "Delinda had one other, older bastard daughter from a different man. Her name was Liecia."

I'm going to puke.

There was a sense of the surreal in Reyna's confession. Words continued to flow from her mouth as if the situation was common. Undoubtedly, two daughters sent to finish their mother's work. It was an outrageous story—a writer of books wouldn't dare come up with such an unbelievable twist.

The wince reflected the growing pain in his head and stomach. "Another daughter?"

"Yes. She was jealous of my relationship with you and told me she'd be 'the one to kill you and be the heroine.' Liecia was going to seduce you and then put a knife in your chest."

Tears streamed down Reyna's face and caused her to pause for a moment. When she was ready to continue, she spoke in a halting voice with not much power behind it. "I ... told Sir Raiimond about ... Liecia ... so ... he would ... kill ... her."

Rycardus scrunched his eyebrows and narrowed his eyes. "What are you trying to tell me?"

Reyna couldn't hold on to her emotional mooring any longer and began to shout and cry at the same time. "I told Sir Raiimond my sister planned to kill you! As I felt myself falling in love with you, the thought of losing you was unbearable. I orchestrated the killing of my sister for your sake."

"No wonder Sir Raiimond hated you."

Nodding her head in agreement with Rycardus was the best Reyna could do as her tears continued unabated.

He had the right to hate me too. Now he's gone ... I can never tell him … I'm sorry … what have I done to myself? I've betrayed the man whose job it was to protect me.

With his head bowed, the shame of all he had done in the name of love came crashing down atop his head like a wave crashing on the rocks. Rycardus recalled the last angry words he exchanged with Sir Raiimond and quietly shook his head back and forth.

Why didn't he tell me?

His conscience shot back. *Would you've believed him?*

Rycardus's stomach roiled with conflicting emotions while Reyna lowered her head and sobbed. It was nearly impossible under the haze of the deceit to discern a course of action. He hated and loved Reyna, further obscuring the truth, and making the knot tighten in his stomach like the hangman's noose.

What if this was a lie to prove her love and gain my sympathy?

"Damn you, Reyna. Can I trust that this isn't a lie?"

Reyna rubbed the back of her hand under her nose and wiped the tears from her eyes with the back of her sleeve.

"Please believe me. How could I fabricate this? Werewolves differ from humans. I wanted you and I did what I had to and besides, she always hated me."

"That doesn't bring me much comfort."

What have I done to myself? I'm in love with a liar who wants to kill me too, for all I know.

The spinning wheel spun in Rycardus's head, and he reached back in time for a clue missed, something said, an observation, anything telling him to stop walking the path he was on. In the last days, months, and weeks, he'd done and said things he never imagined he would, even in the darkest recesses of his mind.

How did I become so foolish to find myself in this situation? It's bad enough Delinda poisoned me with her venom, but to be mixed up with her daughter?

His head hurt as he tried to make sense of the whole

miserable tale of woe. It was almost impossible, given all the thoughts and reactions stirred up in his mind, which was more emotional stewing pot than a thinking organ.

"Why did King Valgerd wait so long for a second attempt?"

"Your father added extra security around you and kept his eye on you at the same time. When we began our friendship, it opened up an opportunity."

"Who did you tell?"

Reyna looked off into the forest shadows, avoiding eye contact with Rycardus, who was untangling lies in his head. He accomplished nothing other than to entangle himself further in Reyna's web and exacerbate his sense of being trapped, which was becoming less of a sense and more of a reality.

I'm nothing more than a fly in a spider's web. Unable to move and waiting to be eaten.

"I told my grandmother, who told King Valgerd. My grandparents opened the cookshop with coinage from King Valgerd in exchange for spying. I was too young to understand that and why Delinda was home one day and gone the next. I was only told Delinda left."

Rycardus shook his head and smirked. "She left without her head. It may still be rolling."

"Rycardus, you've never—"

"You concealed the truth. How can you do a thing so corrupt and abuse my love for you?"

The river of tears began anew as a reflexive action of a true manipulator, but did nothing to move Rycardus. The tears only made him angrier.

"You are older than what you told me."

Reyna sniffled the answer. "I am. Six years older."

The words became louder as they emerged from Rycardus's mouth. "You were fully aware of your actions. You spread your legs to put a collar on me like I was some kind of damned dog."

"Please, Rycardus. I know I've hurt you. If you could only find a way —"

"Find a way to what? Not kill you?"

"Oh, dear gods, don't say that, Rycardus."

Rycardus paused as if someone had tapped him on the shoulder. He became distracted, and his mind wandered until it met *the other one*. The one changing on the inside, the one wanting to take control. That Rycardus was nearing its birth.

With pleading eyes, Reyna inched forward. "What do you want me to do? I'll do anything for you."

The twinge in his muscles made him acutely aware that what was inside wanted out. "Why didn't you tell me this?"

C'mon, think of something else. A partial change only makes you more vulnerable.

"I thought you wouldn't trust me. That I only hoped to end your life."

"I don't trust you now, and you may want to kill me yet."

Rycardus stepped over to the stream and took a deep breath, hoped to cleanse himself of his anger and the dirt from Reyna's dark revelations. Reyna bowed her head as if praying and wept in silence where she stood.

After several breaths brought enough relief to keep the monster at bay, Rycardus turned to catch Reyna continuing in her tears. "A traveling drama wagon was your calling."

"I am truly ashamed of what I've done," whimpered Reyna.

"You should be. What happened before the Knife's Edge?"

"They snatched me and took me into the forest for two weeks, and all they talked about was this book. The seer kept asking me questions about you, as did King Valgerd. They threatened to kill me if I didn't tell them the truth about you."

Reyna clinched her teeth as tears of bitterness and rage

built up behind her light green eyes. One singular tear crept out and ran down her cheek, stinging her face as it rolled.

Reyna gained enough control of her emotions and continued the story. "They were insistent I bring you to the forest. Once they allowed me to leave, I made my way to the Knife's Edge. You were in danger, and I wanted to disappear. I was going to save some coinage and leave the kingdom, but you found me, and now I wish you hadn't."

"Isn't that what you're doing now, taking me to the forest so someone else can kill me?"

Staring out through bloodshot eyes, Reyna began anew. "No, it's something far different."

Something?

"Far different, but still a lie."

"No, I swear upon the name of Trynt, it's true."

Rycardus sucked in a breath and braced himself for another falsehood. "This is it, Reyna. If I think one bit of this story is untrue, I'm leaving."

Some measure of brightness returned to Reyna's eyes and her body released some of its tension. "When I told you of a greater destiny, I had reason. There is a prophecy within that book regarding a coming king for our kind. I think it might be you."

Rycardus closed his eyes in disbelief. *This lie is worse than the ones before it,* he thought. "That's it, Reyna. I can't believe what you say anymore. I'm done."

With a quick turn, Rycardus headed toward the horses, but could hear Reyna coming after him. He spun back around with his hand on the grip of his thirty-eight-inch steel blade, intent on ending the lies forever. When he saw her tear-stained face, eyes wild with desperation, he stopped as if someone had jerked his imaginary collar.

May the gods save me from myself.

Shock replaced desperation as Reyna stopped in her tracks. "You were going to kill me."

"Lucky for you I didn't. More lies, though, might kill you."

Reyna kept her eye on Rycardus's right hand resting on the pommel of his sword. She spoke cautiously, no doubt worried she might not be so fortunate the next time. "King Valgerd and Queen Luana want to meet you."

"And you believe them?"

"Yes. Why wouldn't I?"

The emphatic shaking of Rycardus's head showed his mistrust of Reyna and anything coming from her forked tongue. "You're lying or ignorant."

Reyna pulled her head back and cocked it to the side. "What is there to be ignorant about? I don't understand what you're saying."

"Think about it, Reyna. A king doesn't invite a prophetic usurper to dine with them. Valgerd wants me to come to the forest to kill me."

"Yes, but—"

"Yes, but what? Valgerd's going to bend the knee to me because of what it says in some book?"

"But the king and seer agreed it was a true prophetic book because there were other prophecies that were already fulfilled within it."

Rycardus stared at Reyna while arguing with himself if it were worth the trouble to continue the discussion or be done with it and her. "Who gave them the book?"

"I overheard them discussing the man who gave it to them. They weren't sure if he was to be trusted."

"Did they mention his name?"

"No. I only heard bits and pieces."

"With your ears?"

"I was too far away."

Reyna's eyes pleaded and begged for Rycardus to believe her story.

You can't help yourself. You lie when you don't need to. It's your native tongue and now, your undoing.

Rycardus shifted his gaze downward for a moment and chuckled. He raised his glance with a sardonic smile stitched on his face. "Maybe it appeared via magic."

Surprised by his response, she hesitated. "Rycardus, please don't mock me."

The true characteristics of Reyna, not the one he succumbed to as an immature, sex-driven young man, coalesced in his mind.

My mind hates you, and my heart has turned to stone. There is no truth in you, and I can no longer abide by it. You've set me on a path of ruin apart from my family and for that, there can be no forgiveness.

The words flowed and were sharp, intended to cut to the quick. "Mock? You deserve to be hung in a cage for all to see. You've lied, manipulated, been duplicitous at every turn, and even killed when you needed to."

Reyna stood motionless, eyes wide and lips parted.

"Nothing to say? Has the truth made you silent?"

Reyna ran within her maze of lies with the fury of a trapped rat scurrying after the cheese that was Rycardus. Each time she ran into a wall, she turned in a different direction and continued with a new set of lies.

"I know I've been awful, but if we get on our horses and flee instead, I promise—"

"Wait," said Rycardus. He narrowed his eyes and moved toward Reyna. "Instead? The whole point was to flee."

Reyna swallowed hard. "I said they wanted to meet you. We don't need to go. We just disappear, and it'll all be over."

He steeled himself against the woman he had loved when the day began. Reyna was a miasma, corrupting Rycardus's life with her cunning and conniving, always one step ahead of each lie until today. "It will never be over for you. I simply cannot trust you anymore and I'm leaving—alone."

"Please, Rycardus. I know I've hurt you, but I can make it up to you. I swear it on the graves of my ancestors."

"There are not enough graves for you to swear on in all of Wolfden to get me to believe you."

Rycardus turned his back to Reyna, made his way over to his horse, and prepared to leave. He would ride Indigo and leave Bolt behind. It was a tough decision to leave Bolt and allow Reyna to follow. Taking Bolt would slow him down, and he needed speed to get to the road of his choice.

"What are you doing?"

"What does it look like I'm doing? I'm leaving."

"No, please don't. I need you."

"I don't need you. You've squeezed all the love from my heart."

Like a soaked rag with the water wrung out of it.

Reyna fell to her knees and began to beg and plead with Rycardus.

"Rycardus, please. I'm begging you. Don't leave me out here."

"You're humiliating yourself. Get up, it's over."

"They're going to kill me."

"It's what happens when you play one side against the other. Picture yourself as a woman who borrowed money from two corrupt men and now lacks the coins to repay them. What do you think they'll do?"

Rycardus had placed his foot in the stirrup and prepared to mount Indigo when the words reached his ears.

"There are Doomclaw soldiers out there," said Reyna, "waiting to escort us into the forest."

"What?"

Rycardus stopped and made his way straight to Reyna, who'd eased herself back on her haunches. Rycardus, with his growing strength, jarred Reyna by jerking her up from her knees. "What else haven't you told me?"

"You're hurting me," she said. "Put me down."

With a sneer, he flung Reyna to the ground and hovered over her. "Are you going to answer me or not?"

Reyna wrapped an arm around her stomach and winced. "Ow, that hurt. You toss me around as if I'm an unwanted doll."

"What else haven't you told me?"

"You won't believe me if I tell you."

"It hasn't stopped you so far."

You are with child, aren't you?

"Your child is in my belly."

He cast his eyes upward into the trees and watched for a moment the red hannibirds and yellow-tailed goldenias zipping from tree to tree, hoping to catch an insect. Their songs filled the air, casting a calm over this part of the forest, but not over Rycardus. The thought of wedding Reyna felt repulsive, but having a bastard child wasn't acceptable to any Andairn man.

I was careless about leaving my seed in your belly. Even liars tell the truth now and again, but I won't accept this. No one will believe you, not that it matters. I may lose my life tonight in this damned forest, and so will you.

"You know it's true," said Reyna.

The powerful urge to leave and get as far away as possible from Reyna washed over him as a river carrying his saturation point. Hastily, Rycardus mounted Indigo and turned her toward the path. "Goodbye, Reyna."

Stumbling to her feet, Reyna screeched, "Don't make your child a bastard."

Rycardus moved his hands above Indigo's withers, squeezed his legs just enough to move her forward, and whispered into her ear, "Gallop."

There's a time in each man's life where he must choose a woman's character over the desire in his loins. The wrong choice will shipwreck a man's life as the waves break wood. You were right, Father, but I was too far gone to notice.

Dread joined the knot in his belly, anticipating one if not more Doomclaws intercepting him before he turned east and followed the road toward the Northern Steppes. In some strange way, he desired to confront one of the Doomclaw warriors and make it clear that he did not flee out of fear of a fight.

One of the best swordsmen in all the continent has trained me. He has a black sword, and only courageous and battle-tested men get one. My father is the best of the best. I know he could beat the knight from Brüeland.

Spending time with Reyna and her lies was a waste, and now the escaping light will become an enemy. The best hope was for his changing body to give him better eyesight in the darkness, knowing any Doomclaw could see effectively at night.

Rycardus was going to get his chance whether or not he was ready. There was a dark figure on a horse headed toward him. The rider's mount was one of the great horses used in war by knights who could afford them. This Doomclaw fighter was of some importance or had enough of something to trade for it. Or, more likely, he stole it after he killed its owner.

This is it, Rycardus.

Rycardus placed his hand on the grip of his sword and a finger moved up to touch the rain-guard for good luck, a trait his father hated.

"If you're a skilled swordsman, you don't need any luck."

Shut up, Father.

The stranger closed the gap and Rycardus eased back on Indigo, who breathed heavily as she arched her neck. "Easy, girl, you've met nastier."

Time crawled, waiting for the Doomclaw fighter to dismount his horse and approach Rycardus, who did the same and met the beast between the two horses.

"Prince Rycardus," said Halec. "I've been waiting for you."

Halec was a fierce and frightening creature, standing well over six feet tall. The shape of his head was almost human, and he possessed the loose jaw structure allowing him to speak in the Known Language.

Rycardus swallowed hard and did his best to channel his inner Rycharde. "And you are?"

"Commander Halec. I've come to escort you to King Valgerd."

"I received no invitation. Given the relationship between those in the forest and those of us in the castle, it is customary for a king to send emissaries with an invitation sealed with his signet. It would be foolish of me to enter the forest without guaranteed safe passage."

Halec wasn't expecting such a response. "Where's Reyna?"

Rycardus gave Halec his best smirk. "What does she have to do with this?"

"She was the one to invite you."

"When I say emissary, I don't mean a *duhbrarei* whore who lies better than a devil."

Halec swung his head to each side, presumably searching for Andairn guards in the nearby trees. When he faced forward again, Rycardus focused his gaze and met Halec's narrowed eyes, which were more like yellow flames around pupils, black as coal and infinitely angrier than Delinda's more than a decade ago. His eyes were centered on a large, wide nose more human than wolf, its nostrils flaring at the bottom.

Rycardus's mouth was as dry as a desert, but he pressed forward. "I don't know who sent you or what your intent is, so get back on your horse and return to the forest."

Halec snarled at Rycardus. "Don't test me out here because you think I will not kill you. I can bring you to the king, alive or dead."

"This is the king's land. Don't think there won't be consequences for your empty threats."

You can't talk your way out of this. Reyna's betrayal has led me to this moment, and it's up to me to determine my future.

Rycardus drew his thirty-eight-inch longsword, one of the

finest swords in the land, which had been made by a highly skilled swordsmith sought by knights as far away as the deserts of Ougrar.

The unexpected low growl from deep in the chest of Halec brought reality home to Rycardus, as did the words he barked. "Here's your invitation to death, and I'll seal it with your blood."

The blacksmith fashioned Halec's two-handed sword as the Croikura of old, with a cross hilt of forward-sloping quillons and quatrefoil terminations. It was heavy and hard to control, even for a big powerful beast like Halec.

Rycardus put himself into the Fool's Guard, holding his sword with two hands at the waist, blade pointed outward and the tip touching the ground.

Halec took the bait and hacked downward toward the top of Rycardus's skull, but the young prince brought his sword up and knocked Halec's off its path. Maneuvering inside, Rycardus turned his sword and jabbed the pommel into the face of the clumsy, charging Halec.

Halec called curses down from the heavens or from the under the earth; Rycardus understood none of what he belched out of his mouth. Either way, the heavy end of the sword opened a deep gash on his eyebrow, and the area around the blow swelled. Blood from the cut trickled into Halec's eye, affecting his vision, as did the swollen brow and eyelid.

The reddish-colored gore stained the fine gray facial hair covering most of his face. Halec had less-than-thick, deep black hair with a widow's peak covering his head, which was parted down the middle. Triangular ears peeked out of his shoulder-length hair, wet with sweat.

Halec wiped at his eye with the back of his thin leather gloves, and the sight infuriated him even further. Bearing his fangs, he spat, "You stupid little boy."

Rycardus changed his guard, but Halec again raised his

sword high and chopped it down with maximum effort. Rycardus met Halec's sword higher up this time and stepped quickly into the space created; and like a viper striking, punched Halec twice on the cut along his eyebrow before vacating the area.

Now in a fighting rhythm, Rycardus's nerves calmed, and he was feeling himself, growing in confidence and surprised at the ease with which he was beating the stronger fighter.

I am my father's son.

"Your blood's stained my new leather gloves," said Rycardus.

Halec regrouped for another try. "Fuck you."

Swords clashed again and again as Halec attempted to slow the quicker and more agile Rycardus with little success. Grunts, howls, shouts, and cries of pain filled the darkening evening air. Halec's face resembled a mask of blood from the earlier blows and sharp, quick punches in close when he slipped inside of the beast's wild swings.

C'mon, Rycardus. Dig deep. Don't let him wear you down.

Rycardus looked unscathed save for a few scratches and two short but deep gashes from Halec's claws around his cheek that he did not feel at the time Halec clawed him. As if out of nowhere, the open wounds burned and an awful, bitter taste formed in his mouth. Spitting several times did nothing, and the cheek felt numb.

Weariness crept into Rycardus's muscles, the result of fending off the heavy blows from Halec's strength in wielding his heavy sword. His confidence ebbed as a small leak in a bucket allows drips of water to escape. Both had backed away to catch their breath and prepared to engage again.

The two stood about twelve feet apart and waited. Halec had wised up and abandoned his wild hacks. There was no sense in wasting energy on a risky move. If it failed, the other could exploit it and create a pronounced advantage. Halec wiped his eyes constantly, a ritual of hand and finger movements working in tandem to keep the blood out of his eye. The slit in the mass of his swollen eye showed the small amount of remaining sight.

Rycardus obsessed about the wound. "You dirty animal, what kind of shit do you rummage in?"

"It's the poison," hissed Halec, "that will turn you or kill you."

My face is on fire, I swear it. Damn you—

Halec's impatience got the better of him, and instead of waiting he raised his sword and chopped down one more time at Rycardus, which he blocked as he had all of Halec's predictable tactics, but this time the swords locked around the cross guards.

"No—no," said Rycardus. "Shit."

Halec seized the opportunity to use his greater strength to force Rycardus's sword downward. Rycardus pulled a primal scream from deep within and wailed at the stars with a last-ditch effort to pull out of the lock. The thought struck his mind like lightning.

Drop it and run.

As quick as the idea raced into his mind, Rycardus released his sword and sprinted away. Halec crumpled to the ground and landed on his shoulder, jarring his sword from his hand. Rycardus would've laughed his arse off had he seen the clumsy beast fall awkwardly to the dirt. Instead, he ran as fast as his body allowed down the horse path and ducked into a grove of birch trees to catch his breath.

Once into the trees, he kept as quiet as possible, stepping around branches and sticks, anything that had the potential to make a sound. As he kept a wary eye on his surroundings, he listened for Halec, who was certain to close the distance with his superior speed, although diminished from the energy-draining sword fight. Despite Reyna's failure to turn him completely, Rycardus's senses had improved dramatically, though there was no time to notice.

Fatigue set in, creating the dreaded condition in which men turn to cowards. It wasn't helping that an angry werewolf with murderous intentions was in pursuit. "Please let me live; keep that beast from killing me."

AAAOOOOOWWWOOOO echoed through the forest loud enough to scare the stoutest of men. The hair standing up on the back of his neck proved Rycardus was no exception.

Shit. If he catches me, he'll tear me apart.

AAAOOOOOWWWOOOO. Halec's howl was much louder this time. Rycardus stopped moving and spun 360 degrees, searching for eyes of yellow in a maze of birch trees and shadows.

Good god, I hope he's not calling for his friends.

The stop was a brief respite and Rycardus picked up his pace for a few moments before his body bickered about which part of it would bring Rycardus to a halt. His inner voice interrupted and explained stopping again meant sudden and certain death.

What was that?

Rycardus scanned ahead and to the sides.

I smell him getting closer.

Every shadow was Halec, and each tree trunk was a torso, and its limbs were hands and arms reaching at Rycardus as he passed. His heart was pounding harder and faster, and it threatened to leap from his chest.

He's near. Keep moving your legs. Don't look back.

But Rycardus had to look; needed to know; had to *know*. He glanced over his shoulder and—

Thud.

An errant root sneaking out of the ground like a snake lying in wait dropped Rycardus to the duff.

"Ow, shit …" flew out of his mouth before he belly-flopped into the natural compost of the groves. "Humph."

Rycardus pushed himself up on his hands and knees. The grove was quiet. Even the dwellers within the birch fell into silence. He contorted his body and stared behind him. Nothing. No sound. No Halec.

The prince swiveled his head and scanned the area ahead. "Damn you," he said, "where are you? I can smell you, bastard."

Just start running in the same direction …

Rycardus did not move far before almost tripping over Halec's boots. Halec was closer than Rycardus realized and had leaped at the prince just as the errant root tripped him. Instead of tackling Rycardus, the beast flew over the top of the prone prince and into a tree, knocking himself unconscious.

Rycardus reached for the dagger behind his back, drew it out, and turned his attention to Halec's prone body that lay motionless in the dead leaves. Without stepping on anything capable of sound, he raised the dagger his mother gave him at age fifteen.

"Rycardus, this is for you," Sela said.

"Mother, it's beautiful," said Rycardus.

"Why the sad face?"

"Father told me great swordsmen never carry daggers. If you need to use one, it means you've already lost."

"Sometimes your father exaggerates to make a point."

"Not with me. I think he hates me most of the time."

"He does not. He loves you as his son."

"He doesn't act like it."

Rycardus felt something on his shoulder and swung his arm back to knock whatever branch was tapping him on the shoulder.

That's no branch.

Startled, he turned around and pointed his dagger. It had a fourteen-inch blade with a sharply tapered point and two cutting edges sharpened the full length of the blade. "Damn you. I knew I shouldn't have left Bolt behind."

"Halec's going to kill you," said Reyna.

"Not if I kill him first."

Rycardus turned back to Halec, but Reyna pulled him back by the arm.

"Don't do it."

"Why? So he can kill me?"

"I swear he's playing possum."

"That's stupid. Another lie."

"I've seen others do it."

"Let go."

"No."

"Damn you."

Leaves crackled as Halec showed signs of life by moving his limbs as Rycardus shook free from Reyna's grip.

Do it or run.

CHAPTER 20
FOREVER GOODBYES

"You fine knights are part of the King's Guard," said Renoldus. "What are you doing guarding Lady Evelyn's door?"

"We don't want any trouble, Sir Renoldus," said Sir Ricon, the senior guard of the four guardsmen blocking the entrance to Evelyn's apartment.

"Ah, Sir Ricon the Romantic, everyone says that and then trouble always rears its ugly head."

Renoldus wore his typical burgundy silk tunic with the golden stallion, dark black boots, beige pants, and a matching coat.

"Sir Renoldus," said Ricon, "if you choose to engage us, it's a crime against the crown."

"Who said anything about engaging?"

"Sir Renoldus," said Sir Amfrid, "state your purpose or leave." Renoldus had little respect for Amfrid, a former Naval Officer turned knight—a title he bought rather than earned.

"Well, Sir Amfrid of the Sea, I will state my purpose not because you demanded it, but because the longer I stand here, the odds of killing you rise above this tower. Go to Lady

Evelyn at once and tell her Sir Renoldus the Black wishes to talk."

Amfrid fixed his eye of evil at Renoldus, a look he'd seen from far greater men than the one standing across from him. Renoldus flipped the small golden latch open on his scabbard and placed hand his on the pommel of the greatest sword in the kingdom, and perhaps the continent, and tapped it with his index finger.

"Don't be angry with me," said Renoldus. "Deliver my message to Lady Evelyn."

"Go, Amfrid," said Ricon, "and that's an order."

Amfrid glanced at Ricon, then Renoldus, and finally knocked on the door before going in. The answer was quick as Amfrid returned almost before the door closed. He nodded at Ricon and returned to staring at Renoldus.

"Open the—" said Ricon to Amfrid before Renoldus raised his hand.

"Don't bother," said Renoldus as he moved toward the door.

Amfrid continued posturing and did not leave any room for Renoldus to walk past. With quick hands, he threw a short right cross to Amfrid's jaw, dropping him to the ground. Renoldus glanced at the fallen man, then looked at Ricon. "Have the healer stitch up that cut."

"Bastard," said Ricon under his breath as Renoldus pulled open the door and disappeared.

Evelyn was standing next to a standard wood chair behind the curved oak table where she and Watkin had shared meals together, and she motioned for Renoldus to take a seat across from her at the table.

Evelyn greeted her guest with little respect. "Renoldus."

Renoldus glanced down at the seat of the chair where Watkin once sat to eat his meals and drink his wine. He pulled the chair far enough out to accommodate his size and sat, hoping Evelyn didn't see him pause.

"Don't judge the chair where Watkin once sat. I know what evil has been done on your own table. That's what your whore told me."

I can't say she is wrong. I am plagued by the haunting thought of the lives I'll be accountable for because of my allowance of Ingrid's actions to taint the alliance with House Andairn.

"Lady Evelyn," said Renoldus, "there is not a need to delve into matters in which one of us is guilty of the greater evil. I came here to say farewell."

"I don't know why you bothered considering the princess's boorish behavior, including attacking me with her fist. Look at what she did to me."

Evelyn leaned across the table and pointed to the nearly healed cut on her lip. Renoldus felt like rolling his eyes but thought better of it and instead, landed a verbal jab.

"Princess Ingrid told me she hit you," said Renoldus, "but looking at your face, I'd say she exaggerated the damage."

"Do you find this funny?"

"No, just ironic. You were her lady-in-waiting for a time. Didn't your duties include teaching the young woman how to behave properly?"

Evelyn rolled her eyes before catching Renoldus's glance. "It was all good until you bedded her."

Renoldus hesitated, unsure of how far he should take the conversation, creating an uncomfortable silence.

If I let my emotions take over this conversation, it's a waste of my time and energy. Each of us played a part in burning the bridge of righteousness and nobility.

"Out of respect, I came only to say goodbye."

"It's too late for that now," said Evelyn. "You're here and you'll hear what I have to say."

"Does that include," said Renoldus, "your story about the dirty green *kirattu*?"

"Why talk about it? We both know it's true, and you disgust me because of it."

"That dirty green *kirattu* is twice the woman you've become."

"Grala should strip you of that sword. You've debased yourself beyond belief."

The sound of the chair's legs against the stone floor echoed throughout the apartment as Renoldus stood. As he did so, Evelyn rose from her chair.

"Let's stop this nonsense. We both hold hate in our hearts. Why exacerbate it further?"

I should walk out. But a part of me wants to let out my anger on this conniving and murderous woman.

Evelyn narrowed her gray eyes and blew as a harsh wind through Renoldus's warning.

"Whatever your lying doxy told you about me," she said, "and what I've supposedly done is simply conjecture and a vivid imagination."

"Since you respect neither of us, why does it matter what she said and what I think about what she said?"

"Truth matters."

"Princess Ingrid laid out for me a very detailed and logical argument why you did what she's accused you of."

"To you, the sun rises and sets in the crack of her arse. You'd believe anything she said."

"I was mistaken about the princess."

"Finally."

"She could be the kingdom's smartest woman."

Evelyn's chair crashed to the floor as she fled to the veranda through the open doors. Renoldus started to follow, thought better of it, and stayed at the table.

I will not chase you out there if you're expecting some sort of apology. My father was right in calling off the arranged marriage between us. Cecile was also right in warning me about you. Now it's very clear why Leander arranged for you to be Ingrid's lady-in-waiting. You reported to the king what she was doing, and you tried to tame her. But you failed, and Ingrid played you as she told me. Ingrid is a political savant with an iron will and an ability to, as skilled chess players do, see ahead two moves.

Several minutes passed by before Renoldus extended a courtesy to Evelyn and made his way to the veranda to tell her he was leaving. Evelyn was waiting as he stepped through the doors and onto the veranda.

"I'm leaving. May the gods show you kindness."

"Yes, you are, you hollowed-out bastard of a knight," she said, "and you're never coming back. You will die a knight-errant in some distant land."

"There is no coming back from where your words have taken you."

"Who said anything about coming back?"

Evelyn smiled at her cleverness, but the stone face of Renoldus only got harder.

"Your lack of self-awareness is truly remarkable," said Renoldus, "as is your trafficking in lies and deceptions."

"Ingrid's native tongue is lying," said Evelyn, "and she is the one who speaks with a tongue that is forked."

Renoldus nodded his head at what Evelyn had said and rubbed the beard on his chin. "If she is lying, then tell me the truth."

"What is truth?"

"Truth is truth. You cannot tell me one plus one equals three. Either her version is the truth, or it is not."

Evelyn's self-righteousness and her tight-lipped smile pushed Renoldus dangerously close to his tipping point. The words she hissed through the smug smile were like adding kindling to a long-held smoldering fire within his soul. "I'm done with this conversation and with you."

Stepping forward, Renoldus put a gloved hand around the neck of Evelyn and drove her into the three-foot-high retaining wall at the edge of the veranda. It was not a question of dying if one were to fall off the veranda; it was only a question of how big a splat the body would make.

"What are you doing?" croaked Evelyn.

"What someone should've done a long time ago," said Renoldus.

Tears of fear and pain ran down her cheeks, and her voice was full of panic. "Please don't."

"Did Cecile feel this before she was murdered?"

"I wasn't there."

"Who was?"

"Please don't make me."

"You need to make a choice. Your life depends on it."

"No ... please."

"Tell me, damn you."

Evelyn's words were impossible to hear, so Renoldus loosened his grip around her neck and pulled her away from the retaining wall. What she said again was indiscernible, so Renoldus turned his ear toward her mouth, and she said the name loud enough for him to hear it plainly.

"You're lying," said Renoldus. "There is no way they did it."

Renoldus dropped Evelyn to the floor and left her gasping for breath and rubbing her neck over the top of a large red handprint. She nodded her head, confirming it was true.

"I don't care what happens to me," said Renoldus, "but if you tell the king about this, Ingrid will burn down the castle until she finds you and puts an end to your time in this world."

Renoldus walked out of the apartment with a hardened heart and a mind wondering where it all went wrong.

Stop fooling yourself. It was the night you took Ingrid into your bed.

Renoldus walked out of the apartment, left Tarquin Tower, and crossed over to a smaller tower named after his father, Jeames. When he approached the Omond apartment, two guards were stationed by the door.

"You guardsmen are like cockroaches today," said Renoldus. "You're at every door I approach."

"Sir Renoldus," said Sir Folkes, "you're not welcome here."

"That was a rude welcoming," said Renoldus. "So much for Sir Folkes the Courteous."

Renoldus chuckled, but neither guard found any humor in it, and they maintained their serious faces. "By whose authority am I not welcomed?"

"The king's," said Sir Sanson the Gentleman. "He feared your drunkenness would lead to an unfortunate incident."

"Perhaps he fears the answers I might find beyond the door and what I'd do with that information."

Sir Folkes threw back his cape, freeing his right hand and arm to draw his sword. Both guards didn't want to be there, and who can blame them? The best approach lay in an appeal to Renoldus's sense of honor, order, and discipline. Provoking Renoldus, they had agreed earlier, was a bad thing, yet Folkes was doing just that by showing aggression in his movements.

"Folkes, cut the shit," said Sanson. "This is Sir Renoldus the Black, and he'll take Blackout and shove it so far up your arse your tongue will taste it."

"Well said, Sir Sanson," said Renoldus. "I couldn't have done any better."

"Surely we can talk to Renoldus sensibly," said Sanson. "He's a man of reason."

"You know what we were told," said Folkes. "Absolutely don't have a conversation with him."

"Can we handle him?" said Sanson.

"What are you saying?" said Folkes.

"No two men can beat Sir Renoldus."

"He's drunk and wanting to harm the Omond family."

One more fool to suffer in a day full of them.

When the clasp was flipped, it made nary a sound, but the sound of Blackout flying out of its sheath surprised both guards, who pulled and raised their swords in defense.

"Didn't we agree, provoking him was not good?" said Sanson.

"We did, but here we are," Folkes said.

Bemused by the two knights whom he had trained as part of Brüeland's army, he could no longer stifle a laugh.

"Sir Folkes, you don't want to fight," said Renoldus. "You'll end up dead."

Sanson shot a nervous glance at his partner and sheathed his sword at the same time. "Don't be stupid. If he kills you, I'm telling everyone you instigated it and forced Renoldus to defend himself."

Folkes sheathed his sword and stood with a red face, as if someone had pulled his pants down.

"Sir Terrin has left," said Sanson.

"As I would expect," said Renoldus, "I only want to say goodbye to Lady Gelen of House Bridetomb."

"I will ask," said Folkes, "but if she is unreceptive, do you agree to leave?"

"Of course," said Renoldus, "but Sir Sanson goes in."

Sir Sanson turned and rapped on the door. The door opened slightly, allowing him to enter. Folkes and Renoldus found themselves in an awkward moment.

"You've hated me from the very start," said Folkes.

"I don't hate you," said Renoldus, "but you lack the skills to be a commander in Brüeland's army."

"My father didn't see eye to eye with Sir Jeames, and you hold it against me."

"This has nothing to do with my father. You're only making excuses for why you're lacking."

"You're a disgraced legend and all you have is your damned black sword. Enjoy your exile."

Renoldus wrapped a hand behind his back and gripped his dagger. "You are a fool for speaking to me—"

The door opened again slightly, and Lady Gelen, wearing a purple dress, slid out and gave Renoldus a warm hug. Her beauty was natural, with long brown curls, blue eyes, and a thin, petite body. Even if she wore a burlap bag, she would still turn heads.

The healers and midwives feared for her life after having five difficult births, of which she lost three because of complications related to her small hips. The last loss of a child, a daughter, made her cry out to the gods and ask why they were crushing her soul.

"I'm so sorry," whispered Lady Gelen into Renoldus's ear. "Terrin didn't want to do this. Leander demanded it."

"Let's move away from them," said Renoldus.

They took a few steps, stopping further down the hall, but still within view of the guards.

"Don't weep," said Renoldus, "this is my fault. By my actions with Princess Ingrid, I have made enemies. I have incurred the king's offense, and to be honest, I deserve the punishment that is coming to me."

"I will miss you. And I miss Lady Cecile so. My dearest friend—"

Lady Gelen broke down and wept. The death of Cecile had set into motion a series of unfortunate events building to this day's climax. That Renoldus suffered alone was something she hated. She hated Terrin for the snide remarks he would tarnish a conversation with. She especially loathed her husband for feeding information to Leander, painting an unflattering portrait of the man, using broad strokes with embellishments and lies when necessary.

"Maybe exile is what I …" With his lower lip beginning to quiver, he hugged Gelen tightly and she returned the same.

"I hope you do not live alone for the rest of your days."

"Perhaps it is my destiny to be alone and leave no heir."

"Don't say that."

"I fear it's true."

"Don't let the kingdom's betrayal beat you down like a *k'traat dus*. Go live a life for yourself."

They pressed in, then parted, their tearful eyes locking gazes.

"Lady Evelyn told me who killed Cecile," said Renoldus.

"How does she know?" said Gelen.

"She was married to Watkin."

"I knew he was involved."

"He lied to me, although there was nothing I could do about it. He was dying and beating it out of him wasn't an option." Renoldus forced a smile and Gelen returned it with one of her own.

Lady Gelen's striking blue eyes were misty and red, but she took a deep breath and asked the question. "Are you going to tell me?"

Renoldus leaned in and whispered in her ear.

Gelen's lips parted, and her mouth opened ever so slightly. With eyes as wide as a full moon, her countenance took on a hint of confusion. "I'm sorry, Renoldus. I must've misunderstood you."

Again, he whispered in her ear.

Gelen's eyebrows pointed downward, and she shook her head as if encountering a problem too difficult to answer. Sweat formed on the lady's forehead and her skin turned ashen, and confused eyes stared at Renoldus like he was a stranger. "I think I need to sit down."

Renoldus acted swiftly as Gelen's petite body fell sideways into his arms. Sir Sanson ran over to the two and Folkes walked behind, drawing his sword as he did.

"What happened to Lady Gelen?" said Sanson.

"The lady told me she needed to sit," said Renoldus, "and then passed out."

Renoldus removed his cape and eased Gelen down, placing her head on the makeshift pillow. Renoldus and Sanson kneeled next to Gelen and quietly called her name, and the Black tried to wake her by touching her shoulder. Sanson pulled out a flask—

The sword came down with great speed and pierced Lady Gelen's heart before either Renoldus or Sanson could react. Gelen gasped and grabbed for her heart while Folkes lost no time pulling the sword from the lady's torso. He took several even steps backward and pointed the sword at his own heart with hands on the cross guard.

"Stop!" said Sanson. He moved to prevent Folkes from continuing with his deed, but slipped on the bloodstained stone.

Folkes ignored Sanson's plea to stop and placed the tip of his blade over his heart. Sanson scrambled to his feet but in his haste slipped once more, allowing Folkes to continue undeterred, ready to seal his own fate.

Taking one last deep breath, he leaned forward and dropped to his knees with the pommel of his sword firmly inside one of the large cracks in the stone floor. The blade pierced his heart and exited through the back, leaving two lifeless bodies on the unforgiving, frigid stone, drenched in their own blood.

Stunned, Renoldus acted on instinct. He placed his hand on Lady Gelen's body and pressed on her chest to keep the blood from leaving her delicate body. Renoldus watched Lady Gelen pass from this world with tears streaming down his cheeks. The death of her loyal friend was one more piece of fabric torn from the tapestry of Cecile's life and memory.

Renoldus screamed toward the heavens. "Why have you taken her?"

"Sir Renoldus," said Sanson, "you need to leave at once."

Confused and angry, Renoldus looked at Sanson as if he were a stranger. "What?"

"Leave now. You don't want your name attached to this evil. I swear upon the *Witness Books* I will never mention your name. You weren't here."

Renoldus stood and towered over Sanson, who was still on the floor. "How can I trust you?"

"If I've not earned your trust over the years, then nothing I say will change that."

Seeing Lady Gelen bloody and dead brought the memories of Cecile, Sir Jeames and King Tarquin rushing back like the rapids of a free-flowing river after a storm. "Damn you. Damn all of you."

"For the love of the gods, Sir Renoldus," said Sanson, "get out of here before I have to inform the captain of the guard."

Renoldus shot Sanson a glance and walked out the way he had come into the tower and headed straight back to his apartment, where wine and fresh clothes awaited.

Brutrark Vercis decides who lives and dies in this city. Who leads this consuming viper? Or is it like the r'zrta of old with many heads?

CHAPTER 21
BOTTOM OF THE WELL

*I*n the Great Heil, somewhat hidden behind the raised platform and chairs, two dark wood doors opened to the small council room. The room had sparse decorations, and a singular gonfalon with the sigil of House Ingimund adorning the fading flag hung from the ceiling. Six men had gathered around a table with a base of five orcas carved into small stone pillars that were topped by a long rectangular piece of smooth slate.

Opposite the door, two large windows with simple curtains tied open lit the room. In addition, a large metal chandelier with tallow candles provided secondary light. But it also left an unwanted haze hanging over the room from the smoke. Several individual candles on the table produced the last form of light in the room.

The five members were present and seated at the table, a small number for Ashul's size. People widely considered the harbor and shipbuilding enterprise to be the best on the continent. However, Skuti learned from Thorve's father, Eldgrim, the fewer the men, the less likely they were to breed disloyalty amongst themselves, which he found out in the hardest way possible. His own death through a rebellion within his council.

Skuti rose from his chair and eschewed the normal greetings. The narrowed eyes and white knuckles from fingers wrapped hard around the edge of the table signaled the seriousness of the meeting.

"You've had twenty-four hours to think about the alliance I've made on behalf of Ashul with Lord Taylor Denton, Master of the Seas."

The rest isn't important right now. If I tell them about fighting with his men to expand foreign borders and building a castle for him, they will have me condemned by sunrise. If I speak of the Leviathan's existence, they will lock me up in the Irongate Asylum.

Prior to Skuti's revelation, the councilmen already sensed that an alliance had formed. The tea leaves concerning the Pirate Lord and Ashul weren't difficult to read once Skuti returned from dining aboard the *Vendetta*. When Skuti took to the seas with Taylor, people talked, and a low grumble spread throughout Ashul and beyond.

Lord Meldun Thorgils, steward of the castle, was a short man with the complex to accompany the lack of height. His full and straight white beard left only his creased forehead, blue eyes, and large crooked nose to be seen. There was no evidence of gray in his long and thinning blond hair falling down his back with two loose braids woven in, one on each side of his face.

His detail and organizational skills were a credit to the Aeehrldom, but he was a man unafraid to loosen his tongue and, as such, was the first to wade into the pool of discord.

"You've aligned us with a pirate and a whore of the deep. The Aeehrls of the past warned us never to make such an alliance with evil and untrustworthy souls. Yet you've ignored their advice."

"Dead Aeehrls," said Skuti, "will not face the army Jomar is preparing to march against Ashul. He has risen against us and our relations."

"I don't care if the entire continent has risen against us," said Meldun. "You've aligned Ashul with a man claiming to be Master of the Seas with his dark magic whore and those dark-skinned heathens. You have blasphemed our gods and will dishonor our land by doing so."

"Jomar has raised an army of five Aeehrldoms," said Sir Alfarin, the Outsider. "Would you have us bend over as whores do and take it?"

Jorund Fridmund, a large and gregarious man, was not so affable on this occasion. Despite the droopy eyes and a bit of a stutter, Jorund was a smart man and a master of trade by sea and land. He was also aging, and it showed with streaks of white hairs throughout his reddish-brown beard and also in his hair that came to the top of his shoulders. "Better that than to be saved by Netrix and taken to the underworld."

"This is not the time for foolish exaggerations, Jorund," said Alfarin. "Speak your mind plainly."

"I prefer being forced to speak *Anari* and worship the gods of the Acarians rather than using a pirate and his whore to save us."

Skuti felt himself wanting to reach for his axe and split the head of Jorund into two distinct halves. "Then your faith in our gods is as worthless as salt thrown onto a road to be tread upon. I will allow no one to force their gods onto us, and I don't care who I have to align with to prevent it."

People disliked Slode Brodir because he spoke the truth whether or not they wanted to hear it. In addition, he controlled the Aeehrldom's coinage, which made him universally disdained. Slode was a slight man by Flacian standards, but average when measured against other races. He spoke in a dry and droll voice to further the stereotype. "It's too late to convince Aeehrl Skuti to go against what he has already decided in his heart. The temptation of riches and the power of the Ice Throne has corrupted his soul."

The thought of splitting Slode's head with Blood Spiller was finding traction within his mind as well. Skuti felt his legs move and in a moment, he was standing straight up, his arm reaching down to grab his axe. He caught himself before actually splattering blood against the walls and leaving body parts strewn across the room.

Why don't I just do it?

Skuti's inner voice responded. *You still have some modicum of decency left. But if you don't change your course, it will soon disappear, and you will butcher men much like the Serpents.*

Instead of reaching for his axe, Skuti used his hand to point a finger at Slode. "Who are you that knows my soul? The gods search the soul, not man."

Rising out of his chair, Jorund interjected and fired back. "Your legacy will be that of Vott. Just a usurper, an interloper using blood money and devils to accomplish his bid to sit on the Ice Throne."

Alfarin jumped up from his chair, knocking it over. His brown eyes burned with a fierce hostility when they locked onto Jorund's green. "Dare you compare our Aeehrl with Vott? Have you lost your mind, or do you have a death wish?"

"You're not one of us either," said Jorund, "only a bastard who made good by becoming Skuti's friend."

Meldun sprang from his seat and joined the verbal assaults, directing his ire at Alfarin. "Jorund's right. You're the bastard of a pirate who's been in Skuti's ear since you were a boy. It's no wonder you support to ally with a pirate."

Any hope of a reasonable discussion regarding Skuti's alliance was gone, trampled on by personal accusations and spiteful vindictiveness. The room was filling with anger and bitterness, and together they were certain to spark a fire on bridges never to be rebuilt.

"Why do you short-dicked men wait until now to spit your hate at Alfarin?" said Skuti. "Now you whoresons have made it personal."

"Aenta will turn against you," said Meldun, "for bringing those heathens onto our soil and a witch into our waters."

"Slode knows my soul," said Skuti, "and you know the mind and motivation of the goddess of war. I was unaware that the two of you had godly powers. Perhaps we should worship you."

Meldun ignored Skuti's insult and singled out Commander Nasi, who'd stayed seated and silent so far, preferring to listen before offering an opinion. "Lord Nasi, what say you, or are you still waiting to see which way the wind will blow up your arsehole?"

"I'm a pragmatic man—"

"So you say," said Jorund, "but you're a man without a spine and conviction."

"Damn you both," Alfarin said, "let the man speak."

"Make no mistake," said Nasi, "our Aeehrl will win the wars to come with the dark-skinned fighters on Ashul's side. He will sit on the Ice Throne and rest his feet on the bones of those who doubted."

"Men, I've already told you he has decided," said Slode. "Your choice is to stay and keep your mouths shut or leave the Aeehrldom."

Nasi stood and circled the room with his gaze, making sure he made eye contact with each man. "Whom do you want on the Ice Throne? Aeehrl Jomar or Aeehrl Skuti? You're a fool if you side with Jomar."

The conversation paused as the men sensed their decisions approaching. Just as dark clouds gather in the sky before the deep and loud rumbling starts, and they prepare to unleash their rain.

"The Acarians will bring the judgment of the gods to our shores," said Meldun, "when they find out who it was that sunk their ship and stole the Advocate's homage."

"Taylor will destroy their ships," said Skuti, "before they hit the open seas. We will strangle the snake before it can slither here."

"Pirates are untrustworthy," said Jorund. "Even Taylor's

lies have lies. Yet you aligned with him anyway. This is a fool's folly."

"If you keep insulting him," said Slode, "you'll be in the dungeon before the day is out. Decide and move forward."

"I'd rather die," said Jorund, "than live off a pirate's stolen money and watch his witch wreak havoc in Flace."

"I'll say it again, damn you," said Slode. "Say yes or no."

Cheeks flushed, eyes dilated as if he had gone mad, Jorund searched the eyes around the room and, sensing he was not alone in his thoughts, answered first. "I refuse to be involved in any of this. A man who sold his soul to a whore of the darkest, deepest sea forged this alliance. Aeehrl Skuti has brought shame and ruin upon Ashul."

Alfarin turned and nodded to the guards stationed behind Skuti, and the two responded by drawing their swords and moving toward Jorund. Alfarin raised his sword halfway out of its scabbard and Skuti put his hand on the handle of his axe, Blood Spiller.

Jorund raised his hands and shouted at Skuti. "Swords drawn? How is it you treat me as a common criminal?"

"You're more than a common criminal. You've committed high treason," said Skuti.

The guards sheathed their swords when it became clear Jorund wouldn't put up a fight, and each grabbed him by the biceps and led him out through the entrance doors. Two more guards outside would take him the rest of the way down into the belly of the castle.

There were unmarked passageways, circular hallways, and false doors along the way to disorient the prisoner. Once in the dungeon, Jorund, despite his knowledge of the castle, would have no idea where he was at.

As he left, Jorund shouted back at Skuti. "Someday crows will come and gorge on your flesh for what you've done."

Meldun watched as they marched Jorund out and wasted little time in revealing his answer. "As you live by the sword, you will also die by it. May pain and suffering be the bane of your miserable existence. I pray the gods allow your death to be slow and agonizing—"

"Hold your tongue and save your breath," said Skuti.

Two more guards arrived, took Meldun out, repeating what they had done to Jorund. Meldun also descended to the "bottom of the well," as the Castle Marshal and his staff referred to it as. All eyes turned to Slode, who made eye contact with every man before speaking.

"Regarding the treasure Taylor gave to you, I want to assure you, I didn't touch it and have no plans to do so in the future. I will not engage in business transactions involving stolen treasure or coinage. I'll have a clear conscious when I stand before the gods, something you, Skuti Ingimund, will not."

Alfarin picked up Slode by the collar of his finely made coat and then shoved him against the doors, leaving the Master of Coin in a heap on the stone floor.

"You hypocrite," said Alfarin with spittle flying out of his mouth and onto Slode. "How much have you stolen from the treasury each year?"

The loud crash of Slode's body against the doors caused one guard outside to throw the doors open.

"Get this whoreson out of my sight," said Alfarin. "He turns my stomach over."

Two guards grabbed Slode's semiconscious body and dragged him from near the doors and dropped him on the cold, hard floor between the High Chair and the council room. He too would soon find himself on the foreboding walk deep into the bottom of the well.

Skuti looked at Nasi and raised an eyebrow.

Nasi spoke with sharp eyes and a mind unclouded by old ways and bitter reluctance to embrace a new way of thinking. "The Advocate rising in the west has changed warfare. Without an alliance, no kingdom nor country stops the Acarians when they come knocking at the door."

"And Taylor as the ally?" said Skuti.

"Taylor is an enigma," said Nasi. "He steps onto the stage, without a past, and with a woman of extraordinary power. Even you, who spent time on the ship, know little about them."

Nasi, if you only knew how powerful she is. The Leviathan does as she commands, and it is the most frightening thing you'll ever see. Yet the iron balls belched out of fiery brass tubes elicit their own kind of fear.

"These things you say are true," said Skuti, "but are you loyal to me?"

Nasi moved around the table over to Skuti where he bent the knee in a show of respect and humility before the Aeehrl.

"Stand up, my friend," said Skuti. "When the books of this generation are complete, they will write many things about your ability to navigate the seas and what it takes to govern a navy," said Skuti.

"Thank you, my Aeehrl," said Nasi.

Alfarin followed suit, made his way to Skuti, and kneeled before the Aeehrl.

"And you, Sir Alfarin?" said Skuti.

"I've always stood by you," said Alfarin, "and I will continue to do so no matter who or what stands before us."

"Stand, my friend," said Skuti. "The books that come after us will also contain the story of your bravery, fighting skills, and fierceness."

"Thank you, my Aeehrl," said Alfarin.

In the castle's belly, three former council members locked in a singular cell bemoaned their fate and cursed Skuti for aligning with Taylor and Calena. Although the three came from divergent backgrounds, they shared one thing in common; death by being horse-drawn, hanged, and quartered.

The executioners tied Jorund, Meldun, and Slode to

horses and dragged them to the gallows. They then hung their bruised and beaten bodies until just before death and then cut them down. The executioners spared them disembowelment but quartered their bodies by tying each of their limbs to horses and sending them off in opposite directions, tearing them apart.

Skuti sent twelve limbs to villages outside the castle walls as evidence that he would not tolerate opposition. Alfarin assigned his guards to finish the job by taking the head of each man and jamming it into a stake. The guards placed the heads on a pike along the castle's walls, each head looking in a different direction, as a warning to those contemplating turning against the Aeehrl.

The dire change of one Aeehrl Skuti Ingimund had officially begun.

CHAPTER 22
ROAD TO NOWHERE

*T*he details surrounding the murder of Lady Gelen by Sir Folkes and his subsequent suicide begat rumors so fierce they threatened to cause riots in the streets. People knew Gelen for her gentle spirit and her selfless work with the poor in Crence. The killing of such a woman produced cries of mourning amongst the poor and fanned the flames of intrigue amongst the politically connected.

Renoldus pulled Ingrid's retinue together and drove them hard out of Chirlingstone Castle as if a fire were burning in the keep. The princess's departure, with no fanfare, only served to further poison the well of public discourse with rumor and conjecture. King Leander was furious that Renoldus left the kingdom under the cover of night. However, he took solace in the fact that he had solved two problems. It was time to move on to more important matters.

Evelyn kept her mouth shut about the incident with Renoldus and revealed nothing to Leander. Not because she feared Princess Ingrid, but because she was the only one who knew the truth about the so-called accidents. Knowledge was power, and she intended to keep hers.

Sir Terrin, now Lord of the Brüeland Army, returned

from military training exercises for his wife's funeral. Rich and poor alike filled the Chapel of Ancestors to mourn Lady Gelen. Sir Terrin sat in the front row with his daughter of ten on the left and his son of five to his right. He stared straight ahead with an empty look on his face. Sir Terrin left the castle soon after the burial and headed back to his men.

~

THE WEEKLONG JOURNEY to the Blaen River was uneventful and went to plan. The retinue traveled by day, and noblemen hosted them in their castles at night. Once at Edgewater Landing at Brüeland's far western border, the entourage boarded flat-bottomed boats and prepared to travel north.

There was no way Renoldus was going to keep himself out of Ingrid's clutches in a confined space. With Renoldus, no place was off-limits to Ingrid. No matter the time or situation, when the princess found Renoldus, she would either speak ill of Prince Rycardus or drag Renoldus to her cabin to be "satisfied," as she called it. Sometimes, simultaneously.

After Princess Ingrid arrived at a large landing on the river, the retinue boarded a different set of ships and set sail across the Pusag Sea for two days before reaching the border of Aflana. Still, it took them five days to travel on what people claimed was a good road to reach Wolfden and Wolf's Keep, where King Rycharde and his son Rycardus resided. Three days into the ground portion of their trip, they traveled along a dirt road just large enough to accommodate the retinue through the forest as they made their way toward Wolfden.

The entourage was now only tired and weary of the journey. Ingrid's temper tantrums had grown in frequency and intensity the closer she came to the castle, which would be her new home.

Inside of Ingrid's white and gold coach, her new lady, Madelina of House Edlai, endured Ingrid's outbursts, suffering through blame, scorn, and sarcastic comparisons to Lady Evelyn. Despite Madelina's best efforts to please the princess, nothing seemed to soothe her except for when the conversation turned to Renoldus.

Still, there were instances when Ingrid lamented her eventual separation from the Black of Brüeland, and invariably, this talk would end in a flood of tears. Declarations of her love and eventual reunion with Renoldus replaced the tears, and the cycle would begin anew.

Renoldus, riding at the front of the retinue, caught sight of Josson, his scout and spy, galloping his horse across a large clearing the entourage was on the verge of crossing. Josson was an eager young man who excelled in blending into the scenery and had an innate ability to find reliable sources of information. He also possessed unique ways of extracting information even Watkin would've found resourceful.

Josson approached Renoldus with sweat-soaked hair and a worried and wary face. It was the look of a man who had seen much more than he bargained for. "Sir Renoldus."

"Speak," said Renoldus.

"It's the Acarians, my lord. They ambushed our camp and supply wagons."

"Any survivors?"

"None, my lord."

Renoldus winced and gazed upward, where Vesceron was approaching its zenith. He spoke without looking toward Josson. "They're a long way from home. I suppose it wasn't a random attack."

"It was not. They were looking for Princess Ingrid, my lord."

"Are they headed here?"

"Yes."

"How much time do we have?"

"Very little. Their unit is split, and the other half is in the woods across the field."

"How many?" said Renoldus.

"They outnumber us nearly ten to one, my lord," said Josson.

"That's all? If it were twenty to one, I might be concerned."

Josson smiled but wasn't sure if Renoldus was serious or not. Having heard the stories, the young man hoped to witness the great knight's magic with *Blackout* at least once.

"We're in trouble," said Renoldus. "I don't have enough knights and the Princess Guard isn't up for this type of fighting. I will have to make tough decisions if the fight gets away from us. Be prepared to move in a hurry."

"It shall be as you say, Lord Commander."

Renoldus started the calculations of how badly they were outnumbered. "Horses?"

"Forty," said Josson, "maybe more. Most are foot soldiers."

"Archers?"

"Few."

"What else, Josson?"

"They intend to kill us all, even if we surrender the princess."

The clearing was at its narrowest along the pot-marked road approaching the last forest the caravan would pass through. Soldiers who built the road carved it through the edge of the trees and away from the deepest part of the forest. Small bands of Yelloweyes had long terrorized travelers making their way through the deeper part of the forest, with robberies, kidnapping, and murder.

Despite its being the longest route to Wolfden, it was not worth the risk of saving time and cutting through an area where danger not only lurked, but thrived. Once the retinue cleared the woods, smooth roads across gentle rolling hills awaited the caravan as it neared the end of its trek north to Wolfden and Andairn Castle.

"Did you catch a name?" said Renoldus.

"I overheard two men talking about a Sir Balan," said Josson.

Why would King Jamettus send him?

A pleasant breeze swayed the majestic trees surrounding the clearing. The remains of a tavern consumed by fire a year ago sat at the far end of the field, furthest from the road. The charred remains were silent, unable to tell the tale of what had caused the once-busy Wolf's Head to burn to the ground in the middle of the night.

"What is my Lord's command?" said Josson.

"Sit tight for the moment," said Renoldus. "I need to check on the princess."

Someone with intimate knowledge of this passage sold us out. The Acarians caught us at the exact spot on the route where the retinue would have to slow. They also knew we were traveling with supplies and materials to make camp. Although this sounds like a plot hatched by Brutrark Vercis, it seems on too grand a scale and not subtle enough.

Renoldus trotted his horse down to Ingrid's carriage and peered inside. The princess sat with her arms folded under her breasts, rocking back and forth against the back of the carriage. Madelina, the noblewoman, was across from Ingrid with her brown eyes fixed on her charge.

"Princess Ingrid," said Renoldus, "how are you holding out?"

"I'm not," said Ingrid. "How can I be? I'm going to be kidnapped."

"You will not be ransomed," said Renoldus. "Sit tight. You and Lady Madelina will be fine."

"Then why did we stop?"

"That's for me to worry about."

"Sir Renoldus, she's been like this all day," said Madelina.

"Shut it, Lady Madelina," said Ingrid. "What do you know about having the hero of our kingdom between your legs?"

For the love of the gods and goddesses.

"Princess Ingrid," said Renoldus, "please mind your decorum."

"As if you're Sir Decorum," said Ingrid. " 'Oh my god, Ingrid, take my seed deep inside you.' "

"Ingrid, you're out of line."

"That's Princess Ingrid to you."

Renoldus trotted his horse toward the front of the retinue, where Josson was waiting for him. Josson was shifting in his saddle as if he needed to piss. Renoldus turned his head and took one last look at Ingrid's coach and then turned his attention to Josson.

"My Lord," said Josson, "there's an Acarian knight, tall in the saddle, and he sits in the middle of the meadow under a white flag."

"It's the Butcher," said Renoldus. "Find some white cloth and let's go meet the bastard."

"Right away, my lord."

I need to get the princess out of here. She's going to demand I go with her, but I can't, and I won't. I've allowed her to enslave me via my bedchamber for too long.

Renoldus turned Inferno and trotted back to the retinue and gathered his leaders to discuss strategy to fend off the interlopers on the opposite side. The session was brief for the small set of fighters and knights whom Renoldus had recruited. They faced long odds, and the opposition outnumbered them badly.

"The Acarians have attacked the wagons we sent ahead," said Renoldus, "and slaughtered those with them. They've come here to capture the princess and kill the rest of us."

"May it never be," said Gyrard the Keen, a tall, solidly built man. "I'll die here before I allow this to happen."

The other knights chipped in their approval until Renoldus raised his hand. "I understand how you feel, but I'm not sacrificing lives today. We're badly outnumbered, and we can move the life we're protecting from here."

Renoldus looked toward Hendry, his former squire, now known as knight Hendry the Gray. His maturity was unmatched for his age, and many expected him to inherit *Blackout* and become the next knight to be known as the Black of Brüeland.

He's the only one I trust with this mission.

"I'm sending the princess on horseback to Wolfden. Sir Hendry, you'll accompany her."

"Yes, my lord," said Hendry.

"Get Ingrid's horse. I'm sending the two of you out of harm's way."

"As you have commanded."

"We'll delay them as much as possible," Renoldus said. "I'm going to meet the Butcher in the meadow and listen to what lies he has prepared for us."

"I should've known that rat's dick was involved in this mess," said Gyrard.

Renoldus turned to Hendry. "Listen carefully. Do you remember the fork in the road about three miles back?"

"I do, my lord."

"Veer left at the fork. The path is too narrow for our caravan, but horseback riders can still pass through. When you get to Wolfden, head straight to the castle and explain to King Andairn what happened today."

"What of Princess Ingrid? You know she's not keen on going anywhere near there."

"I'm hoping she'll opt for safety given the alternative. If she bolts, relay it to the king and he can send out his own men to chase her down."

"And you, my lord?"

Renoldus allowed a sly grin to form on his face. "Tell King Andairn my destruction of Sir Balan has delayed me for a moment, but I will soon follow."

Sir Balan, the Butcher of the Forest, sat in the middle of the clearing and waited for Renoldus. His herald carried a spear with the pennon of Acaria, a rendering of the heraldic firebird (often referred to as a phoenix) and a small white flag tied underneath.

Balan sat straight in the saddle of his black warhorse, an animal so powerful and indomitable, no one dared come near him. He aptly named his destrier Beast, and it had no equal across the continent. At twenty-four hands, the Beast had the strength and stamina to wear his own horse armor and carry both Balan and his armor into battle, while still using his legs and teeth as weapons.

Josson carried a wood pole with Brüeland's pennon of a burgundy field with a black bestiary of a raised stallion posed for battle atop a golden crown. Underneath was tied the piece of white cloth Renoldus asked for. He and Josson reached the middle of the field and met the sneering Balan.

The Butcher's full, straight blond hair flowed down to the middle of his chest. In the crook of his muscular arms, he held his golden helm with thick ram's horns coming from the top and curling to about ear level. The perpetual frown on his chiseled face contributed to his fierce reputation.

Balan built his notoriety and fame by practicing mayhem and destruction across the Western Continent. Kingdoms, unwilling to bend the knee and swear fealty to the Zealot in the Tower, found King Jamettus Betan II and his army, along with Balan, at their door.

"Scared?" asked Balan. "I thought you weren't coming out to play."

"What do you want?" said Renoldus. Josson was at his side, itching to spill the blood of the herald in front of him.

Balan eyed the large bag hanging off the saddle of his herald's horse. His suddenly giddy demeanor belied a man who might rather kill you than look at you. "Know what's in the sack?"

The Black of Brüeland rolled his eyes at Balan with a droll voice of a man knowing the answer to a near-rhetorical question. "The body of one of my best scouts butchered into pieces."

With near glee, the herald opened the bag and dumped the contents— a man's body—onto the damp soil beneath them. Flies buzzed off the various body parts into the open air and the stench came in waves so awful it rose to the nostrils of the gods and goddesses for their displeasure. Josson turned his head and coughed but refused to vomit and instead focused his eyes on the herald and flipped the clasp on his sheath open.

"And?" said Renoldus.

"That's how you're going to end up," said Balan. "Cut up in a potato sack."

"What's the ransom for the princess?"

Balan's demeanor returned to his Butcher face, and he scoffed at Renoldus. "I wouldn't be here if there was a ransom."

No, you wouldn't; you're too stupid to understand the concept.

"Do you want to be the one to start the war between our kingdoms?" said Renoldus.

"If you don't want to start a war," said Balan, "then surrender and give us the princess."

Renoldus tapped his index finger against *Blackout's* pommel and locked eyes with the steely blue eyes of the Butcher. Balan broke his gaze and shifted it down toward Renoldus's waist.

"Leave the sword in the scabbard," said Balan. "It causes me no fear."

Your voice says one thing, but your eyes another.

"Move aside and let us pass," said Renoldus. "This alliance holds little significance for the Advocate."

"There will be no alliances between kingdoms," said Balan.

"Then there is nothing to talk about. You'll have to take up arms if you want the princess."

"Arms, it'll be you arrogant prick."

Both parties turned and trotted their horses back to their respective sides. The Butcher was furious, shouting profanities into the air as Renoldus made his way back to the retinue with Josson.

Something about this situation lacks sense. Why send the Butcher here? Is he here to carry out the execution I deserved in Crence that no one had the balls to order or perform?

Renoldus gave the last orders to his head of the Princess Guard and worked his way back to Ingrid's carriage. Tension was mounting as evidenced by the solemn faces and lack of eye contact by the princess's guards and the fighting men Renoldus had enlisted to accompany the retinue.

Men were moving hastily and with purpose, as Balan's fighters pressed the attack, except for Heward of the Rox, the trusted driver of King Leander and his family. He sat on the driver's bench, eyes as big as saucers, reins resting in his hands.

Renoldus caught Heward at the last minute, idle on the bench. "Heward, Heward of the Rox," said Renoldus.

Damn his soul. He's frozen and doesn't know what to do.

Heward was approaching his fifty-second birthday. His eyesight was becoming worse, and his body hurt, but of greater importance was his mind. He was forgetful and remembered little about the details, and his stories often ended without finishing. Knowing his job was at risk, he did his best to hide his failings, but those close to him, including Princess Ingrid and Renoldus, knew the end was coming.

Why did I give him the reins?

"Let's go," said Renoldus, "get the horses moving, Heward. Go!"

Life slowed to a crawl. The sound was awful; a splat, as if an arrow pierced a large melon, but the singular projectile landed in the middle of Heward's balding forehead. His head tilted back, yet his body remained in the same position for a moment as the reins slipped out of his dead hands.

Renoldus leaped onto the carriage bench, using the top of the twelve spoked wheels to propel himself. The commotion spooked the two white horses pulling the carriage, causing them to bolt forward. Renoldus pulled Heward from the bench and pushed him to the ground in a crumpled heap.

Ingrid saw Heward's twisted body on the dirt and gasped at the sight and covered her mouth. Tears escaped her eyes as Madelina slid down the bench, extending her head out of the window for a glimpse.

Renoldus shouted back at Ingrid and Madelina as arrows whizzed by. "Keep your heads inside the carriage!"

It was too late for Madelina, whose head stayed outside the carriage for a moment too long. One arrow intended for the Princess Guard surrounding the coach struck her in the eye and entered her brain before stopping with the arrowhead and part of the shaft sticking out of the back of her head.

Princess Ingrid screamed as loud as she could. "No!"

Madelina's lower body was inside the carriage, and her limp upper body hung out of the window cutout. Ingrid recoiled at the body as she slid on the bench away from the dead woman.

Renoldus grabbed the reins, settled the horses, and turned the carriage one hundred and eighty degrees, so the back end faced the direction of the arrows. At Ingrid's scream, Renoldus jumped from the bench and pulled the doors open.

"Get out and stay down!" said Renoldus. "Use the door as a shield."

Ingrid, dressed in her peasant clothes (as dubbed by those who mocked her), hopped down and crouched behind the door. "Renoldus, those bastards killed my lady."

Renoldus entered the carriage and pulled the top half of

Madelina's body back inside. "For the love of the gods. At least it was quick."

"That's all you can say?"

"I'm sending you with Hendry out of here."

"Hendry?"

"See your horse? Get on it."

"No. You're going with me."

The sound of steel clashing and men shouting was getting closer.

"Ingrid," said Renoldus, "you're going with Hendry."

"No!" said Ingrid. "You're supposed to protect me."

"I am. If you stay, they will either kill you or take you."

"Leave this and go with me."

"I can't and you know it."

"You have to. I have your child inside me."

"Ingrid, this is not the time for lies."

Hendry stared at the two and licked his dry lips as Acarians soldiers moved forward with more shouts.

"Sir Renoldus," said Hendry, "our defense is pulling back."

"I'm not lying, you bastard!" said Ingrid. "What do you think happened to all your seed?"

"Ingrid," said Renoldus, "mount the horse and depart."

"No. I'm not going without you."

"If you're truly with child, then you're getting on that damned horse."

Ingrid's lips quivered and tears ran down each cheek.

"Promise you'll come to me later," she said, "and be a father to our child."

"Promised. Now go."

The princess wiped away her tears and hopped aboard her horse, Red, a smooth-gaited palfrey, and settled into her saddle. She was an experienced rider, but this sprint to Andairn Castle would test all of her skills.

"Are you ready, princess?" said Hendry.

"Dispense with the talk," said Ingrid. "Just ride."

Hendry mounted his horse and gave Renoldus one last look. "Kill the bastard."

Hendry's horse sped off back the way the retinue had traveled, with Ingrid right behind him. They hurried to the fork and took a left turn as directed. They would ride until dusk and find an inn with beds available. When they awoke, the two would need to reach Wolfden by the time the moon had put the sun underneath its feet.

Renoldus watched the two ride away for a moment before he mounted Inferno. As he headed toward the battlefield, Josson approached on horseback.

"My lord, Balan is in the meadow."

CHAPTER 23
THE COMING ONE

*R*ycardus jerked his arm away from Reyna and was on top of Halec with his left forearm on the beast's neck. Although the blow to the head had caused Halec to lose consciousness for a few moments, he awoke in time to play possum long enough for his brain to shake the cobwebs out of his head.

"Die, bastard," said Rycardus.

Time slowed to a crawl as Rycardus brought down his arm with all the force he could muster. His mind concluded that he was going to kill Halec and then turn his wrath against Reyna, but in the blink of an eye, he realized all was not quite what it seemed.

Halec opened his eyes.

Halec stopped Rycardus's dagger six inches from his chest with his muscular hand rising to grab Rycardus by the wrist. The claws on his free hand pierced the prince's shoulder and the revenge-driven Halec pulled his nails, sharp as any blade, down his arm, tearing muscle, ligaments, and tendons from the bone and rendering the arm useless.

Rycardus screamed in agony, a high-pitched wail, and he

tried to pull his body away from Halec with what strength he had left, but the beast held firm to his arm.

"Let go of my arm," said Rycardus. "Please, I'm begging you, show some mercy."

Halec's sadistic laughter was his answer to mercy, and it fueled Rycardus's adrenaline. Instinct took over, and with his free hand, he punched at the beast's face. The blows thrown resembled those of a child taking swings at an adult. Halec blocked or absorbed them, to his amusement, and signaled that the fight was over, and the prince was at the mercy of the beast.

"Get up! Go!"

Rycardus looked up into the dark sky. Or perhaps it was a dream. He felt beaten and noticed the poison in his arm spreading. Halec releasing his arm was only a vague feeling.

"Get up," screamed Reyna into his ear, "go before it's too late."

With vocal cords raw from screaming, Rycardus forced the words out of his mouth, with little understanding of where he was or what he was saying. "Help me."

Reyna reached for his hand but pulled hers back instead. "Dear gods."

Strange visions of a white wolf seated on a grand throne of gold danced through his mind, as did memories, starting when he was a child. Amid it, he briefly moaned. "It must be bad."

Reyna nodded her head but looked away.

Rycardus perked up at the sound of Halec's growls and curses aimed at Reyna for throwing dirt in his face. While he vainly attempted to get the dirt out of his eyes, Reyna turned her attention back to Rycardus.

"Get up," said Reyna. "Come on."

Renoldus stood while Reyna lifted from behind. It seemed he would inevitably fall back down.

I'm dead or dreaming.

"Run, love," she said, "or he's going to kill you."

She let go, and he stumbled off with his ravaged arm down at his side, dripping blood as he staggered toward a clearing nestled in the birch trees by sheer luck. He didn't notice, but his senses transformed, such that he smelled not only the birch but also the creatures in and around the clearing.

Pain racked his body, yet he continued to live and move, a remarkable achievement given the poison in his body and the loss of blood. As his ability to pick up scents increased, so did his hearing. He heard a bark and a whimper behind him, but he didn't see Reyna jump on the back of Halec.

Rycardus walked a few more feet before his wounds got the better of him and he collapsed. Passing in and out of consciousness, mumbling disjointed words and crying out in pain, he was unaware of his surroundings or what was happening behind him.

Reyna hit the ground with a thud next to him and the sound of her body bouncing off the ground caused Rycardus to stir and look in her direction. Still suffering amidst searing misery, hallucinating, and mumbling incoherent words, he did not know it was Reyna who lay a few feet from him. She attempted to edge her way toward him but stopped out of fear, as the howl from Halec, followed by snarls, barks, and curses, meant more agony was on the way.

What is this place? Please make the burning stop ... oh, god, my stomach.

Rycardus shook as if tossed naked into the middle of a blizzard. He blinked his eyes and stared into the sky. The deep claw marks running down his arms and the venom in them spread across his chest, and his heart pumped the tainted blood throughout his body and set it ablaze. He puked a yellowish liquid onto the ground and passed out.

If there are gods, I beg you to make it stop. If you do, I swear I'll go back to my father and never leave. He will have me as a servant in his household. I swear I will shovel shit in the stables and be happy with it. I'll do whatever my father wants, even if it means marrying the ugliest woman in the kingdom. Nothing could be worse than this.

The tormenting sensations maneuvered into his head, blinding his vision, and spread throughout his insides. Another vision came. This one was set deep in the bowels of the castle, and the healer had strapped him to an old wood table.

"What are you doing?" said Rycardus.

"Replacing your blood," said the healer.

"Why?"

"It will be good for you."

"You boiled it. It's going to burn me to death."

"Open your mouth …"

He opened his mouth to scream, but nothing came out. The strength of Halec's poison was a hundred times greater than Reyna's, and there was enough of the vile bane in Rycardus to severely wound him, if not outright kill him.

I'm going to die. There are no gods nor goddesses, and if there are, they don't give a shit about me.

Reyna inched her way close enough to whisper in his ear, "Rycardus, please don't leave me. I love you. I swear, no more lies."

Rycardus turned his face toward her with blank eyes, neither alive nor dead. She used her claws to push the hair out of his eyes and stroke his face as if that were a comfort to him.

Halec put his boot into her belly and sent Reyna sprawling several feet from Rycardus. "Stay away, whore. I'll deal with you next."

Halec kneeled and the grotesque smell of his rancid breath floated into the air and into Rycardus's nose, and added insult to injury. It was bad enough to cause the best of men to vomit. The beast took one set of claws and ripped open Rycardus's tunic and chest with a hard slash. The prince's body spasmed and jerked, and the beast rose and stood over him.

Halec heard the sounds of crackling sticks and pounding hooves and turned to face Rycharde and his horse, Meeko, ride into the clearing. Rycardus, Reyna, and Halec had traveled in a near circle and didn't realize it left them closer to the castle than they knew.

Rycharde dismounted and headed straight for Halec, with *Heartstriker* drawn. He glanced at Rycardus before climbing down from his horse, and it was evident that his son was mortally wounded. Having witnessed many men perish in war, he recognized the appearance and scent of their imminent departure from this world.

Rycharde strode toward Halec, trained his steely gray eyes on the beast, and walked him down as if he were toothless and without claws or weapons. "You're going to meet *Heartstriker*, as did your father."

Halec tried to laugh but coughed up blood. "Doesn't matter. You'll have to live with the fact that I killed the heir."

"Your piss-yellow eyes say it matters. Men, wolves, all the same. No one wants to die. And yours is going to be painful."

Halec became incensed at the flippant threat and a lifetime of hatred spewed out of his heart. "You humans know nothing about pain. From the very first Andairn till now, pain is all we know. Fucking bastards, all of you, for persecuting us and driving us deeper and deeper into the forest."

Rycharde lined up Halec for the kill, and then stopped and shot him a curious look. "What in the name of the gods happened to you? One eye, half a nose, scratches all over. Don't tell me the little whore over there did that to you."

Halec responded as Rycharde expected. These fearless fighters of the forest, incredibly strong and vicious, forever chained themselves to their rage and the violence it produced. And because of it, they were entirely predictable. Provoked to anger, they attacked without considering the consequence of such a decision.

Halec charged Rycharde with snarls and growls as the king

knew he would. Halec was too proud to be laughed at, especially because of Reyna. Hobbled by his injuries and worn down by a night he did not foresee, he took the few steps needed for momentum and leaped at Rycharde with his underbelly exposed.

As soon as Halec left the ground, Rycharde stepped up and let his arms go free, swinging *Heartstriker* flat, and the sharp edge of the Black blade caught the beast just below the ribs, sending him crashing to the ground. The blow landed with precision, and the power and sharpness of the black blade almost cut Halec in half.

"This is for every one of you fucking yelloweyed bastards," said Rycharde.

The king raised *Heartstriker* above his head and with every ounce of his rage-driven strength drove the black blade through Halec's head and into the soil beneath him with an ugly splat.

Although the damage was done and the momentum of what was started was too late to be stopped, Rycardus remained oblivious to the gruesome end of Halec. In all of this, Rycardus felt something odd within his body, an awareness in the agony that he was reaching the bottom of his descent into oblivion.

Someone, please. Stop it. Make it go away. Oh, god, now I can't see nor hear. My disobedience to my parents and belief in Reyna's lies have sent me to a place of suffering.

"You're not dying," said a deep, dark voice in his head. "You're receiving a new body to match what you've become."

What?

Instead of running, Reyna watched the demise of Halec in all of its gory detail amidst her desire to see him suffer and die. Rycharde turned and headed for her with wide and wild eyes that were a tempest for his gray orbs.

"King Rycharde," she said, "please have mercy on me. I

swear I will sit in a dungeon and think about what I did for the rest of my days."

"Don't say another word to me," said Rycharde, "just be quiet and die."

"I loved your son. With all my heart."

Reyna's yellow eyes were no longer filled with desire and lies and whatever else was in her conniving heart. Instead, they were full of fear and expectation, a reckoning to account for her life and all she had done.

She scooched backward like a crab. With adrenaline flowing, she flipped over and got up to run but fell down, unable to get traction with muscles too rubbery from her fight with Halec. She attempted to push off the ground once more, but strangely toppled leftward, landing on her face.

"No!" she cried out into the night.

The swift blade of *Heartstriker* had cut off her left arm at the shoulder. She stared at the arm for a moment as if it was something she didn't recognize until the pointed end of the blade entered her ribs with a loud crackling sound below the heart and pinned her to the ground.

"You won't be remembered," said Rycharde. "Your life was a mist and now it's gone without a trace. Wherever you find yourself in the netherworld, tell them more will follow."

Reyna began the transformation back to her human body postmortem as Rycharde pulled his sword from her body. He sliced her abdomen open and found what he expected. A fetus was growing inside of Reyna, no doubt Rycardus's child.

"Thank the gods," he said, relieved the baby was never born. "It can now find comfort in the heavens instead of being born a Yelloweye."

All was quiet as the king approached the listless body of his son. Rycardus's body lay in a puddle of his own fluids, arms around his body as if he was hugging himself.

He stared down at his son with bloodshot eyes. "This wasn't necessary, son," he said. "Without Reyna and her lies, you wouldn't be lying in a puddle of your own blood. But now she lies dead, and your child was in her womb."

Rycharde walked away, shaking his head. He headed over to Reyna's body, dragged it back, and dumped it on top of Halec's. He motioned to his guards, who stayed back on his command. Rycharde was determined to kill the two responsible for his son's undoing alone and on his terms.

"Burn the bodies," said Rycharde.

"It shall be as you say," said Evrardin.

"When you're finished, check the area for others. I don't want any revenge killers nearby whilst we get my son's body back to the castle."

"As you have commanded, my king."

The unforgettable sound of Rycardus's skin surrendering to the werewolf within him would stay with Rycharde forever. Like the sound of an old cloth being ripped in half, the awful tearing of human flesh echoed one-hundred fold. The splitting of flesh was a fiendish thing to imagine, much less understand or visualize.

Rycardus screamed as loud as his vocal cords would stretch as soon as he felt a pulling sensation down the center of his body. The feeling turned to wicked, brutal pain in seconds, and every ounce of his flesh felt the torture caused by the emerging body underneath his skin.

Rycharde turned his attention back to Rycardus at the sound of tearing flesh and the scream of agony from his son that followed. "No, please, for the god's sake."

After the one cry of insufferable pain, Rycardus was quiet and not breathing. The emerged werewolf had thick, long hair from the neck down to just below the chest and mid-back in an upside-down triangle. Thin white hair covered the rest of his body, with most of it soaked in blood.

The sound of air broke the silence as it rushed into the lungs of Rycardus. He gasped, took in a second large breath, and slowly released it. His breathing was shallow, faster, and it would take some getting used to. But he kept at it, retraining his lungs on what it would take to do the most basic of all things—breathe.

Rycardus gradually came to life. Newfound claws picked off small bits and pieces of skin around his nose and eyes. Once enough of the skin was plucked, Rycardus blinked open his eyes to a different world. Even in the dark of night, nothing was beyond his vision.

Rycardus's eyes were the color of the seas in the faraway tropical places. Spectacularly blue, they gazed upon a world of both age and novelty. Most strikingly, they were intelligent, knowing, confident, piercing, angry; and it was true, not a hint of yellow was in them.

"No, please no," said Rycharde. "The gods of our forefathers have forsaken me."

Triangular ears peaked out from the straight white hair framing Rycardus's face, a close enough incarnation for those that knew him to see his human characteristics. But the werewolf's face was one of a more pronounced forehead, a smallish snout with nostrils flared out, and dagger-sharp canines protruding from his mouth.

I have been reborn.

Rycardus stood with groans and unfolded his body. Bones cracked and popped into place, and when he finished, the newly born Grayclaw was taller than his father by a good measure. His legs weren't stable, but he wasn't a newborn foal either.

"What's the matter, Father?" said Rycardus. "You must've known this day was coming since the night of the attack."

"True," said Rycharde, "but you hope until the bitter end."

"The end is here, Father. Is it as bitter as scarlet's berry?"

"Worse."

The son and father stood facing each other at a short but safe distance. Rycardus stared down at his father with satisfaction. Glaring down, feeling strength and youth on his side felt good.

The sword captivated Rycardus as never before. The history and mystery of the black swords had long fascinated the boy, and now the new creation felt an innate lust for *Heartstriker*. But with his transformation came a dimming of his recollections about the sword. It was as if a fire had scorched his memory, leaving only charred remainders of what once was.

I know the dammed Black sword has rules, but why can't I remember them? There's something about holding one if it doesn't belong to you. Shit. What happened to the memories I need to know?

Shaking off his thoughts, Rycardus put the blame for his presumed evil at the feet of his father and laughed. "You made a critical mistake in not killing me, although I appreciate it."

"Only a monster kills a firstborn son," said Rycharde, "and I was not about to become one."

"Instead, you allowed one to rise up in your own castle."

"You had your choices. That you're a monster is just as much your fault as it is mine."

Rycardus was feeling himself and smirked at his father. "What choices did I have? My choices ended when I was four years old."

Tightened lips marked the facial cues on Rycharde's face. The speed at which he spoke suggested he was on the defensive. He pointed at the two dead bodies nearby. "You act as if Delinda's attack ended your ability to make choices. Reyna was your choice because you enjoyed banging her above all else. Where her legs met was the idol you worshipped."

Anger directed toward his father was nothing new for Rycardus, but this rising tide of resentment was far different from before. Whatever this was, he had no control over it. It was a rage so strong he realized there was enough hate within his body to kill. Worse, he found satisfaction in thinking about it, even sensing the pleasure of killing.

Rycardus growled and bared his fangs. "Good for you. She's dead, and you avenged Raiimond's death. Is this what you're counting as victories now?"

Rycharde seized on the opportunity and went after his son's weakness. "You're no different from those who came before you and failed. You can't control your anger."

I know what you're trying to do. Don't mistake me for a fool.

The battle inside of Rycardus raged between anger and calm. "In your eyes, I'm a failure. Why should this be any different?"

"I never said you were a failure."

Deep-throated growls arose from Rycardus's chest, and he snapped his words at Rycharde. "You didn't have to say it. It was in your eyes, your tone, your actions."

"Your only failure was Reyna, and it cost you everything."

Rycardus called down curses from the heavens, and bloodlust flooded his eyes. "I swear to Trynt if I hear her name roll off your tongue one more time, I'll rip your lungs out."

The menace and danger in his countenance caused Rycharde to pull *Heartstriker* from its sheath.

"Give me the sword," said Rycardus, "and I won't kill you later."

"You've mastered empty threats too," said Rycharde.

Rycardus was the first to hear singular hooves heading toward them. He sniffed the air and placed the scent on one of the royal horses.

It must be mother. Certainly not my brother at this hour.

As the hooves grew louder, Rycharde turned his head toward the sounds, which stopped a short distance away.

"Rycharde, Rycardus," said Lady Sela, "where are you?"

With urgency in his voice, Rycharde turned to Rycardus. "Go. Don't allow your mother to see you like this."

"This is your last chance to kill me."

"Shut up and listen. If you have any remaining love for your mother, depart. Let her last memory of you be that of a son, not what you've become."

"At least Mother loved me for who I was."

"Yes, she did. And now look at you."

Rycardus gave the eye of evil to his father, but before walking away, he made a simple statement. "We will meet again."

Rycharde slammed *Heartstriker* into its hardened leather sheath as Sela approached. "I'm not hard to find."

Rycardus the Grayclaw cut an imposing figure at six and a half feet tall and well over two hundred and fifty pounds, and all of it muscle. He walked with some speed and hid amongst the birch trees and forest shrubbery, out of sight but close enough to hear his mother and father with new, powerful ears.

"Where's our son?" said Sela.

"He's gone," said Rycharde.

"Gone or dead?"

"Gone."

"Did he—"

"Yes."

The guards nearby spoke in hushed voices but not loud enough for Rycardus to pick up. Still hiding, he hoped to hear words, phrases, anything for him to justify his newly gained rage.

"I see you put the sword to Reyna," said Sela.

"With all the rage I could collect," said Rycharde. "Yet, it left me feeling empty, and I received no joy from it."

"If only I could bring her back from the dead, so I could kill her myself."

"I've been a coward. I allowed this evil to escape the castle."

"Don't say that. There were at least four times the pieces were in place, and I talked you out of it. In our god's name, let the blood of those slain by Rycardus fall upon me."

Some believed an oath held true meaning. Lady Sela was one of those. Enough humanity remained in Rycardus to be saddened by the words of his mother, while his new mind tried to wrest away any vestige of emotional connection to her.

"Rycardus," said Sela called, "return to bid farewell."

Don't listen to her, keep moving. She wishes you were dead.

"Rycardus," shouted Sela, "come back and say goodbye to your mother!"

Rycardus mumbled and walked away with his head down. Half of him wanted to return and beg forgiveness, and the other half wanted to kill both of his parents.

Don't be so stupid. They're trying to lure me back so they can kill me.

With conflicted emotions brought on by his mother's calling out for a goodbye, he lifted his head to the sky and let out a deep and powerful howl reverberating from the castle to the forest. The howl had a sense of forlornness in it, as if someone was mourning a loss.

Goodbye, Mother ... you too, Father.

CHAPTER 24
BATTLE FOR THE ICE THRONE—PART ONE

*T*he Freezing Months came early to Flace and stayed longer than usual, giving Skuti extra time to integrate the Serpents into his army. The open window provided an opportunity to forge new weapons and build more ships, both for Taylor and for Ashul's navy. Skuti's highly skilled shipbuilders needed little motivation, but when they heard Jomar was constructing ships for the Advocate, their intensity grew as heat does in a smelting furnace.

Skuti used the coinage from Taylor's treasure to buy the best materials and hire the most skilled laborers found in all of Dapuin to handle the increase in production. If Skuti's army could not defeat that of his fellow Aeehrls, it would be an indictment of his leadership and tactics. He had a small but ferocious group of warriors and commanders, better weaponry, and the finest ships on the water.

Skuti designed and built a warship for himself and named it the *Mostru tal-Fond* as an ode to the Leviathan. His ship was much like Taylor's, but on a smaller scale, with less expensive decor. But there were no openings below the deck of the ship for mounting the brass tubes. He coveted the brass dragons that belched fire and sent iron balls hurtling toward the enemy. Taylor declined without explanation, just stating "it wasn't time."

Ashul's forces, numbering twenty-five hundred, left the harbor on an overcast morning and sailed east for a brief time before turning north onto the Northbonear River. Flowing south from the Thessarock Straights, the free-flowing river separated Ashul from the Eastern Mountains before dumping into the Pusag Sea.

On the first night of the voyage, Skuti invited Alfarin up to his quarters to drink mead and swap stories, as old friends are wont to do. Solvar, Skuti's personal servant, greeted Alfarin at the door.

"Sir Alfarin," said Solvar, "Aeehrl Skuti is expecting you."

"Solvar," said Skuti, "fetch two tankards and a jar of mead for Sir Alfarin and I."

"I brought your favored mead," said Solvar. "It has the X-X marking on it. Is this acceptable, my Aeehrl?"

"Quite."

"Thank you, my Aeehrl. Will you be needing anything else?"

"Yes. Make a posset for me before I sleep."

"Of course, my Aeehrl."

Solvar left the men briefly, returning with the mead vessel and tankards before departing again. Alfarin nodded approvingly after tasting the mead. "I can see why you prefer this mead. The herbs and spices add to the flavor."

Skuti smiled in return and took a large gulp of the honey-based concoction. "Evil descended upon Ashul the last time I consumed this and it changed everything."

"You going to start in about Astrid? Things haven't been the same since she got into your head. And by the way, don't think I didn't notice how much Solvar looks like Astrid."

"Doubt all you want. What she said was true."

And she will return to me when I need her the most.

Alfarin chuckled and rolled his eyes, causing Skuti to burst out with a laugh, and the two men guffawed as if this were the start to a festive evening with no impending trip to be made to engage the United Flacian Army (UFA) in battle.

After the two burned up some of their nervous energy by sharing laughs, the mead acted as a calming substance and changed the conversation to a more serious issue.

"What of Lady Thorve?" said Alfarin. "Any further news?"

"No," said Skuti. "I warned her about Jomar before she left. She disregarded me and headed to visit her deceitful sister."

"What are you going to do?"

"Nothing."

"Nothing?"

"There was no ransom demand, and I will not storm the castle, if that's what you're asking."

Skuti looked away and hoped Alfarin might drop the subject. On the one hand, he owed his friend some answers, but on the other, he was tiring of the subject. He would not have his focus change from the battles to come and let it drift to what may or may not be happening to Thorve.

"Losing Thorve doesn't bother you?" said Alfarin. "To Jomar, of all people?"

Taylor told me she was a millstone around my neck, and he was right.

"It can't and it doesn't," said Skuti. "Jomar is a dead man walking either way. I'm going to humiliate him and give him a very painful death. Now, let's focus on more agreeable matters."

Skuti lifted his mead toward Alfarin and the two clashed tankards, spilling mead onto the floor. "May Aenta allow us to bathe ourselves in the blood of our enemies."

"May she steal the hearts of our enemies," said Alfarin, "and fill their minds with doubt."

The talk slowed, as did the flow of mead, and Alfarin soon

left for his own room on the next level down from Skuti. Solvar brought the posset and herself to Ashul's Aeehrl, finding pleasure and satisfaction together. Like trash falling down from an upper floor to the street, he discarded any thoughts of Thorve from his mind.

Until Astrid's return, of which he had convinced himself was near, Solvar would remain with Skuti as his mistress. Everyone else be damned if they thought he was bringing shame to his lady in the hands of the enemy.

Aside from Skuti's ship, the rest of the fleet were flat-bottomed ships called *sheağs*. The vessels were versatile, designed to be used for cargo or ships of war, making them vital in Admiral Nasi's fleet. Soldiers, horses, weapons, provisions, and all the gear to set up and manage an efficient camp had to be sailed up the Northbonear with the rest of the army.

Besides soldiers, a support staff of talented workers sailed with Skuti's forces. The ships carried bladesmiths and blacksmiths for weapons and armor, cordwainers and cobblers for boots, and tailors for clothes and uniforms. Farrier-marshals came to take care of the horses' hooves and diseases, and cooks to prepare the soldiers' meals.

After three days of sailing up the river, the ships landed in Clearwater, a once important inland port. The abandoned port was on the Northbonear near the confluence with the Wickbonear Stream.

Ashul's army found the damaged and unused port, along with the remnants of Karlsa, a once-thriving port city, to be a perfect landing spot. After docking the ships, the lengthy process of off-loading cargo and setting up camp began. It was hard and time-consuming work, and with the plans Skuti had drawn up, it was of vital importance to set up the camp to match his strategic objectives.

Skuti's scouts were right; the UFA was headed for the Northbonear. Arriving first, Skuti would dictate where the two sides would wage war. On the outskirts of Karlsa was a small forest, a perfect place to hide parts of his army. If Skuti had to retreat, his forces would hide in many of Karlsa's empty buildings and launch attacks on the enemy if they chased him and his army into the city.

On the eve of war, Skuti called his commanders together for one last review of the battle plan. It was a risky play by Skuti, but the Aeehrl of Ashul had always been a risk-taker when he sensed the odds were in his favor, even if no one else saw it. His bet was on the Serpents to be as good on land as they were on the sea. If the training exercises in the Freezing Months were any sign, the enemy was on the eve of destruction.

Skuti and his commanders met in one of the nondescript tents dotting the field on which his army was staying. The tent held the rectangular table from the council room, and on top sat map markers along with a map of the area around the Northbonear River and Wickbonear Stream. Ashul's markers were orcas while the UFA's were coiled snakes.

"First," said Skuti, "there has been no word from our scouts where Aeehrls Jomar, Frostulf, and Bjartmar have headed after breaking off from Aeehrls Steiner and Värmod. They may take the Woodland Route and attack us from the rear, or they could head back on the same road they marched on and wait for us on higher ground."

"Or," said Alfarin, "they ran back to their castles, scared."

Light laughter came from around the tent, but Skuti's frown shut the levity down. "That's not our worry. Our minds are on Steiner and Värmod and the six thousand men across from us."

Skuti's green eyes, glowing from the torches and candles, searched the room for any signs of fear or reluctance on the faces of his commanders.

These men, stout and ready, are prepared to go to war for Flace's unity and glory.

Skuti moved the first markers. "This is where we set up the fake camp. We hold the north and south positions here and here."

Nasi was ready with his war ship positions and strategy. "We'll have two warships filled with archers at each marker. There are two platforms per ship, meaning we'll have four platforms on which to place our archers at each location, besides the use of the ship's deck."

Nasi searched the room for doubting or questioning eyes and then continued. "The archers accomplish three things. One, rain arrows down upon their troops to sow confusion and fear. Two, prevent enemy troops from fleeing away if they've crossed the Wickbonear. Third, the longbowman will aim flaming arrows toward the enemy's camp, leaving them nowhere to turn."

Skuti nodded his head in agreement and directed his attention to the commander of the Serpents. Cikku Toglia was the commander of the Serpents Iswed, Taylor's fighting men, and the most accomplished warrior and best rider of the Serpents.

He was tall, muscular, handsome, unscarred, with an intimidating glare and dreadlocks pulled up on top of his head. Tribal tattoos covered both arms, and the symbols contained within told the story of his life.

He spoke with an island accent, both soothing and quite remarkable to the men of Ashul. In his fighting spirit, his voice lowered a few octaves. Skuti's men had resolved the questions surrounding their mercenary role and fighting on Flacian soil, killing Flacian men. However, it wasn't so for their adversary, and they were certain to fight the Serpents, motivated by an absolute hatred of the island fighters.

"When you start the fire, Cikku," said Skuti, "wait until the enemy is moving forward and can see you and your men clearly. Once you flee, their confidence will rise at the sight of our camp burning and the Serpents fleeing. They will no doubt attack without discipline when they see blood in the water."

Ċikku placed three markers in the forest area where each of his light cavalry fighters would exit the trees. He moved the first marker out of the forest. "The smallest line, the first, will come out here and separate their infantry from the front line."

Scanning the eyes of each man, he continued by moving the second marker from the forest. "The second line will come out here and attack their unguarded flank. They'll assume the forest acts as a natural guard, and they'll leave their flank unprotected."

"How can you be sure?" said Alfarin.

"Even if they guard the flank, it will be light, and we'll cut through it."

Ċikku slid his third and last marker out of the forest and placed it behind the snake markers at the rearguard. "What is happening in front of them will distract the rearguard. My third line will loop and attack the rearguard straight on and push them back into their bowmen. Questions, my friends?"

Nasi looked over at the Serpent Commander with a slight smile. "Do you think they will be too frightened to fight, or will they be determined to kill the heathens?"

"Which do you think, Sir Nasi?" smiled Ċikku.

"They'll want to flee the field."

There was quiet laughter in the room until Skuti signaled for quiet. "Aeehrl Steiner of Gance and Aeehrl Värmod of Laugar, stand ready to test our strength tomorrow. We have prepared a meal to share with our enemies. They will taste our lances, feast upon our arrows, and gorge on our steel. Those who survive will testify to what they witnessed; Ashul's immense power."

The men in the room nodded their heads, and voices rose as men poured out venom on their enemy, made oaths to the gods, swore to show no mercy, and Ċikku recited an incantation in his native tongue.

After the room returned to quiet, Skuti bade his men to look toward the heavens. "It's time to seek the blessing of Aenta."

Skuti lifted his eyes upward. "Great Aenta, goddess of war, grant us victory over our countrymen who've gathered against us. They've betrayed Ashul, Flace, and you, the great Aenta, by creating a war of their own making against their own people. May we be victorious tomorrow."

"May it be so," said everyone.

The commanders filed out and walked back to their tents while a few walked about the camp, telling stories and crass jokes. Alfarin followed Skuti back to his tent to share a mead and pass away time just as they had since they were old enough to take part in the raids led by Skuti's father, Havard.

Early the next day, as Vesceron chased the darkness away, the red-colored sky was the sign for Skuti's army to put into motion their plan of attack. Ashul's army and two Aeehrldoms opposed each other with a wide but shallow portion of the Wickbonear between them.

Skuti's soldiers started the fire in the false camp and before long, the flames were licking the sky. As Nasi predicted, the morning breeze blew the smoke from the fire south toward Skuti's knights, hiding them from the frontline of the enemy. He and his knights were on what was now considered the southern flank of the enemy, hidden by the smoke and the early morning shadows cast by the grove of trees behind them.

Ashul's foot soldiers waited for the enemy's heavy cavalry to react to the fire and then put into motion the planned panic amongst Skuti's foot soldiers, throwing down their pikes as the fire became very visible to the enemy across the stream.

Amidst the sound of loud and panicked voices, the UFA proceeded with their attack, crossing the stream to chase down Skuti's fleeing troops. With the hurriedness of pressing forward, the enemy lost some of its cohesiveness, creating vulnerabilities within it.

Skuti's defenders engaged the first section of the enemy's heavy cavalry as they crossed the Wickbonear but retreated from the camp as the fire continued to burn. The light cavalry of the Serpents sped off from camp in a chaotic manner and fled north, and then ultimately east, into the forest.

Skuti sat atop Avenida, a handsome destrier with a unique coat of gray hair with white spots, white mane, and tail, with black hind legs. Nobleman Ragi Aslaks, the standard bearer, was next to Skuti at the front, carrying the heraldic standard tied to a spear. The flag with a sea-blue background and attacking orca in the center stood firm in the breeze.

Ashul's knights held firm behind him with their iron-tipped lances held in rests which were bolted on to their breastplates. As did Skuti, they all wore black great helms made of steel with pointed crowns designed to deflect arrows. The vision slits were formed between the side and skull plates, and several ventilation holes pierced the lower part of the helm.

"I can feel it, taste it, smell it," said Skuti.

"Yes, my Aeehrl," said Ragi, "the smoke from the fire is unpleasant."

Skuti turned to Ragi a second time with a sly smile. "No, their blood, the blood of my enemies. After the day ends, I desire to swim in a river of their blood."

Skuti raised his battle axe into the air, where it seemed to hang for an eternity. At last, he pulled it down, and with it unleashed a hurricane of strong, well-trained, and disciplined knights to emerge from the smoke at a steady trot.

The enemy front had stopped, confused by the retreat of the defense and the apparent desertion of the heathen fighters all amongst a camp on fire. They fell out of their tight formation as the chaos of war settled onto the field. The anarchy of noise drowned out commands, further exacerbating a situation destined to spiral out of control. Yet the enemy, unwilling to flee, tried to regroup and fend off Skuti's charge.

Skuti guided the knights in a close formation and maintained the horses' speed below a full gallop until they reached the final thirty meters. He targeted a knight in silver armor holding a shield in the silver and red of Gance. The knight was losing control of his horse in the madness and but righted himself just in time to see Skuti bearing down on him.

"I see you whoresons!" said Skuti.

The Aeehrl of Ashul aimed the lance across his body and let out a primal shout before landing a hard and sharp blow to the knight, knocking him from his saddle and onto the ground. The lance splintered and left Skuti with the grip portion of the weapon in his hand. He threw the grip down as if it were on fire.

"Damned piece of wood."

Ashul's vanguard plowed into the enemy's flank with their couched lances. Chaos ensued when the opposing knights fell from their horses after the penetrating power of the lances' strike. As dominos fall, men and horses became mangled together and formed a mound of desperation and death on the field amongst the mud, blood, and bodily excrements from men frightened beyond measure.

Skuti's knights, with either broken lances or no room to use them, grabbed for their secondary weapons and went to work. The weapon of choice was a matter of preference; knights often used longswords, but metal-headed maces and axes made their way onto the battlefield with gruesome consequences.

Individual fights broke out on horseback and on the ground between the two sides in ferocious exchanges. Skuti's knights, with their own squires delivering weapons and fighting alongside them, continued to assault the enemy with no let-up.

Skuti searched the field and found an enemy knight

gaining an upper hand on one of his own. He moved Avenida the short distance toward the two and shouted. "Churl!"

The enemy knight saw Skuti's axe hit his head and knocked him down. Ashul's knight pulled out his dagger and, as Skuti watched, opened the visor and killed the man by driving his dagger into his skull.

An enemy mounted knight appeared out of nowhere and took a wild swing at Skuti with a longsword that he ducked under. Raising his torso back up, Skuti swung his axe and slammed it into the back of the man's helm, dropping him to the ground. Skuti slid off Avenida and attacked the downed knight with his axe, driving it into his helm until the blade pierced the steel and entered the skull, finishing the enemy knight.

Emotion swelled into Skuti's lungs, and he screamed into the smokey air. "Who wants to bleed?"

The cacophony of sounds heard in the heat of a pitched battle filled the air. Men shouted orders, others absorbed blows from steel or iron and screamed in agony, still others cursed at each other and the gods. Horses played their part with groans, snorts, and loud squeals. Mixed with the sound of steel on steel, it created a deafening, dreadful song of death and dying.

Despite being caught in the mass of bodies, Aeehrl Steiner made his way out of the pile of men, horses, and steel, and scrambled to his feet. He was holding an arm to the side of his body but whistled for his horse, then drove the stallion hard toward the forest.

While Skuti scanned the battlefield, he caught Steiner's movement as he fled; he mounted Avenida and squeezed him with his calves and took off after the Aeehrl of Gance. As he pursued Steiner into the forest, the Serpents' second line was in sight and in position to attack the enemy's unguarded flank as planned.

It didn't take long for Skuti to close the gap between the

two, as Steiner was having a tough go of attempting to control his horse with only one hand on the reins. Skuti took careful aim at the Aeehrl of Gance and readied himself to drive the hammer of his axe into the back of Steiner's armor.

As he pulled even with the other horse, Skuti changed his mind at the last minute and swung the axe blade with a backhanded motion at the chest of Steiner. Perhaps it was luck, or maybe Steiner saw the axe coming his way. Either way, Steiner twisted his body and kept himself from receiving a solid blow from the steel blade.

Without landing a clean blow, Skuti's momentum almost knocked him off his horse and left him battling to hold on to the reins and his axe. It was a losing battle as both reins and axe came out of his hands, and the ground beckoned for the Aeehrl of Ashul.

"Ah—shit. Humph ... Humph ... Humph ... ahh."

The welcome from the ground was a hard stop on the path's dirt, followed by the clanking and clamoring of his armor before he rolled to a stop he wouldn't remember.

Steiner's quick defensive maneuver saved him from solid impact, but the glancing blow caused him to teeter in the saddle. With only one functional arm, he lost control of the reins, and as he fell from his horse, his spur caught the branch of the stirrup. The sudden stop broke his ankle and left him dangling from the stirrup.

A third horse, this one a handsome chocolate destrier, arrived and stopped close to the motionless body of Skuti. The man, wearing armor and carrying a triangle-shaped heater shield in the heraldic colors of Ashul, dismounted, picked up Skuti's axe, and hustled over to the Aeehrl.

He kneeled at Skuti's side and lifted the visor of his helm, dotted with several dents. "Aeehrl Skuti, Aeehrl Skuti."

Skuti's eyes were closed, but he was breathing, and there appeared to be no substantial injuries to the outside of his body. Removing his own helm first, he lifted off Skuti's with great care and set it aside. There was no blood to speak of, only scratches on his face and a good-sized knot was developing on his forehead.

"Aeehrl Skuti," said the man, "can you hear me?"

There was no response from Skuti, and shaking his armor was to no avail.

"Aeehrl Steiner," said the man, looking up the path, "you coward."

The man rose, but not before placing Skuti's axe on his chest and made his way to Steiner, hanging upside down with his spur caught on the stirrup branch. The Aeehrl of Gance was laboring to get his spur free of the bridge using his sword's tip. Each time the horse moved ever so slightly, the painstaking process started over again.

"Aeehrl Steiner," said the man.

"Sigewulf," said Steiner, "cut me down."

"Why should I help a betrayer and coward?"

Steiner's face was wet with sweat, and it was clear there was more than just a modicum amount of pain emanating from the ankle, cruelly pointing at an angle opposite of its natural position. "Because I wish to parlay with Aeehrl Skuti and put an end to this bloodshed. You know the Code of War and what it says. Now cut me down and take me to him."

"You forgot what happens to betrayers," said Sigewulf.

"Aeehrl Skuti," said Steiner, "betrayed Flace by bringing the filthy pagans onto our soil. He deserves to die."

"The only one deserving to die is you."

"You ungrateful boy. I trained you, kept you under my roof, and sent you back to your home a man ready for knighthood. Now you threaten me with death?"

"What you did doesn't cover your debt for turning on Aeehrl Skuti. He will sit on the Ice Throne, and I will do everything in my power to wipe your family name from existence."

Sigewulf narrowed his eyes and placed his hand on the pommel of his hand-and-a-half sword.

"You would draw your sword," said Steiner, "and kill a man unable to defend himself?"

"No," said Sigewulf, "I will not kill you."

Sigewulf took his hand off the pommel and picked up the reins of Steiner's horse, a stallion he was familiar with, and led him back to the path, bouncing a screaming Steiner along the ground. "Your horse will do it for me."

Sigewulf slapped the horse on its ass, and it took off down the path, dragging Steiner with him. As the horse ran free, his powerful legs kicked Steiner in the head as he pulled him behind as if he were a child's doll.

As soon as the horse was out of sight, Sigewulf returned to Skuti. This time his eyes were open, and he was sitting, rubbing his temples with the ends of his fingers.

"What happened?" said Skuti.

"You lost your balance," said Sigewulf, "and fell off your horse."

"Where's Steiner?"

"Aeehrl Steiner fell from his horse right after you did," said Sigewulf. "His spur caught on the stirrup branch, breaking his ankle and leaving him hanging from it," Sigewulf said.

Skuti stood, thought better of it, and took a knee instead. "Where is the cowardly bastard and his horse?"

"He's farther up the path. His horse got spooked and took off at a full gallop, dragging Aeehrl Steiner behind. I'm sure he'll be quite dead."

"Did you help him?"

"I tried, but the horse betrayed him."

The smile on Skuti's puffy face told his son he knew the story was a lie, but within it was also his approval. "Cut Steiner out and tie his body to a tree where no one can see him but remember its location. I'll send some men to fetch it after the bloodletting is done."

The ghost materialized from thin air and stood before Sigewulf left to take care of Steiner. Skuti furrowed his brow and Sigewulf's eyes grew larger at the apparition in front of them. It was in the shape of a man, maybe early twenties, in shabby clothes, with a scraggly beard and short hair. He stood just inches above the ground.

The ghost spoke, appearing alive and conversing with the two men. "Aeehrl Skuti, I have a message from the Lord of the Seas."

"During battle?" said Skuti.

"He told me to interrupt you, no matter what."

"Is this a trick, like some of you have done?"

"No, my Aeehrl. I swear it. If I can deliver two more messages, I will have paid my penance and can finally enter the Welkins."

"What did you do? I can tell you've been hanged."

"I stole a horse, well actually, two horses."

"You deserved to be hanged."

"Yes, I did."

"What's the message, before we join you in your netherworld of gray?"

"The Lord of the Seas says: 'Aeehrl Skuti, Jomar has enlisted the help of the Advocate's army, and these troops will arrive soon. Don't be slow in returning to Ashul. Don't engage with this newly formed army. Prepare for a siege until I arrive. My ships will be in the harbor in less than a fortnight. Regards, Taylor.'"

"Jomar and his army have taken the road back to Iziadrock," said Skuti. "I know we can cut them off and destroy his forces before the Blue Horde arrives."

"But, Father," said Sigewulf, "Lord Taylor said not to."

I've never retreated in my life. And I'm going to start now?

"My Aeehrl," said the messenger, "do you have a reply for the Lord of the Seas?"

Skuti threw his axe twenty yards into the nearest tree, and it entered the wood with a thunk. "May the gods condemn me for being a coward."

"Is that your message, my Aeehrl?"

"No. Tell the Lord of the Seas I will return after we've finished Steiner and Värmod's armies. I will await his next instruction."

In a snap of the fingers, the visage was gone, leaving Skuti and his firstborn son staring at each other.

"I may sit on the Ice Throne," said Skuti, "but we both know where the power comes from."

What in the legions of doom have I gotten myself into?

CHAPTER 25
BUTCHERED

"*K*nights?" said Renoldus.

"He's alone," said Josson.

Renoldus and Josson glanced at the field briefly. It appeared Balan was by himself, but one never knew with the Butcher of the Forest. Renoldus glanced back at the battlefield where his fighting men were fiercely holding off the Acarians as they retreated. Two of his knights and several fighters lay dead on the ground.

Renoldus rubbed his bearded chin as he turned toward Josson. Creases formed on his head as he rolled over the plan in his mind one last time. "Take the coach and head back until you reach the fork, then veer right for a short time. Abandon it on the road someplace. You're only a decoy for Princess Ingrid and Sir Hendry."

"It shall be done as you say," said Josson.

"I can't guarantee safe passage after that, but you're free to go. You've served me well."

Josson beat his chest armor twice over his heart with his fist before driving off with the carriage. "It's been an honor to serve you. You have no equal, Sir Renoldus, Black of Brüeland."

Renoldus rode to the left of the field and toward the ruins of the tavern, easing Inferno through the mud covering the ground where the fighting had been. Andreas, his squire, was with him. It didn't take long for him to find Balan and his Beast.

"Get off your horse," said Renoldus.

"The smell of your death," said Balan, as he dismounted Beast, "is in the air."

The Beast rose valiantly on two hind legs and screamed for the forest to hear. Inferno eyed her rival's display, rose on her back legs, and squealed a reply.

"Easy girl," said Renoldus. "You'll get your chance."

The Black of Brüeland wore a black cape atop his shining black armor but shunned his helm. Emblazoned across his breastplate was the sigil of House Blackwood—a warring stallion. The quagmire beneath their feet splattered both men's armor and capes. Renoldus's eyes were clear and focused. Andreas pulled the cape from his knight and led Inferno away from the two combatants.

Balan wore a blue cape fastened by a large gold brooch in the shape of ram's horns over matte gray armor. He wore a gold Barbute helm with the distinctive T shape opening for the nose and mouth and brown ram's horns, the family sigil, mounted on the side. Balan's squire took his cape and helm and led Beast away.

Renoldus and Balan moved toward the other with caution. Unsilenced voices lingered in the field. Screams of agony; prayers and curses of the dying; men begging to be put out of their misery.

The smells rose toward the heavens and may have been worse than the sights. It did not take a deep breath for either man's nostrils to be filled with the stench of bodily waste and disemboweled bodies.

"Do you smell and taste death on this field?" said Renoldus. "May it all be on your head."

"May it be on my head," said Balan, "and the head of my children, and their children as well."

As the two readied for the fight, an odd mist crept over the field, as if the gods had decided that only they themselves would see the battle between the two well-known knights. They were unfazed by the sight. Their clear vision of each other was all that mattered.

"You will drown in this today," said Balan, "and the hope for the continent will die with you."

"How much coinage did the Advocate enslave you for?" said Renoldus.

"Not all of us can be a boy the king's eye fancies," said Balan. "Has your arse recovered from the battering it took?"

"Don't cry for mercy. She is not here today."

The Butcher stared at the Black sword with a lip raised at the famous blade.

"I'm going to break what is unbreakable," he said.

"Many have tried," said Renoldus. "All have failed."

Taking the initiative, Balan swung forcefully from the side. Swords clashed together, sending sparks flying into the mist. Balan advanced and swung heavily from the opposite side. Renoldus's black sword blocked Balan's attempt, again shooting another round of sparks into the light fog. The clang of steel reverberated across the field.

You're stronger than I expected.

The men reset and measured each other. Balan hacked downward at the crown of Renoldus's head three straight times, and Renoldus blocked all. But the weight and strength of the Butcher drove *Blackout* closer and closer to the Black's unprotected head. Balan, not used to the energy spent to make such an attack, took some deep breaths, and parried weakly at Renoldus several times. Renoldus blocked the last slow attempt, sending the hefty sword tumbling into the foul mud like a woodsman cutting down a tree.

Balan looked at his hands as if they'd failed his body and turned to run. Pivoting, he slipped on the deathly slime and fell into the filth of the quagmire and onto his arse.

"Running?" said Renoldus.

"There's nothing to fight for here," said Balan. "My emotions got the better of me."

"Pick it up. Your men have tried to kill some of my best knights and are attempting to kidnap the princess of Brüeland. You will finish what you started."

Balan eyed Renoldus with suspicion as he reached for his sword and pulled it back when it was clear Renoldus would not contest it.

"You'll remember this when I plunge my sword into your heart," said Balan, "you arrogant bastard."

"Hold on to it this time," said Renoldus.

Balan's squire ran out to him, nearly slipping as well, and wiped his sword down with a cloth. The Butcher wasted no time and parried with more force at Renoldus. But Renoldus slipped the stab, swung *Blackout* edge first, and sliced Balan's unprotected hamstring muscle. *Blackout* slid in and out as lighting illuminates the dark sky and is gone in the blink of an eye. The wound, though not fatal for someone as large as Balan, caused significant pain. *Blackout* hurt opponents deep inside their bodies, leaving physical scars and reminders for later when the cold, dank air of the Freezing Months came.

Balan's leg buckled and Renoldus slammed his fist just above the Butcher's eye, opening a deep gash on the eyebrow. The force of the blow dropped Balan.

"On your arse again?" said Renoldus.

Blood ran down the face of Balan and into his mouth. His mind conjured up images of his taller, older brother's fists coming down on his head and face. He pulled his eyebrows down and tightened his lips. In an instant, he was ten years old, sitting on the grass, getting his arse kicked.

Balan signaled for his squire, who ran to his knight and wrapped a tourniquet around the deep cut. He wiped Balan's face and tried to stem the blood from his eye.

"Send your squire off and get up," said Renoldus. "I will not batter a man sitting in shit."

Balan mustered all his strength to rise, but his weakened leg rendered his strikes weak and off target. He tried to swing his sword at Renoldus and nearly fell over. Renoldus evaded the attempt with ease and crashed his fist into the eye this time, opening a deep cut and enough internal damage to cause the Butcher to see in twos.

Renoldus stepped back, anticipating a counterpunch that never materialized. Balan was on his arse once more. He took a deep breath and stood up gingerly on his tormented thigh, swollen to the size of a melon. Balan spit toward Renoldus and reopened his attack by aiming at one of the two opponents his eyes were seeing.

Renoldus moved away from each of Balan's desperate and awkward slashes and hacks. Behind a mask of blood, Balan's eye was a mere slit under the swollen tissue. He sucked air in huge gasps and dragged his tortured leg as if it were a log pulled from the forest.

Balan thrust his sword at the belly of Renoldus, but Renoldus swept it away, knocking the enormous sword into the mire again. Renoldus stepped inside and drove the butt of *Blackout* into the middle of Balan's crotch. As he grabbed for his balls, Renoldus pulled one hand off of *Blackout* and smashed it into Balan's cheekbone. Both blows crumpled him in sections, and he fell back into the foul mud again.

"Did you enjoy playing in the mud as a child?" said Renoldus.

The tip of *Blackout* picked up the Butcher's black-and-white shield and maneuvered it over into his own hands.

Renoldus smiled with satisfaction, deriving pleasure from embarrassing the knight, who the Acarians exalted as untouchable and undefeated.

Renoldus slammed the shield to the ground and stomped his boot on the thick wood. Almost as quickly, he pulled *Blackout* down from the sky, cracked the shield into halves, and sent them skimming across the mud to their owner.

The Beast's forty-five-inch sword lay in the mud as if it had already surrendered. Renoldus retrieved the massive sword and examined it, finding two cracks in the steel. He knew stresses on the blade would always relieve themselves through a weak point. Finding a rock nearby, he struck the blade of Balan's sword such that it fractured.

"I've broken your body, shield, and sword," said Renoldus.

"You're scum," spat Balan. "Even the worst of knights would put their foe to the sword."

"That would be too easy."

"When I return home, I will face humiliation."

"You should. You've slaughtered peasants, butchered surrendering soldiers, and led your soldiers against ill-equipped men."

"I hope you die in a field like this," said Balan. "You're nothing without that fucking sword. Nothing."

The mist evaporated and the clip-clops of hooves grew louder, as five knights under the command of Sir Balan galloped toward their leader lying in the mud with his broken shield and sword next to him.

Although she remained out of sight, Glasha had followed the retinue from a distance upon leaving Crence as the two agreed. The mist had kept her from watching Renoldus's one-sided demolition of Balan, but now that it cleared, she raced her horse toward the men gathered around the stricken man. She was not about to allow the object of her obsession to be undone by numbers in a foreign land.

The five men dismounted and walked toward Renoldus,

who slid his sword across the mud, gliding it to the feet of the knights. There was no mud on the blade, despite it traveling atop the muck.

"Which of you is a true knight and willing to pick up my sword and slay me with it?" said Renoldus.

"Don't pick it up," said Ourri, the senior knight. "Especially you, Aldus."

The blade's shine was more brilliant than gold. As the other men observed Aldus, Diccon, one of Balan's most experienced soldiers, took the sword.

The men's intense concentration on Diccon left them completely unaware of Glasha slipping off her horse a short distance away and silently advancing towards them. Using the covert skills taught to her since she was a child, Glasha stayed in between the knight's horses in silence and waited. All eyes were now locked on Diccon.

"You fool, Diccon," spat Balan from a sitting position. The Butcher's face was a mixture of blood and the disgusting mud he had contributed to. Balan looked toward Sir Diccon as if he were a blind man, gazing but not seeing.

"You're the fools," said Diccon. "Those stories are nothing but lies to keep the swords from being taken by better men. It's mine now."

He took a step toward Renoldus with death on his mind, although it was to be his own. Diccon stopped abruptly, with a pained expression on his face. "What's happening?"

Diccon alternated looks between the grip and Renoldus. He stood frozen, eyes wide, and mouth agape. His four counterparts edged closer to see what was betraying their comrade.

The hilt turned blazing hot in Diccon's hand as if someone lit a fire inside his glove, and he looked in horror at Renoldus. Diccon attempted to drop the sword from his hand, but it remained firm in his clenched fist. Without thinking, he brought his other hand over to pry it off, only to have it stick to the inferno that was the sword's black leather grip.

"Stupid fool," said Balan.

"Get if off!" screamed Diccon. "I beg you, do something."

"Turns out the stories are true, are they not?" said Renoldus.

Diccon dropped to his knees, fell on his forearms, and toppled over onto his side. The smell of burning flesh wafted into the air and joined the stench of the field. The intense and awful screams filled the afternoon sky, and those still alive in the field did their best to cover their ears.

With Diccon reduced to whimpers and passing in and out of consciousness, *Blackout* released his hands. The gloves caused his hands to burn as if made of paper, resulting in a pulp of roasted and bleeding flesh with fingers charred down to the bone.

Blackout glided over the corrupted mud as a steel snake might and stopped at the boots of Renoldus. He grabbed the sword from the muck and gripped it in his hand without a trace of heat. The blade was immaculate, with no trace of muck to be found.

Balan stumbled to his feet somehow despite being bent over at the waist and called for Beast several times. But the imposing horse did not answer his master's call, leaving Balan without the help of his powerful companion. When he turned his attention to his men, they averted their eyes, none wanting to bear the burden of delivering the hard truth. Balan's searching eyes revealed his panic. "Where's Beast?"

Several moments passed without an answer, furthering Balan's alarm. "Are you arseholes deaf?"

Aldus pointed in the direction across the field where the horse lay still in the ooze of death. "It's over—"

"Shut up," said Ourri.

A grimace crossed Balan's face. "Tell me, damn you."

Aldus cast his eyes at the ground. "That bastard's horse killed Beast."

Balan put his head down and shook it back and forth. His

defeat was now complete at the hands of Renoldus and his horse, Inferno. Despite the lack of witnesses, wild stories would persist for years about what happened to the indomitable horse in the mist on a field in Aflana, as they would about its owner.

"Where's my squire?" sputtered Balan. "I need another horse."

Renoldus looked over at his enemy, broken and ruined by the beating and the death of his horse. The moment was brief, but Renoldus felt a tinge of sympathy for Balan, not the Butcher, but the man inside the caricature. It was soon gone as he eyed the four knights in front of him. Within seconds, his mind selected the order in which he would slay the knights and the entry point of the blade in each man.

Glasha sprang to her feet, axe in hand, causing the four remaining knights to spin and draw their weapons. "Lay down your swords, hedge born fools."

Forming a loose circle, the four men put their backs to each other and pointed their swords at the new adversary and a smiling Renoldus.

The woman never disappoints.

"She said drop your weapons," said Renoldus.

"I'm not surrendering to that, puterelle," said Ourri.

"Do it or she'll kill you so quick," said Renoldus, "you won't have time to shit your pants."

Glasha picked out Aldus, who looked like the youngest of the four. "Your balls don't have hair yet. Do you truly wish to perish in this place?"

"You dirty, green-skinned whore," said Aldus, stepping forward.

Balan screamed at his men just as the sound of steel hitting steel begun. "Wait—"

Surprised by Balan, Aldus took his eye off of Glasha, who raised her axe and slammed it down on the top of the shorter man's helm. The blow staggered the man and Glasha followed by shoving him to the ground. In seconds, she had pulled up his visor and drove her dagger into the eyes and throat, killing him. She lept up and pulled her axe out of Aldus's helm and turned on Ourri.

"Put the swords down," said Renoldus to the knights closest to him, named Ragar and Hemmet. "You whoresons don't want to die out here."

Instead, the two attempted to position themselves in front and behind Renoldus to launch a coordinated attack. Of course, the Black of Brüeland was no ordinary knight and instead of allowing them to pull off the move, he jumped at Ragar and overwhelmed him by striking downward with *Blackout*. Surprised by the speed and strength of Renoldus, his attempt to block the black steel lacked conviction and both he and his sword were in the mud in a matter of seconds.

Hemmet was too cumbersome in his armor and didn't react with the swiftness needed while Renoldus's attention was on Ragar. Lacking the aggressiveness necessary, Hemmet assumed a defensive posture. Renoldus spun, expecting his opponent to be closer, but found him several feet away.

You don't want to fight me.

"Put the sword down," said Renoldus, "and go join your friend in the mud."

The loud voice of Balan caused Renoldus to turn around. "You're a barbarian," he said. "Are you going to eat his brain, too?"

Several yards away, Ourri was on his back with his helm several feet away, as was his sword. Glasha showed her blood splattered chest piece and warrior's skirt, as she turned when Renoldus approached. Gray matter dripped from her axe, which she held at her waist. Ourri's head had been transformed into a canoe.

"Hold your tongue," said Glasha, "or yours is next."

"An unarmed, beaten man," said Balan. "Impressive."

"Silence it," said Renoldus. "Have your squire get you on a horse and get out of here."

Balan's squire came into view with a horse he undoubtedly found wandering without its owner, who lay somewhere amongst the dead. Stopping it next to his bleeding and battered knight, it was all the young man could do to assist Balan up and over the horse and into the saddle. Each time Balan's leg contacted the horse, he screamed like a child. When he attempted to settle into the saddle, the hard leather caused his swollen balls to scream for mercy.

The Butcher eyed Glasha, then Renoldus, and spat toward them. "Is this who you're taking into exile? Do you bed her too?"

"What does it matter to you?" said Renoldus.

"I'd rather die than bed a dirty, green-skinned animal. How can someone who claims to follow the Black sard such a thing? It's unnatural."

"You won't be sarding anything after today," said Glasha.

Balan shook his head and motioned for his squire to lead his horse away. "Our work here is done. We've killed enough of your men, and the princess will soon be ours."

Glasha used her boot to turn Diccon face up. The horrid mud ran down the sides of his face, but some stuck to the burns on his nose and forehead.

"Oh, god," said Glasha, kicking the man back over.

"Even if I'm dying," said Renoldus. "Don't pick up that sword. Ever."

Glasha nodded her head and surveyed the field. "You lost too many men. I should've jumped into the fight."

"This was not your fight."

Why was there a fight? Who betrayed us deep within our own castle? Only the Advocate benefits from preventing the alliance and killing me. How would they know our path? Is this Watkin calling from his …

"… Renoldus … Renoldus …" said Glasha.

"Hmmm?"

"What are you thinking about? Your face had a frown."

"Someone inside the castle relayed our travel plans to Acaria."

Glasha's eyes became wide, and she drew her chest and neck back. "We know nothing of it. Better to be thrown into a lake tied to a boulder than commit treason."

"It's a peculiarity found in our castles. Power and wealth prevail over what is right."

Renoldus dropped his head and stared at the ground. He knew well that his desirous lust for Ingrid set in motion much of what transpired in a peaceful meadow now stained with the blood of his countrymen.

I bear the guilt for the blood on this field. All the lye and ash found on the continent can never wash away the blood that stains me. I deserve to be exiled.

The familiar, soft voice interrupted his personal condemnation.

"Yes," said Cecile's voice, "and now you have much more to do because of it."

"I was beginning to think you were done talking to me," said Renoldus.

"It was necessary to interrupt your pity fest."

"I'd rather come to you than continue to slog on. How many men must I fight and kill?"

"Many more, I fear. You were given *Blackout* for a reason."

"Its weight is heavy."

"That's why the sword chose you."

"I know who—"

"I know you do. Don't mention that name to anyone."

"Vengeance will be mine."

"No, it won't. You have more important things to do."

"Such as?"

"Saving the continent."

The moon and stars were chasing away Vesceron, drawing a look from Renoldus. The boundless beauty of the sky gave him a brief respite from the weight of Dapuin landing on his broad shoulders. "Now what?" he said.

"Wed the Af'lam princess."

"How can I do that when my heart aches?"

"Let me go. You'll always have a memory of me tucked away, and you'll see me on the other side."

Renoldus walked a short distance away as an unwanted tear slipped out.

"Carry on with your life and fulfill your calling."

Renoldus wiped the tear away, embarrassed it got out. He breathed deeply, gazing skyward. It was his cue to stop the endless drink and put the affair with Princess Ingrid behind him, although the fear she was carrying his child was gnawing at him already.

"You're right, as usual."

"Of course. Aren't I always? Now, say goodbye."

"Goodbye, my love."

"Goodbye, Renoldus. I have your seat ready at our table."

EPILOGUE

*D*amn Renoldus! He picked the worst time to do the right thing. If he just left with me as I asked, I wouldn't be sitting here in this dreary and stench-filled room. How can I stay mad at him, though? He's my love and the father of the child growing inside me. He will marry me and give our child his name and do everything I tell him to. No more honoring the Black, and I don't care if Grala takes his damned sword.

I'll have the green woman killed too. He denies it, but why trust the fates when I've got the control. He'll have me or he'll have no one. Since I first bled, I knew I'd have Renoldus for myself even if I had to kill every woman in Crence. Any woman who gives him a second glance shall find herself in a grave.

Still, we almost made it. Someone who saw us must've told the Acarians. Hendry fought for me so valiantly, risking his life for me as he should. He was fighting as a young Renoldus would, killing at least three of their men. I should have known with Renoldus as his teacher and mentor.

It's a shame he's going to die here, unless I can convince Sir Fat Arse to save him, which I sincerely doubt. He's better suited to be the king's fool. But it is in my favor, though. I will manipulate him into setting me free even if I have to bed the useless rat.

"Good morning," said Basequin of House Ganslailthe, the nobleman's son. "How is the princess whore today?"

"Worse than I was a minute ago," said Princess Ingrid.

"How's your new gown?" said Basequin. He stood in front of the open door to Ingrid's room with his arms folded across his chest, a bit of a belly hanging over his belt and a smirk the size of his overgrown ego.

It was clever. The first time.

"It's large, yet comfortable, and I actually like the loose fit. The whore you bought it from must've been quite plump."

And the fun starts anew.

"How is Hendry being treated?" said Ingrid.

"Horribly, I'm sure," said Basequin.

"Is he sick again?"

"Yes."

Bastards.

Every day, Ingrid and Basequin engaged in the word dance. Ingrid asking, Basequin responding. He brought his response to her before she asked, some days. The plump mouse was drifting closer to the cat that was Ingrid.

I'm going to get every ounce of info out of you before I go, and I'll start with my love. I know after we left, Renoldus was going to defeat Sir Balan. He had a look on his face I won't soon forget.

Basequin was the worst of the palace guards. But his father was a nobleman and well connected, and his son soon found himself in the most prestigious of the guard battalions. He wasn't a terrible guard, but there wasn't one weapon he was exceptional with. Proficient with staff weapons, he fought defensively, as a means of survival. Everything about him spoke of mediocrity. And as such, they assigned him to manage the political prisoners held in separate rooms within the White Keep.

"There are whispers within these walls," said Ingrid, bearing a wide smile and dancing brown eyes, "that the Black of Brüeland ruined Sir Balan."

Basequin furrowed his brow and stared at Ingrid, wanting to tell her all he'd heard to impress his prisoner, yet still wanting to be true to his call. "Shut up."

Ingrid moved closer to the door, but not within striking distance of Basequin's hand. She'd tasted his slaps and felt his blows since she first arrived, but within the last fortnight he stopped his laying on of hands or even threatening it. Still, Ingrid knew the beatings could start up again if she stepped out of line as she had upon her arrival, taunting Basequin and questioning his manhood.

Ingrid pressed forward, ignoring that a slap in the face was the reward for the use of a wrong word. "Can't you tell me anything?"

It didn't take long for Basequin to crack. "Maybe. One thing."

Ingrid inched closer and was now within Basequin's reach.

"Sir Renoldus," said Basequin, "cut the head off Beast, and let his horse piss all over it."

"Sir Renoldus killed even his horse?" said Ingrid. "I thought that animal had no equal."

"People who witnessed it claim it to be true."

"You must know some men in high places to get that information."

Basequin turned and vanished, disappearing down the hallway. For a moment, Ingrid stepped out of her room. The long hallway was empty.

On a good day, Ingrid's room was stale. The bed needed new stuffing; the blankets were threadbare, and the chair and writing table both wobbled. An unemptied chamber pot sat on the cold, hard floor next to the bed and further enhanced the aroma brewing in her new home.

I'm going to need the help of Basequin to get me out of this room and on to freedom. Ah, speak of the devil. Here comes Sir Chubby Guard again.

Ingrid chuckled and ducked back into her room and waited. It didn't take long.

"Tell me about Sir Balan," said Ingrid. "How bad was it?"

"I don't know," said Basequin. He moved closer to the door to be heard as Ingrid stepped back. "I've heard it was quite bad. They said Sir Renoldus should've performed a mercy killing."

"What else have you heard?"

He looked up and down the hallway, as most fools do, for anyone who might hear them. The ears to fear were already in passageways, closets, and with the castle staff.

"The Butcher had one of his eyes gouged out."

"Seriously? How could someone beat the Butcher so soundly?"

"Some say a strange fog came over the field and sapped his strength. Many believe Renoldus remains the greatest knight."

"What do you think happened?"

Basequin stepped nearer and lowered his voice. "Sir Balan was told not to engage Sir Renoldus, but he did so anyway. Balan is not even a legitimate knight. He got what he deserved."

Ingrid's eyes lit up again and bounced around. "What else?"

"He doesn't walk as he used to. Sir Renoldus nearly severed his leg, is what I heard."

"Can it truly be?"

"Rumor has it he was also kicked in the bag of balls so hard he won't be able to produce children. No woman would want him now."

Ingrid thought for a moment and realized she'd never asked a foreigner for their opinion of Sir Renoldus. She'd risk a beating for this information. "Have you ever seen Sir Renoldus in a tournament?"

Basequin looked down at his boots. "I have once. Long time ago."

"He never loses. Knights from all over the continent come to Brüeland and leave shamed."

Watch it, Ingrid.

"Our best couldn't touch him. But wars broke out, and we were no longer welcome in Crence."

"Still, I hope you catch Sir Renoldus. He left me, the Princess of Brüeland, to fend for myself with Hendry."

"You should forget about the young man."

"You know he's worth more alive than dead."

"It's too late. The die has been cast."

Ingrid gazed around the room that imprisoned her. "I haven't felt a man's touch in so long, and this room is so lonely."

"You'll be gone soon enough."

"What do I do until then?"

"Until then?"

Basequin became the fly to Ingrid's spider, caught in a web of manipulation and seduction. He had no chance from the beginning but was too stupid to realize it.

"Curious about what's under the dress?"

Basequin's eyes conveyed the desire, and Ingrid obliged him by pulling down her dress just enough to show her ample freckled breasts to the mesmerized guard.

"I want to see where your legs come together too," said Basequin.

"To see my honey pot," said the Princess, "I'll need more information."

A frown creased the guard's face. "What kind of information?"

"What do you know about the Advocate?"

THE END

GLOSSARY

Freezing Months—Winter
Growing Months—Spring
Burning Months—Summer
Dead Months—Fall
<u>Languages</u>
Known Language of Old—Language developed amongst the original kingdoms in Western Daupin.
The Known Language—Common language derived from the Known Language of Old. Spoken in most kingdoms and lands.
Writings of the Ancients—First recorded language given by the gods to the first peoples of Daupin.
Anari—Native language of Acaria.
Boejash—Native language of the Island of the Skull
Iskuin—Native language of Flace.
Utari—Native Language of the Af'lam Tribes
Abomination of Yoenia (Writing of the Ancients)—Abomination of the Moon
Birmems dekaaka (Known Language of Old)—Burning disease
Boccromol (Iskuin)—celebration
Cimcier (Utari)—prophet
Chouufsuoum (Utari)—chieftain
Chouufsuoumuss (Utari)—chieftainess
Eahrshe (Iskuin)—great black-and-white whale found off the coast of Flace
Espléndido, the—Splendid, an Acarian ship
Gżira tal-Kranju (Boejash)—Island of the Skull
Heil (Iskuin)—hall
K'traat dus (Known Language of Old)—street dog
Kaarks (Known Language of Old)—seers
Kirattu (Known Language of Old)—half-breed
Kumm omie si kurrmuss (Utari)—Damn you to darkness
Mostru tal-Fond, the (Boejash)—Monster of the Deep, Skuti's ship
Phleaeth (Iskuin)—fleet
R'zrta (Known Language of Old)—hydra
Saeothephol Fleshae (Iskuin)—Beautiful Place
Sheağs (Iskuin)—flat-bottomed ships
Stalŏun (Slang; Unknown Origin)—promiscuous man
Þuriðr (Iskuin)—seer
Vendetta tal-Mejtin, the (Boejash)—Revenge of the Dead, Taylor's ship
Vesceron (Name given by the gods)—the Sun

CAST OF CHARACTERS

<u>In the Kingdom of Brüeland</u>
Sir Renoldus Gwatkin, the Black of Brüeland, Lord Commander of the King's Army
Leander Blackwood, king of Brüeland
Alexia Blackwood of house Stonedwell, queen of Brüeland
Ingrid Blackwood, daughter of the king and queen, princess of Brüeland
Sir Terrin Omand, the Trusted, Battlefield Commander
Lady Gelen of House Bridetomb, wife of Sir Terrin
Lord Watkin Dernesch, Advisor to the Crown
Lady Evelyn of House Rainstrong, wife of Lord Watkin, Lady-in-Waiting to Princess Ingrid
Lord Searl Brewburn, Prime of Law
Lord Valter Cagnat, Master of Ships and Trade
Arnet (The Eunuch) Chatard, Master of Finance
Hendry the Gray, knight in service to Sir Renoldus
Oswald Gloommore, owner of the King's Key
Arlette, whore at King's Key
Johna, spy for Sir Renoldus
Clarenbald Atwood, Master of Mews
Sir Ricon the Romantic, guard at Lady Evelyn's door
Sir Amfrid of the Sea, guard at Lady Evelyn's door
Sir Sanson, the Gentlemen, guard at Lady Gelen's door
Sir Folkes, the Courteous, guard at Lady Gelen's door
Lady Madelina of House Edlai, Lady-in-Waiting to Princess Ingrid
Josson, scout and spy
Heward of the Rox, driver of King Leander and his family
<u>In the Land of Flace</u>
Skuti Ingimund, Aeehrl of Ashul
Thorve of House Hastein, Lady of Ashul, twin sister of Thora
Sigewulf Ingimund, eldest son of the Aeehrl and Lady
Jomar Throst, Aeehrl of Iziadrock
Thora of House Hastein, Lady of Iziadrock, twin sister of Thorve
Sir Beiner Gudmund, bodyguard and confidant of Lady Thora
Sir Alfarin, the Outsider, Marshall of the Castle, personal bodyguard and confidant to Aeehrl Skuti
Sir Harald the Powerful, Captain of the Watch
Eirik the Guardsman, Captain of the Night Watch
Meldun Thorgils, Steward of the Castle

Cast Of Characters

Slode Brodir, Master of Coin
Jorund Fridmund, Master of Trade
Nasi Geirleif, Admiral of the Aeehrl's Navy
Astrid Gretter, seer from Taazrand
Čikku Toglia, commander of the Serpents Iswed
Steinar Anunds, Aeehrl of Gance
Värmod Varin, Aeehrl of Laugar

<u>In the Andairn Kingdom</u>
Rycharde Andairn, king of Aflana
Sela Andairn of house Trulbosh, queen of Aflana
Rycardus Andairn, eldest son of the king and queen, prince of Aflana
Ricaud Andairn, son of the king and queen
Reyna, cookshop worker
Sir Raümond of Winter, Commander of the White Guardians, Advisor to the King
Lord Jasce Lonewhisk, Keeper of the Wealth
Lord Brice Hathawaye, Steward of the Castle
Lord Wymon Reevese, Master of Trade/Information
Sir Evrardin, the Wolf, Master of the Forest
Valgerd, King of the Bloodmoon Wolves
Halec, Doomclaw soldier

<u>Pirates</u>
Taylor Denton, Master of the Seas, Captain of the Vendetta tal-Mejtin
Calena, origin is unknown
Delvin "Grisly" Barre, quartermaster of the Vendetta
Barlow "Artist" Thorne, sailing master and navigator of the Vendetta
Dyson "Coxswain" Crowley, bosun of the Vendetta
Grayson Ainsworth, Captain of the Espléndido
Ġungla tal-Mitluf, Jungle of the Lost
Gżira tal-Kranju, Island of the Skull

<u>Acarian Empire</u>
The Advocate, the most Holy One, Diviner of Wisdom, Interpreter of the Prophetic Word, Ruler over the Empire
Brigida, young woman
Jamettus Betan II, king of Acaria
Helene Betan II, of House Estrish, queen of Acaria
Lord Sanders Lynch, Master of Wealth
Sir Melcher Blackburn, Lord General of the Army
Sir Alleyn Hewelet, Lord Admiral of the Seas
Sir Balan, the Butcher of the Forest, in the service of King Jamettus II

<u>The Af'lam Tribe</u>
Sarg Thall, Chieftain
Ushat Thall, Chieftainess
Glasha Thall, Princess of the Af'lam

Cast Of Characters

Shadbak, seer
Ditru, warrior
Ela, human slave

Derek L. Builteman is a California native who currently resides in San Diego with his wife Leslie. With a passion for Medieval history, Derek has spent countless hours in pursuit of authentic settings and characters. His life experience has been implanted within his characters, giving them a sense of humanity that is common to us all. When not writing, Derek is a cycling enthusiast who enjoys the time he spends chatting with his characters while out on his bike.

www.derekbuilteman.com

FOLLOW DEREK ON SOCIAL MEDIA

facebook.com/Derek%20Builteman%20Author
instagram.com/derekbuilteman

Printed in Great Britain
by Amazon